# Frozen Music

MARIKA COBBOLD

ORION

The right of Marika Cobbold to be
identified as the author of this work has been
asserted by her in accordance with the Copyright,
Designs and Patents Act 1988.

First published in Great Britain in 1999 by
Orion
An imprint of Orion Books Ltd
Orion House, 5 Upper St Martin's Lane
London WC2H 9EA

A CIP catalogue record for this book is available
from the British Library

Typeset by Deltatype Ltd, Birkenhead, Merseyside
Printed in Great Britain by
Clays Ltd, St Ives plc.

For Patrick, P.o.E.

I would like to thank my agent, Jo Frank, and everyone at A. P. Watt and my editor, Rosie Cheetham, and everyone at Orion for the wonderful job they've done for me and for this novel.

My warmest thanks also to Tina and Bjorn Sahlqvist for their invaluable help and advice regarding matters of architecture. Speaking to them has been an inspiration.

I would also like to thank Jeremy Cobbold and Harriet Cobbold, Anne Hjörne and Elizabeth Buchan and Tony Mott for their advice and support. And finally, a special thank you to Lars Hjörne for his endless patience in listening, and for advising me with such wisdom and ingenuity, and to Lena Hjörne for putting up so graciously with my constant interruptions to her life.

## Prologue

My name is Esther Fisher and I'm just about to walk out on the only man I've ever loved. I'm thirty-four and a latecomer to love, which makes this all the harder.

I pause in the doorway of the house before stepping out into the dark November morning. The cold air makes me cough as I feel my way across the garden, my suitcase in one hand. My coat sleeve gets caught on one of Astrid's roses. The blooms are long gone; it's winter after all, but the thorns remain, always there, ready to catch you.

I'm leaving the island on the seven o'clock ferry. I can just see it approach through the mist so I'll have to hurry if I'm to make it on board. But still I linger by the wooden gate. I turn and cast one last glance up at the blue-painted wooden house. There's no one at the window. I pick up my suitcase and walk down the hill towards the harbour, cracking the frost beneath my feet.

I had found love at last, and truth, and that was the problem, because in my life they turned out to be each other's enemies. Like rain and harvest, starlight and sunrise, my mother and reality.

I have to try to make light of it. How else do you survive in a world which seems like a nursery ruled over by a capricious six-year-old?

So where is Nanny? Or God? I don't know.

# PART ONE

# Chapter One

My mother wanted me to be a child prodigy. I wanted to be a psychiatrist. Not that I knew much about what that entailed, I was only nine after all, but I had heard it said that a psychiatrist was someone who looked into people's minds, and I really liked the idea of that: I already liked looking at people's outsides – 'It's rude to stare, Esther, how many times do I have to tell you?' – so to be able to see right inside their heads as well sounded very interesting, almost as interesting as talking to the animals, like Dr Dolittle. And I enjoyed the reaction from grown-ups when they asked me, the way they always do when they can't think of anything else to say, what I wanted to be when I grew up. Then, as often as not, they would answer themselves, 'An air hostess, I wouldn't mind guessing, or maybe a nurse?'

'A psychiatrist,' I'd say. That usually shut them up.

Right now, Audrey, my mother, was speaking to me as she drifted through my bedroom, messing it up. 'Have you practised your flute, darling?'

I didn't answer her straight away. I was busy practising on her, staring at her head, trying to see through her high forehead and into her mind. I was concentrating hard, and just for a moment I thought I had succeeded, as I glimpsed something green, a Harrods bag probably, and something swirling, dancing. Then everything got covered in a pink mist.

'Esther, what are you doing? You look quite demented.'

I frowned at her; it wasn't *my* mind that was covered in a pink mist.

'I asked you if you had practised your flute today?' She picked up my teddy bear on her way through the room and, of course, put him down in the wrong place. I took him from the small wicker chair and put him back on my pillow where he belonged, dead centre.

'Life is Art, Esther, Art is Life. I don't expect you to understand, not yet, but trust me, it's the only truth I know.'

'I know lots of true things,' I said proudly. Audrey was annoying, but she was my mother and I yearned for her approval.

'Oh childhood, childhood, enjoy its rosy innocence while it lasts.' Audrey sighed and absent-mindedly picked up my doll's teapot from the top shelf of the small blue dresser, wandering off to the window, the pot in her hand. 'So pretty,' she mumbled. I couldn't tell if she meant the teapot or the Kensington street below – the cherry trees were in blossom – but I did know that she was going to put the teapot back in the wrong place.

My mother turned away from the window and fixed me with her soft blue gaze. 'Now get on with your practice, an hour at least. That little Japanese girl, Miko . . . Misho . . . you know the one I mean? – Divine – She practises five hours a day, apparently, which is why she is well on her way to becoming a world-class performer.'

'I don't like the flute, I like the trumpet.' In my mind I saw the glinting brass and heard its triumphant noisiness.

'Don't be silly, Esther, the trumpet is a hideous solo instrument, hideous. Anyway, your music teacher tells me you have it in you to be a very good flautist indeed.'

'I have it in me to be a very good psychiatrist who plays the trumpet,' I insisted.

My mother ignored me, the way she ignored most problems. 'And when you've finished, Janet will give you your tea; then you must come and say hello to Olivia.' Audrey had reached the door before she remembered the teapot in her hand. With a vague glance around my room she put it down on my bedside table, rather than back in its place on the dresser. I was pleased; I liked it best when things happened the way I expected.

'And do a drawing for Olivia, will you. I know she'd like that.' My mother blew me a kiss and disappeared out on to the landing, leaving behind her instructions and the sweet scent of gardenia.

I put the teapot back on the top shelf of the dresser (I had to draw my chair up to reach), giving my flute in its velvet-lined case a nasty look as I passed. Then I returned to my game of the French

Revolution. I had managed to construct a guillotine from an old Rice Krispies packet and some elastic bands, but Barbie's and Ken's heads remained resolutely fixed to their rubbery necks. 'Problems, problems, problems,' I muttered as the crowd – two anatomically correct dolls (one boy, one girl), an inflatable crocodile, a Beatles doll (Ringo) and a cuddly rabbit, normally called Rupert but known now as Jean for the purpose of the game – grew restless.

Janet was clearing away the tea. I didn't want to leave the table. I liked the large basement kitchen best of all the rooms in the house and I liked Janet, our housekeeper. Janet was sensible. She wore shoes you could walk in and it didn't seem to bother her if her hair got wet from the rain. She spoke in short, clear sentences and her mood hardly ever changed from its customary brisk friendliness. You knew where you were with Janet.

'Come on, Esther, off you go. Your mother and her friend are waiting for you.'

'She's very tall, Olivia,' I said, staying where I was.

'You say that about everyone.' Janet gave my chair a little shove as she passed on her way to the fridge. 'You're short, have you ever thought about that?'

'I'm supposed to be short,' I protested. 'I'm nine years old.' But I slipped off my chair and ambled upstairs, dragging my feet on the parquet floor of the hall and the cream stair carpet, pausing briefly on the first-floor landing to pinch an apple from the copper bowl where they had been arranged by Audrey in a cider-scented pyramid. I could hear her languid murmuring and the louder, firmer tones of Olivia Davies, her old school friend. I bit into my apple and tried to conjure up a picture of her. All I saw was a mass of hair, darkish brown and wavy, not unlike my own. As I looked at the picture in my mind I ran my fingers through my hair, twisting a strand round and round my index finger.

'Esther, is that you out there?' my mother called and with another bite of my apple I sidled into the drawing-room, feeling shy all of a sudden. 'Darling, what have you done to your hair? You look like a Hottentot. Oh, never mind. Come and say hello nicely.'

I shot Audrey a mutinous glance. Why did she insist on treating me like a child? Then I remembered; I was one. I felt more cross than ever.

'There's no need to kiss me.' Olivia smiled. She put out her large hand to take mine as I approached from across the room, a dutiful pucker already formed on my lips. I released it into a smile as she added, 'After all, Esther, we hardly know each other.'

I had forgotten what a nice, sensible person Olivia was. Transferring my apple to the pocket of my red dungarees, I put my hand in hers and she shook it firmly. I was looking hard at her face, wanting to see if I could count all the freckles on her left cheek before she let go of my hand: one two three four five . . . as I counted I began to get flustered. Suddenly it was really important that I managed them all . . . six seven eight nine ten eleven twelve thirteen fourteen . . . the numbers raced through my mind as if chased by some monster or a wolf. There was still a big bit to go. Fifteen sixteen seventeen eighteen . . .

'Esther, how many times have I had to tell you, you're not to stare at people,' my mother's voice interrupted my counting.

'Can I have my hand back now?' Olivia asked nicely.

I shook my head, counting feverishly, thirty thirty-one thirty-two thirty-three . . .

'Let go of Olivia's hand *immediately*,' Audrey snapped and I dropped it as if it were stolen chocolate. I still had an area on her cheek the size of half a crown to count, but it was too late. I grinned stupidly. 'And don't grimace, child.' Audrey sighed.

'I don't know what's got into her.' My mother's voice followed me like an embarrassing smell as I padded across the room to my favourite chair. It was green, shabby and worn, and very different from the rest of the furniture in our house, but Madox, my father, had decreed that it should stay and my mother, although muttering darkly at it as she passed, had not dared to throw it out. I liked it because it was large enough for me to curl up in and almost disappear, and because it didn't matter if I spilt on it or dropped flakes of chocolate down the side of the seat cushion. In fact, my mother was almost pleased if she saw me eat while sitting there, or if I forgot to take my shoes off when I put my feet up, and normally she was the fussiest person in the world. Tucking my legs up under me I fished out what was left of my apple from my pocket and took a bite, resting my head against the back of the chair. It smelt comfortingly of dirty wool and old pipe smoke.

'So there I'll be,' Olivia was saying, 'the mother of an instant family. A boy of twelve called Linus. Strange little chap, podgy, mostly quiet.'

'That's a mercy, that he's quiet I mean. Boys can be so ... so hideously there.' Audrey lit a cigarette and I sniffed the first tobacco sweetness before the smoke turned acrid, and munched on my apple.

'Then, all of a sudden he'll have these outbursts.'

'Outbursts?' Audrey asked. I stopped chewing and leant forward in my chair.

'Sudden explosions of joy. I think that's the best way of describing it. Very disconcerting and drives his father up the wall, but then, to be fair to the little chap, any child would. Bertil is such a perfectionist, and so utterly in control and on top of life, so bloody good at everything he does. I told you he's an architect, didn't I?'

'Darling, he sounds exhausting.' At that they both laughed, although I couldn't see what was funny. Instead I wondered if Olivia would be impressed to hear that I knew what perfectionist meant. Then again, if I spoke they would remember I was there and I would be told to go away and play, when I much preferred to stay in the large green chair and listen to the grown-ups talk and imagine what I would be like if I were one. That afternoon I very much wanted to have freckles all over, like Olivia, and large hands with big rings set with stones.

'Of course it's hard for a child to grow up without a mother,' Olivia said and I felt like pointing out to her that it was hard for a child to grow up *with* a mother too. 'And the way it happened can't have made it any easier,' she went on. 'Not that the boy knows much about it. Bertil wants to protect him for as long as possible. Actually, I doubt that he'll ever feel ready to speak of it. I certainly can't get much out of him.'

I was confused. What did they need to protect this Linus from? Where was his mother?

'How did she die? The first wife?'

So the boy's mother was dead. I too wanted to know how. We had just learnt about leprosy at school. Lots of people used to die from leprosy and they still did, in Africa. If Linus's mother had died a long time ago as they said she had, maybe that was it. I could see why they didn't want to tell Linus. It's horrible. Their fingers and toes fall off and their noses . . .

'Linus was five or six, something like that,' Olivia said. I liked her shoes as well. They were nicer than Janet's, but they still looked as if you could run pretty fast in them. When we were out together, Audrey, Madox and I, we always had to wait for Audrey to catch up and sometimes we had to stop at some boring old café just so that she would be able to rest her feet. She always said it had nothing to do with those shoes she wore, all pointy and high-heeled, but I didn't believe her. Once I suggested that she bought a pair like Janet's, I even offered to find out which shop Janet got hers from, but Audrey had just laughed and said, 'Honestly, darling, do you think I would be caught dead wearing shoes like that?' Obviously there was something very wrong with Janet's shoes, but I couldn't see it myself. I had thought then, and I thought now, that being caught dead was precisely what she might be if she carried on wearing those silly shoes she liked if some lion or tiger or something chased her and she couldn't run.

'So have you got a photo of your Bertil?'

'Not on me, no.'

'No starry-eyed romantic you.' Audrey laughed and shook her head. 'When I was engaged to Madox I carried his picture in this tiny silk purse around my neck, next to my heart.'

'When Linus's mother died, did he have to wear black clothes?' My voice, coming from the depths of the green armchair, seemed to startle them. They both turned round and stared at me as if they were indeed surprised to see me still in the room.

'I really don't know,' Olivia said finally. 'But I shouldn't think so. He was very young.'

'Maybe he had to wear a black band around his arm?' I suggested.

'Esther, Olivia wasn't there. Now why don't you run along and play? Do a nice picture for Olivia.'

I knew it! Being told to draw a picture was the oldest trick of them all when it came to getting rid of children. 'Why don't you run along to your room and draw me a really pretty picture,' Audrey would say. But then when I'd done one and I showed it to her it was as if she had forgotten that she had ever asked me for one. Honestly, it made you think she never wanted a picture in the first place.

'Come on, Esther, do what Mummy asked you and draw Olivia a really nice picture to take back to Sweden with her.'

I always told myself I wouldn't fall for it again, but what choice did I have? Reluctantly, I propelled myself off the chair and pottered off, pausing briefly in the doorway. 'When Amy Tillesly's grandmother died Amy had to wear a black band around her arm for a whole month.' I remembered because I had wanted to wear one very badly myself. There was no comment from my mother or Olivia so, disgruntled, I trundled upstairs to my bedroom, right at the top of the house. I brought out my coloured pencils and my drawing pad and set to work, lying flat on my tummy on the green rug. When I had finished I sat back on my heels and inspected the result. It was quite good, I thought. There was a tall old man, I had written *Bertle* underneath just in case Olivia didn't recognise him, and next to him stood a small round boy, Linus of course, wearing shorts and a cap. I looked some more at my picture and scratched the tip of my nose with my crayon, then I picked up a black one instead and drew a black band round the boy's arm.

'You will grow up to be the kind of man who sits on his hat.' With his teacher's words ringing in his ears, Linus Stendal trudged through the wintry streets of Gothenburg. He felt the colour rise in his cheeks at the memory of the titters that had rippled through the classroom and he blinked and shook himself. No matter, it was over for that day. He was on his way home and already it was getting dark. The first snow of the winter had fallen the night before, but it had not been cold enough in the centre of town to allow it to rest on the ground. Instead it had melted to a grey slush that seeped through the joins of his black zip-up ankle boots and settled in a mess on the toe-caps. People were hurrying past, their heads bent low against the icy wind, its gusts like a shower of glass needles against the face. Linus pulled his red woolly hat further down his forehead, but he kept his steady slow pace of walking. Dawdling, his father called it and it drove him crazy with irritation.

'When I was your age I ran everywhere, I didn't even know the meaning of the word "walk",' Bertil would say. Well, Linus just wasn't made for running. Not only because of his roundness, but more because of his thoughts; they simply couldn't catch up with him if he walked too fast.

A stream of cars passed, their headlights on, the sound of their tyres

11

squelching through the slush-filled gutters. That sound meant winter had really come and Linus, for one, was glad. He liked being indoors best, and in winter people did not nag him quite so much to go outside and play. Right now his model kit, a Spitfire, lay waiting for him in his bedroom in the large third-floor apartment he shared with his father. Thinking of the model kit made Linus speed up so that now he was keeping pace with everyone else. It had taken him almost two months to save up enough money to buy the kit, and even then he had had to dip into his emergency funds stored in a black-and-yellow tin hidden in a shoebox at the back of his wardrobe. Last night he had brought all the components of the kit out of their packaging, easing each piece from its plastic frame, snapping the little plastic stalks that held them in place, carefully, before arranging them all on his blue Formica-topped desk, ready for today. He crossed the street, his cheeks pink with pleasurable anticipation. Still, at Paleys café he paused for a moment, as he always did, to look through the large windows at the round marble-topped tables and small straight-backed gilt chairs, and at the counter at the front of the shop, laden with pastries and cakes and buns of every kind. Linus and his mother used to go there together before the accident. He had been little then, but he remembered the last time they went. It was winter, like now, and he had burrowed his face into the sleeve of her coat. If he closed his eyes he could feel the coarse softness of the fur against his cheek and the faint smell of camphor. With a little sigh he hurried on his way.

He was about to fish out the key he carried round his neck on a metal chain to unlock the front door when it was opened from the inside.

'Daddy!' Linus rushed inside pulling his knitted hat off his head revealing dark-blond hair, wavy and damp with sweat. 'Why are you home so early?'

'Good afternoon, Linus. And please remove your boots, you're bringing the entire street inside with you.' Linus's cheeks turned a deeper pink as he knelt down, clumsily unzipping the boots. 'When you've washed your hands and combed your hair I'd like you to come into the library. I've got something to tell you.'

Linus could not help himself. 'What is it? What's happened?'

Bertil sighed. It was a special sigh, a mixture of irritation and resignation, reserved just for Linus. 'I believe that I told you a second ago that I would see you in the library in a minute.' Bertil turned on his heels and strode off, leaving Linus still struggling with his boots.

Linus washed his face and hands, and combed his hair, parting it carefully to one side, trying in vain to make it lie flat against his head instead of springing up in those embarrassing curls. On his way to the library he sneaked into his bedroom to take just a little look at his model. On the threshold he stopped, his grey eyes rounder than ever. The blue Formica desk was bare apart from the photograph of Linus as a little boy seated on his mother's lap, the brown imitation leather pencil case and the large pencil sharpener fixed to the side of the desk top. The carefully-laid-out pieces of Linus's model aeroplane were nowhere to be seen. With an anguished little yelp Linus scurried across the room and up to the desk, pulling out the drawer underneath. There they were, the components of his plane, thrown in just any old way among his tin soldiers, the bits of modelling clay, and the handfuls of marbles and pencil stubs.

'It's too bad, Daddy, really it is. She had no right.' Linus was all hot and bothered as he appeared in the library; his cheeks had turned bright pink again and his hair was springing up in those damp curls he detested.

Bertil Stendal looked up from the business section of the paper, taking his pipe out of his mouth. 'There you are, Linus.' He glanced at his watch.

'She's ruined it, that's what she's done. She had no right. It's my . . .'

'Linus, would you please be quiet for a moment and sit down. I've got something important to tell you.'

Linus fell silent, sitting down on the sofa beneath the portrait of his grandfather. Inside, though, he was fuming, churned up with anxiety. In the end he could not help himself. 'I bet she's lost some pieces and if she has then everything is . . .'

'Linus.' Bertil's voice held a warning. There was a pause as he collected himself. Before his inner eye Linus saw his father separate into two, one Bertil striding off angrily as the other followed, putting a hand on the angry one's shoulder and bringing him back to their mutual body. He stifled a giggle as Bertil spoke again.

'Now, you'll be aware that I enjoy the company of Tante Olivia very much. I have been lonely since your mother died.' Linus looked up at his father, surprised at the suggestions of him harbouring emotions similar to Linus's own. 'And, well, what I wanted to tell you is that Olivia has consented to be my wife and therefore your new mother.'

'You and Tante Olivia are getting married?'

Bertil heaved that special Linus sigh. 'Yes, Linus, that is exactly what I've just told you. I hope this arrangement meets with your approval.'

Linus tried to concentrate his thoughts, still hovering anxiously around the question of his model, on his father's news. He liked Tante Olivia. She didn't talk down to him or ruffle his hair. She did not talk that much at all, come to think of it, and she left him alone in his room to do what he wished. His father was in a better mood when she was around and once she had cooked him a really good meal, something English with fish and normally he did not like fish very much. She was English but she had lived in Sweden long enough not to be embarrassing like Johan Falk's mum who came from Argentina. Mrs Falk talked all the time and in a very loud voice and she hugged everyone, even Linus whom she hardly knew. He knew he could rely on Tante Olivia not to be embarrassing like that.

He nodded to his father. 'It's very nice. Are you engaged now?'

His father's rather thin lips parted into one of his rare smiles. 'Yes, Linus my boy, we are indeed.'

Linus liked it when Bertil called him 'My boy', but he thought that if his father would only smile a bit more often he would manage to do it better. 'Practise, Linus,' his gym teacher was always telling him as Linus's legs refused to reach up to the wooden bar. 'Practise and it will stretch.' Maybe if Bertil practised his smile a bit more, it too would stretch.

'Where is she, Tante Olivia?' he asked, remembering that he had not seen her for a while.

'She's been back to England for a visit. She returned this morning. So, have you any more questions?' Bertil's glance passed from his son to the stack of papers on his desk.

'If Tante Olivia comes to live with us can we stop having Fru Sparre? She had no right to come into my room and spoil my things like that and just . . .'

'Linus, stop ranting. I'm going out to dinner in a little while. A small celebration. Fru Sparre left some meatballs for you. You can heat

14

them up in the frying pan if you wish or eat them cold. And there's lingonberry preserve in the fridge. I especially reminded Fru Sparre to get some.' Linus cheered up momentarily; meatballs with lingonberries was his favourite. 'So, my boy.' Bertil got up from the leather armchair and walked across to Linus, placing his hands on Linus's shoulders. 'You're pleased?'

'Yes, thank you.' Linus looked up at his father. 'The other day I had to have my meatballs without lingonberries.'

Bertil withdrew his hands. 'I meant about Tante Olivia and me, Linus.'

Linus's high pale forehead creased in concentration. 'I haven't had time to think properly, but I think I am. And if you're happy . . .'

Later that evening Linus sat in the light of his blue-shaded desklamp painstakingly reassembling the pieces of his model while listening to Bob Dylan singing 'Mr Tambourine Man' on the record player. Outside his room the apartment was dark and silent. Linus looked up from his work at the photograph of his mother with him on her knee and tears began to fill his eyes, running down his round cheeks and into his mouth. He sniffed and wiped them away with the back of his grubby hand, before bending down over his work once more.

# Chapter Two

'The opening of Olivia's friend's gallery went well, apparently.' Audrey was reading her letter, her gold-rimmed spectacles down low on her nose. Now and then she mumbled a sentence out loud, but not loud enough for me or my father to hear, not until she looked up with an 'Oh God, how awful!'.

'What?' Madox, my father, looked up from the pages of the *Guardian.*

'That boy, Linus. It seems he pigged out on pop and crisps, ending up writhing in agony on the floor in the middle of the opening party. He's prone to stomach upsets, Olivia says. Anyway,' My mother scanned the letter before continuing, ' "his father carted him off to casualty, but not before the wretched boy had thrown up all over the main exhibit," ' she quoted. ' "A *Madonna and Child Running in Terror under Attack from US War Planes." '* Audrey shook her head and reached for a cigarette from the black onyx box on the coffee table. My father leant across and lit it, and one for himself too. I wished I smoked. Not smoking was yet another thing to make me feel apart. I was short too, though I knew that was normal for a ten-year-old, and I had to go to bed really early although I was never sleepy, while Audrey, who stayed up on the sofa half the night, kept dozing off in front of the television. Now I watched my parents draw on their cigarettes in unison, identical little smiles of satisfaction on their faces, thin tendrils of smoke spilling out from their lips. As it was Saturday, I had a bag of sweets.

'What was a sculpture of a Madonna and Child etc. doing at a craft gallery?' Madox asked my mother. Audrey shrugged. She looked again at the letter. 'Maybe it was wood.' She put it aside. 'The boy is thirteen. You would have thought he'd have grown out of that kind of behaviour.'

I had finished my sweets. 'Maybe,' I said, making my mother turn to me with a slightly startled look as if she had momentarily forgotten who I was. 'Maybe they should be grateful to him. Maybe the sick looked just like napalm.'

'I told you we shouldn't let that child watch the evening news,' Audrey said to Madox, making me look around the room to see who *that* child was. Then I got up from the upholstered stool where I had been sitting. I looked pointedly at my watch. It was quite new, a present for my tenth birthday, with a small round face and a red real leather strap. It kept excellent time. My parents seemed to regret having given it to me. 'It's eleven o'clock,' I announced from the doorway.

'Thank you, Esther,' my father said, not even looking up from his paper. He had switched from the *Guardian*, now folded on his lap, to *The Times*. Madox had to read all the papers because he wrote for one himself. He was a political commentator and he went on the radio too, and twice already he had appeared on television. Audrey had put Olivia's letter away and now she was studying the flowers she had arranged in an Alvar Alto vase. She frowned at them and I knew how they felt: untidy, in the wrong place, then she put out her hand and tweaked a twig of mimosa. She did that to me too, tweaked bits of me, my hair, the collars on my shirts, whatever offended her view.

'We were meant to leave at a quarter to,' I complained. 'It's now' – I looked at my watch – 'three and a half minutes past.'

'I said be ready to leave at a quarter to, not we are necessarily leaving then,' Madox said.

I looked at him, appalled. Parents were congenitally unfair, every child knew that, but this was going too far. I had to speak up. 'You know that when you say "be ready to leave at a quarter to, Esther" that means that's when we're meant to go and that if I wasn't ready and you were, then I would get into trouble.'

'Oh, do stop going on and on, child,' Audrey snapped. Madox carried on reading.

'It's not fair,' I said. 'If it had been . . .' Madox put down the paper with a little splat, on top of the other one. 'One more word from you, Esther, and the only place you'll be going is your room.' He reached for another cigarette. I felt torn; on the one hand I wanted him to put it out, the cigarette, so that we could leave, on the other hand I knew that Smoking Kills and, right then, I hated him.

'Oh, Esther.' My mother turned to me, a blue iris in her hand. 'What does it matter *when* you leave as long as you do?'

I spun round and dashed out on the landing, throwing myself down on the green ottoman by the window. What does it matter? my mother asks. It's as I suspected for a long time; she doesn't understand. Madox had said be ready to leave at quarter to eleven and we both knew that meant that was when he intended for us to leave. Then he goes and changes the rules just because it suits him and, worst of all, he doesn't even admit to doing it. I hated it when people did that. It made me feel that simply no one could be relied on. Janet had said once that it was just as well I felt like that. 'In this world you'll have to learn to rely on yourself,' she had said. That was all very well, I thought now, wiping an annoying tear from my right eye, then from my left, but I was a child, I didn't have a car, let alone a cheque-book, how would I live? From the drawing-room I heard Audrey's voice. 'It's like living with a sergeant-major,' she said.

'Look on the bright side,' Madox replied. 'At least she doesn't puke all over our *objets d'art.*'

'Dear God, make him smoke a whole packet of cigarettes,' I mumbled. I felt instantly guilty. 'Actually, just one, dear God,' I whispered hastily.

At half past Madox finally appeared on the landing. 'Oh, there you are, Esther,' he said. 'Ready to go? Got your money?'

Silently I held up my purse, which was red like the watch-strap, but made from imitation leather not real. Inside were five pound notes, payment for my appearance as a tooth fairy in a television toothpaste commercial. It had been a disaster. I had been spotted at Peter Jones by a friend of Audrey's. The woman, a complete stranger to me, had rushed out from behind a display of sewing machines, bent down and clasped my face in her hands. 'How darling!' she had exclaimed. 'How absolutely darling.' Then she knelt down on the shop carpet and peered at me. At this stage I expected my mother to intervene; after all, I was not supposed to talk to strangers and this woman was stranger than most, but not a bit of it.

'Darling,' Audrey shrieked as the stranger got to her feet. Then they kissed.

'She's perfect,' the woman said. 'Is she yours?' Sometimes, when asked this, my mother seemed reluctant to answer, but this time she said 'Yes' rather quickly.

'Well, I want her,' the stranger proclaimed.

I began to get worried. I know I complain about my mother, but she was my mother and I was used to her. I think I loved her. All right, there had been that time the other day when I had knelt by my bed and prayed to God that he would strike her dead, but I didn't really mean it.

I tugged at her arm. 'I think we should leave now,' I hissed. 'Just tell her she can't have me and let's go.'

Audrey shrugged me off. 'Esther, I don't know what your problem is, but this is Mrs Debray. I want you to say hello nicely.' I glared and muttered 'Hello'.

'Mrs Debray and I are very old friends,' Audrey went on. 'Mrs Debray is in films.' They decided to go upstairs and have coffee. Mrs Debray ordered a Coke for me.

'I want you to be in a little film of mine, Esther, a commercial, now isn't that something?' She had crouched down again, so that her eyes were level with mine across the table. I looked back at her, wishing that I could suddenly telescope, like Alice, right up and away from her sight. Instead I said, 'Whenever anyone says "Isn't that something" my daddy always says "Well, isn't everything".'

'Don't be cheeky, Esther.' Audrey frowned at me.

'I wasn't being cheeky,' I began. 'Daddy always says that when people . . .'

'That's enough, Esther.' Audrey's voice held a warning of unpleasantness to come. But Mrs Debray just smiled and said again how perfect I was. My mother and I both looked doubtful. In the end, I was offered the part of the Bad Tooth Fairy. I rather liked the idea, looking forward to playing the role. I spent hours hissing and grimacing in the mirror, the way a bad fairy would hiss and grimace. I even coloured my front teeth black with liquorice. The day of filming began and disaster struck. Just minutes before I was due to appear, and was trapped in a dressing-room in just my vest and knickers, the director decided that I was just right for the part of the Good Tooth Fairy. 'All those dark curls and those bright blue eyes. Great complexion. Good teeth too' (my mother had made me clean off the black liquorice).

No one listened to my protests. I tried to tell them that good fairies are supposed to have golden hair and that bad fairies had dark, just like mine, but it was no good, they just wouldn't listen. Instead they milled round me, tugging at my hair, tying ribbons in it, pulling petticoats over my head, and before I knew it I was squeezed into a white tulle frock covered in pink rosebuds. I could feel my face go the same colour, from sheer humiliation, but that only seemed to please them even more. 'What wonderful colouring. Just like Snow White.'

Snow White! A well-known drip. The worst of it was that while all this was happening to me my mother just stood there looking pleased. Who, I asked myself, could you rely on in this world?

But I did earn some money, five pounds which were given directly to me to spend on whatever I liked and I planned to spend it in Hamleys, as soon as my father got us there.

It was Saturday and the shop was crowded, all five floors of it. Madox got tetchy before we had even reached the second. I had watched a man building a Lego castle, then I had moved on to the soft toys. It wasn't often I had that kind of money to spend and I wanted to make the most of it. There was a cuddly giraffe that I liked very much, but it turned out to be too expensive. I didn't mind. It was better not to find what I wanted straight away, that way it wouldn't all be over too soon. Next I moved to the dolls. I paused at the Barbies. I hated Ken. As far as I was concerned he was plain ugly; that short, bristly hair. I preferred his friend, Alan. Maybe I would get an Alan? Behind me, Madox cleared his throat; an impatient sound. Now if *he* had been forced to be a goody-goody fairy on television, *I* would have said he deserved to spend a really long time to choose something nice for his money. But I had noticed before that adults were seldom as fair as children. What happened on the way? Everyone assumed that children grew into adults, but the more I saw, the more I doubted it. Maybe there was an exchange? Maybe, on the eve of their sixteenth birthday children were snatched from their beds and exchanged for adults? That led me to think that there had to be a very nice place somewhere, where all those children were kept.

I ignored Madox and moved on to a display of tiny baby dolls. They each came in their own little pouch and you could buy all kinds of things to go with them: cots and prams and masses of clothes. I picked out one with dark hair like me. She could be my little sister. She cost one pound, ninety-nine pence. I could get a set of clothes or a cot for the rest of my money. I hesitated; it was a big decision and I wasn't sure. Then I saw them, a set of handbells, plump and pastel-coloured: pink, apricot, yellow and blue, lavender and turquoise. *Produces a full and professional sound*, the packaging declared. *Full instructions and a book of easy-to-learn melodies included*. I closed my eyes and imagined myself the owner of the bells. I could practise when I was alone in the house or late at night when everyone slept, standing in my bedroom, ringing my bells. If my parents woke up they would think they were in heaven.

'Come on, Esther.' Madox sounded bored. 'What will it be?'

I took a deep breath and opened my eyes. 'I like those,' I said, pointing at the bells.

Madox picked the cardboard and cellophane box down off the shelf, frowning at them. What was wrong? Were they too expensive? I hadn't seen the price. I looked up at his face, waiting for his frown to clear.

'Aren't you a bit old for that kind of thing? You've got a proper instrument at home. Still.' He handed me the box. 'It's your money. Don't let me interfere.'

I didn't look at the handbells as I returned them to the shelf. 'I was just thinking,' I said quickly, feeling myself turn pink. 'That's really what I want.' I grabbed a box of plastic shapes. 'You make patterns,' I explained.

'I told you,' Madox said, already on his way over to the till. 'It's your money.'

Back home, Audrey glanced at the box with its illustration on the lid of two children, a boy and a girl, both dressed in bright sleeveless pullovers and engrossed in the task of drawing geometric patterns with the help of the plastic shapes. 'Stencils, very nice, darling.' She turned to Madox. 'Now what shall we do about dinner? In or out? Out, I think. I can't bear the thought of cooking. Why Janet has to insist on visiting her mother every weekend I'll never know. The old dear can't remember a thing anyway. "Janet," I said. "Go once a month and just say see you next week as usual. She'll never know the difference."'

I wandered upstairs and put the box of stencils away, unopened, in the cupboard of my dresser. Then I lay down on my bed, clutching Pigotty, the vast red cloth pig my grandmother Billings had given me at Christmas, to my chest. 'He's a prince among pigs,' my grand-mother had said and she was right. Pigotty had teats for a start, little brass buttons running down his striped grey-and-white belly – Audrey had said that that should have told me that *he* was a *she*, but I said that it just made him an even more exceptional *he*. And he was such a sensible pig. He never worried about his weight, for a start, and he had the most even temper of anyone I had ever met. Right now he agreed with me that the pastel-coloured handbells would have been wonder-ful. 'But it's not a catastrophe,' he went on in his calm voice. 'When you're grown up and are a psychiatrist you can buy as many handbells as you like and play them all night if you wish.' Then, because he was such a sensible and intelligent pig, he added, 'Although I suspect that by that time you might prefer something like an electric guitar. Now would you care for a drink? Coke or lemonade?'

'It's a good report.' Bertil Stendal gave his son one of his pale smiles and passed the piece of paper to his wife. 'Fours in most things, but a three in music. Still, five in art and maths.' Bertil turned to Linus again. 'Taking after your stepmother, are you? Anyway, well done.' He allowed a well-shaped hand to rest briefly on his son's shoulder.

'Yes, well done, Linus,' Olivia echoed. But as she looked at her stepson she wondered whom exactly he did take after. Allegedly he looked like his dead mother, the woman whose presence she still felt so clearly in the house on the island and even here, in the large high-ceilinged flat. (Only the other day she could have sworn she heard the keys of the grand piano being pressed, but when she went to check in the library there was no one there.) 'Typical second wife syndrome,' she had written to Audrey Fisher in her last letter. The photographs she had seen of Astrid showed a thin young woman, fair and fragile-looking, and with a lost look in her large eyes. It was that look especially that Olivia had seen far too often echoed in Linus's eyes. Those who had known Astrid spoke of her gentleness and her talent. She could have done something with her life, they said, if only . . .

Maybe she was uncharitable, but Olivia couldn't help feeling that had Astrid lived until she was a hundred she would still not have done very much more than drifted. In that way Linus was not at all like her. In fact, he never stopped working, especially if you counted the hours he put into those cartoon drawings of his. Now, at thirteen, Linus was tall, taller already than Olivia, slim and ethereal looking like his mother, but inside, Olivia suspected, he still felt like the plump little boy she had first met five years ago. So what had the boy got of his father? A talent for drawing. An abiding interest in his surroundings. But if Bertil was a stern Olympian looking down on the world from a plane of unquestioned success and a serenity which it seemed only his son could shake, Linus seemed to live mostly on a small planet of his own, far away from them all. There, in this other place, he constructed his increasingly complex models, drew and listened to music. According to his teachers he was a model pupil, when, as one of them put it at the last parent-teacher meeting, 'he chooses to grace us with his presence'.

'Are you telling me my son is playing truant?' Bertil had asked.

The teacher had smiled. 'Not physically, but there are times when his mind most definitely is. He gets his grades by returning just in the nick of time.' What could you do with a boy like that? Olivia looked at the child, dressed right then in shocking-pink corduroy trousers and a wine-red shirt and black knitted tie, clothes he had insisted on choosing himself. He might be tall and thin these days, but his hair still curled when damp and his cheeks still turned bright pink at the drop of a hat. They had now, with pleasure at the praise received from his father. Bertil made some jokey reference to the brains of the family and as Linus's cheeks turned an even deeper colour, Olivia braced herself for the inevitable high-pitched, abandoned laugh. There it was, rising like pollen in the air, irritating her husband's finely tuned sensibilities, making him frown and sigh.

'Here,' he said, picking out his wallet from the inside pocket of his jacket. 'Buy yourself something nice. One of those plane model kits maybe?' He handed Linus five crisp ten-kronor notes. Bertil's bank-notes were never anything other than crisp and sometimes Olivia imagined her husband staying up late, starching them in the privacy of his study.

Back in his room, Linus put the money in his brown leather wallet.

He had stopped building those prefabricated model kits ages ago, but obviously Bertil had not noticed. Still, Linus knew exactly what he was going to spend the money on. He grabbed his red woollen hat and pressed it down on his head (he had convinced himself that by wearing it almost all the time – he even slept with it on at night – he would finally flatten those curls once and for all). On the Avenue he lifted his face to the sun, squinting up at the pea-green leaves of the limes. At the kiosk by the Park Avenue Hotel he paused, wondering if he should buy himself an ice-cream. He decided against it and walked on down the wide street until he reached the stationers. Inside the large shop he aimed for the display at the middle of the room where the notebooks were: bound ones, soft ones, patterned ones and blank ones. He looked through them for a good ten minutes, carefully turning each one around in his long-fingered hands that were so like his father's, looking inside at the paper, sniffing it. Finally he made his decision.

His notebook was bound in marbled gold and tan, with a tan imitation leather spine, and each page was edged with gold. The pages were plain and quite thin, and as he stood waiting at the till, his fingers itched to begin to fill the book with his cartoons. Once out of the shop he walked so fast he did not even see Ulf and Stig, his friends from school. The two boys were ambling down the Avenue in the opposite direction, on their way to the sports fields.

Ulf, his football tucked under his left arm, reached out and grabbed the sleeve of Linus's blue sweater. 'Want to kick around?' he asked.

Startled, because in his mind he had been far away, Linus narrowed his eyes to focus. 'Hi, guys.' He shifted from foot to foot and burst into one of his high-pitched giggles. 'I didn't see you there. I didn't see you at all. But I have to go home.'

Ulf shrugged his shoulders. 'OK.' And he bounced the ball on the pavement before kicking a pass at Stig. An elderly woman, wearing a long woollen coat in spite of the spring sunshine, almost fell over it and stopped for a moment to remonstrate. 'Sorry,' Ulf muttered, then he pulled a face and the three boys doubled up with laughter as the woman went on her disgruntled way.

By the time Linus reached home, Bertil and Olivia had gone out. He remembered them telling him they were off somewhere for the day, but where they said they were going he had forgotten. He was pleased to have the place to himself. He could keep his woollen hat on, for a start, without having to have an argument about it (last time the subject came up he had declared that he would convert to Judaism if that was the only way he was going to be allowed to keep a hat on inside, but Bertil had threatened to call the rabbi, who was his friend, and tell him that Linus's motives for conversion were less than pure).

Linus went into the kitchen and made himself a chocolate milkshake and three large sandwiches, two with cheese and one with smoked sausage. He sat at the table thinking about his book and once he had finished eating he washed his plate and cup, and wiped the green oilcloth that covered the table. Then, at last, he was ready to start work.

Seated at his desk, he opened the first page of the notebook and wrote: *My Life as It Ought to Be: A Young Boy's Wonderful Adventures (in pictures)*.

In the summer I got a puppy, a little West Highland called Laurence, after Laurence Olivier. I had wanted to call him Jumble after William Brown's dog in the *Just William* stories, but Audrey got her way. I often heard people complain that these days children got their way far too much; well, all I can say is that they had not met Audrey. No matter, both Audrey and Madox had assured me that Laurence was mostly my dog, almost entirely, in fact. The only problem was to convince Laurence. I loved him. I had wanted a dog for as long as I could remember, a big dog who would be my best friend and who went on adventures with me. What kind of adventures I had not decided, but they invariably involved a well-filled picnic basket and a dog on whose powerful head I could rest my hand. Now Laurence was small, and if I tried to rest my hand on his neck we'd both most probably collapse on the floor, but he was *my* dog, almost. Right now, out here on the wide lawn he was making a huge fuss over Granny Billings who didn't even like dogs. Deep inside me a little seed of resentment sprouted a green leaf of jealousy. Why, when I loved Laurence so much, did he seem to love almost everyone better than me?

'Come here, boy?' I bent down and slapped my knees, encouraging my puppy towards me. Laurence, who was busy flirting with Granny Billings's left leg, turned his head for a second before rolling over on his back and wriggling wildly, his eyes, their whites showing, fixed on the adored object of Granny Billings.

'Come on, boy!' I tried, humiliation making my cheeks hot.

'Oh, do give up, Esther.' Audrey sipped her iced coffee in the dappled shade of the large beech tree. 'Why don't you run along and wash your hands. Lunch will be soon.'

I washed my hands in the china basin in the little bedroom that was mine during my visits to the country. Through the open window I could hear my mother telling Laurence not to be a pest. Pigotty in my arms, I sat back in the small wicker armchair and picked up my book, resting it on Pigotty's ample back. Why couldn't Laurence be more like Joey, the dog in the book? Joey loved his owner, a girl called Georgie, and never left her side. In fact, he had been repeatedly punished by Georgie's unsympathetic aunt, with whom they lived, for refusing to leave his place by Georgie's bedroom door at night to sleep downstairs in the scullery where he was supposed to. In the mornings Georgie was woken by Joey's rough tongue licking her face and all day long they played together in the fields. I craned my neck to look out of the open window to the garden below. There was Laurence standing on his hind legs, trying in vain to impress Audrey. Letting her hand drop, she absent-mindedly scratched Laurence's head and Laurence, beside himself with excitement, got down on all fours spinning round and round, chasing his tail. I turned back to my book, Laurence's excited yelps ringing in my ears.

Joey's devotion to his owner was matched by Georgie's faithfulness to him. *Georgie did not need other friends and she despised toys. What would she want with toys when she had Joey? No, Georgie wanted no one but Joey.*

I read that last line over and over again, Pigotty clutched to my stomach. There it was. How could I expect poor Laurence to be my best friend when I was so faithless. I had quite a few friends, usually, and I most certainly did not despise toys. I looked down and there was Pigotty. I clutched him tight to my chest, rubbing my cheek against the rough red cotton of his back. Pigotty was uncharacteristically silent.

'Esther! Lunch-time!' Audrey called.

I hardly slept that night, lying curled up with Pigotty at my centre like a large red cherry in a bun. In his basket in the corner of the room

Laurence yelped in his sleep. I rose at six while the house was still asleep and got dressed. Downstairs in the kitchen I fed Laurence his morning meal of warm milk and Weetabix, putting a couple of spoonfuls in my own mouth before placing the bowl on the floor. I could barely bring myself to look at him, let alone stroke him, and my stomach was churning at the thought of what had to be done.

Three hours later we were about to leave for London. Audrey had already put our bags in the boot of the Rover and now she was calling for me to come downstairs. I could just hear her voice, a faint, angry flutter in the dusty air of Granny Billings's attic. I was sitting in an old armchair, hugging Pigotty tight. Now I got down from the chair, Pigotty still in my arms. 'It'll be lovely,' I whispered in his striped cloth ear. 'Just like a holiday.' Gently, I lowered him into the old wicker shopping basket I had found on top of a trunk. 'A real holiday, just for you.' I opened the white chipped cupboard that stood in a corner of the room, the basket with Pigotty in my hand. On the top shelf of the cupboard lay a battered Panama hat. I put the basket down and standing on tiptoe, grabbed the hat from the shelf and placed it on Pigotty's head. It was a real holiday hat. Next I put the basket with Pigotty on the floor of the cupboard. 'Bye.' I tried to smile. 'Bye Pigotty.' I covered the basket with an emerald-coloured silk throw, which had been draped across an old chair.

'Esther, where are you?' Audrey's voice was coming closer. It sounded annoyed.

'Got to go,' I whispered, but then, instead of closing the door, I tore the throw off Pigotty and picked him up in my arms. Tears streaming down my face I sank down on the floor, hugging him close. 'Oh, Pigotty, I'll miss you so much.'

'Esther, wherever you are, come this minute or your father will hear about it.'

I scrambled up from the floor and put Pigotty back in the basket. I straightened his hat, but I could not bring myself to cover him up completely with the throw so I just placed it gently around him, trying to pretend he was right in the middle of a soft green field. Then I closed the door.

I thought I would never get the picture of his plump red face, his smiling, trusting face topped by that stupid hat, out of my mind.

Laurence was unmoved by the sacrifice and continued to love everyone who crossed his path with equal and abandoned fickleness.

'Whatever happened to that large pig you used to carry around?' Madox asked me months later. It was Christmas time and no doubt the big ham just delivered to the door had put him in mind of Pigotty. I frowned at my feet, feigning indifference. 'Dunno.'

'Don't know, darling, not dunno.' Audrey entered the drawing-room with an armful of gilded fir cones. It was Madox's turn to frown.

'I made this at school.' I shoved the red-and-green Father Christmas in front of her as she stood arranging the fir cones in a large blue china bowl. 'If you pull the string between his legs his arms and legs move up and down, look.'

'Lovely, darling,' Audrey singsonged, but I could tell she was still looking at her arrangement of fir cones.

'You didn't look.'

'Esther, don't be a bore.'

'It's very nice, Esther.' Madox had got out of his chair and picked up the Father Christmas. 'Where shall we hang it? In the window?'

Now Audrey looked up. 'Maybe not in here. It's lovely, but I've got the drawing-room all gold and blue this Christmas. What about the kitchen? Or your bedroom, Esther, then you'll be the lucky one.'

Did all parents assume their children were stupid or was it just mine? 'Actually, it was a present for you,' I muttered, stomping off feeling utterly humiliated, the unwanted Father Christmas dangling from my hand.

On Christmas Day itself even Madox and I ended up colour co-ordinated. I was wearing a brand-new sapphire-blue dress, to match my eyes, Audrey said, but I knew it was actually to match the drawing-room decorations. I got quite worried when I peeped inside the dining-room and saw the green-and-gold colour scheme there; would I be forced to spend the entire Christmas in the drawing-room? Just to be on the safe side I tied a green ribbon in my hair. Madox was wearing a gold silk cravat. 'She didn't try to tell you it matches your eyes, did she?' I asked sourly. We both knew there was no stopping Audrey once she was in the grip of some new fad, interior design being the one for the moment. I fervently prayed that she would be gripped by cake baking, like Arabella Felix's mother. Mrs Felix baked a cake every day for Arabella's tea: chocolate, Victoria sponge, lemon sponge, coffee and walnut. I liked the chocolate best.

'That poor child won't thank her mother when she ends up with clogged arteries and a permanent weight problem,' Audrey would say as she pointed me in the direction of the fruit bowl. I tried to tell her that we could worry about my arteries and my weight in a year or so's time and eat cake now, but she wouldn't listen.

At least we did have a real tree this year. It had been a close-run thing. Audrey hated pine needles, or at least she hated them when they fell on her parquet floor and Trish, her friend who ran an interior design shop, stocked American artificial ones. '. . . Not those dreadful plasticky ones you get from Woollies, darling, I promise,' she had said to Madox, but he had threatened to spend Christmas at his club so we got the real thing after all. 'I warn you.' Audrey had shot the tree a nasty glance. 'Once it starts messing the place up it's out.' She had sounded as if she were talking of some untidy house guest. So to make sure the tree stayed, I went to the drawing-room every morning to top up the water and to check that it wasn't getting too hot in there. And now it was Christmas Day. I spotted a green needle on the floor and bent down quickly to pick it up, secreting it in the breast pocket of my velvet dress. I straightened up and looked again at the tree. It was a murky morning and the room was in near darkness but the tiny golden Christmas lights twinkled like minute stars and cast a warm glow across the blue-and-gold baubles. Right at the back, on a low branch, I could glimpse my Father Christmas, put there by Madox and me the night before.

'So, Linus, did you enjoy your Christmas?' Olivia asked him at breakfast on Boxing Day.

Linus thought about the question and decided that he had not. 'It wasn't anyone's fault,' he assured Olivia. He had known this Christmas wouldn't be right from the very start on the first of Advent when Bertil had said, 'I assumed you wouldn't want to bother with a calendar this year, now you're almost fifteen.' Age, Linus thought, seemed not to be absolute but relative, a convenience that shifted according to the whims of adults. All he could be sure of was that he was never the *right* age. The other day it had been: *What are you thinking about? Of course you can't go skiing on your own with your friends, you're only fourteen.* Now, all of a sudden, he was nearly fifteen and too old for an Advent calender He had to remind himself of this as he woke on the first Sunday of Advent. Not for him lying there, tingling with excitement at the thought of the beginning of Christmas. *He* was too old. He had got out of bed and gone into the kitchen to make coffee for them all as he had done every first of Advent for years. Then they would gather round the kitchen table and Bertil would read the nativity story as Linus lit the first of the four Advent candles. But as he stood there, barefoot in the kitchen, about to measure out the coffee, he thought suddenly that he was probably too old for all of that too. He had left the measuring spoon in the coffee jar and gone back to bed. And Christmas lost its tinsel twinkle magic. To make matters worse, they had stayed at home on Christmas Eve itself instead of going to Aunt Lisa's, as they had every Christmas that Linus could remember. It was no one's fault, he thought again. After all, he was sure that Aunt Lisa had not *meant* to die the week before Christmas, but nevertheless she had. And because of it Uncle Gerald, who was Aunt Lisa's brother and really Linus's father's uncle, and Aunt Marie, his wife, and their daughter Kerstin, who was exactly Linus's age, had decided to go abroad for a change of scene. This meant that on Christmas Eve, Linus and his father and Olivia had been left with only Aunt Ulla. Now she was no one's aunt, not really, but Linus's mother's cousin. Linus had been surprised at how much he had missed the others. Kerstin was just an annoying girl and he got quite cross with her for following him around in the summer holidays when they were all out on the island, but at Christmas he liked her there. She was part of the tradition, like the gold star they fixed on top of the tree. And Uncle Gerald told funny stories about Bertil as a child, which embarrassed Bertil but made Linus marvel at how normal his father had been once. They always played lots of games too. They never did much at other times of the year, but at Christmas it was as if everyone took on an extra shine, becoming more of everything. Uncle Gerald's stories became funnier and Ulla too was funny when she struggled to know the answers to the trivia quiz. She still hadn't worked out that Gerald and Bertil rigged it every year. Aunt Marie sang songs to go with the schnapps, although normally she was really quiet. But not this year. Instead, they were left with Ulla, whom he liked, but she wasn't enough. It was like having the Christmas dinner with just the baked ham but no smoked eel or herring or red cabbage or boiled sausage or any of the other things that showed it could not possibly be any other day than Christmas Eve. Still, Ulla knew interesting stuff and this year she had told him that knowledge was the single most attractive quality a man could have. Linus felt very unattractive at that particular time so he set about reading his Christmas books with greater interest than ever, especially the one with Shakespeare's sonnets. If Ulla was right Lotten, in the year below him at school, could be his by Easter. Linus sighed and helped himself to some soured milk to go on his cereal.

'Audrey called while you were in the bathroom,' Olivia told her husband. 'Wishing us all a happy Christmas.'

'Is she still angry?' Linus wanted to know.

'Audrey? Audrey isn't angry?'

'I meant Esther,' Linus explained, his mouth full of cornflakes. He felt his father's disapproving glance on him and hunched up as if ducking under a low-flying object.

'What do you mean, is she still angry?' Olivia asked.

Linus swallowed and wiped his chin before answering. 'Every photo I've seen of her she looks angry. In that fairy one and the one from her last birthday when she's holding the puppy and well, every one *I've* seen anyway.'

'I haven't really thought of it,' Olivia said. 'But now you mention it, she is rather a cross child.'

## Chapter Three

I had been sent to Coventry by the whole upper school. It was all so unfair. I really liked Jenny Wilde in Upper Fifth and I had only been trying to help. We were all supposed to sew our own aprons for cookery. So last week we were told that those pupils who hadn't finished making their aprons by Friday would have to bring them home and finish them off over the weekend. Jenny, who was no good at all at sewing and had lots left to do, got really upset because she had planned to go to a rock concert with her boy-friend. So I told her I'd finish hers for her. I had liked Jenny ever since the time she told the others to leave me alone when they called me an oddball. I can't remember why they did, that time, but Jenny had been really nice and put her arms round me, and said she thought it was quite nice to be an oddball and that once her father had been told he was one, and now he was something really important in the Post Office and didn't that show them? She was very pretty too, Jenny, the way I'd like to be pretty, all round with soft brown eyes and soft brown hair and soft brown skin.

I worked really hard at the weekend, finishing her apron, thinking how pleased she'd be. I didn't even watch *Dr Who* on television as I usually did. But still, it all went wrong. I was walking down the school corridor on Monday morning when I heard someone yelling. It was Miss Jessop, the sewing teacher, and she was yelling at Jenny, saying how her apron was a disgrace and that only a spoilt little rich girl would waste nice material like that when people in Africa had nothing but rags to cover their poor starved bodies with. On and on she went, yelling at poor Jenny. I had to do something. I mean, it wasn't Jenny's fault that her apron was a mess. It was mine. It was my stitching that was to blame.

I walked up to Miss Jessop and I told her. I said she was not to blame Jenny as it was I who had made a mess of the apron. I felt quite proud of myself for owning up, but only for a second because then Miss Jessop started shouting at Jenny again, saying she was a lazy good-for-nothing girl who forced the younger girls to do her work for her.

I felt awful! I tried to explain, but no one would listen.

Later that afternoon a group of girls from Upper Fifth told me that I had been put in Coventry for being a nasty sneak. It didn't matter what I said, they just turned their backs on me. Even Arabella wouldn't speak to me and Posy McKenzie looked all sad and droopy, and gave me back an eraser I had given her the day before. Worst, when I saw Jenny in the yard she just shook her head at me, really sadly, and turned away.

I ran all the way back home and when Janet asked me what was up I started to cry. I hated crying, but suddenly I couldn't stop myself.

'You've always told me that as long as you do what's right everything will work out.' I wept. '"Tell the truth," you say. But sometimes the truth is just the worst thing you can tell. Then what are you supposed to do? Can no one be trusted?' I looked at Janet, wiping my nose on the back of my hand.

Janet frowned and got me a paper tissue. 'Don't look at me,' she said. 'There's no one who can answer that kind of question but yourself. You must know here.' She slapped her hand in its pink rubber glove across her bosom. 'Inside, what's right. And once you know, then you mustn't let anyone persuade you different.'

'But that's what's so difficult,' I wailed. 'To be sure.'

'Life's difficult,' Janet said.

I tried to do what Janet had told me, to trust in myself, but it just got harder and harder. Mainly because my body had started saying one thing when my mind said another. Like the other day after school. I was supposed to be doing a Geography project with Arabella, but actually I was with this boy I'd met on a joint outing with his school. His name was Mike Hopkins and we were alone in his house. His parents were both working and not expected back until late. I looked at Mike. He was lovely, with his dark hair flopping across his forehead and those big brown eyes and really long eyelashes.

'Why don't we go to my room?' Mike said. 'I've got an ace stereo in there and some really good tapes. We'll be much more comfortable.'

So my body said, *Come on, get in there with him. You know you want him to be your boy-friend. He's probably a really good kisser too. I just bet he doesn't spit like Shaun.* But my mind screamed, *Stop! You can't go into Mike Hopkins's bedroom when no one's in the house but the two of you because anything could happen.*

My body said, *Exactly.*

So it was all very well for Janet to say one must trust in oneself. All very well if one was *one* self.

I went on having those kinds of arguments with myself over the next few months. Usually my body won, which is how I came to be sitting that night on top of the wicker laundry basket in the bathroom, my diary in my hand, scowling at my reflection in the mirror: dark hair, blue eyes, pale skin, lousy character. In fact, one could be justified in saying no character. I read again the latest entry in the diary, made only moments earlier. *Party at Arabella. Lost my virginity.* Then I burst into tears. How had this happened? After a while I stopped crying, raising my head and listening in to the silence as if I were expecting some comforting reply. Silly of me. Audrey and Madox were asleep. And had they heard my tears and found out the truth, Audrey would have been calling doctors and running hot baths and asking where it all went wrong, and blaming my father and saying that now she was almost a grandmother she'd look really silly in Valentino and then what would she wear? She most certainly would not be whispering words of comfort. Madox would feel sorry for me, but not enough to risk the status quo with my mother. I wiped my tears with the back of my hand and fished out a cigarette from a packet in my pocket, lighting it with an old Dunhill lighter of Madox's. So that was it: at fifteen I was no longer an innocent child. Not that I had ever been that comfortable with being one. I had never been able to get away from the feeling that I was really a very short adult playing the part of a child in some interminable play, and counting the moments until I could take my bow, pull off my costume and get on with my real life.

Having a boy-friend (a proper boy-friend, not someone like Mike who said he liked you one day and went out with your friend the next) had been a step in the right direction. Billy and I had been going out for six months now and we loved each other, I think. Working love out defeated me. More than anything it reminded me of filleting a fish, something, Audrey often told me, at which every lady should be proficient. I was very bad at it, separating all those different little bones from the substance of the flesh, and it was the same with all the little bones of emotion: friendship, lust, expectation, fantasy, loneliness, trying to separate them out from the pure white flesh of love seemed beyond me. When I was done, more often than not there would just be an unrecognisable mess left on my plate.

Billy was tall and dark, but not very handsome, although his profile wasn't bad and anyway, as my friend Arabella said, 'It doesn't matter, because when you really love someone they'll look beautiful to you whatever.' On the surface that sounded encouraging, but actually it was just as baffling. Why, I asked myself, if I loved Billy, did I think him plain to the point of ugliness? Was it a) that I didn't actually love him, or b) I loved him but suffered from unusually clear eyesight? These were the kinds of things I thought about when I thought about love. Then this had happened. How? Of course I knew how. You kiss and you press yourself against each other and your breathing gets laboured and a funny ants'-nests kind of feeling develops in your general pelvic area, but how *did it actually happen?* And this was the time I chose to feel like a child, now, when it was too late and the door to childhood had slammed shut behind me, never again to be open.

I felt sick. No, not morning sickness already. I shot the cigarette in my hand – as much a symbol of my decline as a gin bottle to a ruined mother – a look of pure loathing and got up to extinguish it under the tap. I chucked the butt into the flowered sprigged cotton laundry bag hanging on a hook by the door, the one reserved for my father's shirts, before trundling off to bed. I was too miserable even to cry any more.

I tossed and turned in the night gloom of my bedroom. I had broken every rule of decency and I was still barely fifteen. I had even broken the law! And what if I was pregnant? With wide-open eyes I stared at the window, and I imagined sitting on the window-sill and just tipping over, ever so gently. I craned my neck. Was that my broken body I saw out there on the street? My organs ruptured, bodily fluids seeping out on the paving stones. I held on to the sides of the bed, willing myself not to move. To die right now would be a release; then again, to die and only ever to have been a child, that was worse.

I began to wear black, only black. I felt it suited my character. Still, it didn't stop some people from making fatuous comments like 'Oh how lovely to be young, all that unspoilt innocence' (Edith Brookenberry, friend of Granny Billings). Or 'Make the most of these bright childhood days, they pass so quickly' (sentimental old fool visiting school, whose name I can't remember). But at least I wasn't pregnant and my parents never did find out what had happened.

'Life carries on as normal,' I whispered to my reflection every morning, but it was cleverer than me and took no nonsense. 'Now isn't that a pretty lie I see before me,' it whispered back in an Irish accent for some reason. It knew that nothing would be the same. I had trusted my body and now my mind had descended into chaos. Somewhere half-way down I had spotted Audrey drifting along like an autumn leaf on a breeze. (She was too insubstantial to plummet.)

The more I doubted myself, the louder the ding of chaos sounded in my head, the more I craved order around me. I drew up endless lists for every aspect of my life: schedules, What-to-Read lists, What-to-Achieve lists, What-to-Pack-and-Wash-and-Fold-Away lists. Lists of Likes and lists of Dislikes. And the more lists I made the more I seemed to need to make until every aspect of my life was written down somewhere on some piece of paper. I sought out rules and reasons as other teenagers searched for drugs and cigarettes. And I got increasingly interested in what made people fall.

'How did you come to this?' I asked the old drunk who spent his days slumped by the entrance to Kensington underground station. A filthy hand appeared from under the grey blanket, scrabbling round the pavement for an imaginary coin. 'Thank you, little lady, and bless you.'

Impatiently I squatted down in front of him. 'I didn't give you anything, I'm sorry. I just asked you a question.'

'Well, if it's all the same to you,' he sounded peeved, 'I'd rather have a few pennies for something to eat.'

'You know you'd only spend it on drink.'

The old tramp peered at me through bloodshot eyes that might once have been a good shade of blue. 'And what makes you such a know-all, little missy?'

I had to think about that and my legs were beginning to ache from squatting. Passers-by were giving me odd looks, wondering, no doubt, what I was doing down there on the pavement. 'Experience,' I answered finally.

'And does experience teach you to leave an old man to starve?'

I had to stand up, my thighs were killing me. I thought about all the times I had heard Madox and Audrey talk about heartless Tories and selfish acquaintances cocooned in their comfortable middle-class existence, and I made a decision. 'I haven't got much money on me, but if you come with me I'll give you something to eat at home.'

I walked down Kensington High Street, the old tramp shuffling along by my side. I wished people wouldn't stare so. Once a middle-aged man in a pin-striped suit of the kind that looks like a chalk-lined blackboard stopped and asked me if the man was troubling me. 'He's troubling my conscience,' I replied. 'But thank you for asking.'

It seemed to take for ever to reach the house, the old tramp lurching and muttering at my side, but at last we were there and unlocking the front door I stood back to let my guest inside. Just then Janet appeared, coming downstairs with the vacuum cleaner in her hand.

'What on earth!' She put the Hoover down on the parquet floor, careful even in a time of stress not to mark the delicate veneer. 'Out with you, dirty old thing. Harassing a young girl like this; shame on you.' As she spoke, Janet came towards us, shooing the old man out as if he were a stray mongrel and I her pet pooch.

'Janet, this gentleman is my guest and we don't treat guests like that in this house, do we?'

Janet paused and looked hard at me for a moment. 'Oh, yes we do, young lady, if they're drunken old tramps. Shoo!'

'My parents will not be pleased . . .'

'They certainly will not,' Janet snapped. In the doorway the old man was grumbling to himself.

'They will not be pleased to hear how you treated this gentleman.' I lowered my voice and it became eager and pleading. 'Come on, Janet. This is humiliating. I asked him to come with me. I said he'd get a hot meal. And you know how Mum and Dad are always going on about the selfish society and how we should be looking after the weakest and those less fortunate than ourselves.'

'And you, young lady, know very well that that's all talk and has nothing to do with real life. Real life being that your mother would have a fit if she found one of those less fortunate than herself putting their big dirty footprints all over her cream stair carpet and sitting on her pretty chairs. Now you.' She glared at the tramp. 'Out before I call the police.'

'I don't believe you did that,' I said after she had slammed the door behind him. I followed her down to the kitchen. 'That poor old thing could have been me or you.'

'Speak for yourself,' Janet said, putting the kettle on.

'I seem to have spawned a future chairman of the WI,' Audrey said. 'And she's always so disapproving. I'll turn round and find her looking at me with those great big blue eyes brimful of reproach. It's very wearisome.' My mother was in the drawing-room, complaining about me to her friend. Olivia was over for her spring visit. 'And it was definitely a mistake teaching her German. She uses it to hiss at me in shops. I tell you, everything sounds even more censorious in that language. She's changed her mind about becoming a psychiatrist too, which is a real nuisance. There I was, telling poor Caroline whose son's gone completely demented, LSD apparently, that at least she wouldn't have to worry about the future as I was sure Esther would look after him free of charge. He'll need care for the rest of his life, they think, and Julian and Caroline are not well off. And now what do I tell them? And now it's the law. Why? I ask her. She says she likes rules.' Audrey gave a little laugh. 'I suppose she can always sentence him to something. I tell you, I sometimes wonder if she is my daughter.'

I leant against the doorpost, reflecting on my mother's uncanny ability to place herself at the centre of any situation. No wonder she was permanently exhausted. Even my career choice was seen as a calculated attempt to show her up.

'I tell you, in an earlier age she would have been one of these religious zealots, ever ready with a hair shirt and a burning stake.'

'Linus is completely set on architecture, but he seems to be going out of his way to do it as differently as possible from his father,' Olivia said. 'Bertil went to Chalmers, Linus wants to go to school in Copenhagen. He's refusing even to contemplate joining the family firm. I tell you, I love the boy, but he does drive me absolutely demented sometimes. When he doesn't like something he just withdraws, spending hours doing those cartoons of his – "My Life as It Ought to Be", he calls them. Or he just wanders off, for whole days sometimes. "Just looking," he says. "At what?" I say. "Stuff," he says.'

I stepped into the room. My mother looked faintly startled to see me, then again she often did, as if she needed a moment or two to place me. 'Have you got a photo of him. Of Linus?' I asked Olivia.

'Not with me, no. I never seem to carry photos. Don't you remember, years ago you did a drawing for me, of Bertil and Linus, because you felt sorry for me not having a photo.' Olivia smiled expansively at me. Not for the first time, I felt something had gone slightly wrong; surely Olivia was meant to have been my mother. By the sound of it, Audrey could easily have been the cause of Linus, the strange boy dreaming away at his desk or drifting through the streets of his home town.

'He's off to the States once he's done his military service,' Olivia said. 'Just for a few months doing work experience at a firm of architects there. I suppose it will do him good to get away. And then on to Copenhagen.'

'Audrey is trying to make me go to France for the summer,' I said. 'She says it will do *me* good. Sometimes I think that's just a parental euphemism for something that does them good.'

'Don't be precocious, dear.' My mother sighed. 'It's very unbecoming.'

It was my turn to sigh. 'I think it's called growing up.' I left, taking refuge in my room, although I didn't like it very much any more. Audrey had had it redone as a surprise while I was staying with Arabella Felix and her family in Cornwall over Easter. It had been bad enough finding that Posy McKenzie had been invited to the Felixes' without having to come home to a bedroom that had turned into some yucky *House & Garden* teenager's dream, co-ordinated to within an inch of its life. Audrey was working part time at her friend Trish's interior decorating business and anything that stood still for more than five minutes was in mortal danger of ending up swagged, or dragged, or at the very least with a tasteful bow.

'It's so . . . green,' I mumbled. 'And new.'

'It's not new, darling. Your bedside table is Victorian, early

Victorian as it happens, and the dressing-table is Art Nouveau. I thought I had taught you these things.'

'I didn't mean new like that. And it's lovely,' I lied. 'Really. I love it. It's just new to me, that's all. My history is gone.' I pointed at the corner by the window. 'There was a marmalade stain there, just for example, from my Paddington Bear stage. And that old rug, I used to sit on it and pretend it flew.' Then I saw how disappointed Audrey looked. 'But this is much nicer,' I said. 'Thank you so very much.' Audrey, whose happiness depended on her uncanny ability to believe only what she wished to believe, had gone away convinced that I was thrilled with the transformation. She still was.

I threw myself down on the bed with its green-and-blue patchwork quilt and picked up the library book from the bedside table. I was reading according to my reading list, alphabetically according to author. Right now I was on G, G for Goethe.

Linus could feel it. Lotten was expecting him to *do* something. It was obvious from the way she leant back against the sofa cushions, her hands clasped behind her neck, her breasts jutting; from the way she was looking at him through half-closed eyes. He tried to buy time, getting up and changing the record, taking off the Stones and putting on his old Bob Dylan album. Lotten jiggled about on the sofa, sighing loudly, a frown across her clear high forehead. Taking a deep breath, Linus sat back down and slipped his arm round her shoulders.

'What's wrong?' Lotten asked.

'Nothing's wrong. Everything is great.'

'Something's wrong?'

'No, no, nothing is wrong. Really.'

'There's no need to get cross.'

'I'm not cross.'

'Well, you sound cross to me.' Lotten shrugged off his arm and sat up straight.

Closing his eyes, Linus gave her a gentle shove against the cushions, lowering himself down on top of her. In his mind he had always remained a fat boy and he was terrified of hurting her, of crushing her under his weight. Supporting himself on his knees and one elbow he fumbled with the small buttons of her shirt until she pushed him off, undoing them herself with a haste born more from impatience with

40

his clumsiness than passion. Once all the buttons were undone she pulled him back on top of her – she was stronger than she looked – and her hand reached down to his belly and to the buckle of his belt. He kissed her with increasing desperation as he felt her hand undo first the belt, then his trousers. His penis, that instrument of spite, remained resolutely limp and useless, but it sprang up, hard and insistent when he least of all wanted it, like the other day when he was dancing with Beatrice Nilsson.

'Get up, you bastard,' he mumbled between clenched teeth. 'Move!'

'What was that?' Lotten's voice was thick.

'Nothing, nothing.'

'Can't you get an erection?'

Linus rolled off her, throwing himself back against the sofa with a groan. Lotten's voice grew warm with concern. 'It's OK, you know. It happens to most guys at some stage. It's really nothing to worry about.'

She made him tea. She even brought it to him where he sat, slumped on the sofa. His humiliation was complete when she knelt down in front of him and zipped up his trousers and buckled his belt. 'There,' she said, giving him a little pat.

He stayed up late that night, drawing. The old cinema down at the bottom of the Avenue was being redeveloped and Linus had some ideas. It happened to be one of his favourite buildings in the town, a near perfect example of Art Nouveau. On his walks Linus had come across a small workshop specialising in fireplaces and mouldings. There was a man there who would be ideal for the intricate work needed to restore the façade.

The next morning he showed Bertil his plans. 'It's good,' his father said. 'But I'm afraid you're too late. Even if you had been able to back up the drawings with the proper costings and a structural survey.' He allowed himself a small smile at the absurdity of the thought.

'What do you mean, too late?'

'I meant to tell you because I knew you were interested, Stendal & Berglund have got the commission for the new building.'

Linus stared at him. 'New building? Are you saying that they're tearing the old cinema down?'

Bertil sighed and sat down on the kitchen chair. 'I know it's a pity and I have been a strong voice against this course of action, but the decision has been made and that part is out of our hands. When we were asked to take on the design of the new building I didn't hesitate to accept. It seemed to me the ideal opportunity to influence matters in a positive way. It's called pragmatism, my boy, and good sense.'

'It's also called betrayal of ideals,' Linus said in a quiet voice. He looked straight into his father's eyes. 'I can't believe you're doing this. I'm ashamed.' He turned on his heel and walked off before Bertil got over his surprise at his son's open contempt. Linus shut the front door behind him with deliberate care. He ran down the five flights of stairs and out on to the street into the pale March sunshine. There was snow still on the ground and overnight the brown slush had frozen in the gutters. He walked on through town, for once not looking up at the buildings, but down at his feet and the frozen ground. He walked faster than usual, he was almost running as if that way he could escape from his anger and disappointment. He had trusted Bertil, looked up to him, held him up as an example to his friends, dreamt of being like him. Now he felt as much contempt for himself and his bad judgement as he did for his father.

When next he looked around him he had reached the main city bus terminal. There were two buses standing there, waiting to go. One, engine already running, was going out to the island. Without thinking further Linus jumped on board. He slouched in his window seat but as the journey progressed, out of the city and on to the open road, he straightened up. He couldn't remember the last time he had been to the island in winter. It was a summer place and it might as well have existed only for those brief months for all he and the other summer residents knew. And yet, there it was, less than a two-hour bus ride away.

He stood on the small ferry, its only passenger, looking across the short stretch of water that separated the island from the peninsula. It was the same and yet different, like the face of an old friend after years of separation. The softness of summer vegetation was gone, leaving the craggy rocks exposed, its every crevice bare. The bright colours were gone too, the blues and greens replaced by grey and straw-yellow, but it was the same old friend and Linus felt his spirits lift.

Up at the house he got the keys from the large flowerpot by the back door. But before letting himself in he walked around the garden slumbering under its winter cover of snow and ice. He stared at the naked branches of the rose bushes his mother had planted all those years ago. It was silly, but somehow he had imagined them still in bloom.

He didn't stay long in the house. In the sitting-room the furniture was covered with white sheets and the wicker chairs on the veranda were lined up away from the large windows. He played a game with himself, closing his eyes and imagining the sounds and senses of summer, then abruptly opening them again to find the dead of winter in their place. He knew that his mother had died out here one winter day all those years ago. 'She was ill,' Bertil had said.

'How, ill?' Linus had wanted to know.

'Sick. We couldn't help her so she died.'

'Couldn't the doctors help?'

'No one could. In the end she had an accident. You mustn't dwell on it, Linus. Life is for the living. Leave the dead alone.'

He couldn't remember if his mother had looked ill the last time he saw her. He couldn't remember what she had looked like at all. His image of her face was formed entirely from photographs and from a hazy memory of fair hair and a fur coat. Once, out here on the island, when he had been left crying from the effort of retrieving his mother's features from the dim depths of his memory, Aunt Ulla had taken him by the shoulders and swung him round to face the mirror in the hallway. 'Look in there,' she had said, her voice harsh. 'Look in there and you'll see your mother.' Terrified, he had begun to scream, his eyes clamped shut, his fists hammering at Ulla's side to make her let go. Afterwards, when he had calmed down enough to speak, he had told his father that he thought he was going to see his mother's ghost in the mirror. Only later had he realised his aunt had meant that he was growing up into the image of his mother.

He walked round the island tripping once on the slippery rocks as they froze over, abandoned by the dying rays of the sun.

He did not return to town until well after midnight, exhausted and freezing cold.

# Chapter Four

I came to Simon and Garfunkel late. I was seventeen, still only five foot five. Still dark-haired and blue-eyed in spite of a brief flirtation with peroxide and a vague plan to try those coloured lenses and make my eyes bright green and far more interesting.

'Do you like Simon and Garfunkel?' this guy asked. It was a Saturday night and a group of us were at Arabella Felix's house. Mr and Mrs Felix were away.

Did I like Simon and Garfunkel? 'I haven't given it that much thought,' I answered.

This guy put out his hand and said, 'I'm Donald. I'm a friend of Arabella's brother. We're both doing law at UCL.'

'Law's always appealed to me.' I drained my glass of rosé wine and held it out for more.

'What aspect in particular?' Donald reached for an opened bottle on the coffee table.

'All of them. Its humanity, mostly.'

'Humanity? That's not what most people think of when they think of the law.'

'I can't help that.' I could see he was waiting for an explanation, so I tried one. 'To me, the law in a free society shows humans at their best. It's not nature's law, or the law of the jungle, but a law that as often as not goes against those things. A law which is there, set up and adhered to, made to protect the individual and society from abuse. The way a court gives everyone a voice. The way self-interest and revenge are rendered powerless.'

Donald looked at me with wide brown eyes and smiled with firm lips, showing large white teeth. 'You make it sound quite sexy.

Although I'm not so sure that's how it actually works. In fact, it seems to me that it's often misused.'

'But it mustn't be,' I insisted. 'If it is, anything can happen and normally that anything happens to the weakest.' I was getting agitated and I could hear it in my voice too. So could Donald because he gave me a quizzical look from where he stood by the stereo. 'Then we're nothing but animals and then what's the point?'

Donald put on a tape of Simon and Garfunkel, ignoring the groans of the others and pulling me down next to him on the sofa. 'So what are you going to do after your A levels?' he asked, making it sound as if he wanted to know whether I was going home that night.

'Would it surprise you if I told you that I was thinking of doing law?' I said. 'The only problem is, believing in the law doesn't mean I'm sure I want to spend my life practising it. I think I might want to, but I don't *feel* it. Not here.' I put my hand on the place where I supposed my heart was.

I saw Donald a lot after that evening. I kept waiting for the day when I would fall in love with him the way I kept waiting to fall in love with the idea of becoming a lawyer. Both were so right. Maybe it was me who was wrong? There was no point trying to speak to Audrey about it all. I had tried, once.

'But of course you can't be in love with Donald,' she had said, her little laugh indicating how ridiculous was the very thought. 'He votes Conservative.'

'But *you* voted Conservative in the last election,' I said.

Audrey took on a look of infinite patience. 'I know I did, Esther, but I'm not a young man. I always think there's something rather peculiar about *young* men who vote Tory.'

My friends all thought I was lucky having Donald as a boy-friend. But then I suspect that they would have thought I was lucky to have had Lisa Hicks's spotty brother Seth as a boy-friend.

'You're really very pretty when you're not scowling,' Arabella had said only the other day. Behind her was a row of nodding heads. 'But you don't seem to have any idea of how boys like their girls to be. You're so . . . so argumentative. Aggressive, even. You know when you argue a point? You just never give up.' She had looked at me with a mixture of reproach and concern in her soft hazel eyes. 'Boys don't really like that kind of thing.'

45

'It's not for them to like,' I said. 'If I want to argue a point I argue a point.' Behind Arabella the group – Posy, Fee, Lisa and Beth – looked at each other and sighed.

'There you are,' Arabella had said, sighing with the rest of them. 'That's just the worst attitude when it comes to boys. You can think like that, but you must never ever show it. Don't you know anything about how to handle a man?'

I told them I had watched my mother handle my father.

But now I had Donald and all my friends were pleased and surprised, in almost equal measure.

That April I turned eighteen and on my birthday Donald asked me to marry him. Shortly afterwards, while I was still on holiday from school, Olivia Stendal came over for her spring visit.

'What a coincidence, Linus and Esther both getting engaged at the same time, both at an unsuitably early age and both to people of whom we don't approve.' My mother smiled, making out that she was joking, but the smile was brittle as she poured Olivia another glass of Chablis. These days, I thought, as I held out my own glass to be refilled but was ignored, everything about Audrey was brittle: her hair, which seemed finally to have rebelled against years of perming and bleaching and back-combing and lacquering; her voice, pulled thin after years of reaching out to be heard; her laugh, running away from the ever-threatening tears. Audrey herself said it was all due to a decrease in hormones, but personally I put it down more to the constant struggle to keep reality at bay, the strain of stretching truth just that little bit further. She had, in her time, been a painter and a poet, and an interior designer, she had been a garden designer and a student of Post-modernist paintings, but each time the brightly coloured butterfly of success had eluded her. So she had told herself and the rest of the world that she was, at least, the adored wife of a great intellectual. Lately, though, she'd had to resort to statements like 'Men need time to themselves', as Madox went away for yet another vague-sounding weekend or research trip. 'Give them a long enough leash and they'll always come running back in the end.' To me it sounded as if she had already half given up.

'You don't think he might be seeing someone else?' I had asked the other day. It wasn't that I wanted to cause trouble for my father, or that I wished to cause my mother more pain. Far from it. But this was the eighties, a decade for strong women. I wanted to tell my mother that she didn't have to put up with it any more. I couldn't bear to watch as she spent yet another day in Cloud Cuckoo Land.

My engagement to Donald had not helped. Donald had short hair and wore suits. There was also that thing about him being a Young Conservative. And when Audrey flittered around the room wrapped in mental chiffon, engaging him in talk about the latest play or concert or exhibition, he would just smile engagingly at her and explain that he liked art when he had time for it, which sadly wasn't often. He, in turn, tried to speak to her of what he termed Real Life, assuming incorrectly that Audrey would have some idea of what he referred to. Worst of all, to my mother, he was planning to go into . . . hum, ah, there was no getting away from it . . . the City. 'A money man, darling!' Audrey had shuddered – Audrey who loved money and spent more of the stuff in a month than most people got through in a year. But she was born to dissemble. I was sure, for example, that she had convinced herself that there were two completely separate things known as lamb; the white fluffy baa ones that frolicked in the fields as you passed by on the motorway and the garlicky pink-in-the-middle ones that lay very still on your plate.

Olivia had finished her smoked chicken salad and put her fork down. 'It's their beds; they made them, now they have to lie in them.'

'But why have they made those beds?' Audrey lamented. 'There she is, my only child, four A levels, university offers coming out of her ears, the world at her feet, announcing out of the blue that she's got engaged to this . . . this rather ordinary young man and saying that she would take a course in . . .' Here Audrey had to pause and refresh herself with a sip of wine. '. . . In typing.' It was all too much, it seemed. Audrey sank back against her chair and lit a cigarette. 'It's as if you're deliberately setting out to be ordinary yourself,' she said, turning to me.

'What's wrong with ordinary?' I wanted to know.

'Nothing, Esther, for ordinary people.'

'Why are you in such a hurry to get married?' Olivia asked me. 'And can't you go to university first?'

I explained that I no longer wanted to do law and that university would just be another waste of time, like childhood. There are too

47

many people already aimlessly cluttering up courses because someone has told them they *should* have a university education. 'I want to get on with real life and I want to know where I'm heading. Donald and I are right for each other, so why wait? And with all that dating and searching-for-love stuff over with, I can concentrate on what I really want to do with my life. In the meantime, I'll learn to type.'

'Think about what you want to do while you're at university,' Olivia insisted. 'And why marry? There's plenty of time for that later. Being so young, you really are stacking the odds against it working in the long term.'

'That's what I keep telling her,' Audrey said. 'Why can't they just live together? And anyway, I don't even think you're really in love with the boy. Not that I can blame you.'

I looked sternly at her. 'You're my mother, allegedly. You're not supposed to talk like that. And anyway, as I see it, all long-term relationships come under threat sooner or later. It really doesn't matter who you are, what age you were when you got together or even, to an extent, who you're with as long as you're good friends and have stuff in common because in the end it all boils down to much the same: you fall out of love. So why put so much emphasis on being *in* love to begin with? It all comes down to an act of will. I see it as a very exciting challenge.'

'You call that exciting?' Audrey looked at me as if she were trying to figure out where she had picked me up and why.

Olivia sighed and shook her head. 'You know so much for one who has lived so little.' I couldn't work out if she had just insulted me or paid me a compliment. 'Still,' she went on. 'At least you *seem* to have it all worked out. With Linus, I really don't know. Lotten, his fiancée, is his first girl-friend. She's as determined as hell and he, well it's like he's two people, this fey, almost slow young man who looks as if he's just stepped off at the wrong planet, yet, when it comes to his work, he's someone entirely different. Then he's determined, focused, one hundred per cent committed . . .'

'Typing,' I heard Audrey mumble, as she opened another bottle of wine. 'This is my daughter, Esther, she types.'

Olivia raised her glass. 'Well, good luck, Esther.'

Bertil bade Linus sit down on the sofa beneath the portrait of his grandfather. 'About this marriage you're proposing . . .' He got no further, interrupted as he was by that laugh, as high-pitched and abandoned as ever. Bertil's forehead creased into the familiar frown. It was well trained for the purpose, Linus thought and he stopped laughing.

'What I'm trying to say, Linus, is that twenty-one is awfully early to settle down. Can't you at least wait until you've qualified? And what is Lotten going to do with herself in Copenhagen? So far you've done remarkably well. You've got everything ahead of you, so why tie yourself down at such an early age?' As his son said nothing, Bertil continued, 'I have to tell you that your stepmother and I are not at all happy with your decision. However, it is your life and if you persist with this course of action we will go along with whatever is required of us.'

Linus got to his feet and put out his hand, taking his father's and shaking it firmly. 'Thank you. I can't tell you how glad I am to hear that. Thank you.'

Bertil looked sharply at his son. There he stood, tall and lanky, with a huge smile on his handsome face. His grey eyes held no hint of mockery and their innocence and the wayward curl of his fair hair made him look younger even than his twenty-one years. If he had not known better – Linus had come top of his class at the Copenhagen college two years running – he would have thought his only son was a half-wit. 'I'm surprised that Lotten's parents aren't a little more concerned,' he said.

'They like me,' Linus said placidly, as he sat back down. 'And they know Lotten is different. She wants to do things properly. She has this theory about adapting the best of the old values to fit in with our modern existence. She's very interesting about it. She believes that a lot of the so-called feminism of the sixties and seventies was only another way of controlling and ultimately oppressing women. That by denying status to traditional female roles like marriage and motherhood you are playing into the hands of the very reactionary forces you're trying to fight.' Linus had near perfect recall, when he chose to, and he knew he had represented Lotten's views correctly. 'And she really understands me and what I want to do.'

Bertil smiled and shook his head. 'Women always understand what you want to do until the time when it begins to clash with what *they* want you to do, and that normally starts to happen after about two years of marriage. Your stepmother, I have to say, is a notable exception in that she still understands, and what's more she respects and encourages. But she is unusual. It's not that they mean to deceive, it's just bred into them, this desire to please, to be all things to one man. If you like Toulouse-Lautrec they'll like Toulouse-Lautrec. If you like sporty girls with no make-up they'll become sporty girls with no make-up. If you say you can't stand women who worry they'll assume the most carefree air in the world. But it can't last, so eventually they revert to type. Children normally see to that, if time alone doesn't.'

'Lotten is not at all like that,' Linus said. 'She's very much her own person – she just happens to share my interests. She understands me.'

Bertil just went on shaking his head as an annoying little smile played at the corners of his mouth.

Lotten strode towards Westerbergs café where Linus was sitting waiting for her at a small square table by the window. Before he had had a chance to get to his feet she had thrown her rucksack on to an empty chair and sat down next to him. 'So what did your dad say? Was he pleased?'

Linus met her ice-blue gaze and marvelled at her bright-eyed assumption that things were pretty much the way she wanted them to be. 'He was OK.'

Lotten gave him one of her brisk smiles. 'That's fine, then.' She did not bother to ask any further, but got to her feet again and nodded towards the self-service counter. 'Shall we get our sandwiches?'

As they waited in line, Linus said, 'I might not earn that much, at least not to start with, not from the kind of work I want to do. That's all right with you, isn't it?'

Lotten helped herself to a prawn and mayonnaise sandwich, scooping up a prawn that had dropped back on to the serving platter with the cake slice and returning it to her sandwich where it joined the others in a neat little pile on the white bread and lettuce. 'Marriage does not equal serfdom,' she said finally. 'You do what you have to do. Partnership', she continued, as they returned to their seats, 'should be about helping each other towards greater strength and freedom. You should view me, not as a drag, but as a pole on to which you can climb ever higher towards the light.' She cut into her sandwich and put a forkful in her mouth, showing her small white front teeth. Linus gazed at her admiringly as any lingering doubts about his decision vanished.

Lotten raised her glass of low-alcohol lager. 'To us. The future belongs to us.'

'That sounds just like a Hitler Youth song,' Linus murmured.

'Don't be silly,' Lotten said.

## Chapter Five

At first I didn't tell Audrey about my change of plans. I just sent in my application for UCL and said nothing until I needed the money to pay for my first term's accommodation. When I did tell my parents they were predictably pleased. Madox patted me on the head and said he knew I had made the right choice, English too, his subject. Audrey beamed and banged on about smoky student flats and Existentialism, digging out volumes of poetry and quoting from Milton. I just wondered why it pained me so to please my parents. Maybe because they were always pleased for the wrong reasons?

I had told Donald that I wanted to postpone the wedding until after I had graduated. He didn't seem to mind. 'I can wait,' he said. Part of me wished he couldn't.

On my weekly visits home Audrey usually grew misty-eyed as I was about to leave and said things like 'You live for me too'. And 'Enjoy these carefree student days', until I felt like shouting at her that there were no such things as carefree student days and who was the bloody idiot who had said there were in the first place? I realised that I was almost as bad at being a carefree student as I had been at being a child. It wasn't the work that was the problem, it never was. In fact, I shone, getting a first at the end of my first year. It was all that other stuff: being out all night, taking drugs, sleeping around. I did my best, but my heart wasn't in it. I was almost faithful to Donald. (I would have been, completely, but for that afternoon with James Connor.) Dope gave me a headache. I fell asleep in clubs. It didn't matter how loud the music, the moment I stopped dancing and sat down I fell asleep.

I was permanently accused of taking things too seriously. I looked mournfully at Sophie (my room-mate at the start of the second year and the one doing the accusing at that particular moment). 'Lighten up,' she was saying. 'You're only young once.'

'Thank God,' I muttered. Anyway what exactly am I supposed *not* to take seriously? Life? OK. I could go along with that. Life was indeed a big joke. No, it was the little things which cluttered up the road between birth and death that I insisted on taking a little bit seriously, things like war, peace, illness, starvation, the nature of evil, those kinds of things. I couldn't help it. And I kept getting things wrong. When this government minister came to speak to the student union about the possible introduction of student loans, I listened to him. I didn't agree, but I heard him out, or tried to through the heckling and booing. Afterwards I went up to him and told him that I thought he was a misguided fat cat out of touch with real life. That was wrong too. I should have yelled abuse *while* he was talking, like all the other students did and then, the moment he'd finished, I should have elbowed my way out of the lecture hall on my way to the pub. That's when I should have spoken up, telling everyone else there who also hadn't listened what was wrong with the fat-cat bastard. It was all quite difficult to get the hang of.

In my third year I was sharing a flat in Bloomsbury with Sophie, whose father owned the flat, Arabella and Gillian Norris who had somehow slipped in, no one quite knew how. Arabella was doing a secretarial course nearby and Gillian was reading English with Sophie and me.

A couple of weeks before the Christmas break Sophie and Arabella knocked on my door. I looked up from my book and then, as I saw the grave but smug look of the bearer of bad tidings on their faces, I closed the book altogether.

They sat down side by side on my bed. 'It's Gillian,' Arabella said. 'She has to go.'

'Has to go where?'

'Anywhere,' Sophie said. 'As long as it's away from here.'

'Why? What's she done?'

'She hasn't done anything in particular,' Arabella said. 'She's just continuing to be herself.'

'I don't know about you, but I can't stand it any longer.' Sophie sounded close to tears. 'She's always *there*. Have you noticed? Always hanging around. And not in her own room either but in the sitting-

53

room. It must be getting to you too, Esther. Every time you bring Donald back, who's there on the sofa like a blob of left-over custard? And that smelly old dressing-gown she insists on wearing while she just sits and sits there every bloody night. She never gets the hint. She hasn't got a life so she tries to grab bits of ours. David is soon going to refuse to come here altogether, he finds her so off-putting. I mean, just last week I said did he want to come back to the flat for coffee and he said he'd love to, but when we got here and Gillian was sitting there, practically in darkness for Christ's sake, with only the flickering lights of the television screen, he changed his mind. And who can blame him, coming back to his girl-friend's flat and finding Norman Bate's mother?'

'Wasn't the mother Norman Bate all along?' I wondered.

Arabella and Sophie ignored the question. 'If at least she could wash her hair,' Arabella said. 'But she looks so gross. As Soph says, she actually puts people off from coming here. And her mother . . .'

Her mother was a problem, I agreed. Mrs Norris had been a frequent visitor from the very start, but lately she had taken to turning up at all hours and staying the night too, half the time. Last week I had even found her in my bed. I was coming home late after an evening out with Donald and as I walked into my room and switched on the light there she was, in my bed, her head covered in little flesh-coloured curlers like maggots crawling all over her hair. 'Oh, is that you, Esther?' she'd asked, as if it was really surprising that I should be in my own room at night. 'Gillian and I thought you were staying at your young man's.' She had sat up, her beefy arms crossed over her large, low-slung chest. 'So Gillian said, "Mum, why don't you take Esther's bed, saves you kipping on the sofa."' After a pause she had added, 'I suppose you'll want it now, your bed?' Before I had had a chance to answer she went on, 'Well, it'll be cosy for you now I've warmed it up.'

Needless to say, I had slept on the sofa that night.

'And why oh why, if she has to leave her underwear to dry all over the flat, can't she get some decent stuff instead of those enormous grey-white cotton knickers . . .' Arabella was almost in tears by now.

'And the bras. There's nothing wrong with 36 D, but with the elastic gone and those cups just sagging at you from the radiator . . .' Sophie said.

'The thing is, Beth's back from France and she's dying to move in with us.' Arabella looked pleadingly at me. 'Just think of having Beth here. It'd be absolutely perfect. Honestly, I don't think I could stand another week with bloody Gillian.' She paused, then said, her high brow furrowed as if she'd just remembered something, 'Who the hell invited her to share with us in the first place?' We all looked at each other and shook our heads. 'So how did she end up here?' Arabella insisted.

'I suppose she just tagged along.' Sophie sounded vague.

'Well, I vote we tell her to move out at the end of term.'

'She'll be upset,' I said.

'Not as upset as we'll all be if she stays. Honestly.' Arabella had a determined look on her soft face. 'It's for the common good . . .'

'. . . and the will of the majority,' Sophie chipped in.

'Then I think that's it. Who shall tell Gillian?' Arabella asked.

We all did. Gillian did not protest, which made us feel worse, she just hung her head, her lank hair flopping across her chubby cheeks. When she looked up to say 'OK' there was a resigned look in her round bovine eyes that made me wince. Why didn't she scream and shout, and tell us we were bastards, instead of getting up from the sofa, pulling her grubby dressing-gown closer round her lumpen body as if for comfort? 'I'd better get packing, then,' she said.

Why didn't she tell us we had no right to treat her this way, instead of padding off to do as she was bid?

'There's no hurry,' Sophie called after her.

Still, it has to be said that life in the flat improved no end once she was gone, which didn't stop me from feeling ashamed. The will of the majority it might well have been, but what of poor old Gillian?

Donald told me not to be wet. 'It's Sophie's flat, isn't it? Or her dad's, anyway. And you all wanted Gillian out?' I sighed and nodded. 'Well then? There's nothing more to say.' He stretched out on the sofa and kicked off his shoes. 'Snap' went one of his red braces. 'You can always move in with me.' He smiled at me and I smiled back. 'We make a good team, don't we, Esther, old girl?'

I could smell his feet. I wanted to smile indulgently and think, *Dear, sweet boy, his feet don't half pong*. Something like that. I didn't want to turn my head away in disgust, but I did. 'Yeah, we make a good team,' I said, forcing myself to smile back.

I got an invitation to Linus Stendal's wedding. It was to be held in Gothenburg on the seventeenth of July. Audrey was fretting. 'Your father can't get away. Oh darling, you know how I hate travelling on my own. It would be so lovely if you could come. And you'd meet them all at last.'

I would have liked to, but how could I go away in the middle of my finals?

I was told afterwards that it had been a beautiful wedding.

Lotten had refused even to consider getting married on the island. 'That's *your* place,' she had said to Linus, as if that very fact ruled it out. So they had married in the small stone church on the road to Saro where her parents lived. It was a traditional affair: a late-afternoon service followed by a dinner and dance, white tie and tails, speeches, three hours of them as it turned out, and singing, both in the church and at the dinner.

*This is the happiest day of my life*, Linus kept thinking. *This is the beginning of a new life filled with love and contentment.* And there he was now, in the hotel where the wedding feast was going to be held in just a few minutes, waiting for his bride who was in the lavatory.

Uncle Gerald wandered past on his way to the ballroom and gave him a pat on the back. 'Cheer up, old boy,' he whispered. 'It can't be that bad.'

Lotten was taking her time in there. He knew he was being silly, but it felt wrong somehow, that she would be going to the bathroom right then. It was like when he had been little and it was Christmas Eve. He hadn't even liked his father glancing at the papers, let alone making a telephone call or going out for some cigarettes. Those things were in the realm of the everyday and as such had no place at moments of magic. And this was their wedding day. He realised that he had half expected all normal life to cease while it lasted. Still, how could he quarrel with his new wife's need to use the bathroom?

A small girl, not belonging to the wedding party, burst through the double doors that led to the hotel lobby. She was followed by her parents. They played at being annoyed at their child for running off like that, but actually they couldn't help a small proud smile as she stopped to stare at Linus. Taking her finger out of her mouth she said,

'You look funny.' The parents looked even prouder, smiling at Linus in a way that demanded a smile back. Linus tried to, but he just couldn't. 'Why do you look funny?' the child wanted to know.

'Don't annoy the gentleman,' the mother scolded, but her expression said, 'Come on, admit she's cute.'

A waiter appeared from the ballroom and informed the couple with the child that this was a Private Party. They left, looking disgruntled. At last Lotten, his bride, his wife, appeared from the ladies' room. Linus took a step towards her, hands outstretched and took hers that were cool and a little damp from washing. Together they walked into the ballroom, and a sea of smiling faces and raised champagne flutes.

# PART TWO

# Chapter Six

The outside of my little house in Fulham made me think of lemon
meringue pie, bright light yellow with fluffy white mouldings around
the door and windows, and a sand-coloured pebble-dash basement. It
stood on a tree-lined street of pink blancmanges and blueberry pies
and snow-white floating islands. Inside, many of them were camou-
flaged as country cottages, all pine dressers and cotton sprigs, and in
the summer tomato plants grew in terracotta pots in the small
gardens. My basement flat pretended to be Swedish, inspired by the
Carl Larsson posters that Olivia had given me when I was growing up.
I had worked on it, lovingly, doing most of the decorating myself. The
walls were painted a pale pink-apricot. White muslin hung like bridal
veils across the windows. The sofa was covered in white-and-blue
striped cotton and I had bought an old dresser, which I had painted
grey-blue and stencilled with dragon-blood red and green flowers. My
chairs were painted in the same pale grey-blue.

'Faux Suedoise,' Audrey called it, until the look became fashionable.
Then she said, 'That child has got her eye from me.' And my other
eye? I wanted to ask.

'But I still think you need some colour,' she said today as she sat
down. Then she added, 'But thank God you took my advice about
Donald,' as if this somehow made up for my lack of flair with fabrics.

And what was this about *her* advice? Who was it, after I cancelled
the wedding, who had to be carted off to Grayshott Hall for a week of
complete mental rest? Anyway, why go on about it still? I glared at my
mother who reclined on the blue-and-white sofa, one slender, slightly
saggy arm resting gracefully against the back. Her pale-auburn hair fell
in loose waves to her shoulders the way it always had, but the roots
showed grey and her complexion had the texture of tissue paper that

had been crumpled and carefully smoothed out again. I felt a pang of pity for her; she was too easy a target, and I stopped glaring and smiled at her instead.

On a Tuesday almost five years before I had woken up, asking myself, 'What is love?' It wasn't an original question, but it was, nevertheless, a disconcerting one less than two weeks before your wedding day. Like some small furry animal from a fable by La Fontaine, I had scurried around asking my question, 'What is love?' My father didn't seem surprised, but he hadn't appeared especially interested either. Madox seemed to me increasingly like a man whose spirit had taken a long holiday from its body. He went about his business, but the spark was gone and everything about him was thinner, his body and his lips and the hair on top of his head. He was in his study that morning, banging out an article for an American business magazine on his old typewriter and as he answered he barely looked up from the page in front of him. 'I suppose love is to keep paying off your mother's overdrafts.'

I wanted to enquire, too, whom he loved the most, my mother or his mistress? But I got nervous. Let sleeping dogs, or in this case adulterers, lie was the principle my mother lived by. It wasn't for me to go against her.

Did God create man polygamous before He invented the marriage vows? I wondered. And if He did, was it His idea of a joke or was it just absent-mindedness? Then again, it wasn't Madox's love or even Donald's that was in question right now, it was mine.

'What is love?' Audrey had repeated my question, turning to face me as she sat at her dressing-table brushing her hair and piling it high on the top of her head. 'Love is . . . well, it's the pot of gold at the end of the rainbow. It's an ache at the pit of your stomach. It's hope against hope. It's turning a blind eye.' And all of a sudden I felt sad for her and for my father because whatever else love was, it was surely also a disappointment.

Janet gave the brass-and-ebony candlestick one last flick with the feather duster and said, 'In my view, it all comes down to socks in the end.'

'Socks?'

'If you can live with his dirty socks, not to mention the feet inside, and still look at him tenderly, then you love him.'

Arabella got a dreamy look in her eyes as she turned down the radio in her pink-and-blue bedroom. 'When my granny got engaged to my grandfather this other young man, someone she knew only slightly, a quiet boy, not the sort to get noticed, drove up outside her bedroom window on his motor bike and shot his brains out. I suppose that's love.'

'Love is unselfish,' Granny Billings told me over the phone. 'And if you need to ask what it is, you don't feel it.' She was right, of course. By the end of that day I had known beyond doubt that what I felt for Donald was but love's pale impostor.

When I broke it to Donald he took it well, so well, in fact, that I began to feel as if I had done him a favour. But Audrey was a different business altogether. She took the news of the cancelled wedding hard. Now the last thing I would ever expect from my mother was logic, let alone consistency, but this time I had to ask her why she was so upset that I had cancelled the wedding when all she had done since we announced our engagement was to complain. In the torrent of words that had followed, each chased by a sniff or a snuffle, I distinguished Caterers, Flowers, That Beautiful Little Church, Ridicule, Bridge, Laughing Stock and That Bitch Shirley. I'm sure that Immature, Ungrateful and Irresponsible popped up somewhere too, and I said I was truly sorry. When she said that sorry didn't even begin to cover it, I told her that if I had known how inconvenient my not marrying Donald would be for her I would have gone ahead anyway, in spite of my not loving him. The irony was lost on her, but she thanked me for the thought.

'Now you can concentrate on getting yourself a decent career,' Madox said and there had been something malicious in the way he looked at my mother, as if he took pleasure in her discomfort.

I had decided some time earlier that I wanted to be a journalist. Donald had not approved, wrinkling his nose and looking pained as if I had been discussing taking up a career as a low-rent prostitute. When I had got a fetch-and-carry job with *Chic and Cheek*, 'The Magazine for the Woman of Today', he had turned patronising, referring to Esther's little job. But I enjoyed the work and the atmosphere at the office, although secretly I thought that if I ran a magazine I would make it for the woman of the past, as she was a) seriously under-represented and b) more likely to have the time to read the stuff.

After cancelling the wedding and breaking off our engagement I had to move out of Donald's flat, where I had been living since I graduated, in rather a hurry. There was nothing for it but to return to my parents' house while I searched for somewhere to live. I ended up staying for six months. Then Grandma Billings died and left me fifty thousand pounds, so I was able to take out a mortgage and buy the flat. Now I had a place of my own I could have had Laurence with me, but he refused to move – I had packed his toys in a box and he went straight off and picked them out and put them back next to his basket – and who could blame him? For twelve years he had refused to play the part of faithful hound; why should I expect him to start now, in the evening of his life?

I was happy in the flat. I had my own front door and a tiny paved area below the pavement where I could put a chair and some pots for plants. The couple who occupied the rest of the house, the Bodkins, were quiet and elderly and uncomplaining. We were friendly, but left each other alone. I loved living on my own. When I put something down, it remained where I'd left it until I decided to move it. And no one interfered with my systems. For example, I liked to store my tea in order of strength and the time of day one was likely to drink it: starting with English Breakfast on the left-hand side of the shelf followed by Darjeeling, Earl Grey, Lapsang and finally green tea. I liked to use my blue-and-white Spode mugs in the sitting-room and the pink-and-green ones in the kitchen and bedroom. I kept one scrubbing brush for the sink and one for the dishes and I knew no one would mix them up and, best of all, I could use every available wardrobe space myself.

'You're so set in your ways,' Audrey complained and to her friends she said, 'My daughter is twenty-something going on fifty-five.' I didn't bother to explain that I was twenty-something and feeling that if I took my finger out of my particular dike, in a manner of speaking, I would be swept away on a tidal wave of chaos. I did talk to Arabella about it, though.

'I go with the flow,' Arabella said, turning off the video. It was Friday evening and we had just finished watching *Casablanca*.

'You can afford to. Your flow goes in one direction. You've got serenity. You're at peace with yourself and the world. I'm not serene, I'm not at peace. It's as if I've got a whole courtroom in my head, judge and jury appraising my mind, judging and evaluating every thought: the bad, light-fingered thoughts that barge through the walls of decency with crowbars. Indecent ones. Cowardly ones that turn the other way, the lot. I tell you, I get really tired of it sometimes.'

'I'm not surprised you've always got a headache,' Arabella said. She picked up one of my little wooden animals, a cicada, from the coffee table. 'Pretty.' She turned it round in her small, strong hands. 'Feels nice.'

I nodded. 'That's down to hours of sanding.' I had taken up wood-carving the summer after I left university. I'd been in the States teaching English to underprivileged Spanish kids and one of the boys carved. Apparently he had taken a lot of persuading to stop carving people's chests and take up carving wood, but once he'd made the transition he never looked back. (There was that time with the parole officer, but it was a one-off so everyone said.) Anyway, he was a wonderful teacher and at the end of my time there I was quite good. I liked working with my hands; it gave me a measure of peace. Right now I was working on an ark.

'Although I can't remember any cicadas on the ark,' Arabella said.

'Someone simply forgot to mention them. But they were there. I'm doing the animals alphabetically. So far I've got Anteater, Bee, Cicada . . .'

'Do insects count as animals?'

I nodded. 'Sure they do, just as much as Mr and Mrs Noah. Anyway, then there's Dolphin and Elephant . . .' I brought the rest out from a small wooden box and lined them up in front of her on the table. 'And right now I'm working on Giraffe.'

'I'm on G too,' Arabella said. 'George. He's so cute. And he's got a really nice friend, Holden, I meant to tell you about him for ages. He's half American and a barrister, so you'd have a lot to talk about, what with you having worked over there and almost married someone who did law.'

Two days later I was off to dinner at Arabella's flat in Notting Hill. She had only recently moved in and there were still packing cases by the window at the far end of the living-room.

'You have no idea, have you, Esther.' Arabella tucked her arm under mine. 'That's not a packing case, it's my new dining-table. A friend of mine, Boris – he's to die for, by the way – is a cabinet-maker. This is one of his pieces.'

'You're quite sure that isn't what the actual table came in?' I asked. Arabella rolled her eyes and sighed. 'Only checking,' I said hastily.

Holden turned out to be a large, ruggedly handsome man of about thirty, with the kind of look about him some American men have, of making you feel he loved his mother. 'So what do you do?' he asked me as we sank down on to low chairs round the table I still suspected of being a packing case. 'If that's not a boring question.'

'It isn't to me,' I answered politely. 'How could I possibly think that anything which gives me an opportunity to talk about myself was boring?' I went on to tell him about my work on *Chic and Cheek*.

'Sounds like a porn mag,' George, Arabella's alphabet boy-friend, said.

'Well it isn't.' I looked at him, irritated. 'It's a magazine for "The Woman of Today".'

'Same thing,' George said, making me wish that Arabella would hurry up and move on to H. Holden maybe? Holden, in the meantime, was looking interested in the way people did when they didn't know what the hell was going on. 'At the moment I'm assistant to the features editor. I look out for stories that would make good features and do the preliminary research, that kind of thing. But eventually I want to do my own features. I love finding out what makes people tick, seeing inside their heads.' Warming to my subject I went on, 'Give me a really interesting internal landscape to delve into and I'll be happier than a honeymooner at Niagara Falls.'

'Esther also spends her Christmas holidays serving food to the homeless,' Arabella interjected, as if she was trying to advertise me and I glared at her, embarrassed. 'In fact,' Arabella went on, undaunted, 'the only thing stopping Esther from being a modern-day saint is a bad temper and a slight tendency towards sin.'

Holden's handsome face, square-jawed and tanned, took on a keen, focused expression. It was hard to tell whether it was the word 'saint' or the word 'sin', that caused it, but the world being what it is, I could

66

guess. I longed to tell him I was celibate as well, but that would be a lie and I tried not to lie.

'No one could accuse you of being a saint, could they, my darling,' George cooed at Arabella, taking her hand across the table. He looked as if he wanted to eat her then and there, and who could blame him? We were all starving as Arabella was a shocking cook at the best of times and tonight she had surpassed herself with a bouillabaisse, which proved beyond all doubt that fish didn't keep well.

Holden walked me home. 'I won't ask you in,' I said as we reached the flat, 'because . . .'

'. . . because you're tired,' Holden filled in with a little smile, as he raised his hand and touched my chin with the tip of his middle finger.

'Because I'm all talked out for one evening and I don't know you well enough to sleep with you,' I corrected him. He left pretty quickly after that.

'So what was Arabella's place like?' It was Saturday and Audrey had popped in on her way from buying silk flowers from a small shop on the edge of Parsons Green. ('The secret is to mix them with real ones, darling.')

'Arabella's new flat,' I said vaguely. 'Oh, it's nice. I didn't like her dining-room table, but otherwise it's really nice.'

'Bad taste runs in that family.' Audrey sniffed. 'Arabella's mother completely ruined that beautiful mews house she got in the divorce settlement.'

'Big windows,' I said, trying to be helpful. But try as I might, all I could see were pictures of Arabella's mind, all cosy and rosy and rounded, with comfortable thoughts floating gently around against a baby-blue background. 'Really nice.'

'Nice. That word says nothing.'

People always said that, but I didn't agree. Nice meant what it said: pleasant, agreeable, satisfactory, kind, good-natured. Now what was wrong with that?

I was working late one evening, finishing off some research on a new American woman novelist, when the wail of a siren interrupted my thoughts. As I looked out of the basement window an ambulance blasted into the narrow street, screeching to a halt outside the house. I rushed to the door to see the men hurry inside the Bodkins' door. Within moments they were back out on the street, their stretcher weighed down by the elderly frame of Mr Bodkin. Mrs Bodkin stood on her front-door step, frozen, while her husband was being loaded aboard. As the last of Mr Bodkin disappeared she seemed to snap into life and, walking towards the ambulance, she was helped inside. I turned back from the window, tears in my eyes. Oh dear, oh dear, oh dear, I wailed to myself. I prayed he'd be all right. They were such a sweet old couple. Jim and Elsa Bodkin, forty-three years together in that same house. Jim and Elsa Bodkin, inseparable, wandering down the road to Safeway, hand in hand, gardening, feeding the birds, taking a stroll in the spring sunshine.

The next day I heard from another neighbour that Jim Bodkin had died. I knew that the Bodkins had no immediate family and that most of their friends had died or moved from the area, so later that day I rang Elsa's doorbell to ask if she might need some company. She opened the door wearing a bright blue jogging suit with pink socks and brilliant white trainers, very different from her normal tweed skirt and cardigan. 'Oh no, dear,' she said. 'Don't you worry about me. I quite like my own company.' And that was that, she practically pushed me out of the door, closing it quickly as if she was afraid I might force my way in with tea and sympathy. I still kept an eye out for Elsa; grief could do strange things to people's minds, but apart from her clothes, one brightly coloured jogging suit after the other, she seemed fine as she pottered down the road to Safeway or worked in the garden. She was mostly indoors, though. Then the music started. Always opera, always loud. It began to get on my nerves as I came back from work or sat reading on a Sunday afternoon. When she started playing it in the middle of the night I had had enough. The next morning I rang her doorbell. 'I'm all right, dear,' Elsa said impatiently, barely visible through the crack in the door. 'But thank you for asking.'

'I've come about the music,' I said, wedging my shoulder against the door. 'I don't suppose you could keep it down just a little.' Elsa pulled it wide open. Today she was wearing pea-green. I hadn't seen a pea-green sweat-suit before. 'Goodness gracious, have I been disturbing you?' she enquired. I admitted that actually she had. 'Jim never cared for opera either,' Elsa said, beckoning me inside the narrow hall.

I told her I liked opera very much, but in its place. Then I saw it, the object on the wall above the stairs. Elsa followed my gaze.

'What do you think?' she asked me.

What did I think about a huge pink plush penis? 'It's very interesting.'

'I don't intend to keep it in the hall,' Elsa said. 'People might think it odd.' She led me into the small front room. In pride of place, on top of the cabinet where before there had been a fish tank, stood a pair of lush cherry-red lips. A pair of soft plush hands were mounted like antlers on the wall above the fireplace and on an opposite wall hung one huge perfect ear. On the hearth, a hollow foot on a hollow leg housed the fire tongs and poker. 'All my own work,' Elsa stated. 'I always had a mind to do something artistic, but while Jim was alive there never seemed to be the time. He wasn't what you'd call a difficult man, he just liked things his way. They do, men. Then, when he passed away, I thought, well at least now I can get on with it.'

'It's an interesting choice of subjects,' I said. We were sitting down and Elsa had made us a pot of tea.

'Well I've never been one for landscapes myself.' Elsa sipped delicately from her Royal Albert china cup. 'And maybe it's my eyes, but I've always seen people in bits: a mouth or an ear, a nostril even. I'll be honest with you, if you ask me to describe someone I'd be giving you just one bit.'

My mind went to the large plush penis.

'Jim and I were very happy together,' Elsa said as if she had been reading my thoughts.

Before I left I asked her if I could do an article on her for the magazine. Elsa and her 'Plush Pieces' was included in the Christmas issue. The feature made her quite a celebrity. Within days of it appearing it had gained her a spot on breakfast television and an offer of a one-woman show at a well-known gallery. In the new year I had a phone call from Chloe Sidcup, the features editor at the *Chronicle*, inviting me up to her offices for a talk.

'Don't be fooled by all that "I'm just one of the girls" act,' a colleague at *Chic and Cheek* warned before my interview. 'She's as tough as they come.'

Chloe Sidcup got up from her desk and put out her small hand to greet me. She was around thirty-five, bottle blonde, red-lipped and dressed in an electric-blue trouser suit with the kind of padded shoulders that made me think she would have to walk sideways to get through the doorway. She looked me up and down. 'Love the jacket,' she said. 'Whose is it?'

'It's mine,' I said, momentarily piqued. To be fair, she was right to ask because it had once belonged to Madox. When he didn't want it any more I had appropriated it, thinking it lent me a kind of Annie Hall chic. Chloe explained that she had meant who was the jacket by. I was about to take it off to check the label for the name of his tailor when Chloe stopped me: 'Never mind.'

We sat down and I showed her some of my work. We talked about various ideas I had for future pieces and a week later I got a call offering me a job as a feature writer for the *Chronicle*.

I toasted my success with Arabella and Sophie. As I looked across the Carl Larsson room at my friends I felt content with the world, just for once. I had done a good job and I had not had to compromise my principles. I hadn't had to dish the dirt, instead I had brought recognition and a following to someone I respected. It seemed to me then, as I poured us out another glass of champagne, that there was, after all, some order and justice in the world. I raised the glass, my third, to them and said, only half joking, 'To virtue and its rewards.'

'To virtue,' Sophie echoed.

'To rewards,' said Arabella.

Linus was working late at the office. He did most days, and most days he returned to be shouted at by Lotten. Lotten always had supper ready at half past six; she was a very organised woman. Half past six was later than she would have liked to eat, later than anyone else eats on weekdays, she pointed out frequently and with a frown, but on this point Linus had stood firm. He could not leave the office before six. Lotten pointed out that the office closed at five. 'Everyone else leaves at five or earlier.' Linus tried to explain, without sounding pretentious but simply as the only truth he knew, that he was different from the others. But how was Lotten supposed to understand? 'You're different, all right,' she said bitterly. 'You're never home. You walk around with your head in the clouds, half the time you don't seem to hear what I say, or care. You never want to join the others for tennis or an evening out.' 'The others' being the group of friends of about the same age whom they had mixed with since schooldays.

At his desk, Linus sighed and began to put away the drawings he was submitting for a new bridge to join the mainland to one of the islands in the archipelago. On his way over to the large computer screen he passed the plans for a small block of flats left out by his colleague Jonas Berg and, looking closer, he saw the beginnings of a solution to the problem of living space which Jonas had complained about earlier. He slipped on to the chair and picked up a pencil.

A while later Linus looked up at the clock on the wall above the office door. It was six forty-five. Home was a good quarter of an hour's walk from the office so whatever he did now Lotten would be screaming at him as he returned. He might as well stay and finish what he was doing, it was a matter of getting value for money, so to speak. And there were a couple more things he wished to do with the bridge drawings before the ideas went out of his head. This was a commission he really wanted. The west coast and its architecture was in his blood. He loved the brightly coloured extravagant shapes of the buildings. The turrets and wooden carvings that decorated verandas and balconies, and the way it stood in such contrast to the stark beauty of the surrounding landscape of granite rocks and grey-blue sea. He had visited the site over and over so that all he had to do now was to close his eyes and he would see it in his mind, complete with his bridge. A bridge which swept across the water in a perfect white arch, a cloud walk across the sound. In winter it would stand almost deserted, against the unremitting grey of the sea and the sky and the rocks. Then, in summer, when all of Sweden emerged, bright and vibrant, as from a huge sodden winter coat, it would carry hundreds of cars on a daily crossing to the other side.

Reluctantly, at seven o'clock, he got ready to leave. Turning off the computer with one hand, he doodled on his drawing a tightrope dancer in a pink tutu, a green parasol raised in her left hand as she balanced across the line of the handrail along the side of the bridge.

'What the hell do you think you're playing at?' Lotten stood, eyes blazing, in the hall, her arms crossed over her chest. 'Dinner is ruined and I was about to phone the hospitals. Why didn't you call to say you were going to be late, huh?'

Linus, taking off his coat, was about to ask why she had not thought to ring the office before she called the hospitals when he remembered that he had switched on to answerphone and not checked his messages. And how could he explain why he had not phoned himself? The truth? *I didn't call because I knew you would make a fuss and I was far too engrossed in my work to want to bother with all that.* 'I'm sorry,' he said. 'Tram tracks iced up again.'

'Very funny. It's May and you don't take the tram anyway.'

Linus bent down to kiss her, but she ducked out of his way and marched into the kitchen where she removed a casserole dish from the oven, noisily scraping its contents into the bin. 'I could have eaten that,' Linus protested.

'So eat it, then.' Lotten fished out a spoonful from the bin and chucked it on a plate. 'Enjoy.' Suddenly her face crumpled and to his horror she burst into tears. 'I'm two weeks overdue,' she sobbed, her slanted coldwater-blue eyes brimming as she rubbed at her sharp little nose. 'I'm never late, never.'

Linus stared at her. 'I think I'm pregnant, you retard. I'm pregnant with your child and look at you!' Now she stopped crying and began laughing hysterically instead. 'Just look at you, you great big lumbering . . .' She broke off, choking, and sank into a chair. Linus knelt by her side and took her hand, patting it clumsily. She did not withdraw it and after a while her sobbing stopped. 'We're going to have a baby,' she whispered. Linus kept on patting her hand until she straightened up, saying in her normal voice, 'Well, aren't you pleased?'

Linus got to his feet, then sat back down on the chair next to her. 'I'm overwhelmed,' he said finally. 'I don't quite know what to say.'

'But are you pleased?' There was a sharp note to Lotten's voice.

Linus wished he were not so slow. His thoughts were anything but, racing through his brain, darting hither and thither, but it was precisely because of that that he needed time. Time to weed out the true and real from the bluster. Linus was on a quest for the right word, the sincere reaction, the truest feeling. But time was something Lotten was not prepared to give him. She, like everybody else, seemed to want instant feeling, immediate reaction. He did his best to oblige. 'Of course I'm pleased. It's wonderful news. I'm thrilled.'

This time Lotten did not pursue the subject. All at once she seemed to have lost interest in him as she sat picking away at the congealing food, chewing the cold mushrooms and carrots and pulses, a far-away look in her eyes. Linus was left to try to work out what he really felt about the possibility of a new life, his and Lotten's child, growing inside her. Put like that, it scared him. The thought of a foreign body making itself at home inside that of his wife. How must that feel, to be two people all of a sudden? And one of them a stranger. And what does he say when he sees his pregnant wife come towards him? There go my wife and child, hello you two. But no one else seemed to see it that way. The convention was to ignore the person within the person until it was on the other side. Lotten pushed the plate closer towards him. 'Have some.' Obediently he picked up the fork. Was he, he wondered, at that precise moment having dinner with one or with two people?

'Do you love me?' Lotten asked suddenly.

'Of course I love you,' he said.

'You never say so any more.'

'I don't think about it very much, that's all.' He was immediately aware that he had said the wrong thing, again. Furious with himself he watched Lotten's face harden into that familiar air of dissatisfaction: small mouth pursed, eyes narrowed.

'What I meant to say was that loving you is so much part of my life that I don't have to give it much thought, I just take it for granted and I suppose I expect you to do so as well.' His voice trailed off as he met his wife's stony glance.

'Yes, you do take it for granted. You take me for granted and our marriage for granted and I'm fed up with it, do you hear?' Her voice rose dangerously. Linus moved closer to her and put his long arm round her shoulders. He felt desperate. It was always the same; she wanted him to express his feelings, but when he did, something always went wrong. He knew what he wanted to say, in his mind he did, but before Lotten's clear-eyed gaze the words seemed to slip off in all the wrong directions like the legs of a calf on an icy road. Then she'd challenge him and he was lost, no match for his wife's verbal dexterity.

'You know that's not what I mean,' he tried once more. 'It's not taking for granted in the way you seem to think, more like, well the way you take the pleasure of the feel of your favourite pencil for

73

granted, or your favourite sweater, the one you can't do without,' he added hastily, but he knew even before she tipped the plate with the remaining casserole over his lap that as usual he had failed to explain himself.

His plans for the bridge were rejected as too costly, but instead of handing the commission to one of the other firms of architects, the council asked if he could modify his proposal. His boss, Lennart Karlsson, sighed and shook his head. 'You do this every time. Why? Why do you submit something you must know will be deemed unsuitable? You do it over and over and then, when you have to, you go back and redesign, effortlessly it seems to me, producing something to everybody's satisfaction.'

'Not to mine,' Linus said tiredly. 'Never to mine, not those second compromise drawings.' He looked up at Lennart. 'Those first drawings, they are from the soul of an architect. The second ones, well, they come from the mind of an engineer.'

'I understand about being true to one's vision.' Lennart looked up with a small smile. 'Don't think I don't. We've all been there, more times than we care to think about. But things have changed. You know that. The architect has had to step into the background as rational architecture and industry take over the building process. We are co-ordinators, technicians. We have to learn to leave behind the creative side of our work for most of our working lives. It's the way things are, Linus.'

Linus had stood hunched over his desk but now he straightened up and looked Lennart in the eyes. 'Not for me, they aren't.'

Lennart put his hand on the younger man's shoulder. 'Be content, Linus. You've already achieved more in your short career than many in the profession do during a lifetime of work. Take my advice and quit the tortured-genius routine.'

'How can I? I detest seeing my work, my vision, turned into a crude caricature of its original self. If you think getting prizes for some of those caricatures makes it any easier, think again.'

By the time the revised drawings for the bridge between the mainland and the small island off the west coast were being turned into reality, Lotten was nearing the end of her pregnancy.

'Not long to go now,' Bertil said during lunch with his son in a small restaurant equidistant from both their offices. He raised his glass of light beer and he was actually smiling, not that thin, unpractised twitch he usually reserved for Linus, but a broad grin. 'Olivia is getting positively clucky. I even caught her pressing her nose against the window of Erik & Anna, her mouth watering at the sight of all those baby clothes.'

'Lotten wants everything to be able to be tumble-dried,' Linus said tiredly. 'I wanted to buy this gorgeous little shirt the other day, but she said absolutely not. It needed ironing too.'

'And how is Lotten?'

Linus thought of his wife spending her nights seated upright in bed to lessen the effect of heartburn. He thought of her distended stomach that looked as if at any moment it would split open like an overripe tomato and of her poor swollen legs threaded with thick ropes of blue veins. 'She says she's fine, but I can't see how she can be. She looks so terribly uncomfortable. But she says that everyone at the clinic has much the same problems. God, women are amazing, aren't they? Then again, if they hadn't been I don't suppose they'd have been picked for that particular job.'

'If she says she's fine that probably means she is.' Bertil looked hard at his son. 'You look pretty done in yourself actually.'

Linus thought of the endless sleepless hours of the early mornings, lying twisting and turning next to Lotten. Usually she told him to get up and do something useful if he couldn't sleep anyway. 'The baby's room still isn't ready,' she complained, but he was too exhausted to move. The night before he had woken at four. Lotten was snoring gently beside him, comfortable for once. Outside a man was revving his bike, on and on went the shrill engine noise through the dark winter morning. He lay there, his teeth on edge as the sound stopped for a moment only to start again ... and stop, and start again. He could always get up and close the window. It was triple-glazed so few sounds penetrated, but he seemed unable to lift his legs over the side of the bed and on to the floor. The noise had stopped, it had been quiet for a good ten minutes now. Linus felt himself relax as the tension left his body. The bed was soft, moulded to his shape. He floated off to sleep.

Wroom wroom wroom! The motor-cycle engine started up again

and before he knew it he was lying there in the dark, weeping, for what, he did not quite know.

Two days later Lotten gave birth to a son, Ivar. Linus was at the birth. He had asked Lotten right at the beginning of the pregnancy if she would not prefer some privacy; he knew he would have. She had refused to speak to him for almost a week after that. When she did finally address him it was to ask in a small tight voice if he felt that childbirth was something disgusting, something to be ashamed of, something best kept to oneself? And Linus had known that this was not the time to discuss the mass of conflicting emotions he felt on the subject. Instead he assured her that he would be there. When the time came, he was in the middle of a meeting with the town council on the future of a large development on the western side of town. He had been called in as an expert adviser and was due to make his presentation as soon as the quick coffee break was over. He looked at the secretary who had come into the room with the message that his wife had gone to the hospital, then at the file in front of him. With a small sigh he rose to his feet and made his excuses.

'I had to force him to be with me at the birth,' Lotten grunted to the midwife between contractions. The midwife glanced at Linus as if he had just tucked into a meal of fluffy puppy dogs. Every time he tried to sneak up to stand by Lotten's shoulders, the midwife shooed him down towards her feet. 'Daddy doesn't want to miss anything now, does he?' she hissed threateningly.

Daddy jolly well did, Linus thought as, with a concerned look at Lotten's red face, clenched in pain and concentration, he shuffled off to the foot of the bed.

'Now, Daddy, you hold Mummy's leg.'

Then Ivar was born and Linus fell in love.

# Chapter Seven

You hear people say sadly of someone, 'He left before I had a chance to say goodbye.' It seemed to me that Madox left before I had a chance to say hello. I stood in the drawing-room of my parents' house, reading the note from him that my mother had just passed me. It was addressed to *My Dear Audrey. Maybe I should have done as the Florida OAP who when asked about the future by his elderly mistress, croaked, 'We'll have to wait until the children are dead,' but the problem with that is that in the scheme of things so would I be. I have set up generous monthly standing orders for you and the house has been transferred into your name. Tell Esther I love her.*

I realised that I never really knew him. When I had been a child he hadn't had the time or the inclination to get to know *me* and as I grew up and he grew older, it was *I* who ran out of time, and interest too. I had got used to doing without him.

I put the note down, watching my mother's face for signs of distress. My shoulders tensed in anticipation of a scene, screams, fainting fits, threats, tears, but there was nothing. Her face betrayed no emotion. She just sat there in the old green armchair, quite still, only her fingers moving, twining and twisting. After a while she stood up and smoothed down her skirt. 'At least now I can get rid of this blasted thing.' She aimed a little kick at the chair with the tip of her Ferragamo-shod foot.

I told her that I'd stay the week with her. She said, 'At least I can eat whatever I like now there's no need to worry about my weight.'

'Not that I think you should worry,' I said. Having learnt that fat was a feminist issue I added, 'If you ever did, surely it would have been for yourself, not to please Madox?'

Audrey turned a surprised gaze on me. 'Why should *I* mind? But my generation was brought up to believe it was our duty to look good for our husbands; clean and neat, and attractively turned out at all times. It was part of the bargain, that's all.'

And boy could she eat. She told me that for thirty years she had left the table while still hungry. Now she was catching up. It was as if there were a gaping hole at the pit of her stomach that just couldn't be filled. I watched her as she had her breakfast: two soft-boiled eggs with white bread soldiers, followed by two slices of wholemeal toast with honey, followed by fruit yoghurt and rinsed down with tubs of Orange Pekoe tea. And lunch . . . baguettes filled with tuna fish and sour cream and avocado and tomatoes and Beaufort cheese, and apples and pecan nuts. Teatime was an orgy as she munched through platefuls of jam doughnuts, scones with Cornish clotted cream, cinnamon bagels, milk chocolate digestives. She had pasta most evenings, smothered in cream and garlic and Gorgonzola cheese, and at bedtime she brought a mug of hot chocolate and a plateful of biscuits upstairs with her.

'Stay another week,' she pleaded with me, turning those long-lashed baby-blue eyes on me, eyes more suited to the visage of a child or a doll than to an old woman whose still beautiful face was creased and sagging.

How could I say no? After work that Monday I went by my flat to pick up the mail and water the plants. There was a message for me on the answerphone from Holden. Holden who? Oh, Holden: *Remember me? Dinner at Arabella's three years ago. Goodness how time flies.*

You could say the call was completely out of the blue if you didn't know that I had just got an award for journalism and featured in a cringe-making article in *Watch Out* magazine titled 'Smart Little Daddy's Girls' about women following in their fathers' footsteps.

'Not all the way, darling,' Audrey had said sadly as she read the dreadful piece. It was one of the few times she made a comment about the fate of her forty-year-old marriage.

Anyway, Holden wanted to take me out to dinner, so his message said. I shook my head at the machine. I was too busy and anyway, I wanted a rest from men. Since breaking up with Donald I had had a series of short and ultimately unsatisfactory relationships: a jazz musician, Mike, who wanted to be mothered; a fellow journalist, Chris, who liked me working as long as I wasn't as successful as he

78

was; and finally David, who turned out to have a thing against breasts, which was tricky since I had two.

Holden was still talking on the answerphone, his voice with its slight American twang warm and deep and, it had to be said, opportunistic: *I've meant to get in touch all this time, but the days and weeks . . .*

'And months and years,' I filled in, speaking to the empty room.

*. . . rush past and suddenly you find, well anyway, it would be just great if you could give me a ring back on 326 4247 so we could fix a date. Beeep!*

By the time I got back to my mother's house, she was in bed although it was only just gone eight. 'What do you mean he's opportunistic?' she wanted to know.

'I mean that he didn't ring me after we first met. Instead, he calls now, out of the blue and just when I have achieved some modest professional success.'

'Don't be paranoid,' Audrey said. 'Anyway, success is very sexy.'

I frowned at her. I didn't think one's parents should speak in terms of sexuality. Most people felt like that, it seemed, at least until they became parents themselves. Why children should view the particular act which gave them life with quite such distaste, why they should find any reminder of it so excruciatingly embarrassing, I don't know. There's no real reason for it, you simply preferred your parents asexual. I took the view that if God had wanted us to be comfortable with our parents' sexuality, he would have made us conscious at the time of conception. Luckily, we weren't.

In front of my mother, resting on her lap, sat a tray with her supper of cold chicken salad, cheese and figs, and a whole tub of Häagen-Dazs strawberry-and-banana ice-cream. 'It's all right,' she assured me. 'It takes ages for that ice-cream to thaw sufficiently to be eaten. There's plenty of chicken for you downstairs. Why don't you bring it up and eat here with me?'

I told her I'd eat downstairs if it was all the same to her.

'So what is he like this Holden? Is he handsome?' she asked as I got up.

I shrugged my shoulders. 'Yeah, I suppose so, in a kind of old-fashioned Vietcong-bashing kind of way.'

'Why don't you ask him round for dinner?' Audrey had her bright voice on and I wondered how she could still be so keen on romance.

The next day she had a television installed in her bedroom and she told me they were coming to connect her up to cable. 'Aren't you ever going to get out of bed?' I asked.

'Why should I?' Audrey replied. 'Janet comes in every morning and I've got everything I need here.' She made a sweeping gesture with her silk-clad arm across the array of books and magazines and papers that lay scattered over the powder-blue counterpane. She reached for the television remote. 'If you don't mind, it's *Barry Jones Today*.'

I was working at my mother's that day, in my old bedroom, writing up an interview feature with a former Stasi agent, Hanna Holst, who had started a new life working as a vet in the Orkneys. Half-way through the afternoon the doorbell rang and I picked up the entryphone on the landing. It was Holden. 'Arabella gave me the address. I've been trying to get in touch,' his disembodied voice told me.

'I know. I picked up your answerphone message.'

'You know?' He sounded amazed. 'Why didn't you get back to me?'

I pressed the entry button to let him in and walked downstairs to greet him. 'I've been busy,' I answered. He still seemed surprised, one dark, heavy eyebrow lifted, a quizzical look in his squirrel-brown eyes. 'I'm just finishing this article.' I stepped back to let him in. 'But would you like a cup of coffee or something?'

'That's what I like about you, you're so gracious.' I expect he was being ironic. 'I was just passing on my way to see a client whose offices are nearby. Coffee would be great.' He followed me down into the kitchen. I put the kettle on and wondered if my mother would get out of bed if I told her Holden really was very attractive. She had always admired the dark, rugged type.

'So this is where you grew up?' Holden took the mug from my hand, our palms touching for a second. I nodded and sat down opposite him at the kithen table. 'My mother still lives here, but my father has just left.'

'How do you mean, just left? Gone for a trip? Gone to fetch the newspaper?'

'Gone to live with his mistress on a small Scottish island.'

Holden's keen brown eyes took on a compassionate look. 'I'm so sorry. Really I am. Christ I'd feel so hostile if my dad ever did that to my ma.' He sighed and shook his head. 'How's your mother taking it?'

'She's eating a lot.'

Holden nodded gravely. 'Comfort.'

'No, I really don't think so. I think she just likes eating and now my father has gone she isn't worried about her weight.'

'I don't think you're being quite fair to your mother. I'm sure there's more to it than that.'

'You don't know my mother.' Holden had to admit that he didn't. 'I'm not saying she isn't upset, I'm just saying that she likes eating and she likes television and she likes her bed, and now she can sit in bed and eat and watch television. Maybe that's what's known as making the best of something.'

'It's not much of a life.'

'I don't know,' I said. 'At least she knows where she is.'

'Do you have to stay in bed to know that?' Holden wanted to know. I told him of course not. 'But it makes it easier to find yourself.'

'Now you're kidding me?' I agreed that I was, a bit, but secretly I wondered. I had always felt that for your mind to be free it had to exist in a supremely organised body, which in turn lived in an organised environment. Once you were in control of your environment your mind could roam unfettered. Bed was a very controlled environment, as long as you were in it alone of course.

'What about dinner tonight?' Holden interrupted my thoughts. I relented.

I asked Audrey if she minded me going out. She hushed me. 'Angela Andrews,' she said.

What she meant was that the chat-show hostess cum Agony Aunt, Angela Andrews, was coming on with her evening show. It was only six o'clock and I had finished the article, so I perched on the edge of the bed and reached out for a raspberry jam brioche from the plate on the tray. That evening's show was subtitled 'Unfathomable Tragedies'. To rapturous applause a small dumpy woman of indeterminate age took her seat on the sofa opposite Angela Andrews. Her name was Karen Dempster and she was thirty-four. Goodness, was that all? She must have had a hard life. She began her story and I could see from the way the camera was already zooming in on Ms Andrews's tear-filled eyes that this was going to be *sad*. It wasn't long ago, Karen told the audience, that she had been a happy wife and the mother of three strapping lads. Then tragedy struck and she was as we saw her now, *alone*.

What happened?

'First it was our Gareth.' Karen looked up under her frizzy bleached fringe. It turned out that poor little Gareth had fallen under a truck. It was a terrible thing to happen, but slowly, as the weeks went by, she and the rest of the family had begun to pick up the pieces.

'Of little Gareth?' Audrey asked. She had no heart, that woman. Karen and her family had picked up the pieces of their lives, helped and sustained by the kindness of friends and strangers alike.

'It was amazing to see how people cared,' Karen said. 'They just couldn't do enough for us. We had flowers and cards, our local church collected money for us all to go away and have a break. We went to EuroDisney.' The memory seemed to perk her up, but then her eyes grew moist once more. 'Then it was little Andrew and his father's gun.'

I turned away from the television. I could hardly bear to listen. As it happened, little Andrew was all right – for a while. It was his brother Shaun who got shot in the head. Of course Andrew hadn't mean to shoot Shaun. He didn't even know his father's gun was loaded. Again, it was the kindness of friends and strangers alike that carried the remaining family through. 'We were in all the papers,' Karen said. I nodded to myself. I remembered the story now.

As it was, little Andrew didn't have to carry his burden of guilt for long. He was retrieving his skateboard from under his father's parked Montego when his father got in and drove off. When he discovered what he had done, the wretched man killed himself; an overdose of paracetamol.

Poor, poor Karen. I stared at the pinched little face. How much could one soul take?

Karen was writing a book: *Survivor!* She was doing it 'as part of her own healing process', she told us, but mostly to help others. 'To show', she said, a catch in her throat, 'that however terrible the events of your life, you can survive and come through with a new understanding.' The audience wept. I thought of the seemingly unquenchable human spirit. Audrey reached for the remote with one hand and a doughnut with the other. I wanted to weep, but somehow I couldn't.

'That perm,' Audrey said with distaste. I longed to believe that Karen's unfortunate choice of hair-style was not what prevented me from showing true compassion. So what was?

A couple of months later I saw an advance copy of Karen's book in the office waiting to be reviewed. I read it twice. I thought of little Karen blinking at the cameras from under her frizzy fringe. 'I'd like to do a profile,' I told Chloe. 'I really want to know what makes this woman tick.'

I approached the publishers who called me back later that day to say that Karen had agreed to the interview, but only because I represented a serious and respected publication. Oh, and Karen's press agent would be present.

Karen sat straight-backed on the rust-and-green sofa in her neat-as-a-pin house on a leafy estate on the outskirts of Farnborough. 'I chose this' – she stroked the patterned cloth – 'because it doesn't show the dirt. With three boys . . .' She gave a little laugh that caught in her throat and died. I felt like a ghoul at the scene of an accident, one of those people who slow down their cars and crane their necks to catch a glimpse of the human wreckage within the metal one. Then again, I was a journalist, I was used to feeling like that.

'You've never thought of moving, starting afresh somewhere new?' I asked. The press agent, Debbie, had gone out into the kitchen to make us all some coffee, but I had a feeling she was listening from behind the half-open serving hatch.

Karen shook her head. 'Never,' she said. 'My memories are all I've got left now and they're here.' She made a forlorn gesture around the room. 'Here in this house. And my friends and neighbours, what would I do without them? Everyone knows me around here. They look out for me.' Suddenly she smiled, a coy little smile. 'You could say I was a bit of a celebrity.'

Behind us, standing in the doorway with a tray, Debbie emitted a warning sound from the back of her throat. Debbie the watchdog, I thought. 'Why don't we talk about the book?' she said, as she placed the coffee tray in front of us on the table. 'If you've read Karen's book most of your questions will already have been answered. But if Karen can clarify . . .' Her mouth stretched into a brisk smile, like a rubber band being pulled, then as quickly it had sprung back again into its former tight-lipped expression.

'The photographer will be arriving in about half an hour,' I said, glancing at my watch. 'So we have plenty of time.'

'I'll show you the letters,' Karen sighed. 'You wouldn't believe the letters I've been sent, thousands of them. Still get them. Especially since that telly interview. The postman sometimes has to make a special delivery just to here.' She shrugged and stifled a sound much like a giggle. 'And to think there were whole weeks when I didn't get a thing other than that awful junk mail. Not even bills.'

Next she showed me the children's bedroom. 'It's just like they left it.'

I stood on the threshold gazing into the room, trying to get the sense of the three little boys who had lived there once and who were gone now, dead at an age when most of us haven't even started properly to live. A bunk bed stood against one wall, made up with brightly coloured duvet covers. The top one was red and black with a pattern of aeroplanes and the bottom one had football players in yellow and green. A single bed stood against the opposite wall. This duvet cover had blue air balloons on it and was thrown back as if the bed's occupant had only just got up. Toys lay scattered across the brown carpet, cars, Lego, some *Star Wars* figures. A poster of Oasis was Blu-Tacked to the wall above the desk.

'Just as they left it,' Karen said, her voice quiet. 'The top bunk was Gareth's and the bottom one was Shaun's. Andrew slept there.' She pointed at the single bed.

'Did Andrew continue to sleep here after his brothers' deaths?'

Karen closed the door gently behind her. 'Oh yes,' she said. 'It was a comfort to him, and to Shaun before he . . .' Her voice faltered. Debbie, who had followed us upstairs, put a comforting arm round her as she shot me a mean look.

'I'm sorry,' I mouthed.

'There's something odd about this whole thing,' I told Chloe the next day. 'I'd like to go back again. See if I can talk to her without the minder.'

Karen's book became a best-seller. I called her, having copied her number down from the phone in her house.

'Debbie doesn't like me talking to the press without her there,' Karen confided to me over the phone. 'But she's away with another client now, touring if you like. I said to her, "What if I need you?" I said. No, I can't agree with that. I need to tell my story, to help other people who are suffering.'

'Quite right,' I mumbled. 'So true.'

This time Karen herself opened the door. I hardly recognised her. Gone was the frizzy bleached perm, replaced by a glossy helmet of red hair. Gone, too, were the leggings and the white cardigan. Today she was wearing a sharp suit with padded shoulders and a short skirt showing off surprisingly shapely legs. Spotting my gaze she smiled that coy little smile of hers. 'It's my publishers. They smartened me up now I'm a best-seller. I have to say I was a bit of an old frump before.'

We sat once more in the neat little sitting-room with its one shelf of books, its pale water-colour prints hung too high, the small teak dining-table at the far end by the west-facing window. 'I might be going to America,' Karen said as she poured us a cup of tea. 'On tour.' She handed me a Rich Tea biscuit. 'Whoever would have thought? Me who's never been anywhere, apart from that trip to EuroDisney, that is. I always wanted to travel, when I was young like, but then you marry, have kids.' She shrugged. 'Things change.'

'Where do you get your strength from? The enormity of your tragedy would have left most people broken, yet you seem to have got your life back together in a remarkable way.'

'I am strong.' Karen nodded, each strand of shiny red hair remaining in place, rendered immobile by everything modern hair care could throw at it. 'But most of my strength has come from others.' Her voice rose to an almost evangelical pitch. 'The many thousands of hands that have reached out to mine, the many voices ringing out in comfort. You know.' Her voice lowered a note. 'Passers-by recognise me in the street and come forward to touch my hand. It's been said that I should consider going into Healing.'

'That's good,' I said. 'People not being shy of you, I mean. So often you hear bereaved men or women complain that friends cross the street to avoid having to confront what happened. It's as if loss were contagious, they say.'

Karen nodded again. 'But it's different with me; they know me from the telly, the newspapers too. You're not the first person to write about me.'

'Oh, I'm well aware of that.' I smiled at her.

'I'm giving out the prizes at the darts comp at our local, Saturday.

Last year they had that old boy from *Coronation Street*, what's his name . . .?'

'Call me a cold-hearted hard-headed bitch,' I said to Audrey as I perched on her bed that evening, 'but the woman does revel in all the attention given her. She'll be on *Good Morning* next week.'

'I would never call you a *bitch*, darling.' Audrey turned down the volume on the television. 'Such an ugly word. Anyway, I blame the Americans. All that talk of being famous. All these people prepared to humiliate themselves and their families the moment a television camera is pointed in their direction. In my day the distinction was made between fame and infamy – in fact, it was the all-important distinction – but not these days. All that matters now is to get your face on that screen. Apparently that makes you Somebody. And your lot, Esther, are as much to blame as anyone. As for that little Dempster woman, I can't help feeling that losing all your family one by one like that in totally different circumstances smacks of the most awful carelessness. Carelessness can be a terrible thing.' She passed me a doughnut from the plate of mixed ones: chocolate-covered ones, cinnamon, jam, ones with icing. I took a cinnamon one and bit into it. It was soft and slightly warm. I looked around the bedroom. 'Don't tell me you've got an oven in here?'

'Microwave.' She pointed to a shelf by her wardrobe. 'They're a frightfully good idea. Anyway, I still think there's something fishy about the whole thing.'

'If there were something suspicious about those deaths, you would think the police would have done something about it by now?'

Audrey shrugged her plump shoulders. 'I suppose.'

'She'll sue,' Chloe, my boss, said when she had finished reading my feature on Karen. 'I'm not sure what it is you're saying exactly, but you are saying something. Something libellous, I should think. You know me, I'm not one to be soft where work is concerned, but don't you think that poor woman has suffered enough?'

'That's what I'm not so sure about,' I said.

A couple of the papers that previously had written pieces full of tears and sympathy about Karen's Tragic Story, began to turn. WHY GRIEF SHOULD BE A PRIVATE MATTER read the headline of one article, by a well-known woman columnist. It was full of talk of the good old virtues of suffering in silence. Smiling while your heart is breaking.

Keeping up a brave face; rolling up your sleeves and battening down the hatches. It was made clear that Karen Dempster lacked these qualities in spades. Then there were the neighbours who appeared suddenly, like embarrassing memories, and told of Karen's fondness for nights out with the girls, and of family rows and smacks around the head. Little Gareth was always running away from home. It had only been a matter of time before he ran under a truck, in that good neighbour's humble opinion. Little Shaun was locked out all night once when he failed to return home before his parents went to bed. And little Andrew spent most of his time throwing stones at crows and stamping on baby birds. Oh dear!

Next the police reopened the investigation into the death of the Dempster children and their father. Karen went on television telling about the hate mail she was receiving and revealing that she was two months pregnant by a family friend. 'People have said it's too soon,' she sobbed. 'But I say to them, what do they know? I've suffered enough and now it's time I thought about me and my life. I mean if you don't look out for yourself, who should you look out for? What business is it of anyone's anyway? What am I? Public property or something?'

A couple of days later it was revealed that Karen had spent the previous night in custody. While she was away, someone set fire to her house and the same neighbours who had championed her as a modern-day tragic heroine didn't call the fire brigade until it was too late to save anything from the burnt wreckage.

Two weeks after that Karen Dempster was arrested for the murder of her husband and of two of their three children.

*It was the attention,* her sister Mandy pronounced. *I'm not saying that Karen did any of it, or anything, but she had always missed out on attention and when little Gareth died she got it, lots of it. I was always the pretty one and Mum and Dad just worshipped my two little girls, but with Gareth dead, it was Karen and her other two lads who were the centre of attention. I think she just missed it all when the months went by and life got back to normal. She'd always wanted to be famous had Karen, and with the boys dead and her husband and all, she was.*

There was a lot of discussion after that, about the part the media had played in the Dempster murders, sensationalising personal tragedy and crime, endowing fame on people like Karen Dempster and turning death and disaster into nothing more than a spectator sport.

'You have no cause to hang your head in shame,' Chloe said to me. 'You helped expose the woman.'

'So I did something right on my way down the road to media hell,' I said.

'Don't be so bloody melodramatic,' Chloe said.

THE *CHRONICLE* POINTS FINGER THAT LEADS TO ARREST, my paper boasted and I got a pat on the back and lots of free drinks bought for me at the pub by colleagues.


The day before Bertil's sixty-eighth birthday, Linus went shopping. Not for a present for his father – he had got that a long time before – but for Ivar. This was to be Ivar's first occasion with the whole family since he was a baby and Linus had promised him some new party clothes. It was lunch-time. Linus often wandered round the galleries and shops in his break. He seldom bought anything, but he loved looking and as a result he knew just about every shop in town. To his wife's embarrassment he was able to join in a conversation about women's fashion keenly and with as much authority as he would speak on the subjects of art and books. Lotten's thin lips would set in an ever firmer line as Linus discussed the best place to buy knitwear or the wonderful new shop in Kungspassagen which sells scarves to die for. 'I don't want to seem sexist or anything,' she said. 'But it gets a bit embarrassing having one's husband being one of the girls with quite such ease.' Lotten said that she believed that the New Man thing was dead and buried, and that men and women should be true to their gender specifics. At this, Linus looked confused and said he was just doing what came naturally to him.

This particular lunch-time he was strolling happily along the pedestrian walkway that led to Erik & Anna, still after thirty years the best children's-wear shop in town. He wanted to get Ivar something special. Uncle Gerald and Cousin Kerstin had not seen him for years. He and Lotten had brought Ivar to the rambling old house on the island the summer after he was born. Lotten had agreed reluctantly to them joining the rest of the Stendal family for the annual summer break, but the visit had not been a success. It had ended prematurely with Lotten storming off towards the ferry, the baby in a sling around her neck.

'Whatever is the matter?' Linus had asked, as he caught up with her in the car parked on the other side, as she had surely meant him to do.

'Do you want a list?' Lotten glared at him. Actually, Linus did not, but he knew he was going to get one anyway. 'For a start, I can't stand the way there's always so many of you,' Lotten said. 'And always so noisy; arguing and bickering . . .'

'Discussing. I think it would be fair to say we were discussing,' Linus interjected.

'Oh, you would, would you? Well, to my untrained ear it sounds mightily like arguing. But that's just part of it . . . that dreadful Ulla.'

'I've always been rather fond of Ulla. She's a brave old thing in her own way. I know she can be a bit annoying . . .'

'She's frightful and you know it. And that bloody seagull she keeps, it's as vicious and smelly as she is.'

'I never noticed that Ulla smelt.'

'Well she does, of fish mostly, fish and peppermints. Yuk! And Olivia, perfect, condescending Olivia.'

'Oh, come on now; Olivia has been nothing but kind and welcoming, and she dotes on Ivar.'

'Olivia is condescending and interfering, and I wish she'd leave Ivar alone, always babbling away to him in English.'

Linus had tried to remain patient. 'I thought we'd agreed that he should be brought up bilingual and that it was a wonderful opportunity.'

'Yeah, all right.' Lotten had sounded grudging. 'But she just can't stop interfering. And as for Gerald. He farts, don't say you haven't noticed? He just keeps doing it. And you all pretend that nothing has happened with that silly singing. I mean it, I can't stand it another minute, any of it.'

The long and the short of it was, Linus thought sadly as he walked into the shop, that Ivar had not been back on the island since and Linus had been able to go on just the shortest of visits. Lotten wanted nothing much to do with his family and as a result, Ivar too was kept at a distance. They saw Bertil and Olivia, of course, but even that was made as difficult as possible.

Linus looked around the racks of little suits and shorts and shirts. It was warm for April, so shorts would be OK. A pair of those nice long ones that French and Italian boys wore. Navy-blue velvet perhaps? And a white shirt to go with them. He explained to the assistant. They did not have velvet, she told him, but she could show him a very nice pair in navy cord. 'And this little shirt?' She held up a white shirt with blue edging round the collar and cuffs.

'Perfect.' Linus smiled at her. 'He's four, but he's not very big for his age.' At the last minute his eye was caught by a sleeveless Fair Isle jumper and he added that to his purchases. He left the shop, carrying the bright-yellow-and-orange bag, and feeling pleased with himself. He could already see Ivar wearing his new clothes.

'No, Linus,' Lotten said. 'I'm sorry to spoil your fun, but you really should have checked with me before spending all that money. Mummy has made Ivar a really great little denim suit. No, I'm afraid this will have to go back.' She handed him the bag with Ivar's clothes.

Linus looked downcast. 'I don't know that denim is quite right,' he said.

'Oh don't be such an old stick-in-the-mud. What century are we living in, for heaven's sake?'

'Look what Granny made for me.' Ivar, wearing his new denim suit, the shirt buttoned the wrong way, was tugging at Linus's arm. Linus woke with a start and sat up, resting on one elbow. He turned on the reading light by his bed and squinted at the alarm clock. 'Ivar, my little friend.' He sighed. 'It's five thirty in the morning.' Then he grinned and lifted the boy into the bed. Next to him, Lotten snorted in her sleep and turned on her other side.

Ivar wriggled in his arms. 'When's the party?'

Linus yawned and folded back the duvet, swinging his legs over the side of the bed. 'Pass me my dressing-gown, there's a good boy.' He got out of bed and wrapped himself in the soft tartan cotton. 'The party isn't until this evening. You'll have to be patient.'

In the kitchen he yawned again, staring at the cupboards, then, shaking himself he asked Ivar, 'So what shall we have?'

'Party food,' Ivar squealed, jumping up and down until he tripped on the long hem of his trousers and fell flat on his behind. 'Party food,' he chirruped, undeterred.

'Don't you think we'd better have cereal?'

'No.' Ivar had got up from the floor and now he shook his head so hard Linus thought he'd do himself damage. 'Party food because it's a party day.'

'Be careful shaking your head like that.' By way of a reply, Ivar nodded violently instead. Linus sighed, then he smiled. 'Maybe you're right. Maybe we should have party food.' He peered inside the cupboard. 'What do we have? O'Boy, chocolate powder ... and ... marshmallows!' He pulled out the half-empty bag sealed with a green plastic clip. Lotten had a whole store of those clips which she used to seal things with, the inner bag of cereal packets, bags of rice and flour, of sweets. 'What have we here?' Triumphantly Linus held up a jar of popping corn. 'Now you get a mixing bowl,' he told Ivar. Ivar scrabbled round the cupboard by the cooker. 'This one?' He held out a large Pyrex bowl for his father to see.

'Perfecto,' Linus said, pouring some cooking oil into a saucepan. Next he covered the base of the pan with corn, before putting it on the hot plate with the lid securely on. After a moment he beckoned Ivar closer and lifted him up. 'Can you hear it popping?'

Ivar listened, his small mouth set in concentration. Then he turned to Linus, wide-eyed. 'Can I look?' He put his hand out towards the lid but was stopped by Linus.

'You mustn't take the lid off.'

'Why?'

'They'll all pop right out of the pan,' Linus said. 'It's hot and they want to get out.'

Ivar stared at him, open-mouthed, then he started to sob. 'You have to let them,' he wailed. 'Daddy you have to let them out.'

Linus put him down on the floor and took the pan off the heat. Kneeling down in front of Ivar he explained as best he could that he had only been joking; popcorn did not have feelings.

'Why?'

'Because they're not alive.'

Ivar's sobs started anew. 'You mean we've killed them,' he wailed. 'Have you never watched when Mummy makes you popcorn?'

'No.'

'But I know you've had them before.'

'But Mummy never killed them.'

It took Linus ten minutes, at least, to explain about corn growing in fields and as much about the nervous system and theory of life and pain as he could reasonably explain to a four-year-old. Finally Ivar was reassured and Linus put the saucepan back on the hob. 'Pass me the bowl,' he instructed Ivar. 'Syrup.' He nodded towards the larder cupboard. Ivar had to pull up the kitchen steps to reach. Huffing and puffing with the effort, his face bright pink, he handed the bottle of syrup to Linus who squeezed large toffee-coloured globules of it over the popcorn before mixing it all with a wooden spoon. He bent down with the bowl, holding it out to Ivar. 'Now you stir.' Ivar grabbed the handle of the spoon with both hands and stirred, every muscle in his body tensing with the effort. Linus brought the chocolate powder across and sprinkled a good handful into the bowl. Ivar mixed some more.

'Breakfast time.' Linus grabbed two plates from the washstand and brought them over to the table. He patted the chair. 'You come and sit down.' He dished up a goodish spoonful of the mixture for Ivar, and a smaller one for himself. 'Yum, yum.'

Linus felt Lotten's eyes like drops of icy water on his back. He turned round slowly to find his wife standing like a vengeful angel in the doorway, if an angel would ever be seen dead, which come to think of it is the only way an angel could be seen, in a washed-out grey-white towelling dressing-gown and white clogs. Ivar, stuffing another fistful of popcorn into his sticky chocolate-smudged mouth, grinned at them both. 'Look, Mummy, we've made breakfast.'

Lotten ignored him. 'For God's sake, Linus, what do you think you're doing?'

'We've made breakfast, that's what I told you, we've . . .'

'Do be quiet, Ivar,' she snapped. 'Look at the state of this kitchen.' She grabbed the bowl from the table and tipped the sticky contents into the bin, scraping off the last, tenacious few bits with the wooden spoon. Ivar, squealing in protest, slid off his chair, revealing his chocolate-smeared self in full figure. 'I don't believe this,' Lotten hissed, turning to Linus. 'You did this deliberately, didn't you?'

Linus stared at her. 'Did what?'

'The suit. You couldn't stand the fact that Mummy had made him something nice instead of that stuff you'd bought, so you wrecked it.'

Ivar sidled out of the kitchen. 'You don't really believe that, do you?' Linus asked. Lotten just gave him one more long stare before turning her back on him. 'I've had enough. I'm going back to bed.' As she left she stepped on some toffee-covered popcorn. Cursing, she picked up the clog and prised off the sticky mess. She turned back and stared at Linus, and for a moment it looked as if she was going to throw the clog at him. But she just sighed and shook her head before disappearing back to the bedroom. Linus sank back in the chair with a sigh of relief; Lotten had been a mean shot-put in her schooldays and her aim, still, was as accurate as her arm was strong.

Linus made himself a cup of coffee and went in search of Ivar. He found him in the bathroom where he was busy soaking the front of his denim shirt, desperately trying to get the stains out. 'I'll do that, little man.' Linus smiled at him. 'You take it off for now and I'll get it clean for you in no time.'

Lotten was still angry as they arrived at Bertil and Olivia's apartment. Her back, as she stood waiting by the heavy oak front door, turned rigidly the way only angry backs do, her neck stiff. 'Ho, ho, ho,' Linus said, trying to lighten the mood. The neck and back remained rigidly turned away. 'Well, Ivar,' he said. 'I don't expect you remember much about Aunt Ulla, well she's not really your aunt, or mine for that matter, and Cousin Kerstin and Uncle Gerald, now he's really my father's uncle which makes him my great-uncle and your great . . .'

'Do we really have to listen all the ins and outs of your family relationships?' Lotten snapped. The door was opened by Olivia who knelt down instantly to kiss Ivar, chatting away with him in English. They followed her inside, Ivar chatting back in a mix of both languages.

'My goddess of the dawn sulks,' Linus whispered in Lotten's ear. 'I love you.'

'Don't be cheesy,' Lotten hissed.

Once inside the apartment, they went into the drawing-room. Ivar headed straight for the piano, climbing up on the stool and wriggling round, his little legs swinging, proceeding to bang out a tuneless melody. Olivia carried on with her conversation, raising her voice only slightly.

Ulla appeared from the kitchen carrying a tray of canapés. 'So this is Ivar.' She glared at the child, who ceased his playing to meet her gaze.

Then he smiled. 'I'm playing the piano.'

'I heard.' Ulla turned to Linus. 'Children seem to be allowed to wear denim on any occasion these days.' She placed the tray on the rosewood pedestal table by the sofa.

'One more word from that poisonous old hag and I'm leaving,' Lotten muttered. 'I mean it.'

'They're cowboy clothes,' Ivar said.

'And very smart they are too,' Linus said.

'Of course children still fall for the myth about the clean-cut denim-clad cowboy, but the reality was very different. Very different indeed,' Ulla said.

'Now that's very interesting.' Olivia smiled politely. Linus, too, smiled. Ever since he'd known Ulla she had displayed a near religious fervour when it came to imparting information. She was at her most enthusiastic with children. Like a bird she would pull out worms of knowledge from even the most infertile soil and hurry to pass them on to the young. The problem was that her worms were mostly dry, unappetising things, giving neither pleasure nor much nourishment. Linus had always listened, though, like the time that Christmas, when he was fourteen, she told him that nothing was as attractive in a man as knowledge. Linus, feeling distinctly unattractive, had taken her words to heart. As a result he had embarked on a schedule of self-education, which had lasted for the best part of six months. He had listened to music, gone to galleries, stared at nature programmes, mugged up on dates, listened to political debates and read Shakespeare's plays, every single one of them. Because of all this learning he was beaten black and blue by a gang of boys in his class who thought him a show-off, and scorned by the girls for being a pasty-faced swot. The experience had left him with a small scar just above his right eyebrow and a lasting love of Shakespeare. For the latter, he was eternally grateful to Ulla.

'So where's the birthday boy?' He turned to Olivia.

'Your father had to go and fetch Gerald and Kerstin; Kerstin's little car wouldn't start again. They should be here any minute.'

And indeed it was not long before the doorbell rang. 'Happy birthday, Dad.' Linus put his arms round his father, who shied away just slightly before returning his son's embrace. It always happened and Linus barely noticed any more.

'And Uncle Gerald. Ivar, come and say hello to everyone.' He shook hands with Gerald and kissed Kerstin, his cousin, on both cheeks.

Kerstin, at thirty-five, favoured the kind of whimsical clothes that said the wearer was still just a kid at heart. This evening she wore a short pleated navy skirt and a sweat-shirt with tobogganing hedgehogs on it. Her short, straight-cut hair was held in place on one side by a Minnie Mouse slide. As Ivar skipped into view, Uncle Gerald knelt down painfully, emitting a loud fart, like a gunshot, on the way down. Olivia had appeared from the kitchen and, exchanging glances, she and Linus both broke into a hearty rendering of 'Happy Birthday', followed, as Gerald let out a little trio of farts on his way to stand up, by the Swedish version, '*Ja Må Han Leva*'. Linus was glad that Lotten was safely at a distance, stirring some sauce in the kitchen; she did not really understand about Gerald.

The final guest, Gerda Holmberg, arrived shortly afterwards. Gerda had managed the accounts and other office matters for Stendal & Berglund for thirty-five years until her retirement five years earlier. 'I thought this was a Family Occasion,' Ulla hissed in Olivia's direction.

Olivia pretended not to hear. 'You know Gerda, everyone,' she said instead, ushering them all back into the drawing-room. Ulla proceeded to be condescending to Gerda, showing her around the room as if Gerda had never set foot in the apartment before. Linus was about to come to Gerda's rescue when Ulla remembered about her food. She had insisted on preparing the main course: Caribbean sole. It was a speciality of hers. She had cooked it for the family once before, out on the island the previous summer, and no one had much liked it then, so she was trying it again; she felt that they ought to enjoy it. Ivar was allowed to have his fish scraped bare of any sauce; he was only four, after all. He was seated next to his mother. In Linus's family any child unfortunate enough not to be attended by a nanny was placed next to his mother.

'He did it again.' Ivar pointed an accusing finger at Uncle Gerald across the table. 'It's rude, you know,' he added conversationally. 'Hasn't your mummy told you?' The last part of the sentence was drowned out by a rousing rendering of 'For He's a Jolly Good Fellow!'

Lotten picked up Ivar's napkin, which had slid to the floor, and as she popped up again, above the level of the table top, she rolled her eyes at Linus who annoyed her further by smiling back inanely.

'I meant to ask you.' Gerda turned to Olivia. 'How is your poor English friend? Didn't you say her husband had left her? I remember her very well from the wedding. Nice woman. A little vague perhaps, but really very charming.'

'Actually, she's doing much better than I'd have expected,' Olivia said. 'When I first heard Madox had departed I expected her to collapse completely; she seemed utterly to depend on him, but she's fine. Spends most of the time in bed, watching television, reading, that kind of thing. But she's quite happy. She has a rather enviable way of turning her back on anything that displeases her.'

'You mean she refuses to face the truth?' Ulla said.

'I suppose you could say that, yes.'

'Abandon hope all ye who face the truth,' Linus said. 'If we did all face the truth, we'd give up before we even got started on life.'

'So you're advocating a life built on illusion?' Bertil asked.

Linus opened his mouth to answer, when there was a scream from Lotten, followed by violent coughing. He leapt from his chair and rushed across to his wife, kneeling by her side, patting her back. Ivar started to cry.

'Good God, girl, what is the matter?' Olivia too had jumped to her feet.

A strangled 'that' could be distinguished between coughs. And Lotten pointed an accusing finger at her plate. She was handed a glass of water and drank it down. Linus was still kneeling by her side, patting her back. She shrugged him off. 'Chilli,' she snapped now she had stopped coughing. 'A huge piece of chilli. That really could be very dangerous you know.' She turned to Ulla. 'If I had been allergic to spices I could have choked to death.' Ulla looked as if in Lotten's case an allergy or two would not have gone amiss.

Giving his wife a worried glance, Linus said soothingly, 'But as you're not, there's no real harm done. Thank God,' he added quickly. Ivar had stopped sobbing and was listening instead to Uncle Gerald telling him that regular bowel movements were the key to a contented life. Ivar wanted to know what a bowel was.

'Well, I'm sorry, but I believe in speaking my mind,' Lotten said. 'And . . .'

'Why?' Linus had not meant to annoy her further, but he was genuinely interested in her answer. She frequently said how she believed in being direct and speaking her mind at all times and he'd often meant to ask her about it.

'What do you mean, why?' Lotten asked between gulps of water.

'I mean that people often say that, about speaking their minds, but I'm not sure that it always is such a good idea. People tend to get hurt and anyway, someone else's mind is so often both kinder and more interesting.' Lotten shot him a furious glance. Linus didn't seem to have noticed, but carried on in his quiet voice, 'Of course I'm not saying that that's true exclusively of you. It goes for most of us.'

Opposite him, Bertil and Kerstin were discussing the merits of the recent Sibelius evening at the Concert Hall but the sharpness of Lotten's voice made them stop and turn to listen. 'Don't be silly, Linus. One speaks one's own mind because how can one know anyone else's?'

'One can't know for sure, of course, but one can try to imagine, try to put yourself in someone else's shoes and think about what they might have to say in the matter. I wonder what Strindberg or Meryl Streep would say in this situation, or Churchill or Mick Jagger or Mother Teresa . . .'

'But you'd just be guessing so what would be the point?' Kerstin asked.

'You could make an educated guess and it would be a very useful exercise because you would be forced to try to see a situation from someone else's point of view. At the very least it would make you have to stop and think.'

'I'm sorry I'm so boring,' Lotten said.

'Why do you always have to bring everything back to yourself?' Linus sighed. 'I'm speaking generally. It just happens that you triggered off the thought. Do you have to take everything so personally?'

'I think it's a very good idea, Linus,' Gerda said. 'It makes for an excellent game. Bertil, Olivia, isn't that a good idea of Linus's? We all take on the part of someone else, then we pick a topic and argue it according to whoever we are supposed to be.' She beamed at them all from her place at the head of the table.

'Bowels bowels bowels,' Ivar chanted, bobbing up and down in his chair.

'And no, Ulla, you can't be Jesus Christ.' Bertil raised his glass to her.

'I've always rather fancied myself as Charles the twelfth,' Gerald said.

'So what's the topic?' Olivia asked. 'And I want to be Picasso.'

'You always did, dear.' Bertil gave her a small smile.

'Bowels, bowels, bowels,' Ivar singsonged.

'Maybe not, dear,' Gerda said. 'As for a topic, what about the Common Market, or that wonderful film, what was it called again, that they tried to censor.'

Lotten stood up. 'Time for little people to go to bed.' She grabbed Ivar by the hand.

'But we haven't even finished dinner yet,' Linus protested. 'Surely it won't hurt for him to stay a little longer, just for once.' But he knew it was no use. Lotten was an expert in exerting her revenge under the cloak of concerned motherhood.

'Yes, come on, Lotten.' Bertil smiled at Ivar. 'It's not often I get to see my little grandson.'

'There're meringues to go,' Olivia said. 'With chocolate sauce.'

'I'm afraid I believe in regular bedtimes,' Lotten said. 'But you stay here with your family, Linus. I'll see you later.'

'I don't want to go.' Ivar pulled free and clung on to the side of his chair with both hands. But his protest was pitiful in its futility as children's protests often are. Lotten's mind was made up and he was led sobbing from the room. Silence followed in their wake, then Lotten returned briefly to the dining-room to say good-night. The few moments away from them all seemed to have restored her good humour, Linus thought. Either that, or it was the pleasure of having scored a point that made her smile.

'Don't be too late, darling,' she said, honey-voiced, to Linus. She leant over his chair and gave him a kiss on the cheek. 'You won't mind walking back, will you?'

'Strange girl,' Uncle Gerald said, helping himself to some meringue and bitter chocolate sauce from the pyramid in front of him.

## Chapter Eight

Holden signed me up to his gym the morning after the night we first made love; I had pulled a muscle in my thigh.

'You're not awfully athletic, are you, my dear?' He had twinkled at me over breakfast in my kitchen. 'But don't you worry. A few work-outs and you'll be a new woman.'

'Promise?' I asked sourly.

Holden just nodded in an earnest way. 'Promise, baby. In fact, once you get into it you'll wonder how you ever managed before,' he said, the light of evangelism glinting in his eyes. He also mentioned that it was all about self-discipline. Well, that did it. Self-discipline was my thing (although sometimes I suspected that it wasn't at all and that was why I set such store by it). Anyway, I now rose at a quarter to six, four mornings a week. I had always lamented the fact that I wasn't a morning person and now, thanks to Holden I was, reluctantly. I walked through the quiet streets, admiring the blossoming cherry trees, the sound of bird-song from the garden square, and the superiority that came from being up and about when most other people were still tucked up in bed. At the bus-stop stood a bench, how thoughtful, and on it was a huge turd. I suppose it could have been produced by a large and unusually athletic dog, but it wasn't that likely. I resolved never to sit on a public bench again. Cherry blossom, bird-song, large turds; had I been an artist I might well have chosen to paint the scene. The picture would be entitled *Life*. Whoever had constructed the universe must have had a sign above his desk saying *Remember the other side of the coin*. Sex – Shame. Baby – Pain. Love – Hurt. Cherry blossom – Turd. Life – Death. That theory of the earth being flat made a lot of sense to me; you have the nice side, the one you sell to embryos thinking of becoming babies, with the sunshine and the pretty fluffy bunnies and the yummy food and love. The flip side you keep to yourself until they're past the point of no return. No wonder babies arrive screaming.

I was deep in thought when I narrowly avoided bumping into a man coming out from a block of mansion flats, a navy baseball cap pulled down low over his forehead. I mumbled an apology and for a moment our eyes met. We walked on our opposite ways, but I was sure I had seen him somewhere before. It was only as I tried to chase away the boredom of my three-mile walk on the treadmill that I realised that the man in the baseball cap was Barry Jones, hugely popular quiz-show host and the nation's foremost family man. And if it wasn't him, it was someone looking enough like him to be his twin.

A week later I saw him again, at almost exactly the same time, coming out from the block of flats, looking right and left under his blue cap before stepping out on to the pavement. I peered at him and before he had a chance to turn away I had established that it was definitely The Nation's Favourite Husband.

'Doesn't Barry Jones live in St John's Wood?' I asked a colleague.

'Yes, he does. Why?'

'Oh, nothing.' I shrugged.

I could have set my watch by him. He popped out of the heavy oak door, like a cuckoo from a clock, albeit a silent, rather stealthy cuckoo, Wednesday and Friday, at six a.m. sharp, cap drawn low across his forehead.

'He's cheating on his wife,' Arabella said when I told her. 'No doubt about it.'

'But this is Barry Jones we're talking about,' I protested. A man as famous for his perfect marriage to Tammy and their idyllic life with their three perfect, spotless children, as he is for his television work. A man who had been seen so many times with his arm draped around his wife's shoulders that ungenerous minds had accused him of having had it surgically attached. A man who had had more things knitted for him by little old ladies than a royal baby. Barry Jones? Surely not!

'Don't be naïve.' Arabella sighed.

'But this is the man "Who Restored the Nation's Faith in Marriage".'

'I think', Arabella said, 'that the operative word here is man. So are you going to do a piece on it?'

'I don't know. Probably not. I'm not in the business of wrecking people's lives truffling around for scandal, real or imagined.'

'Odd.' Arabella shrugged. 'I could have sworn you were a journalist.'

You get that sort of comment all the time when you work for a newspaper. I try to rise above it. 'I'm a feature writer,' I said. 'Not a reporter.' Then I threw a cushion at her. 'I have my own rules and standards. All the same,' I caught the cushion as she threw it back at me, 'I suppose I should tip off the news desk. It's my duty. And the man is a complete hypocrite. Anyone else and one might say it's nobody's business but his own, but this guy has made his name from being the perfect bloody husband.'

'So tell the news desk.'

'Do *you* think that Barry Jones is capable of cheating on his wife?' I asked Audrey on my regular Saturday-afternoon visit. (My mother liked visits on a Saturday afternoon; nothing but sport on the television.)

'Of course he is.' She reached out for a second scone.

'But Barry Jones. He represented The Cardigan for the association of English wool merchants last year.'

'Clotted cream, darling? It's delicious. Cornish.'

'Have you heard from Dad?'

'He called this morning, actually. He says he's happy. Now try the strawberry jam; it's to die for.'

Holden rolled his eyes. We were having dinner at this new Indian restaurant and for a moment I thought the spices had got to him, but then he said, 'Are you planning to start some kind of witch-hunt against this Barry Jones character? You know my opinion on that aspect of your career?'

'I've told you hundreds of times,' I protested. 'I am not an investigative reporter, I'm a feature writer. I don't snoop, well not much, nor am I interested in exposing the duplicitous love life of Barry Jones, but I should pass the information on to the news desk. That's my duty to my colleagues. In fact, it's my duty as a journalist.' Holden was shaking his head and muttering something about gutters, but I ignored him. 'If he's not up to something,' I said, 'then no harm will be done, but if he is cheating, well, then he's the biggest hypocrite in a decade of hypocrites and I don't see why he should get away with it. He isn't just any old bloke. What we've got here is a man who's made his name and his living from this whiter-than-white image. And, in his time, he's not been averse to pronouncing on the frailties of others. This guy has his own Christmas broadcast, for heaven's sake.'

'Well, it's your decision, Esther.' Holden helped himself to some more Basmati rice. 'I'm just afraid I don't share your fascination with the sordid details of other people's lives.'

Why did he love me when I was so full of faults? Pondering about whether and why he loved me tended to stop me from worrying whether or not I really loved him. Holden put his hand over mine and smiled into my eyes. 'You look lovely when you're puzzled.'

I was pleased about that, seeing I spent most of my life wondering what the hell was going on. Maybe that was what attracted me to men like Donald and Holden; men to whom doubts rated somewhere down there with quiche. 'Do you like quiche?' I asked him.

Holden looked surprised at the question, but then he smiled. 'Real men don't eat quiche, isn't that what they say?'

I thought as much. I returned to the subject of Barry Jones. 'I really care about getting this right,' I said. 'Not only for Barry Jones' and his family's sake. I set myself some pretty strict rules of behaviour. You have to or you open the door to chaos.'

'Maybe you're a little bit obsessive about it. All those lists. Like today. I like Indian food, it's not that, but to be coming here because one of your lists said you couldn't go to an Italian restaurant again until you'd been to an Indian one seems, well, a bit odd.'

'Do you know the origin of the word obsessive?' I asked him. Holden shook his head. 'It means battlement, barrier. In medieval times being *possessed* was a serious problem. It was very much a matter for the stake. But if you were *obsessed*, then you were highly respected because, far from having allowed the devil to get into you, you were busy erecting barriers: obsessions. So if I seem a bit obsessive at times it's simply because I'm putting up barricades against the devil called chaos.' I sat back, feeling that I had explained myself rather well.

'If you hadn't noticed, we've progressed a bit since the Middle Ages. And anyway, what does that have to do with whether or not you eat at an Italian or Indian restaurant? You know, I used to think you were really together.'

'I am, I am. And that's all because of my systems. A lot of people say things like, I really should try and eat something other than Italian, or Thai or whatever it is they're always eating, then they still go back to the same old place they always go to, because it's convenient or whatever. But when I say something like that to myself, I set it into system. I don't leave things to chance or whim.'

The next day was a Wednesday. I was running a few minutes late when I spotted Barry Jones already half-way up the street. As he hurried along I noticed a burly man in his mid-twenties following him. Photographer? But I saw no camera. Reporter? Private detective? I guessed as I walked along. The burly man caught up with Barry Jones and . . . oh my God! Mugger! In seconds, Barry Jones lay sprawled across the pavement deprived of his shoulder-bag, then almost nonchalantly the attacker aimed a kick at his victim's head. 'Stop it!' I screamed, running towards them. 'Stop that!' The man turned round and stared at me, and then, not even bothering to run, he was off.

I knelt on the ground by Barry Jones's side. Cars drove by and if their drivers and passengers noticed anything they showed no signs of stopping. There were no other pedestrians in sight. 'Someone call the police,' I yelled up at the windows of the apartment blocks. 'Call an ambulance, please.' Barry Jones opened his eyes wide and let out a groan. 'It's all right,' I assured him. 'I won't leave.' He tried to speak. 'What was that?' I leant closer, my ear almost touching his lips. I hastily grabbed hold of my hair to stop it falling into his face. 'Can you try to speak again?'

'Go away. I want to be left alone.'

I sat back up. 'But you need medical attention,' I told him.

Above our heads a first-floor window was flung open and a woman's head covered in pink curlers popped out. 'Did you say call the police?' she yelled.

'Please! And an ambulance!' The woman's head disappeared back inside. Was it my imagination or was there a shadowy figure behind the lace curtain of the window next to hers?

'You don't understand.' Although his voice was unsteady, Barry

Jones managed to raise it. 'I don't want anyone. Just help me to my feet.'

But within minutes the ambulance and the police arrived. I gave a description of the attacker, as best I could, having explained that I had been some distance away.

'You're very observant, miss,' the constable said.

I smiled modestly. 'Oh, it's my training. I'm a journalist.' An anguished cry from Barry Jones being carried past on a stretcher made me turn round. I watched as he was manoeuvred into the back of the ambulance. 'Can't they give him something?' I asked the officer. 'The poor man is obviously in great pain.'

I was asked to step into the police car. 'It's common procedure, miss, if you don't mind. We're instituting a search of the area and would be much obliged if you could accompany us for identification purposes.'

I got into the back of the car. 'You mean you want me to go along with you to see if I can spot the attacker?'

'That's what I said, miss.' Off we drove through the nearby streets.

There were still very few people on the pavements, but the road was getting busy with traffic. 'There,' I shouted suddenly as I spotted a lone figure by the window of a computer hardware shop. The car screeched to a halt and a dog, out on his own, his leg lifted against a rubbish bin, leapt with fright and ran off in mid-stream, leaving a trail of pee on the pavement. The man by the shop window turned round. 'No. No, sorry, mistake,' I said just as the two policemen were about to leap from the car.

We drove on. Half an hour later we gave up the search. 'Sometimes we get them; it's amazing how many of them hang around the area of the crime,' the constable said as they dropped me off at the house after a brief stop at the police station where I signed my statement. 'We'll be in touch if we get him.'

The news of how 'Barry Jones got Brutally Mugged on Quiet London Street', would be out instantly and then it would be a matter of time before the story, if there was one, of his infidelity broke. I couldn't justify not alerting my own paper.

The next morning the *Chronicle* sported the headline, SECRET THRUSTS OF NATION'S FAVOURITE HUSBAND END IN BRUTAL WEST END

MUGGING. Underneath was a photograph of Barry Jones leaving hospital, his face bruised and his arm in a sling.

I stayed late at the office, working through the notes for a series of articles I was planning under the heading of 'Passionate Lives'. The idea was to explore the engine in people's lives, and also what happened if there was no engine. As I was preparing to leave, Lennie, the office junior, came in with the hot-off-the-presses edition for the next day. MEET THE OTHER WOMAN IN BARRY JONES LOVE TRIANGLE! (*Turn to page five.*)

I did. Our reporters had found out that the woman whom Barry Jones had spent the night of the mugging with was a Ms Virginia Kitchener, a divorced mother of three. There was a picture of her in one of the tabloids, eyes staring, chin sagging in surprise, trying in vain to shield her face from the camera. Next to it was a photo of Barry Jones's wife, looking immaculate and beautiful in a touchingly fragile way. *I have nothing to say*, dignified Mrs Jones announced. *But I've brought you all some tea. You must be getting cold out there.*

What a woman!

'You landed that guy well and truly in it,' Holden said at dinner that evening. We were sitting in my little kitchen finishing the goulash I had prepared. Holden had stated it was far too warm an evening for goulash, but he still ate it all.

'What do you mean, *I* landed him in it?' I knew precisely what he meant, having thought the very same thing myself, but that didn't mean I was ready to accept it from someone else. 'He landed himself in it by being a cheating hypocrite. If I hadn't told them, another paper would have had the story all the same. I was doing my job.'

Holden sat back in the chair and stretching out his legs in front of him he smiled an infuriating little smile and shook his head. I wanted suddenly to slap him right across his ironic expression.

'Anyway, why should you care?' I asked. 'The guy is a sleaze ball.'

'So stop moping and come and give me a kiss.'

I was torn between needing approval and wanting to tell him to piss off.

Piss off won.

Holden stood up, scraping the chair back on the stone floor. 'Don't be vulgar. I'll see you tomorrow.' He marched out of the kitchen and a few seconds later I heard the front door slam shut.

Five minutes later he was back. 'I forgive you.' He grinned as he sat back at the table and picked up his knife and fork.

'Are you in love with me?' I asked him. 'I mean really, passionately?' I asked because if he was, I wanted to know what it felt like. I could feign in love for long enough to fool most men and even myself for a while. I lusted with the best of them, but deep down below the layers of pretence that constitute one's character I knew that at the age of thirty-two I had never really been in love (that's not counting Pigotty).

'Don't start.' Holden sighed the sigh of male martyrdom. Most men were like that in my experience; treating any conversation threatening to become emotional as if it were a dog with unfortunate personal habits that insisted on curling up at their feet. They'd brush it off with an embarrassed laugh or a frown, or ignore it in the hope that it would slink quietly away. Holden was no exception. Then I thought, why should he be? That was one of the troubles with relationships these days; we expected each other to be the exception. I mean, when a woman referred to her husband as 'a typical man', it was not usually meant as a compliment. And how many times have you heard the phrase 'That's so like a woman' said in a tone of awed respect?

'If you wrote a list of all the things about me that irritated you most,' I said, 'I bet it would go something like this: "She talks at breakfast. Reads bits aloud from the papers. Fiddles with my hair when I'm trying to watch sport. Says, 'You don't like it, do you?' every time she wears something new. Talks about problems even when there's nothing one can do about them. Talks about feelings. Uses the word Relationship as an offensive weapon." Shall I go on?'

Holden gave me a long look. 'So if you know these things get on my tits, why do you do it?'

That was a fair question, but I had to think about it for a moment. 'Because', I said at last, 'I think doing all those things is utterly reasonable. I suppose that's why I feel such despair for the future of heterosexual relationships.'

Linus left Katya's flat, stepping straight out into the pouring rain, barely noticing the water running down the back of his open-necked shirt. 'What have I done?' he mumbled as he walked off towards the office, but the words ended up more triumphant than remorseful. He tried again. 'Oh God, what have I done?' But it sounded more like a moan of pleasure. He could not stop thinking of how Katya's thighs felt encircling his hips and of the expression of surprised delight in her eyes as they made love. She had looked as if she had been given a present she had spent years yearning for. Not like Lotten, who looked more like someone dispensing a favour with varying degrees of reluctance. 'Oh Lotten,' he groaned. 'What have I done to you?' But all he felt was the warmth of being wanted. As the afternoon went on his remorse became more real, helped by the images he conjured up of his wife, his helpmate, the mother of his son. 'What have I done?' And this time the words carried genuine pain. It was late afternoon before he got down to some real work, but then, as always, it absorbed him. He paused briefly only to observe to himself that he was a monster, a cold-hearted, amoral bastard, before bending down once more towards the drawings in front of him.

The sitting-room window of the flat was lit up and Lotten had not yet drawn the blinds. He could see the familiar outline of the reading lamp with its green shade by the armchair and a hazy display of books at the back of the room. The flat was on the second floor of the yellow-brick forties block, above an undistinguished lobby with an efficient lift and a sensibly proportioned stairwell. He and Lotten had lived there since the year before Ivar's birth and in spite of Lotten's talk of moving out of the city they remained. Lotten accused him of being passive to the point of inertia when it came to all things domestic and practical. She was probably right. As he walked up the stairs to flat five, he resolved to make amends. If Lotten wanted to move out of the city, that's what they would do. He would design the house himself, the way she had always wanted. By the time he turned the key in the lock he had almost come to believe that his infidelity would turn out to be a godsend for him and Lotten both.

'You're late,' Lotten said from the drawing-room sofa. She was watching television with her feet up, her hand dipping rhythmically into a bag of dried apricots. He suddenly realised that she didn't really care if he was late or not, in fact she had not for quite some time. He, in turn, had been too relieved not to be greeted by sulks and dramas to ask what had brought about the change.

'Ivar's been in bed for ages,' Lotten said, her eyes still on the television. 'There's some chicken in the fridge and some potato salad.' Linus stayed for a moment, watching her. She seemed unaware that he was still in the room. This was what he had prayed for, a quiet, uneventful evening with nothing to challenge him or confront his guilt, but now he felt let down. He wanted attention, damn it.

'Come and eat with me.' He smiled at her. 'Let's eat together.'

Lotten glanced up briefly, a slight frown on her forehead as if she was surprised and not altogether pleased to find him still there. 'I told you, I've eaten.'

Linus strode up to his wife and took her hands, pulling her up towards him. 'Let's have a glass of wine.'

Lotten's level eyes looked into his. 'What's wrong with you? I'm trying to watch this programme.'

'Why should there be something wrong?' He tried to make his voice light, but had he been singing he would have struck one false note after the other. He tried again. 'Does there have to be something wrong for a man to want to spend some time with his wife?'

'Yes, in my experience.'

He had to pause and think about that. 'Oh, come on,' he said finally, trying to pull her up from the sofa. 'Let's talk.'

Lotten shrugged free. 'What about?'

'Oh, anything. Just let's talk the way we used to. Let's get drunk and talk and be like we used to be.'

Lotten looked round for the remote. 'We *used* to be younger. We *used* not to have a child. *You used* to have time to listen. *You used* not to work every hour God gave you.'

His guilt made him aggrieved. '*You* told *me* that you understood about my work. You told me you couldn't live with someone who wasn't passionate about what they did and that allowing each other space was essential.' He gave a joyless bark of a laugh, a million miles away from his usual abandoned giggle. 'Of course, that was before we were married.'

'I know what you're implying, you bastard.' Lotten was screaming all of a sudden. 'And you're wrong. I meant what I said.' She quietened down. 'I could, because back then, before we were married, you made it seem as if nothing, your work included, could ever mean more to you than I did. That's why I could say those things and mean them.'

The anger left him. He had no right to be angry in the first place. He was the one who had cheated. He understood, too, exactly what she was saying. Illogical it might be, but he understood precisely. He held out his hand towards her. She didn't take it so he let it fall back to his side.

'I'm sorry,' he said. 'About everything.' He sat down on the sofa, stretching out his legs, leaning his head against the back. He was dog-tired.

'Why do we live in this place?' he asked. 'What are we doing in a dump like this?'

Lotten too had sat down, but in the armchair. She had stopped shouting and said, quite calmly, 'We live in this dump, as you chose to call our home, because you refuse, or should I say put off, designing us a real home. It's like doctors' families,' she continued as Linus opened his mouth to protest. 'They can be dying before the great man gets round to checking them out. If Ivar and I waited for you to design our house we'd still be waiting in fifty years' time. As always we come a poor second to your work. Well, maybe we don't care any more. Maybe you'll just be in for a great shock one day.'

Later, on his way to bed, he popped in to check on Ivar. All that talk of original sin, he thought and yet, was there a child born who did not look like an angel when he slept?

Lying back in the bath he got an erection thinking of Katya. 'Shit!' He splashed his fist down into the water. 'Shit shit shit,' he sobbed quietly.

The next morning he went over to Katya and told her he couldn't see her again. As he walked on to the office he felt like a prisoner who had, for a few brief moments, been allowed out from his cell and into the sunlight, only to be led back inside the dark once more never again to see the light.

# Chapter Nine

'What is love?' I asked, the way I had years before.

'Love.' Audrey shrugged her plump shoulders. 'Love is an illusion. Lasting love is a lasting illusion.' She bit into her *pain au chocolat* sending a cascade of flaky pastry down the front of her lavender-blue bedjacket.

'Love is when you can't keep your knickers on,' Chloe, my boss, said. 'Or is that sex?' She might not have been the right person to ask as she had just been through a divorce.

'Don't worry about it,' Holden said. 'Just relax.'

LOVE HAS ITS PRICE FOR TV'S BARRY JONES, read one tabloid headline.
LOVE RAT BARRY GETS HIS JUST FROMAGE AS SECRET LOVE CHILD IS DISCOVERED IN FRANCE, another announced breathlessly.

It seemed his wife had left him, or rather, she had thrown him out of their north London mansion. His mistress had been offered a job as an agony aunt on Cable.

I had some holiday due to me so I took a week off to redecorate the flat. I had my schedule already worked out: *Monday morning, clear sitting-room and prepare walls. Afternoon, apply undercoat. Call Holden and ask him and Arabella and her new boy-friend, Peter, for supper while still in possession of kitchen. Call Mother and ask how she is. Invite Mother to dinner as there's not the slightest risk that she'll accept, but it'll make her feel wanted.*

By Wednesday I had finished the sitting-room. I was pleased with the result. I had painted the walls in a soft pale brown, which might seem an odd colour to choose, but it worked extremely well with the new pink-and-white sofa and with the gilt mirror I had inherited from Granny Billings, which hung above the fireplace.

'Pink?' Audrey had said when I described the room to her. 'I hardly have you down as a pink person.'

'It's love what does it,' I had said.

'Oh darling, you and Holden, how marvellous. He'll do absolutely as well as anyone.'

'It's not me and Holden, as in love's sweet young dream,' I corrected her. 'It's love as in absence of. That can turn your thoughts to pink just as much as having it, more maybe. Anyway, I just liked the sofa.'

The dinner party went well insofar as Arabella and Peter had a lovely time. The problem was they would have had a lovely time in a damp coal cellar. I knew it was serious the minute Arabella told me she had abandoned her plan to go through the whole alphabet and skipped from I for Ian, straight to P for Peter. I couldn't help comparing the look in their eyes with the look in Holden's and mine.

'What's wrong?' Holden asked me over the washing-up. But what he actually meant was: I know something is up, but can you please deny it so we can forget about it and go to bed.

'Peter looks at Arabella the whole time. You hardly looked at me all evening. And I don't count we-need-some-more-garlic-bread looks.'

'What are you on about?' Holden inspected a glass for smudge marks after I had wiped it. I snatched it from him and put it away in the cupboard.

I turned round to face him, gazing into his handsome, mildly puzzled face. It was the face of someone who didn't know what on earth the fuss was about, but who was determined to be patient. The face, in other words, of a man confronted by a woman wielding words like Emotion and Relationship. I sighed and shook my head. 'Oh, nothing.'

Holden smiled and pulled me towards him. 'That's all right, then. Anyway, I didn't have you down as the romantic type. That's what's so refreshing.'

I pulled away from him. 'It's not bloody all right,' I yelled. 'It's absolutely not all right at all. And what am I that everyone wants to categorise me? A novel? Esther is not the type for pink. Esther is not the type for love. What do you know? What does anyone know?' I was sobbing now.

Holden looked hurt. 'What is wrong with you, Esther? Is it your period or something?'

'Don't you use my period as an excuse,' I yelled through the sobs.

'This really isn't like you.' Holden tried to grab my hand, but I snatched it away. 'You're not some hysterical over-emotional female. How much wine have you had?'

Suddenly I felt calm. 'There you are again, telling me what I am. No, I haven't got my period and I'm not drunk, I just want to know what it's like to be in love. I'm thirty-two years old and I've never been properly in love.'

Holden slung the tea towel over one shoulder and took my hand. This time I let him. 'Come and sit down.' He led me to the sitting-room. 'Let's talk.'

'You don't like talking.'

'What do you mean, I don't like talking?'

'I mean, you don't like talking, you like what you call a Companionable Silence. By that you mean me sitting silently, but with an air of rapt attention, in case you should choose to speak, in which case I would answer briefly and uncontentiously before shutting up once more.'

He laughed softly. 'Who's telling who now?' He stroked the back of my neck. 'You and I get on so well precisely because neither of us believes in all that in-love stuff. We know that having fun together and respecting each other is what it all comes down to in the end.'

At that I began to cry again, quietly at first, then louder and with growing conviction.

'I really don't know what's got into you.' Holden pulled back.

'Nothing, nothing's got into me, that's the problem.'

Holden's puzzled expression cleared. 'You mean we haven't had sex for a while. Why didn't you tell me? It's nothing personal, I promise you that, I've just had rather a lot on at work and . . .'

'*I'm not talking about sex!*' I yelled.

Next door, the Potters knocked on the wall. 'I'm not talking about sex,' I hissed. 'Please leave now. I want to go to bed, alone.'

'I thought you wanted to talk.' I heard his voice, complaining, uncomprehending, as I disappeared.

I kept on with my decorating, trying to take my mind off Holden. I missed him, but at the same time I knew I couldn't go on for ever waiting to love him the way I thought I should. By Saturday evening the kitchen was finished. It was blue on blue. Pale-blue-and-white striped wallpaper, a darker, grey-blue shade for the cupboard doors and cornflower-blue for the wooden-backed kitchen chairs. On the Sunday, like the Lord, I planned to rest. Holden called just as I sat down with a heap of newspapers. 'I think we should take a break from each other,' I said to him.

There was a long silence. 'You don't mean that.'

'Yes, I do.'

'You don't.' His voice sounded almost playful now.

'I do.'

'I don't think so.' His voice was singsong.

'I bloody well do.'

'I wish you wouldn't swear.' There was another pause. 'If this is about me not wanting to go to all those French art-house movies . . .'

I put the phone down and then I sat down and wrote him a letter: *Dear Holden, It's over.*


Back to work after my break and Barry Jones was in the papers again. *'"I was punched in the face by disgraced TV star." News photographer tells of moment of fear outside fashionable Knightsbridge eatery.'*

I stared at the picture of Barry Jones's face, wild-eyed and unshaven as he was being restrained by two dark-suited men from inflicting further damage to the newsman. I remembered him on the ground that morning, pleading with me not to call for help.

'I feel so bloody responsible,' I told Chloe at the office.

'That's because you are,' she said. But as I yelped in anguish she laughed. 'Don't be silly. He brought it on himself and you know it. You did your job. If he had stuck to doing his instead of sticking it up his mistress he'd still be the housewife's favourite. So don't you go blaming yourself.' She made a reassuring figure, Chloe, small and compact, looking even sturdier this morning in her fashionable knitted lace tights. She had spent two hours queuing outside Harvey Nichols on her morning off to get her hands on those tights. 'Anyhow,' she said, 'I want you to do an interview with Tammy Jones, the wife. Apparently she's taken him back.'

'I'd rather not. I've done enough damage to that man and his family, whatever you say.'

'You did what you thought was right at the time. Now pull yourself together and get on with it.'

'That's what worries me. If you can do that much damage by doing what you think is right . . . God knows what kind of harm one can inflict by just pottering about one's daily business.'

'Think like that and you'll go mad,' Chloe said. 'Now use your common sense and stop fretting. Where would we be if all journalists thought like you?'

'Karen Dempster's family might still be alive today.'

'You're not blaming yourself for that? You were party to bringing her to justice, you had nothing to do with what went before.'

'Not personally, no, but I'm part of the world which created the ethos which in turn bred this type of media monster.'

'OK, OK. But think about this one. Without us, Cecil Parkinson might be prime minister.'

'All right. I'm not saying we're all bad. But what about that MP who killed himself?'

Chloe shrugged. 'You win some, you lose some. Think of Rwanda, Bosnia, Algeria. Who would care or even know if it weren't for us?'

'All right, then. So what about the Royal Family? Think of all the famous people, hounded for no reason other than that people love sticking their beaks into other people's business.'

Chloe shrugged. 'I'm thinking.'

'All right, then. What about the not so famous people and their families hounded by the press and the rest of the media?'

'I'm still thinking. Now take Watergate.'

I nodded. 'OK.'

'BSE,' Chloe said, a note of triumph in her voice. 'Who makes sure the public is informed? And think back to the time when there was a real threat to the lives of haemophiliacs through HIV-infected factor 8. They tried to gag us, but who was proven right?'

'All right, all right.' I sighed. 'I'll do the interview.'

I got Tammy Jones, Barry's wife, on the telephone. The Joneses' number was ex-directory, of course, but I had got it from a mutual friend in television. Tammy agreed to meet me the following day. 'You're sure you want to do this?' I asked. It just slipped out.

114

'Of course I'm sure,' the wispy little girl's voice held a hint of sharpness. 'What an odd question for a journalist to ask.' Quite. I fixed the time, three thirty the following afternoon. And the place? Her house. Excellent!

Returning home that evening I thought I smelt gas as I passed the house three doors up from mine, the Hammonds' place. I stopped and retraced my steps, sniffing the air. Yes, definitely gas. I walked up to the front door and rang the bell. I waited a couple of minutes, I could hear the television from inside, before ringing a second time. 'Yes.' Mr Hammond stood glaring in the doorway, in his checked felt slippers and vest tucked into his grey trousers.

'I'm sorry to bother you, Mr Hammond, but there's a smell of gas coming from right outside your basement. I'll show you.' I took a step back.

'I'll see to it.'

'You should probably call the gas board,' I said. 'It could be dangerous.'

'Tony, *EastEnders*'s starting.' Mrs Hammond's voice reached us from the sitting-room.

'I said I'll see to it. Good-night then.'

'I could make the call if you're busy.'

'I said I'd see to it.' Mr Hammond shut the door in my face.

I could still smell gas as I stepped out on to our street the next morning. I stopped at the Hammonds' door, about to ring the bell, when I changed my mind and walked on past. I must stop interfering, I told myself. The Hammonds might be unpleasant, but they weren't idiots. They would have called the gas board by now. Anyway, I wasn't in the mood for an early-morning rebuff; my interfering days were over.

I went to my mother's for lunch before setting off to north London for the interview with Tammy Jones. Audrey was sorry to hear that I had broken off with Holden.

'You want grandchildren, I know,' I said sympathetically.

'No, no, I don't particularly,' Audrey said. 'I just thought he was rather a nice young man. 'Not much imagination, but let's face it, neither have you.'

'But I wasn't in love with him.'

'Who was it who said that as you never end up in love with the man you choose to share your life with, you might as well not be in love to start with?'

I shrugged. 'Me?'

My mother nodded. 'Now.' She passed me a plate of asparagus quiche. 'Have some of this. It's delicious. Janet made it this morning.'

I took the plate. 'I would just like to see for myself what I'll eventually be missing, rather than take other people's word for it. I don't want other people's second-hand disillusions, I want my own brand-new ones. I want to know what that particular folly is all about. Is that so unreasonable?'

Audrey sighed. Then she smiled and shook her head. 'No, no, I don't suppose it is. But you know, even if you did find it, love that is, you wouldn't like it. Love is everything you don't want. Love is the enemy of rules and logic. It's the Antichrist of order and reason. No, it's not your thing at all.'

I sat on the boudoir chair by the foot of the bed, the plate on my lap. I felt like a five-year-old who knew the white pointy shoes with heels would damage her feet, but who really really really wanted them anyway.

Audrey, as usual, was reclining against a hillock of white lace pillows. She was getting plumper by the day, but she was looking well. That morning she was wearing an oyster-coloured silk bed jacket and her nails were varnished to match. If it weren't for the bulge extending beneath the bedclothes I might have suspected that she'd done away with legs altogether, like newscasters, but then she wiggled the end of the bulge as well, so I deduced they were still there. 'Ten perfect little fingers,' I muttered, 'and ten rosy little toes.' Then I asked, 'You do get up to go to the loo still, don't you?'

Audrey frowned at me. 'Don't be disgusting. Of course I do. Anyway, how is poor Holden?'

'I don't know. I haven't spoken to him since it happened. You know, men seem to take a pride in reserving talking, proper talking I mean, until there's a crisis. I just wish they'd realise that if they had got into the habit of speaking little and often, there probably wouldn't be a crisis in the first place. It's like having a house and refusing to do any maintenance, then acting all hurt and confused when the roof collapses and they're faced with doing some major

116

work. I ask you, where is the man who likes nothing better than settling down with a bottle of wine in front of a fire for a really good talk?'

'Nowhere, unless he's gay. Now dear Robbie, you remember Robbie Spink?' I shook my head. 'Of course you do. Anyway, he was a wonderful chatter. He would ring up and say, "Audrey, darling, let's chat." And did we chat . . .'

'Why?' Lotten asked again. She sounded tired. Not angry, just very tired and rather sad. 'I need to know why?'

Linus had been sitting with his head in his hands. Now he looked up, his eyes aching as if they had had to be squeezed into their sockets. It was four o'clock in the morning and they had been talking since before midnight. He couldn't think what to say any more. Or rather, there was too much to say, words that would shatter what was left of his marriage. Feebly he shrugged his shoulders, hating himself for not at least being able to give her the comfort of a reason.

'Did you ever stop to think about the effect of what you were doing on the rest of us?' Lotten's voice had recovered its hard edge. Linus just looked at her with his aching eyes. 'God, you're pathetic!' Lotten slammed down her fist on the kitchen table.

'I'm sorry.'

'I'm sorry,' she mimicked. 'Well not half as sorry as I am, and not half as sorry as you're going to be either.'

They had been past this post before. Several times. Tears, threats, resignation, anger, round and round. Linus knew he had to listen, it was the least he owed her. A friend of Lotten who also knew Katja had told her about the affair.

'How could you?' Lotten said again. What was he supposed to answer? The truth? They would never survive the truth.

'What were you thinking of? Not of your family, that's for sure.'

'It only happened once,' he said for the tenth time.

'You creep, as if that makes it all right.' But her voice was resigned. She stood up. 'D'you want some coffee?'

He nodded. 'Please,' he said, as he watched her fill the kettle, get the mugs out, his 'Genius at Work' one given to him by Lotten when they were first married, her 'Wild Thing' one sold in aid of an animal charity. Small everyday rituals observed in the middle of a war.

'I might consider forgiving you,' Lotten said, quite calmly, as she sat down again, pushing his mug towards him across the table. 'But there will have to be some changes, and some promises.'

Linus listened to the list of changes required and to the charges against him. He was obsessed with his work. He was a weekend dad. He was inattentive to Lotten's needs. He took her for granted. He left everything at home to her. He didn't do his share of the housework. He was self-absorbed and, while he was about it, could he do something about that ridiculous laugh.

That, Linus thought, was some list. 'You have to address all these things,' Lotten continued and Linus imagined doing so, taking the complaints one by one. The first one would be a brown envelope: Linus Stendal, The Office, Escape Route One. The next was a small white one with childish writing. To Dad, Weekend Street . . .

'Linus, are you listening to me?'

Brought back to the present he said, 'Yes, yes of course.'

'And I will have to try to learn to trust you again and that won't be easy. Maybe I never will.'

Two things struck Linus. One was that Lotten had not once appeared to doubt that he wanted to remain married, the other that it seemed almost as if she must just have been waiting for an excuse to pour out her dissatisfaction with him. She must have worked out her catalogue of complaints a long time ago, then tucked it away for a rainy day.

Lotten went to the bathroom. Linus sat back and closed his eyes. It occurred to him that he might have a list of his own. Be interested in my work, it would read, not just its rewards. Allow me a chance to be the kind of father I *can* be, not the kind you think I *ought* to be. *Want* me, don't just *let* me. Don't talk everything to pieces. Allow me some space. Don't shut me out of the running of our home. Have some dreams of your own. Love me for who I am, not for who you think you can turn me into.

But he was the sinner; what business did he have making requests?

'So what will it be?' Lotten had returned from the bathroom and stood before him, feet level, hip distance apart as if she were about to do a knee bend, her hands on her hips.

'I'll try,' he said. 'Really, I'll try.'

# Chapter Ten

'So you and your husband are back together?' I asked Tammy Jones. There was a moment's hesitation from the woman in the apricot-coloured armchair opposite me, a woman so well preserved that she might well survive two hundred years below the sea and still come up looking good. A manicured finger swept away an invisible strand of hair. I could have told her that it would have been easier to escape from Alcatraz than from her lacquered chignon, but instead I just waited, looking interested. That's a good tip, by the way, for any aspiring interviewer, just wait and look interested. Few people can face a silence and not yearn to fill it and even fewer can resist filling it with little titbits of themselves.

'In a way, we are, yes,' Tammy Jones said at last. I waited and looked interested.

'Oh, it probably all sounds pathetic to you. You're young, you've got a career, your life ahead of you.' Tammy Jones leant towards me. 'But what have I got?' She looked at me intently. 'You tell me. I gave up my career to look after him and our children, I was quite a successful model once, you know.' I nodded sympathetically and she continued, 'I've given my life to being Mrs Barry Jones. So what choice do I have? Of course I've taken him back. It's either that, or having to admit to the world and myself that I've wasted my time on someone totally undeserving. I'd be like those wretched Russians who'd spent their lives sacrificing everything for the revolution, only to be told it was all a dreadful mistake in the first place.' She paused again, then she looked me straight in the eye. 'And he's not a bad man, Barry.'

'I'm sure he isn't,' I said. 'And for what it's worth, I'm truly glad to hear you're back together.' I meant it. The Greek Chorus in the background of my life, announcing the progression of Barry Jones's

119

downfall, had been a constant reminder of my part in it. I wanted things to pick up for him and his family.

'It's nice of you to care,' Tammy Jones said. 'I'm afraid I always think of journalists, especially female ones, as completely ruthless and unfeeling.'

I wondered if this was the time to tell her that it was I who had started the ball rolling downhill? Instead I asked, 'So you don't blame the *Chronicle* for exposing the affair?'

She shrugged. 'It would have come out sooner or later. These things always do.'

'And anyway,' I said, pushing my luck, 'who wants to live a lie?'

'Oh, lots of people.' She smiled a pale smile. 'But with you lot around that's getting increasingly difficult.'

'But you've decided to forgive him.'

She nodded sadly. 'Forgive, yes, but not forget. Never forget.' Her expression changed to one of contempt and she lunged forward and reached for a cigarette from the silver box on the glass-topped coffee table. 'Can you believe how plain that bloody woman is? None of our friends could. They'd look at me and at pictures of her, and they just thought the man had gone mad.' She lit the cigarette and inhaled deeply as her features rearranged themselves back into a sad but dignified mask. 'Normally, in a man his age I would say it was sex, you know the thing?' I nodded, of course I did. 'Middle-aged man wanting to prove to himself that he's still attractive, still got what it takes, that kind of thing. But with her . . . he would have had to put a sack over her head.' She laughed shrilly and stubbed out the cigarette, jabbing it down in the ashtray as if it were the much despised face of her rival.

'And what about Barry's television career?' I asked. 'Many commentators believe it will never recover.'

'The public adores him,' she said in a flat voice. She gave a small smile and shrugged. 'But who knows? If it's over it's over.'

I wondered if maybe she'd be quite happy if it was. 'But you have forgiven him?'

Tammy Jones opened her wide eyes even wider. 'Oh yes,' she said.

I drove off back south through the rush-hour traffic, thinking that Barry Jones's penance was just beginning. I arrived home exhausted and went straight to the fridge and brought out a bottle of white wine.

The bang as I closed the fridge sent me reeling backwards into the kitchen table. Next I saw the debris flying through the air outside my window and I rushed out into the street, the bottle still in my hand. The air was so thick with dust that at first I couldn't see for more than a couple of inches ahead. Coughing, I bumped into Elsa. I grabbed her by the shoulder just as the second explosion erupted, diving behind the hedge for cover as a television aerial flew through the air, landing with a clank and a rattle just feet from were we were crouching. Seconds later it was followed by an arm.

'An arm!' I shrieked. 'Elsa, oh my God, an arm!' I hid my face on her shoulders and when I looked up again the dust had cleared a little and I could see that the arm, draped across the low hedge and looking eerily like one of Elsa's 'pieces', was hairy and adorned with a tattoo of a leering mermaid. Last time I had seen that arm it had been attached to Mr Hamilton's shoulder. 'Oh Elsa,' I whispered into the terrible silence. 'Where is the rest of him?'

The street was full of noise once more. Someone sobbing, me. People shouting questions, dogs barking and, just as I got to my feet, the sound of sirens. The police car arrived first, followed by two fire engines and an ambulance. Elsa and I, together with everyone else on the street, were hustled away to safety in a nearby church hall as our road was cordoned off.

It was gas. Elsa nodded sagely over her cup of tea. We had been allowed back into our house and were in her kitchen. 'It's as Jim always said, "Gas is a mixed blessing." We were always electric. He insisted on it.'

I looked at the plush ear above the kitchen table and shuddered. Elsa followed my gaze. 'My pieces giving you the heebie-jeebies?'

I nodded. 'A bit.'

'Don't look at them,' Elsa advised. I burst into tears and Elsa leant across the table and patted my hand. 'It's only natural that you should have a cry,' she said. 'I lived through the Blitz so nothing much shocks me, I'm afraid, but you young people, you're different.'

'But you could do nothing about the Blitz,' I said, wiping my eyes with the back of my hand. 'It wasn't your responsibility.'

Elsa straightened in her chair. 'It certainly was not. No, the responsibility for that rests fair and square with Mr Hitler and don't anyone try to tell me differently.'

'I smelt gas yesterday,' I mumbled. 'Outside the Hamiltons'. I told them. I rang the doorbell and I told them. I suggested they call the gas board. I even offered to do it myself. He practically slammed the door in my face; *EastEnders* was about to start. I assumed they'd do something about it. Even when I smelt the gas the next morning I assumed they'd called and that it was being looked into. I shouldn't have.'

Elsa looked at me. Her eyes were blue and deep-set, and surprisingly sharp. 'Maybe you shouldn't, but it's easy to be wise after the event.'

I told the investigators from the gas board everything I knew. They told me that they had not received a call from the Hammonds. 'So you decided not to report it yourself?' the inspector, a Mr Fenton, asked me.

'It wasn't so much a decision.' I paused, looking for understanding. 'But they told me they were taking care of it, so I assumed they had.'

Mr Fenton looked up gravely from his notes. 'It's as we say, Miss Fisher, never assume with gas. We didn't lodge any call from the Hammonds and now they've lost their home and Mr Hammond his arm. Mrs Hammond is in a state of shock from which, we've been told, she might never recover. And as for her leg . . .' Mr Fenton shook his head.

I dreamt about destruction. Each night there were different scenes: an explosion, a burning building, a sinking ship, an outbreak of a deadly virus, different calamities with one common factor: me. I would be there, in the thick of it, its undisputed cause, the queen of disaster.

'Audrey is very concerned about Esther,' Olivia said. 'She called me this morning. Apparently she's lost all her oomph, all her get-up-and-go. She dithers about the smallest decision, mopes around asking questions about life . . . it's all since that gas explosion on her street.'

'It sounds as if she should join the Merry Group,' Lotten said.

'Your what group?' Olivia wanted to know.

'Merry Group. I'm sure I've told you about it. It's all about finding your inner . . .'

'Self,' Olivia suggested.

Lotten frowned, her thick blonde eyebrows meeting above her nose. 'I'm not quite as stupid as you seem to think, Olivia,' she said. 'What we learn at the Merry Group is real. It's about relying on your own quiet centre, the base core inside you. About not blowing in the wind of other people's actions and opinions. Instead, we learn how to trust ourselves and to dare to go with our instincts. Since the . . . since Linus's little episode, it's been invaluable to me.'

Linus shifted uncomfortably in his chair. Any social occasion lately had been a minefield of embarrassment as Lotten confessed, sooner or later, on his behalf. 'I don't think we need to go into all that again, do we?' he mumbled, clearing his throat and feeling himself turning pink. How he hated that tittle-tattle complexion of his, how he hated everything about himself from the hair that still curled ridiculously when damp or wet, to his long-fingered hands with their insistence on drawing what no one seemed to want or understand. How he hated his fickle heart and his act of betrayal. He could feel it, all that self-hatred, seep into every part of him like some terrible exercise in reverse relaxation. Now hate your toes, feel it creep up your ankles and up your thighs. Now it's at the pit of your stomach, feeling sick yet? Your fingers tingle with it, feel them tingle, and your arms . . . feel that hatred seep into every pore, every cell. Your limbs are growing heavy with it.

'No, let's just leave it for now shall we?' he said. Lotten turned to him with a faintly surprised look on her face as if she had not expected to find him there, in his own parents' flat, drinking after-dinner coffee.

'I don't think that it's really your place to object, do you?' she said.

No, no of course not. As a sinner he had no rights, Linus had learnt that, if nothing else lately. 'So anyway.' Lotten turned back to Olivia. 'The group has been a life saver. Did I tell you why it's called the Merry Group?'

'Because you're all frightfully jolly?' Bertil said from his chair in the corner of the room.

Lotten ignored him. 'It's rather a lovely story. The founder of the programme . . .'

'. . . American?' Bertil interjected again.

'Dutch with an American mother, actually. Her name is Merry van Heuysen, but wait for it, her real name was Joy van Heuysen.' There was a pause while everybody tried to work out what the point was.

'Ahh,' Olivia said, but she still looked confused. 'She decided to change her name from Joy to Merry because . . .'

'Wait for it,' Lotten repeated. 'Her mother who was this strict religious woman, very cold, would tell her as she grew up, "We named you Joy and J stands for Jesus, O stands for Others, and Y stands for You, yourself. You must never forget that you come last, after Our Lord and your fellow men." Can you imagine what that kind of thing would do to a young mind? Anyway, she then met this young man and they fell in love and she told him the story of her name and that it all was the reason why she had no confidence and no self-esteem. And do you know what he said? He said, "I'll call you Merry. M stands for Me. Now you can put yourself first." Isn't that the most wonderful story?'

Linus rubbed the bridge of his nose with his index finger as Bertil cleared his throat, then they both looked at Olivia who got up and asked if anyone wanted more coffee. Lotten smiled, unconcerned. She certainly seemed more contented these days, Linus thought. And even more sure of her opinions. He had always envied Lotten her certainties, imagining her topping them up at the supermarket together with the coffee and cereal and cartons of milk so that she could sit there at the end of the day, brim-full of them. And waking up every morning with the knowledge that you were more sinned against than sinning was probably as helpful in strengthening your beliefs as attending the meetings of the Merry Group. Lotten had taken to shaking her head and saying 'Men' a lot, too. At first it had just been a minor irritation, but it had become something of a worry since Ivar had appeared for breakfast wearing his mother's night-dress.

'I've decided to be a woman when I grow up,' he had announced as he climbed up on his chair.

Linus had put down his mug of coffee and looked searchingly at his small son. 'That might not be all that easy, you know,' he had said gently.

'But I want to.' Ivar's voice had become agitated.

'But why do you want to, darling?'

'Because then when I'm really grown up and have a wife, she'll like me better,' Ivar had declared, kneeling on his chair and reaching across the table for his cereal.

Lotten was busy sharing more of those excruciating little confidences he had learnt to dread. 'And do you know, Olivia, Linus and I have never been closer.' She glanced around the room. As her eyes fell on Linus, she lowered her voice as if he were the one person in the room who should not hear. 'Even our, you know what, has improved no end.'

Olivia looked helplessly at Linus and got up from her chair with an air of relief. 'I just remembered, I promised to call Gerald. About a book,' she added. 'Help yourselves to more coffee.' And she was off as if carried by a little gust of relief. Linus wished he could have followed. Actually, he could. 'I'll just run down and get some cigarettes,' he said, leaping up and ignoring Lotten's sigh and the disapproving shake of her head.

Outside, the air was fresh and clear, and a brisk wind sent the autumn leaves swooshing along the pavement, but Linus saw summer sunshine and bright, warm-weather clothes, and Lotten with her flaxen hair dancing round her shoulders. Lotten some ten years ago, smelling of lemon and looking at him with her straight gaze. 'Grapefruit, Linus, not lemon, grapefruit.' He was yanked back into the present by an impatient voice asking him if he meant Marlboro or Marlboro Light. He muttered 'Light' and, pocketing the cigarettes and his change, strode back to his parents' apartment. 'I love her,' he muttered to himself as he walked, his collar up against the chill wind. 'I love her. She's my wife, the mother of my child, of course I love her. And who said it should be easy, marriage? Who said it should be rewarding and warm and companionable and stimulating? Someone should.'

Someone should.

## Chapter Eleven

I was meeting Chloe for lunch. I was on time, as always, and Chloe was late. She finally arrived, brimming with the kind of excuses – traffic, roadworks on the Cromwell Road, telephone ringing – that the terminally tardy keep handy the way a young mother keeps wet wipes.

Once we were seated we ordered, salade Niçoise for both of us and Chloe asked for mineral water, fizzy, no ice and a slice of lemon. I wanted wine, but I had a rule not to drink on my own at lunch-time. 'No wine?' I asked.

'No, I fall asleep.'

'Why don't you have a glass?' I coaxed. 'It'll do you good.'

'Look, Esther, if you want some, have some.'

'Me, no, no, I'm absolutely fine with water.' I ordered some for myself, feeling disgruntled.

'This lunch isn't entirely pleasure,' Chloe said as our salads arrived. 'In fact, I won't beat about the bush . . .' Oh do, I wanted to say, do if it'll stop you saying something I don't want to hear.

'Your portraits, they're lacklustre these days. I'm sorry, but that's the truth of it. The wit is gone, the bite and the irony. They're bland, lame to the point of paralysis. That interview you did with Tallulah Pinkerton Taylor, for example, it was about as thrilling as a kiss from one's brother.'

I sighed. Chloe was right. I had tried to ask the girl some searching questions, but as I had looked into her large empty eyes, trying to find something interesting behind, as I listened to the inane platitudes spoken with the earnest fervour of someone about to reveal the secrets of life, I froze. 'That's a very pretty frock you're wearing, Tallulah,' I heard some idiot say. 'Where do you go for your shopping?' The idiot, of course, was me.

'It depends, Esther,' Tallulah said, stretching out her long legs in their high Gucci boots. 'It depends on the season. For autumn wear there's nowhere like Milan. Of course my winter cashmeres I get from Scotland, like everyone else. Spring, well, spring is Paris.' Her eyes lit up as if someone had just popped a chocolate fondant into her carefully painted mouth. 'Summer is New York, of course. No one, but no one understands what's required for summer travelling like the New York designers. If you've ever travelled with anything else you'll know what I mean.'

And so the interview had continued. I had got hundreds of handy hints: Where to go to get Mummy's old pearls jazzed up. Where to find those little baskety handbags that were like totally to die for. She told our readers how to get to the top of the queue for the three-thousand-pound Hermes Kelly bag and which restaurant in the Swiss Alps one simply must not miss on this year's skiing holiday.

Chloe frowned at me over the lunch table. 'You let that girl get away with the most inane load of drivel I've ever seen south of *Hello!*. What's up, Esther?'

I shook my head. 'Maybe I'm just tired, my mind plays tricks on me when I'm tired.' I could have added that these days the little blighter played tricks on me when I wasn't tired as well. I sighed. 'All right, I suppose I've lost my nerve. It's as simple as that. Lately I've come to see how every action, even ones that could be deemed reasonable or justified, can have the most disastrous and far-reaching consequences. You can literally destroy someone's life with the stroke of a pen.'

'I've told you, you can't think like that,' Chloe said. 'Or you'll never do anything. If we all thought about every possible consequence of everything we did there'd be no newspapers, no TV either, for that matter, and then where would we all be?'

We'd been over that one before. 'It's happened to me twice now,' I said instead. 'First with Barry Jones: I interfered and practically ruined the man's life, his family's too and they were completely innocent. Then there was the gas explosion. Can you imagine what it's like knowing that if I had just bothered to interfere some more the Hammonds would still have a home, let alone all the requisite number of arms and legs. You know me, I'm as sane as they come, but it's enough to send anyone mad. You do what you see as the right thing and the consequences are awful. You do the wrong thing and what d'you know? The consequences are still awful. And God knows what damage I've done without even knowing about it, simply by existing.'

'You can't think like that,' Chloe repeated.

'I can't see how you can fail to. As a child I made up my own rules, constructing them, *Blue Peter* style, from bits and bobs: keep your room tidy because that means you can find your favourite things in case there is a fire. Always finish a book once you've started it or the characters you left unread might come back to haunt you, say your prayers every night and never forget to include someone once you've thought of them because then God might let them die, that kind of thing. My parents only believed in discipline when my crime interfered with their comfort. That kind of attitude is confusing for a child. You have your own idea of what's right and wrong, of what constitutes a misdemeanour. Then they go and change the goal posts. You think that breaking Great-Aunt Doris's china pitcher and using the pieces for a mosaic will get you into serious trouble, you actually accept it as quite fair, but then it's laughed off as creative. The next minute you're treated like the spawn of Satan and all his little right-wing followers because you spilt some Ribena on a chair cover. As I said, it's confusing and you end up losing your antennae.'

'You certainly lost me somewhere along there,' Chloe said. 'But Esther, be this as it may, we have a problem.'

'And the same with goodies and baddies,' I carried on, oblivious. 'Black and white. Bit by bit you come to see that what you thought was black and white was just grey and beige, and that the goodies were only looking after their own interests and the baddies weren't all that bad, just hormonally challenged. It makes you kind of insecure, don't you think? Apt to cling to any passing certainty as if it were a lifebuoy.'

'Not really, no,' Chloe said. 'Coffee?'

'I can live with the thought that the likely consequences of a bad act are bad. That obviously makes sense, there's a logic and a fairness in that. But when doing what you think, after due consideration, is the right thing, or when you commit some seemingly small act of neglect and all hell breaks loose, then the confusion starts all over again. I've always tried to do the right thing and look where it's led to. And responsibility, how far do you take it? Think about it. You cross the road which makes a car slow down, which in turn makes that car reach some point seconds later than it would have otherwise. In turn, that means this same car gets caught up in a fatal crash which, if you had not crossed the road in front of it, it never would have done. You walk blithely on, wheeling along your shopping . . .'

'You don't use a shopping bag on wheels?'

'I most certainly do. I'd kill myself lugging those heavy bags around. Anyway, you walk blithely on, with or without a shopping bag on wheels, and meanwhile this poor sod who let you cross the road is lying in a morgue.'

'That's life and destiny; that kind of thing. You can't hold yourself responsible.' Chloe put her hand over mine on the table. 'Look, Esther, you're a friend as well as a colleague, I want nothing better than for you to get back on form, but quite frankly, right now you're sounding like a lunatic.'

I liked people to be straightforward, that way you knew where you stood, but just then, I thought I might have preferred to have been kept in the dark. 'Are you saying you're sacking me?'

Chloe sighed, withdrawing her hand. 'I thought you might like to go free-lance. Have a break, check yourself in somewhere . . .'

'Broadmoor?' I suggested helpfully.

'A health farm, that type of thing. Then use your contacts to spread yourself around a bit. There's a huge market for your kind of "portraits" and I'll obviously use you as much as I can, once you're back on form.'

'What do you mean you've been sort of sacked?' Audrey asked. I wished she wouldn't talk about private matters in front of the manicurist. Lisa came to do my mother's hands and feet every Friday morning together with her friend Abigail who did my mother's hair. Abigail had left a few minutes earlier. I liked Lisa, she was a sweet girl, but this was private.

'Coffee anyone?' I asked brightly.

'Tea would be lovely, dear.' My mother waved a completed set of left-hand fingers in my direction.

Once Lisa had gone, Audrey asked again, 'How can you be sort of sacked?'

'I've been sacked as a feature writer and asked to write for them as a free-lance.'

I was back living with Audrey, back in my Audrey-designed childhood bedroom. It was only a short-term measure until I found a new place of my own, but I had found it unbearable to remain in my old street in Fulham, with the gaping hole that was once the Hamilton residence almost next door. I had found a buyer for the flat, but I was yet to find I place where I wanted to live myself.

'You were so rigid as a child.' Audrey sighed. 'I always knew you would break.'

I glared at her across the pale-blue counterpane of her bed. 'I don't know what you mean, "break". In fact, I'm doing a piece on Lydia Garland. There's an ill wind, etc. Apparently she's only agreed to an interview because I've got a reputation for being "nice". For nice read harmless and ineffectual, but it'll do for now. It's work.'

Lydia Garland wrote heart-warming and hugely popular novels about 'people like us', holding up a mirror, it was often said, reflecting our everyday lives and struggles. It was interesting to see how many people saw themselves as 'people like us'. Judging by her sales, most of the population. Her latest novel, due out next month, was called *Charlotte Alone*. On the dust jacket it said that the author lived in a converted windmill on the Sussex coast with her dogs, Heidi and Gretel, and her husband. It didn't mention her husband's name.

'I quite like her books,' Audrey said. She read a lot these days, in between television soaps and films, and she read widely, novels, travel, biographies, popular history, with the result that, since taking to her bed, my mother knew more about the world than ever before in her life.

But she didn't know everything. 'What do you mean break?' I asked again. 'For that matter, what do you mean rigid? I just thought then, as I do now, that an ordered life was the best way of freeing your mind for greater things.'

'And what greater things would they be?' Audrey asked gently. She could be so cruel.

'I don't know,' I said. 'I suppose we all imagine we're destined to do great things, it's just the time when we accept we're not that varies.' I reached out for another of Audrey's doughnuts and bit into it, not really noticing I was doing it. 'Right now I would just settle for some rhyme and reason,' I said. 'Some justice and order and system and meaning.'

'Don't be silly, Esther,' my mother admonished me. 'If God had wanted us to see any of that he would have given us a bigger brain.'

'So you believe there are all of those things, but we just can't see them?'

'Oh, yes,' Audrey said. 'Now it's time for my Open University class so you'd better run along.'

'Open University?'

'I'm sure I told you. I'm doing Renaissance art at the moment. Fascinating,' she said, her eyes already on the television.

'But what's the good of there being a point and order and a system and rules and justice, if we can't ever see any of it?'

'I don't know,' Audrey snapped. 'Why do you ask me?'

'You're my mother. I suppose that the forlorn hope that mother knows best, or at least something, is hard to quell. It's inborn, no doubt.'

'Well, I know nothing. Now run along and frown at someone else.'

The next morning I had a call from the estate agent about a house newly on the market. 'It's bijou,' she said. 'And it does need some work on it.' Everyone joked about the language of estate agents, but at least you knew where you were with them; they were consistent. Every child knows that 'bijou', in estate agent speak, means tiny, and that 'in need of work' means it's about to fall down. 'But it is in Chelsea, just off the King's Road.'

'Is it in my price range?' I asked.

'As I said, it is bijou and you will have to do some work.'

My house, because I knew straight away that it was meant for me, looked as if it had elbowed itself in between its taller, more elegant neighbours. Narrow and squat, it was badly in need of paint; in fact, as I went inside, it was obvious that the list of things the little house was not badly in need of would be short.

'This is a rare opportunity', the estate agent said, scenting success with a near telepathic ability, 'to acquire an unmodernised house in this sought-after area.' Say what you will about estate agents, and people did, but you had to admire their almost lunatic ability to see the best in a situation.

The house consisted of a kitchen, sitting-room and cloakroom downstairs, and two and a half bedrooms – two double, one single to my cheerful friend – upstairs. 'What about a bathroom?' I asked.

The estate agent looked at me as if she was just a teensy-weensy bit surprised that I should want one. 'I suppose you could turn bedroom three into one, well a shower room anyway.' She suddenly got defensive. 'I did warn you the place needed some work.'

'I like it,' I said.

'You do? I mean, that's great. Great!'

Back home I did my sums. The purchase price was not much more than what I had received for my flat, but then there was the modernisation. My savings would hardly cover that. I could do most of the decorating myself, but things like gas and electricity worried me, especially since you know what. Then again, the upkeep, once the work was done, would be minimal. What were the chances of a free-lance getting a mortgage?

I was planning the colour of the sitting-room walls as I drove up and parked in front of Lydia Garland's charming windmill home. Lydia herself greeted me at the door, hands outstretched. I recognised her handsome, strong-featured face from countless publicity photographs, but she was much taller than I had expected and the hands she proffered were large and strong. She had not, to my knowledge, admitted to a particular age, but was believed to be in her late forties. She chatted on amiably as she led the way through the house and into the large farmhouse kitchen at the back. As we sat down at the huge oak kitchen table I asked her what had happened to her toe; the big toe on her right foot was bandaged and she was limping slightly. 'Just a silly accident,' she said breezily. 'Gardening.'

I brought out my pad and my pencils, and my list of prepared questions and Lydia Garland quotes from previous interviews and articles.

'You're very organised,' Lydia said.

I nodded, gratified. 'I try to be.'

We chatted a bit about her *Charlotte Alone*.

'I'm just an ordinary English countrywoman who happens to have a gift for telling stories,' Lydia confided charmingly, as she poured us both some tea from a brown earthenware pot. 'Milk? Sugar?' There was milk on the painted tray in front of us, but no sign of a sugar bowl. Like ashtrays, they were an endangered species these days.

'Both, I'm afraid,' I said, watching as Lydia Garland made a move to get up. She might stumble and fall, with that bandaged toe, I thought. And break something else, her neck maybe? Cause and effect, cause and effect. I leapt out of my chair. 'Let me get it,' I offered.

'Thank you, my dear,' Lydia Garland said, looking slightly surprised. 'It's in the top left-hand cupboard over the sink.'

Once seated again, I asked her, 'Your success as a writer is said to be largely due to your extraordinary ability to empathise with ordinary people's lives and struggles. It's a gift that's envied by many lesser writers.'

'It is a gift, you're right. I put it down to compassion, an open mind and heart, and a firm belief in the triumph of the human spirit.'

I wanted to ask her how one went about acquiring those things when the phone rang. She got up awkwardly from the chair and limped across to it. She mumbled something into it, then moved it away from her ear and turned to me: 'If you'll excuse me, I'm going to take this in the drawing-room.' She hobbled off.

Chloe had speculated as to the shape of the rooms of the windmill. 'Round, I expect,' she had said. But the kitchen was a perfect rectangle. It lay, like most of the rooms, in an extension built on to the west-facing side of the mill. There were plenty of straight walls for the old oak cupboards and the large dresser stacked with blue-and-white china plates and jugs, and Staffordshire figurines. As I sat there, sipping my tea and waiting for Lydia Garland to return, the back door opened and a middle-aged man with a shock of dark hair speckled with grey stepped inside, carrying a basket of onions. He seemed startled by my presence. 'Who are you?' he asked as he bent down to remove his black gumboots.

I got up from my chair. 'Esther Fisher. I'm the journalist who's come to interview Mrs Garland.'

'Oh,' he said, standing the boots carefully on a newspaper that lay spread out on the floor next to the doormat, before placing the basket with onions by the sink.

'She's on the phone,' I said. The man – I assumed he was the gardener – didn't reply but made his way across the kitchen to the table with the teapot and, grabbing a mug from the dresser, poured himself some. 'Her toe,' I said, making conversation, still not knowing who I was speaking with. 'It looks painful.'

The man looked down into his mug of tea. 'Got a kick like a mule, that woman,' he muttered.

'Kick?'

'Like a mule.' He drained his mug and got up just as Lydia Garland returned, two red setters criss-crossing in front of her. 'You haven't met my beautiful girls.' She sank down on to her chair, patting her knee, beckoning the dogs towards her. 'This is Gretel.' She pointed to the smaller of the dogs. 'And this is Heidi.'

I bent down and patted the nearest one, Gretel, admiring her glossy coat. 'But I have met . . .' Here I paused. Whom exactly had I met? I looked around for the man, but he seemed to have disappeared. His gumboots on the newspaper by the door had gone too. 'The man who brought the onions in.'

'You've met my husband.' She looked surprised at the thought.

'Dark,' I said. 'Average height . . .'

'Of course it was Bob. I was just surprised to hear he'd come in. He has his office in the old grain store at the back and he normally doesn't set foot inside the house before five. He's my tower of strength,' she added briskly as she sat back down by the stove.

'Would you say you were a disciplined person?' I asked. 'Your productivity is legendary.'

'I believe implicitly in discipline, discipline and application. As George Bernard Shaw was fond of saying, "Genius is the ability to apply the seat of one's pants to the seat of one's chair."' Lydia Garland's shrewd grey-blue eyes twinkled. Then they turned steely. 'I write every day from eight to one in the morning and that includes weekends, then I break for a light lunch, some soup and bread and cheese, usually, then it's back to the desk for another three hours' work. I stick to my schedule religiously, come what may.'

'And you never get blocked? The inspiration is always there?'

'Inspiration is just another term for hard work. If you work on it'll be there.' She gesticulated in the air above her head. 'All around you, yours for the taking. If you sit around waiting for it to appear out of nowhere, it never will. At least that's my experience and that of most professional writers I know.'

'I read somewhere that you eschew the use of computers, preferring to do all your writing in longhand using a fountain pen. Is this still true?'

'I find that there is a flow, a connection if you like . . .' She was interrupted by a crash from somewhere in the house followed by a man's voice, cursing. After a brief pause Lydia Garland went on in her even, calm voice, telling me about her working day and her writing foibles. 'I can't have my morning coffee in anything but a white mug.'

I asked her where she got the ideas for her stories from. She gesticulated into the warm, scented air of the kitchen. 'From nothing and from everything.'

I coaxed her into being more precise. 'Ordinary life is my inspiration and the little people my heroes,' she said. 'Didn't Chekhov say that the writer's art is to find a miracle in a blade of grass? Well, that's just how I see it. Find the extraordinary in the very ordinariness around us. The Arctic explorer is all very well, but give me the pensioner struggling to keep warm during an English winter any time.'

The door to the kitchen opened and the two dogs unfurled from their places on either side of their mistress's feet and made as if to get up. But when they saw it was her husband they remained seated. Now he was limping too and it was easy to see why, as his left foot appeared to be stuck in a large earthenware pot. What was it with the Garlands and feet? Bob didn't speak as he shuffled past us and out of the back door, but he gave his wife a reproachful glance.

'The number of writers, or would-be writers, who fall by the wayside are legion and often it's not because of a lack of talent but of application. You need staying power.'

I left an hour later with a notebook full of harmless answers to my harmless questions; I'd been given my chance and I'd blown it. On my way to the car I passed Bob Garland sitting on a garden chair, looking out at the fields, his foot still stuck in the pot. 'Traps,' I heard him say as I passed. 'She sets traps.'

I stopped and walked up to him. 'Who sets traps? Your wife? Are you talking about your wife?'

A look of cunning spread across his round face. 'That's for me to know and for you to find out.' He winked.

I tried again. 'You said she has a kick like a mule. Does your wife kick you?'

135

'I'm tired. You've talked to her, you've got your interview, don't bother me, there's a good girl.'

A window opened upstairs. 'Bob!' It was Lydia. 'Bob, I need you inside please.'

Bob Garland got out of the chair and hobbled off in the direction of the house. Then he stopped for a second and turned back towards me. 'Normally we keep begonias in it.'

Did I follow it up? Did I try to find out if Bob Garland's words were the ramblings of some jealous nobody or the truth? Like hell I did. Was Bob Garland really a battered husband? Well, if he was, I wasn't going to tell anyone. I didn't dare because now every act was followed in my mind by a pack of hounds of disaster. I simply lacked the courage to risk unleashing them. Instead, I wrote a 'portrait' which wouldn't have disgraced a chocolate box. Chloe phoned to say she'd take it because it was about Lydia Garland, but that otherwise it was a saccharine piece of inane rubbish. I agreed with her. 'Take some time off,' she told me. 'Get your head together before you do your reputation more harm.'

'I'm about to buy a house. I need my income.'

'Well,' Chloe snapped. 'You should have thought of that before you developed a conscience like a bloody trip-wire.'

'It's not a matter of conscience really,' I said.

'Well, whatever it is, you can't afford it.' Chloe rang off.


Lotten had something to tell Linus. 'So, Linus, I would appreciate it if you came back from the office at a decent time for once.' She put away the breakfast cereal. 'Oh, and Ivar is staying with Nils tonight.'

He arrived home just after six o'clock to find Lotten at the door, waiting. He could see straight away that she was fit to burst with things to say and he prepared to make his escape. 'I'll just have a wash and change,' he said quickly, darting past her through the hall.

'I've got supper on,' she called after him. 'I couldn't be bothered to cook so I got some pasta from the deli.'

'Fine,' he called back. 'I like pasta.' He took his time washing his face and hands, and changing from his chinos and tweed jacket into jeans and a sweater. Lotten was calling from the kitchen, 'Come on, will you. You know pasta can't wait.'

'So you've had a busy day?' Linus said, sitting down at the kitchen table.

'Not more than usual.'

'Oh, right, I just thought because you hadn't had time to cook.'

Lotten slammed her fork down on the plate. 'It's always the same with you, Linus, isn't it? You just have to make one of your little snide, superior remarks. You just have to find something to pick me up on.'

Linus blinked. As usual he must have missed something, that vital something that would make sense of what his wife was saying, the magic key to unlock her mind and make him understand.

'I didn't cook tonight because I didn't feel like cooking; there, will that do?' Lotten picked up her fork again and stabbed a piece of ravioli with such violence that Linus winced; he knew she wished that was a bit of him she was piercing with her fork.

'I wasn't criticising,' he tried to explain. 'I was just making conversation. You said you hadn't had time to cook so I assumed you had been even more busy than usual, that's all.'

'That's another thing I can't stand. You have absolutely nothing to say to me, which is why you keep coming up with these meaningless remarks. I presume you did better with that little tart.' Lotten's voice rose to a higher pitch. 'You betrayed me, you know that? You utterly betrayed me, and Ivar. No wonder it took me so long to cotton on to what you were up to with that . . . that slut, you'd been in love with your bloody work for so long anyway. Have you ever stopped to consider what I want out of life?'

Reeling from this sudden attack, Linus could not decide whether to ask Lotten not to refer to Katya as a tart, when she continued, 'You're a stranger in our midst, do you know that. You're a stranger in everybody's midst. One thinks one's seeing Linus, oh yes. You seem to be there all right, but actually, you're back home on planet Zog.'

'Aren't you going to eat?' she said suddenly, waving her fork at him.

'I'm so sorry,' Linus said. 'I had no idea I have been making you so unhappy. Of course I know you were miserable over my . . . me having been with Katya that time, but everything else? Things aren't perfect between us, but I thought . . .'

'You thought? Well, that makes a change. But it's too little too late. Quite frankly I don't want to go on. I feel as if trying to make this one-sided relationship work is draining me of energy that I should use to make something of my life. I want us to separate. Linus, Linus do you hear me?'

Slowly it sank in that his marriage was at an end and for a wild moment, as he looked across at Lotten seated in her place at the kitchen table, the same place she had sat for the past eight years, he was filled with exhilaration. Before him the world stretched out as if seen through a wide-focus lens and life seemed full of possibilities. Then he remembered Ivar and suddenly all he felt was panic. 'I want Ivar to stay with me,' he blurted out.

Lotten looked at him, eyes narrowed, then she laughed. 'That's all you've got to say? Well, dream on.'

All that night as he lay, uncomfortably furled on the study sofa, that laugh rang in his ears and each note spelt out his powerlessness.

Bertil was taking Linus out to lunch. 'Talk to the boy,' Olivia had told her husband. 'Tell him we're there for him.' So at twelve forty-five precisely he rose from his corner table, left far side, to greet his son. 'Make an effort, Bertil, dear,' his wife's voice rang in his ears.

'Linus, good to see you. And perfectly on time too.' He really was making an effort.

Linus looked mildly surprised. 'I usually am, aren't I?' He sat down in the chair opposite his father.

'I heard you sleep in the office,' Bertil said once they'd ordered, smoked herring and mash with beer and schnapps. 'But I thought you said that Lotten had left *you*.'

'Apparently' – Linus sighed – 'Lotten leaving was a euphemism for Linus being kicked out.'

'For heaven's sake, Linus, why are you so wet? Did it never occur to you to refuse to go?' Bertil winced at the sound of his own voice, irritable, impatient, just the way he had been determined not to sound, just the way he always ended up sounding when speaking to his only child.

Linus looked up at his father, but he didn't look hurt, just vague. 'No,' he muttered. 'I suppose it hasn't. I can't stand being where I'm not wanted,' he explained.

'What has that got to do with anything? I really don't understand you sometimes, Linus. It's your home and your son lives there. You're not the one who wants to end the marriage. Why should you leave?'

'Because Lotten asked me to,' Linus explained, nodding a thanks to the waiter who had just placed the food in front of them on the red-and-white checked cloth. To him it had seemed obvious; if you are not wanted you leave.

'You can stay with us, of course, until you've sorted yourself out.' Bertil too nodded a passing thanks to the tall young waiter.

'It's all right,' Linus said. 'Sten has offered me a bed for the rest of the week and I think there's a good chance that I'll get this sub-let just around the corner from here. It'll be good to be so close to the office.'

That afternoon, Linus remained at his table, his head in his hands, thinking. He was not much inclined to self-analysis, in fact, he was not much inclined to any kind of emotional analysis. Lotten was, which was why she always won the argument. Right now, though, he felt like blaming Bertil. Of course he could try and blame his mother for dying and leaving him with the cold bastard, but he loved her, the memory of her, too much. He remembered in childhood a feeling of being permanently in the way, present only on sufferance, never quite at ease. In his mind's eye he came and went in his father's study as if it had a revolving door. 'Yes, Linus' – sigh – 'what is it now? I really am very busy. Haven't you got any homework? You run along and leave me to it, there's a good chap.' It had got better after Olivia married his father, but the fear of being where he wasn't wanted had never really left him.

Back at the office the air, full air-conditioning, automatic temperature control, was humming with excitement. Jonas was the first to tell Linus. 'Take a look at this.' He shoved a fax in front of him. 'That English guy, Stuart Lloyd, is building an opera house and he's invited a handful of firms all across Europe to submit designs.' Linus took the paper and sat down with it at his desk.

'Huge budget.' He looked up at Jonas who nodded back. 'Innovation, modern design, new thinking . . . whoa, is this guy for real or the ideal client as dreamed up by a panel of architects?'

Jonas grinned at him. 'I know. Sounds too good to be true.'

'I have to go over to see the site,' Linus said. 'We'd better have a meeting this afternoon, go through the thing in detail. I tell you.' He smiled up at Jonas, a small, far-away smile. 'This project is ours.'

*

I bought the little house and had the outside painted eggshell-blue. In the end, though, I had to share it with Posy McKenzie because I couldn't afford the mortgage on my own. Posy needed a friend; she had just gone through her third divorce. We had known each other for ever, but we had never been especially close friends, not until we met again at Arabella's last year. Then we had discovered that at thirty-three, shared memories were as potent a recipe for friendship as shared interests ever were. I think that at school my problem with Posy was that she reminded me of my mother and one Audrey is enough for most people. Posy was kind of dippy and arty, the way Audrey used to be, before she took to her bed and became quite sensible. Posy was the kind of girl who, when all those years ago I had told her the story of being forced to wear that awful fluffy dress and be the Good Tooth Fairy, had sighed and said she would have loved to wear a pink-and-white frock with rosebuds on. Posy had not been a beauty back then. Now she was. In fact, she was so beautiful that she could cross a dual carriageway in rush-hour, confident in the knowledge that every last car would screech to a halt at the sight of her. Being so beautiful meant that no one who met her tried to figure out whether she was clever, or funny, or learned, or kind, or anything else that mattered with most people who didn't have huge dark-green eyes the shape of almonds, long, thick dark hair and a dew-kissed complexion. In fact, Posy was very smart in her dippy kind of way and one of the kindest people I knew. She dressed in floaty lace that she picked up from market stalls and second-hand shops, and she was given to saying things like, 'I was born in the wrong age, at heart I'm an Edwardian.' To give her a fairer perspective on the thing I tried to point out the little matter of the First World War. 'That', I said, 'is after all where most Edwardians of a certain age ended up. And then there was the Spanish flu. Have you any idea how many millions were killed by the Spanish flu?' But Posy seemed to think she could have been the kind of Edwardian who skipped all of that. Posy made a living from making jewellery, rather badly. When she had told me, a few weeks ago, that she was getting divorced from Philip, her third husband, I had asked her if she might ever consider sleeping with someone without marrying them. It just seemed simpler. She answered that she was an Edwardian at heart. Well, I knew that.

The day Posy moved in, a week after me, she arrived late, way after the small removal van bringing her belongings. She drifted inside with that serene Mona Lisa smile of hers, not in the least concerned with her possessions. The first thing she did was go into the kitchen to make a cup of tea and ended up getting the tassels of her shawl caught in the waste-disposal unit. It happened so fast; she arrived, drifted into the kitchen, carrying a carpet bag, her skirts trailing on the stone floor, moved over to the sink to fill the kettle and there all of a sudden she was, or nearly wasn't as it happens, being gobbled up by the waste-disposal unit. I arrived to switch it off, just in time; she was already bent double over the sink with the shawl tightening round her neck.

'I don't understand these modern things,' she said once she was sufficiently recovered to say anything at all. 'Really, I don't belong to this age.' Her voice still hoarse, she added, 'Thank God you came when you did.'

I started to tremble then and it was a full half-hour before I could hold a cup and not spill it, my hands were shaking so much. It had been such a near thing that I had not arrived on time. One of the removal men had started chatting out in the hall as he placed the last of Posy's boxes on the bare floor-boards. 'This must be one of the smallest houses that I've moved anyone into,' he said companionably. 'In fact, it reminds me of one of them doll's houses that my youngest lass keeps nagging me to make her.'

Normally I would have stopped and chatted back, but that day, as most days lately, I was feeling tense and mildly irritated with the whole world, so instead I had muttered some reply and hurried on to the kitchen to speak to Posy about where she wanted her turn-of-the-century steamer trunk put as the men were leaving and that had been when I found her on her way down the disposal unit. It was enough to make anyone tremble, the thought of how tiny were the actions that decided between life and death. To chat or not to chat? Something as minute as that.

'But you saved me,' Posy insisted. 'So it's all right.'

'Yes, I did,' I said darkly. 'But I might just as easily have been chatting about doll's houses next door while you were having your last breath squeezed out of you.' I felt my voice rise. 'I simply can't stand the randomness of things, the arbitrary way that people's fates are decided. How can we be expected to go on when we have no control over the things that really matter?'

'So what are you planning to do about it?' Posy asked.

'Go mad,' I said. I was joking of course. 'Maybe then it won't bother me so much.' We finished our coffee and I helped her settle in. After supper I went to my bedroom and worked. I liked it there. It was a tiny room, with only just space for my desk and chair, my bed and a chest of drawers. (The wardrobe was inbuilt.) It was a room that fitted round me snugly, leaving no space for thoughts to roam out of control. I had got a job writing a weekly story for a magazine called *Modern Romance*, edited by an old colleague of mine, Mary Swanson. Mary was a good woman, a born-again Christian who had resigned from the *Chronicle* rather than investigate Bishop X's rumoured weakness for altar boys. 'It's for God, not man, to do the exposing,' she had said at the time. At the time, too, I had been spiteful enough to add, 'Tell the bishop that.' But I had come to respect her decision even if I didn't agree with it.

Writing the stories for Mary's magazine was hard work, mainly because each one obviously had to be about romantic love and I still hadn't figured out the first thing about that, and also because, to make matters worse, three out of four stories had to have a happy ending. I did not have a natural talent for happy endings. Now and then I cheated, killing off the heroine, say, but allowing her dog and the hero's to live happily ever after. Or sending the hero off to Alaska to find a different kind of romance, the romance of the wild; that sort of thing. Sometimes I got away with it. Sometimes I didn't and a story would be returned with a terse note to the effect of 'Anyone would think you didn't believe in romance' or 'Where's your heart?'.

Where indeed? 'In San Francisco?' I crooned to myself, remembering the old song. But I needed the work so I kept trying, writing of love at first sight and of trembling knees and sightings of heaven, of descents into hell and wounds to the heart and love that transcends all. Things, in fact, of which I knew next to nothing, but had learnt second-hand from books and films, and other people's lives. 'Your readers will always notice if you're not sincere,' Mary told me. 'Tongue-in-cheek writing simply doesn't succeed.' So I tried hard to believe my fantasies and to my surprise I sometimes did, at least for as long as it took me to write them. It was four o'clock the next morning before I got to bed, having finished the latest story. I set it in Italy and it was all about a man who was in love with his wine cellar, neglecting his poor wife and spending all his love and attention on tending his bottles, a dozen in particular, all from the same vineyard; taking them to be recorked each decade, tenderly turning them at frequent and exact intervals, checking the temperature, until one day, many years on, when he opened the first of them to drink. He raised his glass, smacked his lips, drank. Just then his wife appeared on the terrace, and as he caught her sweet smile he realised that all the years had not marred her beauty because it came from within and nothing could wither it. The bottle, on the other hand, whose beauty could also be said to come from within, was past its prime and tasted sour on his lips.

The next morning I got up at eight, feeling light-headed with lack of sleep. Posy was already at the breakfast table and she made me some coffee while I leafed through the paper. Barry Jones had been out of the news lately, but that morning's tabloid carried a piece about him drying out in a Welsh clinic. I read on over my bowl of All-Bran. 'We work hard here,' he was quoted as saying. 'Real work tending sheep and making our beds. I feel more like my old self with every day that passes and I'm looking forward to being back on your screens before long.'

Personally, I just wished he'd go away. 'A bad conscience sweeps its debris under the carpet,' Audrey had once said and at the time I hadn't understood what she meant, but now it fitted in with how I felt. I was fed up with feeling guilty about the man.

That morning, over my bowl of All-Bran, it seemed to me that God, the God who had laid down the laws of the universe, was uncannily like Audrey. The more I thought about it the more plainly it was there to see; the inconsistency, the despotic whims – Audrey would spoil you rotten one day only to be on a frugality drive the next. God did exactly the same. One day you would have it all, just like Barry Jones, the next – poof! – it was all gone. Or think of poor old Job; that story had always made me extremely uneasy. And there was more. 'You can tell me everything, darling,' Audrey would say. 'I'll always be there for you.' So, lulled into a false sense of security, you would come to her with your problem. And *she'd* say: 'Darling, not now. Can't you see I'm busy. You have to learn to sort your own problems out.'

Same thing with God. 'Come to me with your prayers.'

'Please, dear God, help those who are starving and whose land is ravished by war. And while you're about it, please could you cure me of this nasty illness.'

'Sorry, but you see, I can't interfere. Child murders? Bosnia? Auschwitz? I thought I explained all of that. I have a strict policy of non-interference. And about that illness of yours. Haven't you heard the one about God helping those who help themselves?'

So there it was, God had created Audrey in his image and, as usual, I was left to set my own rules.

# Chapter Twelve

'Angus thinks you're wonderful,' Posy said. Angus was her brother and he had taken us out to dinner the night before.

'That's nice,' I said. I had just emerged from my room after finishing the first draft of a story set in Sweden.

'Why Sweden?' Posy asked. 'You've never even been there.'

'It's because I've never been there,' I replied. 'It makes it more interesting to write. And my mother's been. Her oldest friend, Olivia Stendal, you know who I mean, lives there. She even had me learn the language. It was years ago, when she was in her "children's minds are like sponges just waiting to soak up information" stage. A Swedish friend of Olivia's was over here and needed a job so she came to the house once a week and read Strindberg to me. Audrey said that Swedish was especially useful because hardly anyone speaks it, there aren't even that many Swedes, but somehow I think there is a flaw in that argument.'

'So you speak Swedish? I never knew.'

'Not much. I read it better than I speak. The lessons didn't last long. Audrey sat in on one and after that it seemed she decided that children didn't have minds at all, sponge-like or otherwise, and that the money was better spent on other things. I kept it up myself though, for a while, reading some books that Olivia Stendal had sent me, listening to tapes, that kind of thing. Mostly to prove Audrey wrong, about my mind, I mean.'

'Say something in Swedish,' Posy said, the way people always do.

And the way people always do when asked to say something suddenly in another language, I felt stupid. 'What?'

'Anything.'

'*Det ar synd om manniskan,*' I said.

'What does that mean?'

'Mankind is to be pitied.'

Posy looked unconvinced and returned to the subject of her brother. 'Angus really adores you.'

'He doesn't know me. Before last night we hadn't seen each other for twenty years.'

'That explains it.' Posy smiled at me.

'And I fell asleep over coffee.'

'He thought you were cute. "Just like a puppy," he said.'

I frowned. 'Call me peculiar if you will, but I would prefer to be admired for, say, my scintillating conversation and my sparkling personality, rather than my canine ability to fall asleep in public places.' But my curiosity quickened. To be honest, Posy's brother had not made a huge impression on me. I remembered that he worked in advertising, but seeing he was so kind about me, the least I could do was to recall what he looked like. Tallish, dark, sensitive mouth, nice but unremarkable eyes of unspecified colour.

'Anyway.' Posy shrugged her lace-wrapped shoulders. 'He's going to give you a call.'

Two days later I was having dinner again with Angus, just the two of us this time. 'You're much less forceful than I remembered you,' Angus said. 'Much softer seeming.'

'Dithering, you mean?' I asked. 'I haven't been on top form lately, that's all.'

Angus put out his hand and placed it on mine, which I had carelessly left at the side of my plate. 'Don't do yourself down. You've changed and it's really nice.'

I sighed. What could I say? People always believed me least when I was speaking the most truth. Instead I studied him across the table, wriggling my hand slightly to see if I could throw his off. As children, Angus and Posy could have been taken for twins. As grown-ups they still looked alike, but somehow he was a little less of everything. Posy had waves and Angus had the odd stray lock. Posy had two dimples whereas Angus had one, in the left cheek, and it showed only when he smiled. Posy's eyes were large and dark-green, Angus's were hazel. There was a dreamy energy about Posy. Angus's movements were slow and he seemed to be content with everything the way it was.

'To think we've known each other since we were children,' he said, his hand still on mine. It was a dry hand, warm but dry. I decided to stop wriggling and to leave his where it was. 'But I'm not just Posy's annoying little brother any more, am I?' His smile was sweet but a little unfocused. We had drunk almost two bottles of wine.

I looked at his unremarkable but handsome face and at the warm dry hand on top of mine. Then I looked up and into his eyes. 'No, no you're not.'

'Angus really thinks you're terrific,' Posy said some days later as we settled down to watch television, each with a large bowl of pasta in walnut sauce.

'I'm glad,' I said and added hastily, 'I think he's pretty terrific too. But I'm not sure I'm really ready for a relationship.'

'Do you still miss Holden?'

I sighed. 'I miss something, but whether that something is Holden I don't know.'

'But you like Angus?' Posy insisted.

'Of course I do.' And he really was very nice. In my view nothing recommended someone to me more strongly than a high opinion of me. I thought they were mad, of course, but that was another matter. And I seemed to be making Angus happy, and I hadn't even gone to bed with him yet. I had been thinking a lot about making people happy these days and I had decided that it was one of the few useful things left to me. So far, I had failed dismally, just ask Barry Jones or Mr and Mrs Hammond (so all right they had both got the latest in artificial limbs, an arm for him, a leg for her, fitted at the Roehampton Hospital, but I can't really see them thanking me for that). I had let Chloe down after all the support she had given me over the years. I'd even disappointed my mother. The poor woman had wanted a little golden-haired girl with great musical ability and a fun taste in clothes, and look what she ended up with. No, it felt good being with Angus, sunning myself in his admiring gaze. When I looked at him I saw reflected an altogether more acceptable Me. Maybe that was what true love was? Someone in whom you saw a pleasing reflection of yourself. I had been a bit lonely lately, as well. Working at home, I had lost touch with many of my old colleagues already. And even when someone did call they had to be really patient. Everything I did took

147

so long these days. It was as if the tiniest decision required the kind of deliberation normally reserved for matters of national security, or in Audrey's case, whether red lipstick was a strong fashion statement or merely ageing.

I painted *Angels can fly because they take themselves lightly* on a piece of cardboard and pinned it on the wall above my bed. I was looking at it now, upside down, as I lay on my back, with Angus beside me. We had made love, or to be more exact, we had added sex to our friendship. As far as I knew I had never made love in the true sense. I would have enjoyed sex with Angus more if I hadn't been so busy thinking about all the things the child that would not result from the act (Angus was wearing a condom, of course) might have achieved for mankind. As Angus lowered himself on top of me I saw a meeting of world leaders deciding on the future of our overpopulated undernourished world. I saw before me the large table with the solemn delegates seated round. And I saw the empty chair where my child would have sat, had Angus not been wearing that condom.

As Angus moved inside me, his warm sweat-damp chest pressed hard against mine, I saw our daughter receive the Nobel Prize for Medicine after discovering the definitive cure for cancer. Then, at the moment of triumph, accepting the honour from the King of Sweden himself, she grew transparent and vanished altogether, and with her the hopes and salvation of millions, and I let out a moan of despair. Angus thought it was a moan of pleasure and got even more excited, quickening like a crab in boiling water. OK, I thought, it was quite possible that the child would have turned out to be a perfectly harmless minor player, working as an inspector for the water board, for example, but like most mothers to be, or not to be in my case, I couldn't help having big plans for my offspring.

Angus had shuddered and let out a moan of his own. Then he had kissed me a little clumsily on the neck before rolling off, on to his back. It was then I arched my back and looked up at the cardboard sign.

*Angels can fly because they take themselves lightly.*

I had to admit that when the fairy godmothers were busy doling out gifts at my christening, the gift of taking myself, or anything else, lightly had not been on their list. Then I remembered that I wasn't christened.

'Did you have a nice time?' Angus's voice reached me, fuzzy and a little coy.

I mumbled something vague, hoping to convince him I was still in the throes of post-coital ecstasy.

'So how is it going, you and Angus?' Posy asked over breakfast, her eyes wide with the expectations of good news, lovely news, life's-young-dream kind of news. She must have been listening at the door last night.

'Not too good,' I said, pouring myself a bowl of All-Bran.

Posy didn't lose her starry gaze. She could afford to be chirpy, I thought, breakfasting as she was on crusty white bread with butter and apricot jam. Posy looked at me, her head a little to one side. 'I expect you're only *saying* that.'

'What do you expect me to do? *Write* it down? Tap dance it in Morse code? Send a singing telegram?'

Posy bit into the soft thick bread and the golden orange jam rose over her even white teeth. 'You old grouch you,' she mumbled through her mouthful.

What could you do with someone like that? Kill her? 'If you ever get caught in the waste-disposal unit again,' I said, 'don't call us, we'll call you.'

Posy giggled. 'Always joking.'

'Not always,' I said, putting the spoon into my bowl of All-Bran.

I was having lunch, that day, with Mary Swanson, the editor of *New Romance*. We had decided on one o'clock at her office in Covent Garden. I arrived at quarter to two. Mary was in the grip of one of those controlled furies which make the sufferer speak very slowly, stringing out each sentence as if it were a straining leash. 'I was expecting you an hour ago.'

'I had problems getting here.'

'Traffic?'

I sighed and shrugged my shoulders. I didn't want to lie. The traffic had been its normal demented self and anyway, I had taken the tube. No, it was simply that nowadays everything took so long: where to cross the road, which route to take, which charity box to put my money in . . . every step was hounded by the need to make a decision about something and it all took time.

I tried to explain it all to Mary, but she wasn't interested. 'Let's get on, shall we?' she said, nudging me towards the door. 'I called and the restaurant is keeping the table.'

Once there (it was intimate and Italian, and I forgot the name of it as soon as we left) we ordered and Mary got down to business. 'Normally I don't talk business over lunch, as you know, but with the lack of time' – here she looked pointedly at her watch – 'at our disposal, we'd better get down to it straight away. I like your stories. A lot of us do, but there are rules in romance writing, particularly in magazine stories such as ours.'

'Rules,' I interrupted. 'I like rules. I spend my life trying to find some. The problem is that as soon as you do find one, what you think is a nice firm one, to hang your principles on, it turns out to be as soft and yielding as a branch of pussy willow.'

'Well, the rules for our kind of writing are quite firm. Our readers demand it. One of these rules is that the hero and heroine actually meet.' She stabbed a rocket leaf with her fork and looked expectantly at me.

I looked back, not quite sure what response exactly she was waiting for. Then I remembered the story she must be referring to. 'Oh, that one. I kept putting the meeting off because I got fond of the characters. I just couldn't bear to see them disappointed.'

'Esther, that's the problem. It's up to you to create characters who *are* suited to each other. Characters who will not be disappointed in each other but who will live happily ever after. That's the job of the writer of romance fiction. That's what we pay you to do and that's what our readers pay us to provide. And you can do it. I wouldn't bother if I didn't think you could. Often, when your characters do meet, it's all fine – up to a point.'

'Which point?'

'What did you say?' Mary had to ask. I had had my mouth full of pumpkin risotto.

I swallowed. 'At which point exactly?'

'Oh, well, passion. Our readers like their passion.'

How? I wanted to ask. Black, white with one sugar?

'There's a coldness at the base of your writing, a distance. Look,

Esther.' Mary leant closer to me across the table. 'I like you and you're a good journalist, a good writer, I'd like to go on using you, but you have to change gear.' She moved back again in her chair. 'Think of your boy-friend. Sit back and close your eyes and think about him when you write your heroes and your love scenes.'

A couple of hours later I was back at my desk, thinking of Angus. Closing my eyes, I tried to think passionate thoughts. Angus undressing in front of me as I lay waiting in bed; shirt, socks, trousers . . . those crumpled Popeye boxer shorts. I opened my eyes. After a few minutes I tried again. 'I want you,' Angus said, unbuttoning his trousers. They fell down to the floor and . . . Now it wasn't that I expected him, or anyone, actually to iron their boxers, but one would have thought that he could at least fold them as they came out of the dryer.

Just after five, I turned off my computer and went outside for some air. (When did we drop the 'fresh' part of that phrase?) I used to walk fast, paying appropriate attention to what was around me. On the King's Road I would be mindful of carelessly wielded umbrellas avoiding, as best I could, getting my feet caught up in the spokes of a basket on wheels emerging from the general direction of Waitrose. I looked in the shop windows and when I drew money from the cash machine I peered about me furtively to make sure that no one was standing by to pounce as I left, my purse replenished. When I returned home at night I would have my keys ready and glance around the quiet little back-street and down the basement steps to make sure that there was no dark figure lurking in the shadows. In the streets around the office I used to put my arm protectively around my large bag. London streetwise, no more, no less. As for the rest of the time, I looked up at the sky at the sound of bird-song. I glanced at the face of a good-looking man or the legs of a fat girl in a short skirt. I gazed into shop windows and in summer I checked out the people sitting at the pavement cafés. I looked up endlessly at the buildings I passed, finding a plaque new to me here, or a gargoyle I'd never noticed there. Like any big city, London was a cache of delights in a dustbin, and I paid as much attention to it as most people and more than some.

But lately it had been different. Now, almost every step I took brought its own problem. Pass a beggar without a second glance and you might turn your back on genuine suffering and need – or you might not. It was cold for March. The scruffy, ginger-haired boy, slumped on a heap of blankets in the shop doorway, might die that very night from the effects of malnutrition and exposure, his body found the next morning, lying like the Little Match Girl by the window of the Body Shop, his unseeing eyes turned towards an unobtainable paradise of apricot bubbles and strawberry washes and goat's milk cleanser, none of it tested on animals. And he was so young. Poor, poor, wretched boy. On the other hand, give him a wad of cash and he might leap up from under his mound of blankets and head straight for the nearest drug dealer and would end up every bit as dead.

I spent more than ten minutes just walking up and down and round the block deciding whether or not to give him some money, before dropping five pounds in the glass jar by his side.

And you don't have to look far to come upon more problems requiring decisions. There was a woman outside Boots. She was young, early twenties maybe, with lank, greasy hair down to her shoulders and a pinched, pale face. A small boy with a crew-cut was pulling at her hand and whining, and at first the woman didn't seem to notice, then all of a sudden she twirled round and whacked him across the back of the head. The child opened his mouth and cried in that heart-rending abandoned way that children do. Was the woman his mother? She could be the nanny from hell or even an abductor. Was she a habitual child beater? Was this a case of abuse? Should I report the incident? I hovered for a moment, watching. The woman knelt down by the child and shook him. 'Be quiet, you little sod, do you hear me? Just shut up!'

I stepped forward; I felt I had to. 'Are you his mother?'

The woman looked up at me, pushing a lank fringe from her eyes. 'What's it to you?'

The boy stopped crying. 'Mum, who's that lady?'

'No one, poppet.' She got to her feet and took the boy's hand. 'Come along now. Dad will be wondering where we've got to.' She shot me a contemptuous glance over her shoulder and off they went, down the road. My heart was beating furiously and I could feel the heat rise in my cheeks. I felt awful: itchy, scratchy, breathless. The more you think about things the more you see the connections. How could one be expected to make any decisions? What was that saying? The best-laid plans of mice and men . . . Well, what about them? All I knew was that they were a joke, our plans. What was the other one? Men plan and angels laugh? Something like that? I would laugh too if I were safely tucked up in heaven, away from the madness down below.

Plan? Why, when any seemingly random act could be the one that determined the course of someone's life? Stop to answer the phone on your way out and because of it, that three-and-a-half-minute delay, you end up bang in the middle of a motorway pile-up. Turn left and walk straight into the path of a killer. Reap what you sow, that's what the Bible says. I think. I had nothing against that concept in itself, but it simply didn't work that way. What I objected to was when you went merrily along sowing your furrows of grain only to wake up with a view over a field of poison ivy.

Deep in thought, I passed a café and suddenly I felt exhausted. I forced myself to walk straight inside without prevaricating, finding an empty table in a dark corner at the back. Someone nearby, a middle-aged man, lit a cigarette and three people instantly turned towards him and pointed to the No Smoking sign on the wall behind him. Kick a pensioner to death on a public fairway, I thought, and you'd probably get away with it, but light up in a No Smoking area and you were sprung within seconds.

Someone cleared her throat, interrupting my thoughts. 'Were you ready to order, then?'

I looked up to find a waitress dressed in a floor-length pinafore and with a mob-cap pulled down over her dirty-blonde hair. I hadn't noticed any of the other waitresses dressed that way, but looking around me I saw that they all were.

'Tea please. I'd like a pot of tea.' The most difficult thing to come to terms with, I thought, was that you could do absolutely the right thing and still be the cause of everything going hideously wrong. And it never changes. When we are little and our parents' children we frequently get into trouble for doing the right thing. I remember being about six and hearing Madox talking admiringly of this girl Ruth, the teenage daughter of a friend of my parents. This wretched Ruth could sing and play the piano. She sailed and skied, and she read novels. She was so brim-full of energy that she got up every morning at five so that the day would be long enough for her to fit everything in. I assumed that the sailing and the skiing were done at different times of year, but still. Madox sang Ruth's praises. He had been rather irritated with me earlier in the day; something about not knowing my times tables. That night I set my alarm for half past four. I woke with a start in the still dark morning and clambered out of bed. The house was quiet, the kind of quiet you listen to, waiting for it to be broken. But it wasn't. I wandered up and down the stairs, pausing anxiously outside my parents' room, looking at my watch. I was exhausted and soon it would be ordinary morning and my father would never know what an early riser I was. In the end I couldn't stand it any longer. 'Onward Christian Soldiers' I sang, in a kind of whispery voice at first, then louder and louder. It was the song Janet always sang when she was in an especially good mood. 'Marching as to war,' I squeaked. At last the door to my parents' bedroom opened, and I took on an alert and energetic expression.

Madox practically leapt towards me. 'Shut up,' he hissed. 'What the hell do you think you're doing? It's half past five in the morning.'

Something had gone wrong, horribly wrong, but I persevered. 'I've been up since half past four,' I said.

'Well, you're an idiot. Now go back to bed before I lose my temper.'

However old we got, we were all God's children, allegedly, and that kind of thing just kept on happening.

'Indian or China, madam? Madam, I said Indian or China, madam.' The bored voice of the waitress reached me. I felt other-worldly, other-planety, as if any communication had to travel millions of light-years through the ether to reach me. I blinked at her. The girl sighed and shifted from foot to foot.

'Indian or . . .'

'I don't know,' I snapped. 'But I really do wish you'd all stop asking me these things. Indian or China? Condom or plain? Train or plane? Black or white? Interfere, don't interfere? Do the right thing and get a kick in the teeth. Do the wrong thing and get a kick in the teeth. What do I know? Could you please get it into your head that *I Don't Know*!'

'I'm sorry if I upset madam, but there is no need for madam to shout.'

Was madam shouting? Apparently. Now that kind of thing can't be allowed to go on. But what to do about it? I lowered my voice to a polite level and said, 'Now would you please just bugger off and leave me in peace.'

'I'd rather madam didn't use language like that.' The young waitress had metamorphosed into an officious young man with a moustache. It was a real skill they possessed, these restaurant managers; disappearing and reappearing with such immaculate timing. Never there when you wanted them, always there when you did not. 'Our customers don't like it.'

What was that old joke? *Mother wouldn't like it. That's all right, mother ain't gonna get it.*

'And I don't think it's a laughing matter.'

Who was laughing? Whoops, I was.

'You're not feeling well. Why don't you let me help you to the door. A nice little lie-down in the comfort of your own home would do the trick I shouldn't wonder. Shall I call you a cab?'

I was bustled through the door of the café and out into the street – where was that cab? – and I began the walk home, slowly. 'Tread softly,' I heard a voice in my head. 'Tread softly because you tread on my dreams.' So I trod very softly, all the way back to the house, where I was met by Angus and Posy. Angus was livid and Posy just looked pained in a wilting-flower kind of way.

'Where the hell have you been?' Angus grabbed me by the elbow and pulled me inside before I had even had time to wipe my feet. 'Do you know what time it is?' He sounded like a wrathful father, but he looked genuinely frightened.

'We've been really worried,' Posy chimed in.

'What time is it?' I asked, taking my coat off. Looking at my watch I answered myself, it was half past seven.

'We should be at the theatre by now,' Angus said. 'We'd agreed I was to pick you up here at half past six. Where have you been?

I shrugged my shoulders like a child. 'Nowhere.'

'Oh, that's great. You waste tickets to the hottest show in town and you worry us half to death and that's all you have to say.'

I walked into the kitchen and poured myself some water from the tap. Angus and Posy followed me in and Posy put the kettle on. She looked beautiful in her long brown cotton trimmed with white lace and her large green eyes were full of concern as they fixed on me. I

155

was sweating and I pushed my damp hair away from my forehead. 'I'm sorry,' I said, looking at them both, brother and sister, my lover and my friend. 'I think I'm going mad.'

For once in my life everyone seemed to see things my way. No one disagreed with me.

Chloe: 'I thought something odd was happening.'

Mary: 'Anyone so completely lacking in romantic sentiment must have serious problems with herself.'

Posy: 'She's a tortured soul.'

Angus: 'She really has been rather odd lately.'

Audrey: 'Esther seems perfectly normal to me.'

I thought that the most damning statement of all.

My GP gave me a certificate to enable me to draw sickness benefit and he also suggested I saw a therapist.

'I wanted to be a psychiatrist once,' I said conversationally. The therapist, whose name was Anthony Peel, looked me straight in the eyes as we sat facing each other. He said nothing for a long time. At first I stared back, then I felt ill at ease and glanced over his left shoulder. When I got bored with that view, and that was pretty soon since there was nothing to see but an insipid water-colour of a beach, I looked over his right. I wasn't one of those people who can't stand a silence. I liked them, in fact. They were either restful or embarrassing and either would do me. But this was different. I was paying this man – and very expensive he was too, at fifty pounds an hour – to sort me out. This silence did nothing other than bore me, apart, of course, from costing me money.

'Decisions have begun to worry you to the point of paralysis,' he said finally. 'You are a doubter. This led to a nervous breakdown in a café the other night.' Well, full marks to him for reading the letter my GP had sent him.

A flicker of a smile passed across his long face. 'It's perfectly normal for you to feel hostile towards me initially.' Now that was perceptive. 'But that hostility will disappear as you gain confidence in your therapist.'

Wanna bet? Then I smiled at him. It was intended to be a nice smile because it had occurred to me, suddenly, that everyone was a smart aleck with their shrink and that it wasn't remotely clever or funny, just banal. Again he said nothing for a long while. He obviously counted on no one being able to remain silent for long in the presence of another mortal, be it man, cat or therapist.

Finally, I cracked: 'I know this isn't an original thought, but it's struck me that my breakdown, although I don't think it was as bad as that . . . no? Yes? Well. Anyway, that it was more a result of my seeing the world and my place in it for what it was, rather than any illness. But as I said, that's probably what all your loonies say. The mad are the only sane people, that kind of thing.'

Sitting back in his chair, Anthony Peel said, 'We prefer not to use terms like "loonies" and "mad".'

'Right,' I said. 'Well, maybe I've just gained a painful degree of insight into the buggering-up factors of life. Maybe it's God's way of silencing you when you've seen the light, or the dark, rather; make you a gibbering wreck so no one will listen to you. An old trick, no doubt.'

'Do you believe in God?'

I shook my head. 'No, not really.'

'So why did you talk just now about God silencing you?'

'Well hearing it like that, it does sound a mite pretentious. I mean, why should God bother to silence me? I'm really not that important.'

'But you just told me you don't believe in God.'

I looked at Anthony Peel. 'You must have heard of agnostics?' I said. 'So anyway, what do you think?'

'It's not for me to tell you what I think. We're here to discover what *you* think.'

'But I know what I think already.'

'Ah, but do you?'

There was no answer to that other than, 'I thought I did.'

Anthony Peel rested his clasped hands on his tummy and raised his chin a little as he spoke. 'You're not "mad", to use your phrase. You've had a breakdown precipitated by certain events.' He waved my GP's letter at me and the form they had made me fill out. 'Events which were aggravated in your mind by a personality and background which already dispose you towards an exaggerated sense of responsibility for people and events. You have to learn to let go. To trust in something other than yourself.'

'But I, and I alone, am responsible for what I do and say. I mean, if I'm not, what's the point? And', I said, feeling a ten-year-old again, 'who else is there? For as long as I can remember, I've known, deep inside me, that there's no one you can trust but yourself. Then I found that I can't even trust me. I make one lousy decision after the other, causing mayhem as I go. So here I am, with nothing to hold on to, not even myself. Have you any idea how terrifying that feels?'

'You tell me.'

I didn't approve of this aspect of the session: *he* gets paid and *I* give the answers. Surely it ought to be, *I* pay and *he* answers? 'No, no, you tell me,' I insisted.

'I'm not here to hand out answers.'

'Well that's exactly what . . .'

He ignored me. 'I'm here to help you find them within yourself.' He looked at his watch and stood up. 'Same time next Thursday?'

It was a fine day; cold, but sunny with a light breeze from the west. The leaves on the trees in the park outside Linus's rented flat were in bud. The long dark Scandinavian winter was on the wane at last. Linus was standing by the window, waiting, and when he spotted Lotten's car he rushed out of the front door and down the two flights of stairs. He had not seen his son for almost three weeks and had missed him badly.

Ivar was wearing blue jeans and a fluffy pink sweater. Apparently he still had problems with his 'gender identity', as his mother put it.

'You like pink, darling, do you?' Linus made his voice casual.

'Not really,' Ivar admitted, putting his hand in his father's. 'But it's a good colour for little girls.' He sounded matter-of-fact. Linus thought about pointing out to his son that he was a little boy, but Lotten had expressly told him not to broach the subject. 'It will just confuse him further. It might even make him feel a failure,' she had said. (Lotten had started a course in child therapy and was, by all accounts, doing very well.) So Linus said nothing, but just picked up the child's overnight bag, and hand in hand they walked upstairs to the flat. It was Maundy Thursday and Linus was taking a week off. He and Ivar were going to the island. He turned to his son and grinned. 'We're going to have a lot of fun.'

'Are we going right now?'

'Almost,' Linus said. 'I'm just waiting for a phone call, a very very important phone call.'

'What about?'

'Well, Pappa has designed an incredibly beautiful building for a man in England. The man in England is looking at several different plans made by all these different architects from all over the world, then he'll decide which one he likes best and build it. I'm waiting to see if he's had the wonderfully good taste to pick mine.'

Ivar was looking at his smiling father with a grown-up look of indulgence on his small winter-pale face. He liked it when his father smiled like that. Lately, both his parents had taken to bending down low and looking him in the eyes until he felt embarrassed, and saying, 'Mamma and Pappa just want you to be happy.' They didn't seem to understand that Ivar wanted *them* to be happy. They weren't very often these days. His mamma cried for no reason at all sometimes, or no reason that she would tell Ivar about, and his pappa seemed to be far away even when he was sitting right next to Ivar and there was a sad look in his eyes even when he laughed. But not now. Ivar's pappa was smiling all the way to the eyes and that made Ivar feel really happy too. 'Is it a really, really beautiful house?'

'The most beautiful house in the world.'

'How beautiful is that?'

'As beautiful as . . . as a sunset over the sea.'

'As beautiful as the Peter Pan grotto at the funfair?'

'Oh, yes.'

'As beautiful as the girl in *Holiday on Ice*?'

Linus had to think for a moment. 'There were lots of girls in *Holiday on Ice*.'

Ivar began jumping up and down. 'You know, the really beautiful one with the blue spangly dress and the hat with fur on.'

'Oh, just as beautiful,' Linus said, not remembering the girl at all.

'As beautiful as ice-cream?' Ivar giggled.

Linus put his head to one side and scratched his head. 'No,' he said finally. 'Not *that* beautiful.' Then he laughed and Ivar did too.

Suddenly Linus looked serious. 'You know, Ivar, I really want this to happen. I've dreamt that building, sung it, slept it and eaten it, and I can't believe that it won't be the one they pick. I know I've had problems getting my designs through before . . . sorry, Ivar, what was that?'

'I said, why did you eat your design?'

'I didn't.'

'You said you did.'

'I meant it figuratively. And before you ask, figuratively means roughly that I didn't mean what I said, exactly the way I said it.'

'So why did you say it?'

'Never mind.' He picked Ivar up in his arms and gave him a noisy kiss on the baby-soft cheek. 'The point is, Ivar my boy, that your father's design is, if I may say so myself, heaven. It's an opera house, which is a place where people come to listen to other people singing stories. There's a foyer, that's the place where you spend the time before the performance and in the interval, which is built in a semicircle skirting the lake, and the outer wall is all in glass so that you feel as if you're actually walking on the lake itself. That part of the opera house faces west so that in the summer you'll catch the last of the evening sun. There'll be a bridge, a covered bridge, connecting the foyer with the bar and restaurant on a small island in the middle of the lake. When there is no music, when you stand and wait for it all to start, you'll hear water, water from everywhere, but never too loudly. And just as music flows the rooms of my opera house will flow one into the other, over the bridge, through the foyer and finally into the auditorium where the most wonderful music ever written by man is performed.' Linus stopped suddenly, remembering that he was speaking to a six-year-old child.

But Ivar's large blue eyes were fixed on his father's face and he looked as if he was listening intently. 'Are you an architect?' he asked.

'Yes, Ivar, that's exactly what I am.'

'That's what I thought,' the child said. 'But the other day, when they talked on TV about professions, Mamma said you were a professional bastard.'

'Ah, well, I expect Mamma was joking.'

Ivar shook his blond head. 'No, she wasn't.'

'Anyway, as I said, then you have the auditorium. In that room you have to have all special shapes and materials to help the music to sound its best. And masses and masses of seats for people to sit comfortably, and balconies . . .' The phone rang. Linus made himself walk up to it slowly. 'Hello.'

It was Lotten. She wanted Linus to stop off at Domus and buy Ivar a pair of wellington boots. Linus felt his heartbeat slow down and steady as he listened and agreed.

Ivar was drawing a picture of an opera house. He added a sun to his picture. The phone rang again.

'You did it!' It was Sten, his colleague from the firm. 'We've just had a fax through with the result of the competition. You won. The commission for the Stuart Lloyd opera house is yours. They want to talk to you as soon as possible. I know you're on your way to the island, but . . .'

'Sure. Sure, I'll call them right now. Give me the number again, would you?' He jotted down the numbers on the back of a brown envelope he'd picked up from the floor. 'Will that get me through to Stuart Lloyd direct?'

'I said, can I have another drink?' Ivar sounded impatient.

'Drink?' Linus had replaced the receiver. 'Drink, yes of course. What would you like? Champagne? Lingonberry?'

'O'Boy chocolate milk, please.'

'O'Boy. Right you are.' His heart was thumping hard against his chest and the excitement he had felt when first hearing the news kept growing, slowly filling his body from the pit of his stomach up towards his chest, until it almost squeezed the breath from him. Trying to concentrate on Ivar, he brought the tin of O'Boy out from the cupboard. Next he needed milk. He opened the fridge and stared into it, in the idiotic hope that a carton of milk would miraculously materialise. It did not. 'Sorry, little man, we seem to be out of milk.'

'Mummy said you would be,' Ivar stated. 'She said, "Eat all your breakfast because your father is bound to have nothing but beer in his fridge." I can't drink beer,' he added.

Linus closed the fridge. 'I tell you what,' he said. 'Why don't we just get on our way. We can stop off at the kiosk at Ytterby and buy you an ice-cream. One call, I'll just make one call and then we'll be off, promise. You see, I won. My design won the competition.'

'Will Grandpa be there when we arrive?' Ivar asked from the back of the car. Linus nodded in the rear-view mirror. 'And Grandma Olivia?'

'Yes, she'll be there too.' He went over in his mind the conversation he had just had with his client, Stuart Lloyd, who had confirmed the fax and congratulated him on the design. As soon as the Easter break was over he wanted Linus to fly over to London for a meeting. 'We intend you to have a free hand, though, believe me. We'll expect consultation, but you'll have the final word at each stage.' If Stuart Lloyd had been a fairy godmother waving a magic wand, instead of a middle-aged man with a beard, he could not have brought things to a happier conclusion, Linus thought. God, it was frightening getting everything you'd ever wanted.

'I like Grandma Olivia. I don't think she's a smug old bat at all,' Ivar said.

'Of course she isn't a smug old bat. Whoever put that idea . . .' Here Linus broke off, knowing suddenly all too well whose words Ivar was repeating.

'Mummy says men are weak.' Ivar's voice fluted towards him. 'But I saw this muscle-man on TV and he could lift a whole car. It wasn't a very big car, but I still think he had to be quite strong.'

'Absolutely, Ivar.' There was silence.

Then Ivar spoke again: 'Mummy says that women are strong like silk thread but . . .'

'Look at all those balloons,' Linus said, pointing to the balloon seller by the gates to the Municipal Gardens. 'Have you ever seen so many balloons?'

'Yes, I have.'

'Oh. Where?'

'At Torvald's party. There were bunny balloons and doggy balloons and kitty balloons . . . I wouldn't have called them that myself, I would have said rabbit balloons and dog balloons and cat balloons but the balloon man . . .'

*I have been given a chance few men are given*, Linus thought. *The chance to fulfil my dream. Bloody hell!*

'Of course balloons are fat, but they're not at all strong,' Ivar told him. 'They go bang.' He tried the word again, raising his voice to a high-pitched squeak. 'Bang! As soon as you touch them, almost.'

'They sure do,' Linus said, changing into the fast lane as they joined the motorway.

Ivar sucked on a sweet he had found in his jeans pocket. 'I sometimes wonder why sweets take so little time to eat when Brussels sprouts take ages. Ages and ages and ages and ages.'

'Because you like sweets and you don't like Brussels sprouts.'

'But I do like Brussels sprouts.'

162

'Oh.' Linus slowed down and changed lanes again, keeping right and filtering off on to the smaller road leading to the island.

'Could Grandpa lift a car?'

'No.'

'Has he tried?'

'Not to my knowledge.'

'So how does he know he can't?'

'Some things you just know, Ivar. You know a fire burns without putting your hand in it. When you wake up in winter and see snow you know it's cold before you've even gone outside.'

'But that's because I went outside in the snow last year. And Torvald's little sister put her finger in a candle flame and she screamed for ages so it must have hurt.'

'Ivar.'

'Hm.'

'Would you understand if I told you that I'm so pleased right now that I don't want to talk for a little while?'

'Daddy.' Ivar's voice was careful, as if tiptoeing towards him. 'Daddy?'

'Yes, Ivar.'

'Who else will be there?'

'On the island? Oh, everyone.'

'Are they nice, everyone?'

'Don't you remember? Don't you remember meeting Uncle Gerald and Cousin Kerstin and Aunt Ulla?'

Ivar thought for a moment. Then he shook his head vigorously. 'Not very much.'

'Well, you'll see them all in a little while. Then you'll remember.'

## Chapter Thirteen

'It strikes me', Audrey said, 'that you have to be young in order fully to appreciate the concept of ageing gracefully. I have to admit that the charm of the idea is completely lost on me these days.' My mother was reclining against a stack of lacy pillows, holding a silver-backed looking-glass up to her face, pouting into it, frowning, smiling, raising her chin and lowering it again. With a sigh, she put it down on the chest of drawers next to her bed and reached for a sugar-dusted apple doughnut. Across the soft blue counterpane shiny golden toffee wrappers lay scattered like melted stars and on the floor stood a silver ice bucket, a bottle of champagne periscoping over the rim. Audrey glanced at her watch. 'Time for a drink. You'll have one, won't you darling?' My mother was the only one left in my acquaintance who still expected me to make decisions. I rewarded her with a nod followed by a shake of the head. 'Better not, I'm driving.'

'But you sold the car when you moved. You told me you couldn't afford to keep it.'

Found out. 'All right, then, it clashes with my medication.'

'Oh, Esther, you're on something at last! I *am* pleased. I know you've always despised that kind of thing, but I was sure it would help to stop you being so *serious*.' She smiled contentedly and bit into the doughnut, her free hand beneath her chin to stop the sugar from falling on to the sheets. 'Mother knows best.' She leant over the side of the bed and pulled the dripping bottle out of the bucket. 'You know, life is so much easier since they invented champagne stoppers that really work. It keeps fresh for days with one of these little gadgets.' She waved what looked like a silver spinning top at me and poured herself a glass. 'I really don't like all this trouble at Covent

Garden,' she said suddenly. 'Things are not well with the arts, I tell you.'

'What do you care? You never go out.'

'I know I don't, but I'd like other people to have the benefit of these things. Anyway, I watch the televised performances. I have my books.' She gesticulated towards the newly installed bookcase, its shelves filled already but for a small space, about four hardbacks wide, on the bottom left. 'But music is the key, I'm sure of it. Even the coarsest thug would respond to Mozart, the hardest heart could not fail to soften at the sound of Beethoven's 'Spring' Sonata. Oh, Esther, why did you give up the flute?'

I sat back in the blue-and-white checked armchair at the foot of my mother's bed and closed my eyes. I saw myself being attacked by a burly mugger holding a knife to my throat as I pull out my flute and begin to play. The shock might kill him, of course, but I wouldn't like to bank on it. But I was too tired to argue the point.

'So how are you anyway?' Audrey asked.

I thought about it for a moment. 'Well,' I said. 'Considering that I'm out of work and have been forced to attend a psychiatric clinic while Angus has decided that the best way of standing by his woman is buggering off to Chicago for six months, things are going remarkably well.'

My mother looked pleased to hear it. 'And have you heard from your father lately?' she asked.

I nodded. 'He wants me to come up for a visit. He says he's strong enough to overcome the siren song of family ties by now. Insanity obviously runs in the family.'

'Not on *my* side, Esther. Now if you don't mind I'll just finish my letter from Olivia.' Audrey picked up the handwritten pages that lay folded on her lap and resumed her reading. 'Apparently they're all on the island. Bertil is taking to retirement just as badly as she thought he would, refusing to do all the things he'd always planned to do once he had the time.' She glanced up at me. 'That's so typical. It's easier for women, on the whole. Life never allows us to be as single-minded as men, so we have more resources to fall back on.' She read on. 'Oh and Linus's divorce has come through, which is very sad, but a great relief all the same. Still, Lotten spends a lot of the time ringing up to speak to Ivar and ending up screeching down the phone at Olivia blaming her and Bertil for it all.' My mother's voice and the sun shining straight in through the tall windows made me drowsy and I felt my eyes close. I opened them again as Audrey shrieked, 'Darling, how exciting. Linus has got a huge commission. Very prestigious, very hush-hush.'

I tried to look alert and interested. I wanted to be interested, damn it. 'What kind of commission?'

Audrey turned to the next page in the letter. 'Olivia doesn't say.'

'Ah.'

Audrey read on. 'That Ulla person is there, as usual. Why Olivia puts up with it all I'll never know.' She continued, 'Bertil's cousin Kerstin is training for the Wasa Run, jogging round the island every morning before breakfast and . . .'

'What's the Wasa Run?' I interrupted, eager to prove to myself that I hadn't lost all interest in life. But it didn't really work because while Audrey explained – it had something to do with skis – my mind drifted along its now familiar routes: you get up in the morning, all ready to get on, work, do well, be good, do the right thing. Then a man's sneeze, as he drives along the M40, reverberates through the atmosphere and, before you know it, the walls of your existence come tumbling down. So what is the point? you ask yourself.

'Gerald is showing no signs of improvement.' Audrey went on mumbling aloud as she read her letter. I gave her a brief kiss on her cheek, which was plump and wrinkled like a prune that had been left overnight to soak, and left.

'I don't know if my mother stating so categorically that there's no insanity on *her* side of the family actually means that there is some on my father's side,' I said to the therapist.

'I told you, you are not insane.'

'So what am I doing here? Not an original question, I know, but pertinent nevertheless.'

'What do *you* think you're doing here?'

There we go again. I sighed. 'Have you *no* answers? Not even an itsy-bitsy tiny one. I mean, I came here for answers.'

Anthony Peel told me that in that case I had come to the wrong place. 'You'll only find true answers within yourself.'

I tried to be patient. 'That's the whole point, though; I don't want

166

*my* answers, they don't work. I want someone else's. And while we're about it I wouldn't mind some absolutes back. You know the kind: "Just because Mummy threw a Pyrex bowl at Daddy and Daddy called Mummy a demented cow, it doesn't mean we're not the best of friends and love each other very much." Or: "Virtue is its own reward." Or even: "God loves you."'

'I think I can detect a little bit of irony there.' He sounded playful, all of a sudden, as he leant forward in his chair and looked deep into my eyes.

What was it with this looking-in-the-eye business? I used to do it when I was a child, to intimidate my friends, but I had given up because once we all started to wear make-up, I ended up too involved in checking how they'd made up their eyes. 'I mean it, though,' I said. 'I really need to find some of my old absolutes. So how do I go about it?'

'But what I'd like you to see is that it's precisely this obsessive need for what you term absolutes which led to your breakdown in the first place. Of course it's frightening to go out and face the world unshielded, undressed if you like.'

'Not frightening,' I said. 'Just confusing. I'm confused, that's all. Wouldn't you be if you suddenly realised that you'd spent the best part of your life reading the instructions upside down?'

He said he would be. I was glad we agreed on something. He told me that I had to go out there and start making decisions again.

'I thought I might find someone extremely bossy to make all the decisions for me, have a little rest.'

'So you think that's the solution? Returning to some childlike state of dependency?'

'I don't know about that,' I said. 'I was actually a very independent child. Someone had to make the decisions about the place and, like most children, I worked out early on that my parents certainly weren't up to it.'

The therapist leant forward and looked sternly at me. 'Either you want to get better or you don't.' He didn't wait for me to decide which I wanted before going on, 'So I want you to make at least two decisions every day. They don't have to be big ones, but they have to be firm.' He glanced at his watch and taking the hint I stood up immediately.

Anthony Peel smiled and shook my hand. 'See you next week, Esther.'

'That', I said, 'is surely in the hands of the Almighty.' I walked out of the office feeling that somehow, in spite of my best efforts, we hadn't really bonded.

As it was, I didn't see Anthony Peel again. I got home that day and poured myself a Whisky Mac, one part whisky, one part ginger wine. I had a couple more after that, then I wrote a piece on psychotherapists and faxed it straight to Chloe at the office. It came right back with *Unpublishable and probably libellous* written across it and the words *but thanks anyway* added at the end. Still, I decided, I had made a start; I had written a sharp, decisive piece, a little too sharp, perhaps, but it was erring on the right side, and I had the Whisky Mac to thank for that, not Anthony Peel.

In the next couple of days I drank a lot more and I wrote a story for *Modern Romance*. That too was returned. *Too explicit*, the comments read, *not to say pornographic. And quite frankly, I'm sure that none of our readers would even contemplate putting a razor blade* THERE!? Oh well, I thought, Rome wasn't built in a day.

'You're drinking.' Posy wrinkled her tiny, perfect little nose at me or, as it seemed to me at the time, her two perfect little noses. Then her large eyes grew sad and brimmed with tears. 'I can't believe Angus left like that just when you needed him most. I've written and told him exactly what I think of him.'

I wished I could do the same, but I didn't know what I thought of him. In fact, I thought about him very little. I had tried to ask Anthony Peel about it. How it was that a man with whom I had slept quite a few times, a man whom I had watched Ingmar Bergman films with until he begged for mercy, a man I had spent a weekend *and* a bank holiday in a rented country cottage with, could up and quit my life leaving barely a trace in my heart.

'You feel betrayed by his leaving?' Anthony Peel had asked.

I had told him: 'Yes.'

'So you're hurt?'

'Angry,' I had explained.

'You're angry because you're hurt,' Anthony Peel had informed me.

I had contradicted him: 'No. I'm angry because he proved himself to be a spineless little shit and I can't believe I wasted any time on him.'

'So you're hurt?'

'No,' I had explained patiently. 'I'm angry.' Then my time was up.

'But you're drinking,' Posy repeated. I told her she was right and asked her if she would like a Whisky M. She said she didn't. 'What's a Whisky M, anyway?' She sat down opposite me at the kitchen table.

'It's a Whisky Mac with an ever-decreasing amount of Mac in it,' I elucidated, pouring myself one, six parts whisky, one part ginger wine.

'How revolting.' Posy frowned at the glass in my hand. I was about to point out to her that she was not to blame the drink for being drunk, I mean, it didn't seem fair, when she handed me a letter. 'Read this. Daddy showed it to me, it's from one of his constituents.' (Posy's father had been elected Liberal Democrat MP for Sunning and Tyne in the recent by election.) The letter was handwritten and as I squinted at it, trying to decipher it, Posy snatched it from my hands.

'You can read it when you're not pissed. I just thought it was the kind of story that might interest you. You heard about Stuart Lloyd's plans to build what he calls a People's Glyndebourne on his Kent estate?' I nodded but I soon stopped, it made my head hurt too much.

'Well, George Wilson and his sister Dora, both in their seventies, are the victims of these grand ideas. They own the cottage which is being demolished to make way for an access road. It's all here in the letter.' She waved it at me. 'You want right and wrong, well you'll get it in this story. I told Daddy I'd get you on to it; power of the press and all that.'

'You hate the press.'

Posy nodded. 'I know. Who doesn't?' She had a point there. 'But you have your uses.'

'Like a kind of laxative suppository,' I suggested. 'No one likes it, but you're grateful for it when all other avenues are blocked.'

'If you like, yes.' Posy gave me back the letter.

I read it a couple of hours later, having had nothing to drink but coffee and water. I went over to the office and looked up everything I could find on the Stuart Lloyd project and the Wilsons. I also got the name of the firm of architects: a European firm by the name of Keppel & Rooth. Back home again I phoned Posy's father and got some more information about the plight of the two old people.

'Three generations of Wilsons have been born in that cottage,' Posy's father said. 'The cottage might not look much to an outsider, but to George and Dora it's their whole life. George only managed to buy the place a few years ago; until then the family had been tenants. They're baffled, Esther. Old George came to my surgery and he said, "But we own the place now. It's ours. How can they just take it from us?" It's enough to make you weep.'

Next I called Chloe at home. I told her the basics and asked if the *Chronicle* would be interested in a story. She said they would if it had teeth. I told her it would have a serious mouthful. Which is how I came to be in Stuart Lloyd's office the following morning.

# PART THREE

## Chapter Fourteen

It was a Tuesday in late April and the kind of day which gives that month its bad name: blustery, wet, with moments of brilliant sunshine teasing through the clouds just long enough for you to put away your umbrella. Right now I was trying to get to see Stuart Lloyd at his office at Terra Nova Enterprises. His secretary was firm, which didn't surprise me, but polite, which did because I always imagined mothers up and down the country cautioning their small offspring never to be rude, unless, of course, they're dealing with a journalist.

'As I said, Ms . . .?'

'Fisher. Esther Fisher.'

'As I said, Ms Fisher, Mr Lloyd is tied up in meetings all morning. I'm afraid you'll have to make an appointment. The next available one is . . .' she ran a polished finger-tip along the pages of a large desk diary '. . . two weeks Monday. Ten o'clock.' She looked up at me with the contented air of someone who'd just put a spoke in somebody else's wheel, but she remained polite. 'Sorry.'

'Come on' – I peered at the name plate on her desk – 'Ms Morgan. It's not as if I'm asking for a hip replacement. I just want two, no, five minutes of his time. I'll do this piece about the People's Glyndebourne one way or the other but would prefer to hear both sides of the story first. I like to be fair.'

'I'm sure that's very laudable, Miss Fisher, but as I said, Mr Lloyd is tied up.'

Just then the door to the inner office opened and a tall, fair man stepped out, followed by a shorter man with dark hair and a neatly trimmed beard, Stuart Lloyd.

'I'm Esther Fisher from the *Chronicle*.' I hurried forward, barring their escape. 'I'd like to ask you a few questions about your proposed building of an opera house on the land adjoining your estate, Dora and George Wilson's land.'

Helen Morgan rose from her desk. 'I'm sorry, Stuart. She got past the front desk somehow.'

Stuart Lloyd flashed a smile at me before turning to his secretary. 'That's OK, Helen. I've got a minute.' He turned to the fair-haired man, who, I noticed, was gawping at me. 'You don't mind if I talk to Ms Fisher?' The man, a very good-looking man if he'd only shut his mouth, shook his head. Then he opened his mouth and laughed. Well, not so much laughed as giggled, high-pitched and abandoned. Dear oh dear, I thought, the man is a moron. A beautiful moron, maybe, but a moron all the same. Stuart Lloyd, however, didn't seem fazed by the noise – I suppose he'd heard it before – but I noticed Helen Morgan flinching at her desk. Just a small, discreet flinch, but a flinch nevertheless.

'Esther Fisher, I can't believe it.' The moron had stopped laughing. 'Not Audrey Fisher's daughter?'

I nodded, mute.

'So you're the cross English girl?'

Well, that was one way of putting it. 'How do you know?' Then I corrected myself. 'I mean, how do you know of me? And my mother? Are you a friend of hers?' It wasn't impossible. Audrey had got a veritable little salon going in her room these days.

'What's going on here?' Stuart Lloyd looked at us both, a small frown on his bearded face. He was the kind of man, I thought, who liked to be in charge at all times, the sort who had probably remained in the driving seat even while making love in his first car.

'This is extraordinary,' the blond man went on, ignoring Stuart Lloyd's question.

'You two have obviously met before,' Stuart Lloyd said.

I shook my head. 'No, no we haven't.'

Stuart Lloyd looked confused, then took charge again. 'Let's go into my office.' He waved us towards his door. 'And Helen, could you bring in some coffee?' Helen nodded, but she didn't look pleased. She knew a snake was being let into the bosom of her office and now she was asked to give it coffee too. I shot her an apologetic smile over my shoulder as I disappeared into the other room.

My mother's odd friend turned and gave me a heart-stopping smile,

174

extending his hand to shake mine. 'I'm Linus Stendal. Olivia's stepson. You must have heard about me? I've certainly heard about you. For years and years.'

'Good God!' It was all I could say. And who was gawping now? I clamped my mouth shut. Then I opened it again. 'Good Lord! Don't tell me *you're* the architect.'

'That's me.'

I took a deep breath. 'I have to tell you both that my paper is entirely opposed to the building of the opera house on this particular piece of land and that we are doing everything we can to publicise the plight of George and Dora Wilson.'

Stuart Lloyd threw himself down into one of the two large cream leather chairs which flanked a glass-topped coffee table. Now he looked up at me with a small, tight smile. 'Well.' He jabbed at his thigh with the tip of a pen. 'At least we all know where we stand.'

I glanced across at Linus Stendal who looked as if he had no idea where he was, let alone where he was standing. 'But if you've made up your mind,' Stuart Lloyd continued, 'why bother to come to me with questions?'

'Because I believe in giving both sides of the story, regardless of my opinion on the subject. I must give our readers the chance to make up their own minds with as much material as possible at their disposal.'

'Are you telling me that you actually believe things you write?' Stuart Lloyd shook his head.

I gave him a stern look. 'Yes, I do. I believe in all kinds of things and one of them is the right of two old people to remain in their home however inconvenient this might prove to be to you and your company.' Stuart Lloyd just smiled and went on shaking his head.

'I know I'm a journalist, Mr Lloyd,' I said. 'But I live by my principles.' At least I would if I knew what they were, I thought.

In the corner by the window Linus Stendal stirred and I felt his gaze on me. 'I live by my work,' he said in his faultless English. 'This is going to be a beautiful building.'

Stuart Lloyd was looking at me, his head a little to one side, his small dark eyes alert. 'I tell you what. Seeing as you two almost know each other, why don't we all have lunch together. See if we can find some common ground, Miss Fisher. And I'd really like to explain what we're trying to do here.'

I wasn't fooled by that old 'Let me take you into my confidence' trick. But I smiled and said, 'Love to,' adding a *'Hej, hej'* to Linus. This was Swedish for hello and about as much common ground as I could muster for then.

On my way out I thanked Helen Morgan for her help. She had been absolutely right to find me a pain.

We went to an Italian restaurant right near the offices of Terra Nova Enterprises. Once seated, Stuart Lloyd made it clear there was no time to dither over menus, so I said I'd have what he had so as to be decisive and make someone else responsible, both at the same time. Stuart Lloyd ordered grilled vegetables for us, followed by cod in a herb crust. Linus looked at the menu as if it had some hidden depth that no one else had noticed, before ordering pasta with four cheeses, followed by breaded veal.

'You eat veal?' I said.

Linus opened his grey, dark-lashed eyes wider. 'Shouldn't I?'

'Doing what you're about to do, I suppose you should.'

'I don't quite follow you,' he said in that almost too perfect English of his.

Luckily my glass of wine had arrived. I thought of giggling prettily and saying something like 'Gosh, am I the only one here drinking', but I was never very good at that kind of thing and anyway, I didn't want to waste time. I took a deep gulp from my glass of red house wine and said, 'You evict defenceless old people from their lifelong home and turn their land into a hymn to élitist culture, so it figures you should eat veal.'

'Now, now,' Stuart Lloyd said. 'You're being just a bit unfair there. Linus is the architect chosen to design my opera house. He has nothing to do with acquiring the land. And I can't agree with your term élitist culture. The whole point with this development is to bring culture to people who might otherwise feel excluded. And the building itself, Linus's design, is a quite spectacular merge of art and functionalism. Think about it; that building will be there for countless generations to enjoy. Anyway, you're forgetting that it's the council who's evicting the Wilsons, not Terra Nova Enterprises.'

'Surely that's the height of hypocrisy on your part. If it weren't for you and your promise of jobs and tourism, let alone the huge sum of money you're no doubt offering for the council-owned land adjoining the Wilsons', the council would not be slapping a compulsory purchase order on the place.'

'It's all legal and above board, I can assure you, Miss Fisher, Esther. We've had our lawyers crawling all over those papers.' He picked up his glass of water and drained it. Then he leant back in his chair and looked at me, his head a little to one side, his keen eyes slightly narrowed. 'Do you really believe that the whole of that part of the country should suffer because two stubborn old people don't know what's good for them?' he asked.

'May I quote you on that?' I enquired. 'Or is this off the record?'

'Nothing is off the record. I'm here to answer any concerns you or your readers may have about this business. Still, I'd prefer, as we are having lunch, that you didn't use a tape recorder.'

I was about to haul mine out of my tote bag but instead I brought out my notebook and pen. 'So the rights of the individual count for nothing?'

'I'm not saying that. But I really do fail to see what the fuss is all about. The council is offering to pay the full market price plus the cost of the move. I've seen the place. In my view, anything would be better than that rat-infested hovel.'

I made a note of *rat-infested hovel* Stuart Lloyd looked at my glass, it was empty. 'More wine?'

I nodded decisively. Hadn't the therapist told me to be decisive?

Stuart Lloyd turned to Linus, who had been sitting happily doodling on the napkin like a large backward child, until you looked closer at the doodlings, that was. 'What was that you said to me this morning about the architect's task?'

As Linus opened his mouth to answer I nodded towards the napkin and said, 'That's not paper, you know.'

Linus turned bright pink and muttered 'sorry', pushing the napkin away, then changing his mind and placing it on his lap. 'It was Alvar Alto, the Finnish architect and designer. He said, "The architect's task is to restore a correct order of values . . . it's still the architect's duty to attempt to humanise the age of machines."'

'I would have thought that was the worst possible quote for you all to use,' I said.

'They're good words,' the godlike moron insisted.

'So you're saying that the correct order of things is throwing two old

177

people out of their home to make way for your design? That's your way of humanising our age?'

'No.' Linus looked at me. 'No, I'm not.' The sudden vulnerability I glimpsed in his dark-grey eyes gave me a jolt. 'Stuart asked me to repeat the quote, that was all.' He looked away.

I reminded myself that I was fighting, not only for my career, but for what was right, and that this therefore was no time to weaken. 'Still.' I sat back in the chair, the glass of wine in my hand. 'You should think long and hard before you accept this commission. The old defence of "I was only following orders" has lost its ring of late.'

Linus narrowed his eyes at me and I realised I had been mistaken: Linus Stendal was no more vulnerable than any other amoral environmental vandal. He stood up. 'If you'll excuse me,' he said. 'I've suddenly remembered an appointment. I'll see you this afternoon, Stuart.'

I followed him with my gaze as he manoeuvred his way out between the tables, then I turned back to Stuart Lloyd who said, 'Now don't forget to tell me the name of your Charm School before you leave.'

I smiled as sweetly as I could. 'I would really appreciate it if you would outline your side of the story to me, give me an idea of your vision, because that's what this is all about.'

Stuart Lloyd pushed away his empty plate, but he didn't relax in his chair, remaining forward in the seat, one elbow on the table. He spoke well. He had passion as he told of his desire to leave something behind that would benefit people, ordinary people like himself. 'Opera was my father's solace and his inspiration. He slogged away in a dingy office all his life, working nights in a warehouse just to pay the bills. But when he sat down in his own front room and listened to his music he felt like a king. He never saw a live performance; the mere thought of it was beyond him. By the time I was able to get him tickets to every performance he'd ever wish to go to he was dead. So you see, it's precisely the élitist label you spoke of that I'm trying to remove. And Linus Stendal's design is as exciting a piece of modern architecture as anything I've seen. It stands up to the best you come across in places like New York and Chicago. It's perfectly in tune with its lakeside setting, and with the existing house.'

'But what of Dora and George Wilson?' I asked. 'I'm sorry, but nothing you've said has convinced me that you have a right to cause them to be evicted from their home. Anyway, I would have thought it's green belt.'

Stuart Lloyd shook his head. 'Nope. They might be keeping a few animals, but it's not designated farmland and it's not green belt. Years ago there was talk of a bypass going through and it was all dealt with then, although the council ran out of money before the bypass could be built.'

'And the access road and car-park absolutely have to run through that particular piece of land, the Wilsons' land, and nowhere else? Not just a bit to the left or right?'

Stuart Lloyd stifled an impatient sigh. 'If you had been down there and seen the layout for yourself you wouldn't have had to waste either of our time with questions like that.' He glanced at his watch. 'Well, there we are. I've explained my position and that's all I can do. I can't force you or your paper to agree with it. Still, I would hope that you'll give it some more thought before you write your piece. There are more nuances by far in this world than the black and white we see on the pages of newspapers.' He signalled for the bill. 'Now I must get back to the office. It was a pleasure talking to you, Miss Fisher.'

Once home, I faxed an outline for a feature to Chloe at the office. I got a fax back saying, *Are you sober?*

I faxed back, *You want sober, you go somewhere else.*

The machine whirred out, *Fine!*

I sent my grovel by return: *What I meant to say, of course, is if you want sober, you'll get sober.*

*And sane?*

*What do you want? Blood?*

*Cut the crap and get writing!*

*OK.*

I had found out that Linus was staying at the Metropolitan so I faxed him there asking if I could see the proposed plans for the building. Next I called Directory Enquiries for the Wilsons' telephone number. It turned out that they were not on the phone. There was nothing else for it other than to get across to Kent to see them. There was no time to write to ask for an appointment so I just hoped for the best and got into my car. Well, Audrey's car, really, but she was always on at me to use it. I had my road map and the drive down looked pretty straightforward. I was a good map reader. Both my parents had taught me that women were congenitally unable to read a map, Madox by telling me so and Audrey by example, so years ago I had set about learning. After weeks of study I had found myself secretly agreeing with them, but I had persevered. Just because a prejudice was justified, there was no need to give in to it. Once off the motorway the road narrowed, from dual-carriage road to single-lane B road, to narrow lane that wound its way through countryside that seemed forgotten by the developers. The small industrial estates and neat mock-Tudor housing developments gave way to farmhouses and barns. The sun was shining, but it was chilly for late April. The lane snaked its way up a hill and over a small railway bridge and a few yards after that I spotted a neglected wooden sign saying Rookery Cottage. I turned left off the road and on to a mud track leading up to a rusty iron gate. I parked and got out.

Rookery Cottage, built in a dip between two small hills where even now, at midday, the sun didn't quite reach, looked like the ginger-bread house after the witch had fallen on hard times. I opened the gate and narrowly avoided stepping on a large hen picking its way through some debris. Free range, I thought happily as I continued up the dirt track and into the small front yard. Two rusty old tractors stood in an open-sided corrugated-iron shed and what would once have been an engine was piled in its component parts right outside. As I approached the house I saw a net curtain move in an upstairs window. Good, someone was home. People say that the quiet of the countryside is a myth, but it seemed pretty quiet to me as I looked around, drawing in another breath of country air, quiet until a large dog appeared from nowhere, bounding towards me barking hysteri-cally. There was nowhere to run.

'Back, boy.' I heard a voice, a man's voice with a countryman's accent. It sounded beautiful to me. A small elderly man emerged from the broken-down greenhouse at the back of the main building. The dog gave one last shrill bark, as if to say 'I'll deal with you later', and looped back towards its kennel.

'Mr Wilson?' I called to the man.

'And who might you be?' The old man had stopped some ten yards away and stood looking at me.

'My name's Esther Fisher. I work for the *Chronicle*. I wondered if I could ask you and your sister some questions regarding the building of the proposed opera house?'

There was a silence while George Wilson, because I was pretty sure it was he, thought about it. Then, remaining standing where he was, he called back, 'You better come on in, then.'

'Dog happy where he is?' I asked as I approached.

'Dog's not there to be happy.' George Wilson's voice was puzzled. 'Dog's there to do a job.'

'What I'm saying is, he's not going to attack me?'

Again, George Wilson seemed surprised at my question. 'Not unless I tell him to,' he said.

The narrow hall was dark and damp smelling. A carved oak chest, black with old polish and grime, stood against the back wall and above it hung a photograph of the cottage in happier days. There, roses bloomed round the door and the fowl picking in the yard looked like ladies browsing through their favourite store not harassed mothers desperately searching for bargains at the local jumble sale like the hens I'd just seen.

'You'll want to meet Dora too, then,' George Wilson said.

'I'd love to meet your sister.' I followed his stooping figure into a medium sized square kitchen. It too was steeped in gloom and the light from the one small north-facing window was filtered through a pair of grubby net curtains. Dora Wilson was standing by an old Rayburn stove, stirring a pot. She was as round as her brother was skinny and she smiled, showing a mouth that made do with only a small selection of teeth, as she turned to greet me. George told her who I was and what I'd come for, and Dora's smile grew wider. 'Has Mr McKenzie sent you?' Mr McKenzie, of course, was Posy's father, the Wilsons' MP.

'Not exactly.' I smiled back. 'I did see your letter, though. I'm a friend of Mr McKenzie's daughter. I've spoken to Mr Lloyd and to his architect already, and now I would really like to hear your side of the story.'

Dora Wilson took the pot off the stove and replaced it with a huge kettle. 'We'll have some tea,' she said. We sat down at the stained Formica table and Dora pointed to the carved dresser, as black and ornate as the chest I'd seen in the hall. 'Our father made that.' Her voice, with its soft country accent, was proud. 'That and the bed we were all born in. I'll show it you upstairs. He worked for old Mr Merrick up at the farm all his life. Never owned this place, though. Our family never owned anything much, not until now, that is. We bought the cottage off old Mr Merrick's son only five years gone. Bought it, lock stock and barrel, and no help from anyone. There's been Wilsons in Rookery Cottage for over a hundred years but we, me and George, were the ones to buy it. There was talk once before of us being thrown out. Nearly killed our old ma. Then George bought it and he said, "It's ours. Now let them try and evict us."' She nodded at her brother. 'That's what you said, George, I remember it as if it was yesterday. But now they are. They're coming here and telling us that they can just throw us out. How can they?' She twisted her red swollen hands in her lap. 'This is *our* home.'

I had barely wanted to admit it to myself, but until that moment I had had doubts, the all too familiar question mice gnawing away at me. Was the compulsory purchase order justified, after all? Should I interfere? If I did, what would be the consequences? In fact, all those ethical questions that it was fatal for a journalist to consider. Meeting Stuart Lloyd and finding out that it was Olivia's Linus behind the design had only increased my discomfort. But as I looked at poor distressed Dora Wilson and listened to her words, I felt my old decisiveness return, its tattered standard waving.

'Well, maybe we can stop them. Sometimes public opinion can move mountains, even opera houses.' I smiled at her. 'I'd like to start by giving our readers an idea of what your life here's like. Tell me, how have things changed for you through the years?'

George scratched his head. 'We get lots of visits from people wanting to sell us things. We never used to.'

Dora reached for the teapot, brushing a kitten off the table on the way. The animal landed on the floor, letting out a little mew of distress.

'There's the man from double glazing, he calls twice a year, regular as clockwork. We did get a television set last year. We pay monthly. We're thinking of having one of them discs.' George held his mug out to be refilled.

'We're by way of being famous for our eggs,' Dora said, then she cackled with laughter. 'But these days folk seem to like them better the dirtier they are. In the old days I used to clean them off to make them more appetising like, but not any more. The dirtier the eggs the more folks around here seem to like them. That's the new people come in. Give them a box of lovely clean even-shaped ones and they turn their noses up, isn't that right, George?' She turned to her brother who nodded, joining in with a wheezing laugh of his own.

They gave me the bones of their existence and I marvelled at the thought that bones were maybe all there was. They didn't seem to read – 'Never had much cause to,' George said. Nor did they have any hobbies other than watching television. 'Friends?'

'We've never been much for socialising.'

'Work hard and sleep easy.' Dora's voice broke. 'Well, that's what we thought.'

I left feeling humbled. Back home I sat straight down to work. I headed my piece: THE WAGES OF A LIFETIME'S HARD WORK ARE EVICTION. When I'd finished I faxed a copy to Stuart Lloyd.

Chloe ran the article and the response from the readers was huge and supportive.


'Come for lunch, darling,' my mother said on the phone. 'You've been working so hard, I'd like to spoil you.'

I'd like to see her do it, so I went. As I walked along the narrow hall passage I heard voices, my mother's fluting tones and a man's deeper ones. The man, seated in the boudoir chair by my mother's bed, had his back turned to me, but I recognised Linus Stendal from the hair; the colour of straw and curling slightly at the nape of the neck. As my mother greeted me, he got up from his chair, the look of surprise on his face mirroring my own.

'I felt you two just had to meet each other,' Audrey said.

'We have met, you know that.' I remained standing and so did Linus.

'I read your article.' Linus spoke lightly, but his eyes searched mine, for what? An explanation?

'I'm sorry if it offended you,' I said, sitting down finally, on the far side of Audrey's huge bed (I swear it grew with every visit). 'But right is right, not might.'

'She's rather pompous, my daughter,' Audrey explained. 'Used to drive her father and me up the wall when she was little.'

'Thank you, Mother.' I shot Audrey a furious glance.

'I can't possibly argue with right,' Linus said quietly. 'So why don't we talk about something we agree on.'

I felt small. I racked my brain for anything that would fit the bill. 'It's cold for late April.'

'Not if you're used to Sweden, it isn't,' Linus replied with a smile. Audrey just sat there propped against the pillows, wearing an emerald-green velvet dressing-gown and the satisfied smile of a hostess whose party is going with a swing.

'But it is for England,' I pointed out. 'And England is what most people in England are used to.'

Linus picked up his glass of white wine from the small table next to him. 'Well, I suppose everything is relative.' He looked faintly bored.

'That's where you're wrong,' I said. 'Everything is not relative. Thinking that it is is why we're all so confused these days. Relative religion, relative morality, relative relatives even. But some things just *are*, whether we like it or not.' In the background I heard Audrey mention something about lunch being ready any moment.

Linus didn't raise his voice or change his expression, the colour just darkened slightly in his cheeks. 'And rigid attitudes like yours, principles set in stone, are the cause of untold misery through the ages.'

'If you're talking about your precious opera house not being built, well, I weep!'

Just then the door opened and Janet appeared with a tray.

Janet was the reason why Audrey had turned my father's old library on the ground floor into her new bedroom and bathroom. She had, quite reasonably, refused to climb all those stairs carrying heavy trays any more. 'Look, there's Janet with lunch,' Audrey exclaimed now. 'And what have you prepared for us today?'

'Exactly what you asked for.'

'You clever thing, how did you guess?' Audrey beamed at her. My mother was of the surrealist school of conversation, maybe all mothers were.

'From what I hear you're very successful,' I said to Linus as I transferred from the end of Audrey's bed to a chair at the round table by the window. 'Surely you don't have to rely on dodgy commissions like this one.'

There was a chair for Linus too. He sat down, hard, as if he imagined it was me he was squashing and not a perfectly harmless though frilly cushion. 'I don't *have* to do anything. And this is anything but a dodgy commission. Stuart Lloyd is a well-respected businessman, one who does a lot for charity. He is a good employer and above board in every sense. And I happen to believe his idea for a People's Glyndebourne is an excellent one. I am given an almost entirely free hand when it comes to the design, something of a dream of mine, in fact.' He turned to Janet who had just poured him some wine. 'Thank you.'

He looked so calm as he sat, slightly crouched over the too low table, cutting into his fried fillet of sole. Very Swedish, Linus, I thought. So tall, so blond, so cool and controlled.

'Esther used to guillotine her dolls when she was a little girl,' Audrey said conversationally. She had, of course, remained in bed, where she sat propped up against her many pillows, with a papier-mâché tray in jewel colours perched on her knee.

I turned to glare at her when Linus laughed, that high-pitched, abandoned giggle of a laugh, as disconnected as Audrey's conversation. Maybe, I thought, there had been among all his handsome, dour Swedish ancestors an unusually tall goblin.

'So how's darling Olivia?' Audrey asked. 'She's so proud of you. I don't think anyone who knew you as a child could have imagined you growing up to be so handsome and successful.'

Linus took my mother's remark well and I decided he deserved a break, at least over lunch. 'Tell me about your work?' I said. Linus looked up from his plate and straight at me with those grey eyes. I found that what I really wanted to know was whether he dyed his lashes; they were dark enough.

'When I was quite young, ten or eleven, something like that, I saw this quote in one of my father's books. "*Architecture in general is frozen music.*" That was all, but since then that's all I've wanted to do, to create frozen music.' He looked down at his plate again.

'Your mother, I mean your real mother, was a singer, wasn't she?' I asked him.

'Yes, yes she was.' Linus's voice was light, but I saw the tension in his jaw. I wanted to ask him some more questions – after all, questions was what I did – but something in Linus's expression stopped me.

Janet came back and cleared the dishes. 'Fruit and cheese, that's all we're having,' Audrey said, as Janet returned with fresh plates. 'Nice and simple. You young people insist on being so formal, starters, three puddings and goodness knows what.'

'I've never made three puddings in my life,' I protested.

'I was talking about *people*,' Audrey corrected me.

Linus looked as if he were about to laugh again, but I glared at him and it worked. He cleared his throat and smiled at his plate. Suddenly I found myself wishing that it were at me he was smiling. I was softening at the edges like the weeping Camembert on the dish and I didn't like it. 'So you think I should speak to Stuart Lloyd again?' I asked him.

'I can't guarantee that he'll wish to speak to you, but yes, hearing the other side of an argument does tend to help one form an opinion.'

Not when you're in my profession, I thought. For a journalist, the other side of the story was like the bad fairy at the christening; it buggered things up. 'I'll make an appointment,' I said, so meekly that Audrey shot me a motherly look of concern. Help me out here, someone, I thought, as I fought off the old doubts with everything at my disposal: rusty old bits of arguments, chunks of therapy speak, sharp and painful memories. 'Of course one needs to hear both sides. But sometimes, in order to get things done and in deference to the cause of justice, you have to trust your instincts and go with the bigger pictures and to hell with the nuances.'

'I think you'll find that that's how all the great injustices of this world came about, people ignoring the nuances in favour of the bigger picture,' Linus said.

'But surely', Audrey said, 'Esther's old things on the farm are the nuances and your opera house is the bigger picture? So you seem to be arguing each other's points.' Linus and I looked at each other and I shrugged my shoulders.

'Now don't tell me your head hurts,' Audrey warned. She turned to Linus. 'That's what she used to say when she was a little girl and you argued with her. "My head hurts."'

Now I saw the point of motherhood. It gave you a unique ability to humiliate under the cloak of sentimentality: *And this is little Johnny when he was three and didn't know better than to stand naked in a sand-pit and twist his willie round his finger as if it were a rubber band. Oh and look;*

*there's our Daisy on her fourth birthday; you wouldn't think she'd be able to fit a whole finger into that tiny little button nose, now would you?*

'I would get this funny buzzing sound in my head when my father was having a go at me, as if my brain was hosting a party for a swarm of bees,' Linus said. A brief look of mutual understanding passed between us.

'More cheese, anyone?' Audrey offered.

Soon after that Linus stood up to leave. As I sat back down in the boudoir chair by Audrey's bed I felt his absence even more strongly than I had felt his presence.

Audrey sank back against her pillows with a contented little sigh. 'I think that went very well, don't you?'

I looked at her, appalled. It was just this attitude of hers – this 'I'm not just looking at the world through rose-tinted glasses, I'm strangling it with a rose-coloured ribbon' – that I felt was to blame for my desperate need for clear-cut answers. 'And', she continued, 'who would have thought that podgy little Linus would grow up to be such a handsome man?'

I hauled a cigarette from my pocket and lit it. 'If you like that tall, blond, chiselled type, yes I suppose you could call him handsome. I myself prefer the more earthy look.'

'You've taken up smoking again,' Audrey said. 'Why?'

I exhaled a perfect circle of smoke (an old skill remembered). 'I've fallen victim to the incessant advertising by unscrupulous tobacco companies. And it's something to do with my hands when I feel like strangling you.'

Audrey gazed at me fondly. 'You always were rather gullible behind that cynical façade.' This was news to me. 'Anyway,' she went on, 'I'm not surprised to hear you say Linus isn't your type. You seem to have a preference for men with the kind of looks and personality that fail to engage your feelings too deeply.'

I stared at her. What was it with this motherly insight all of a sudden? 'I have to prepare for tomorrow,' I said, standing up. 'I'm going down to see the Wilsons again.' I stubbed out my cigarette on a saucer.

'You mean after I got the two of you together for lunch and we all had such a lovely time you're still intent on carrying on this silly vendetta?' Audrey was outraged; I knew from the way she gripped the cream silk counterpane so hard that her plump knuckles whitened.

'It was very kind of you to have me for lunch,' I said, 'and I don't wish to be ungrateful, but I have to do what I think is right, in spite of having had a nice lunch. It's called principles . . .' My mother sighed, impatient with the very concept. 'I don't do these things just to sell newspapers, you know. Obviously I need to get my career going, but I do believe in right and wrong.' I paused for a moment. 'What else is there?'

I hadn't expected an answer, but I got one. 'Everything,' Audrey said. 'Everything between heaven and earth. Linus has a passion, can't you see that? He wants to create something lasting, something of beauty. What do you want?'

'In this instance, justice. However beautiful the proposed building, it does not justify evicting those two old people. Stuart Lloyd's vision doesn't and nor does Linus's passion. Rookery Cottage is Dora and George Wilson's home and they don't wish to leave.'

'And that's all there is to it as far as you're concerned?'

'Yes.' I picked up my tote bag. 'That's all there is to it.' I stopped in the doorway and turned round. 'Passion without justice is a danger-ous thing.'

'And so is blind justice.'

'And what do you know, stuck in your bed for the last couple of years?'

'It's not where you go but what you see when you're there that matters,' my mother said. That was it, I'd had enough. What did Audrey think she was playing at, carrying on like some cut-price oracle?

'Shall I tell Linus you're reconsidering your next article?' she called after me.

'No,' I barked. Looking back I could see her reach for the telephone. 'And you can say the same to Olivia.' I was out of there.

## Chapter Fifteen

The entrance to Utterly village hall smelt of lavatory disinfectant, the kind you get in a little icy-looking white block and hang on the inside of the rim. As I paid my fifty-pence entrance fee I searched the rows of stalls for Dora and George. There they were, right at the back of the hall, just below the podium. I waded through the scrum of punters, muttering apologies as the tote bag on my shoulder knocked into arms and backs. There did not seem to be a lot of buying going on among the Spanish fans and old patchwork quilts, the old-fashioned dolls, the china coffee cups and the Wedgwood blue vases, but there was a thinly veiled air of excitement generated by legions of *Antiques Roadshow* viewers hunting for a bargain. Their excitement didn't seem to be shared by the vendors who stood or sat behind their stalls. One man was engrossed in a science fiction paperback, while chewing his way through a packet of biscuits on his lap. A woman seated on a low stool was munching a huge sandwich, oblivious, it seemed, to the would-be buyer asking for a music box to be wound up for her to hear. Only when the customer, a middle-aged woman with permed ginger hair, had given up and wandered off to the next stall did she look up, sigh, and return to her chewing and staring into nothing. Dora and George were not eating, but they each had their hands clasped round cups of strong milky tea. George looked up and nodded briefly in my direction. Dora smiled a big, gummy smile.

'You've got some nice stuff.' I put my finger out and touched the base of a brass paraffin lamp crowned by a cranberry-coloured glass shade. 'My grandmother had one very like this,' I said, smiling back, aware with a sudden rush of pride of my own even white teeth.

'And these are lovely.' I pointed to a little group of carved wooden animals: a duck, a hedgehog, a fox and cub. 'I used to carve, but I was nowhere near as good as this person. Where do you get them from?' I looked up at George.

'What was it you wanted, then?' was his only reply.

'George was pleased with the job you did in the paper,' Dora said hastily. 'We've had ever so many calls and letters from people wanting to help. I've saved them all so that you could do something with them. Maybe print some of them.'

George stood with his back slightly turned, paying no attention to his sister and me, but when a man came up to ask the price of a wooden tea caddy, he didn't seem to hear him either. I gave Dora a little nudge. 'Customer.'

Dora waddled across and the man repeated his question. I took some shots of the stall and of George looking into the distance. A photographer had been down already taking pictures of the Wilsons At Home, but this kind of picture was always worth having. 'I'm after a kind of "Day in the Life of" thing for the Saturday supplement. I'll just follow you around as you go about your business here at the hall and at home.'

We were back at Rookery Cottage and I looked around the musty-smelling hall where damp made the kind of pattern on the tobacco-yellow walls that people paid a fortune to reproduce. 'I think Terra Nova Enterprises would be willing to add a substantial sum to the money already offered by the council,' I said as I followed them into the kitchen. 'You could get a . . .'

George sat down at the table. 'You're saying we should accept charity?' His voice was harsh with outrage. 'A hundred years and more there's been Wilsons at Rookery Cottage and we've never taken charity from no one. Everything we've got we've worked for and earned.' His hands were shaking and his old-man's eyes filled with tears.

'I'm sorry.' I hung my head. 'I wasn't thinking.'

Dora waddled across to the stove and put the huge kettle on the hotplate. 'This is where our roots are.' She gesticulated out across the fields. 'Other than during the war when I had to go and work in the munitions, that view has been the first thing I've seen every morning of my life, and the last thing as I draw the curtains at night. This is *our* place. Why should we be made to leave?'

I sighed and shook my head. I'd always felt that the reason 'For the common good' was less persuasive when you directed it to the sacrificial victim on his way to the altar.

I had left my car outside the village hall a mile or so away. The weather had had a sudden April mood-swing and turned warm, and I was glad of the walk. I breathed in the clean country air and listened to the birds twittering away like the guests in a TV talk show. I was meant to feel a pang of regret for returning to the city, but in fact I couldn't wait to be back in London. I lit a cigarette and inhaled. In the city you had the results of hundreds of years of human endeavour at your finger-tips: opera, ballet, theatre, cinemas, restaurants, museums, all-night shopping and ready-made food. In the country progress was represented by tractors and combine harvesters and satellite dishes on the thatched roofs. It was seen in the turkey farms along the road to my right, huts like prison-camp blocks, spreading a rancid smell and a ghostly silence. Whoever heard of a quiet turkey? Whoever heard of two hundred quiet turkeys? Well, I had now. Further on, I passed a small farmhouse to my left and gazed idly into the garden as I went. A rusty old Rover stood parked in the overgrown driveway. A young man was sitting on a seat in the garden. He was busy, bent low over some work. Craning my neck I saw that he was carving. Was this the creator of the little wooden animals on the Wilsons' stall? 'Afternoon,' I called out. The young man looked up, still frowning with concentration, then his round face split in a grin. 'Nice day for it,' he called back before bending over his carving once more. I would have liked to have gone over to look closer at his work, but it was getting late and I had an article to write.

Two days after the latest of my articles appeared Stuart Lloyd announced that he was putting the construction of the People's Glyndebourne on hold. Chloe offered me a permanent position back at the *Chronicle*. I looked up Pyrrhic victory in my dictionary. It said, *a victory in which the victor's losses are as great as those of the defeated.*

'Pyrrhic, schmyrrhic,' Posy said. 'What are *you* supposed to have lost?' She was getting ready to go out for a job interview with a large PR company, looking like a pre-Raphaelite who had been told by her mother to smarten up.

'D'you know,' I said, nodding in the direction of her short black skirt, 'I think this is the first time I've seen your legs since school.'

'What have you lost?' Posy insisted. 'You're getting your old job back and it looks as if the Wilsons are going to be allowed to stay on at Rookery Cottage.' She pushed a black beret down on her thick dark hair.

I handed her the briefcase. 'Where did you get that from?' I asked. 'Oxfam.'

'Ah.' I scuffed the toe of my heavy black shoe against the carpet. 'It's my old insecurities rearing their wobbly little heads,' I explained. 'And you know how it is when you're in the heat of battle? You're all fired up by the cause. Then the battle is done and there's calm and in that calm the sound of doubting voices can be heard. And I kind of liked Linus. He was passionate about this thing. The opera house, this People's Glyndebourne, it wasn't a bad idea, they just went about it the wrong way. Audrey is furious with me. What with her best friend being his stepmother and all that.'

'Since when did you care what Audrey thought?'

I sighed and shrugged my shoulders. Then I looked up at her with a smile. 'Winning is always scary. I know I did the right thing. We all know that there are times when the rights of the individual have to be sacrificed for progress, for the good of the community, but the day we just accept it as a matter of course, with a shrug and a "That's life", that's when we, as a society, are in danger of losing our humanity.'

'You're a bit pompous for a journalist,' Posy said.

'Certainly,' I agreed.


Audrey announced that she was going on a trip.

'They don't take beds on aeroplanes,' I said. 'Not unless you go in the hold.'

Audrey frowned at me and reached out for a chocolate doughnut. 'Don't be silly.'

'Ah, you're going by train.'

'I said, don't be silly. I'll get up, of course.'

'You're getting up?'

'That's what I said. Why do you look so surprised?'

'Oh, no reason. Well, all right then, it hasn't escaped my notice that you've barely left your bed in the last couple of years. Anyway, where are you thinking of going?'

'To Sweden to visit Olivia's island. It's ages since I've been. And you're coming with me.' She bit into the doughnut.

'You must be joking.'

'I never joke.' This was true.

But I said, 'Why should I want to go there? I've just scuppered darling Linus's dream project.'

'That's precisely why we're going. Olivia is my oldest and dearest friend. She's the sister I never had. Neither of us can stand the bad blood that has developed between the families over this opera house business. You and I are going across to mend fences. And you could do with a holiday. I know you don't start work again full time until September.'

I shook my head. 'I'm sorry. It's a dreadful idea. Linus did what he thought was right. So did I. We were both doing our jobs, that's that. Either they accept that or they don't. I can't see that forcing myself on them at this stage is at all a good idea. But you go, you like it there, just leave me out of it.'

'Maybe you're right,' my mother said thoughtfully. 'Maybe letting them get to know you better isn't such a good idea.'

## Chapter Sixteen

The phone rang just as I was about to get into bed. 'Esther, this is Olivia.'

'Hi, Olivia,' I said.

'I'm afraid your mother has had an accident. She's in hospital.'

Audrey, unused to walking, had slipped on a wet paving stone in the Stendals' garden and, as well as suffering a broken hip, had severe concussion. She was comfortable, but as Olivia said, at her age and at her weight you couldn't be sure. 'I think you should come over. She could be in hospital for some time. She can't be moved, flying right now is out of the question. And although I don't want to worry you unnecessarily, as I said, at her age you never know.' There was a pause. 'She's frightened.'

'You don't think Audrey did this deliberately, do you?' I wished I hadn't said that, but it just slipped out.

'I'll pretend you never said that, Esther.'

'Thank you,' I said meekly. 'I'll book my ticket first thing tomorrow morning and ring you back. Oh, and Olivia . . .'

'Yes, Esther.'

'She will be all right, won't she?'

'I don't know, but the doctors are hopeful. The hospital is a good one and she's getting the best possible care.'

'And what about Linus?'

'What about him?'

'Won't he mind? First I'm instrumental to his project being put on hold, maybe indefinitely, then I appear on his island.'

'Linus will understand that you'll have to be with your mother. He's always been fond of Audrey.' It was a continuing surprise to hear that other people liked one's mother.

194

I couldn't sleep that night. When I closed my eyes it wasn't sleep that came, but images of Audrey, frightened in a narrow hospital bed and dressed in an insulting white gown, split at the back, instead of one of her voluminous silk négligés, as rich and colourful as any butterfly's evening dress. Like so many women before me, I had been so busy running from my mother that I hadn't noticed when I had turned a corner and was heading right back.

Posy gave me one of her shawls as a goodbye present. 'It gets chilly out there,' she said.

'It gets chilly here,' I argued. 'But you've never given me a shawl before.'

'Ah, but you're going away, thank God.'

'That's not very nice.'

'No, but it's true. I love you, but you've been an absolute pain lately. It'll be bliss to have the house to myself for a while. Of course I'm desperately sorry it's in these circumstances and all that, but I'm looking on the bright side.'

One of the things that had always annoyed me with Posy was her tendency to dither and not get straight to the point, but just now, a little dithering would have been quite nice. 'You're not really glad to see me go?' I asked as I dragged the suitcase downstairs.

'Yes, I am.' She gave me a hug. 'Now look after yourself and I'll be praying for your mother.' She opened the front door. 'You're sure you can manage?' she asked.

I was walking to the tube station to catch the train to Heathrow. 'Yeah, it's got wheels.' I kicked the case with the toe of my canvas shoe.

'Off you go then.' Posy gave me a little shove out of the door.

Once down the three front-door steps I turned round. 'Anyone would think you'd like to get rid of me.'

'Get on with you.' Posy blew me a kiss.

I had brought along my old Swedish books to study on the journey. On the plane to Gothenburg I sat between two silent and unsmiling Swedes, one who asked for, and received, a steady flow of miniature bottles of brandy, which he either drank or hoarded in his attaché case. Liquor is very expensive in Sweden I had heard. Every time the hostess handed him one he nodded gravely and said '*tack*'. That's the

Swedish for thank you. Apart from that, the journey was spent in restful silence.

Everyone knows that Swedes are serious-minded, hard-working and very gloomy – we've all seen those Ingmar Bergman films – so I had been confident that I would feel right at home among them. I was ill-prepared, therefore, to find the arrival hall at Gothenburg airport thronged with chatting, laughing people looking like extras in a Kodak ad in their brightly coloured summer clothes. Not one of them seemed an even half-decent candidate for suicide. Never mind, I thought, trying to cheer myself up; from what I had heard of Olivia's family, things were bound to darken.

'Your mother is doing all right,' Olivia assured me as soon as we had greeted each other. 'It's done her a power of good, you coming.'

'And she really has got concussion and a broken hip?' I asked as I pushed my trolley along the polished floor of the arrivals hall towards the exit.

'Really, Esther, I don't know what you mean. Why should poor Audrey have made something like this up? And there are such things as X-ray machines, even in this northern outpost.'

'I'm sorry,' I muttered. '*Tack, tack,*' I went on, to show willing. 'It was just that she was so keen for me to come with her . . . you know after this business with the opera house. She had this bee in her bonnet about bad blood and stuff.'

'She was keen, but not that keen, believe you me. She's in a great deal of pain.'

That really worried me. Some people withstood physical pain better than others. Audrey, most definitely, belonged to the 'others' group. 'Are we going straight to see her?'

Olivia nodded. 'The hospital is about half-way between here and the island.'

As she manoeuvred her dark-grey Volvo estate out of the car-park she asked, 'So how are you doing, in yourself? Audrey told me you have been having some problems.'

'I'm much better, thank you,' I said, shielding my eyes from the bright sunshine streaming through the windows of the car. 'I've been told to fight indecision at every turn. To embrace uncertainty and learn to accept that nothing is perfect, or even ordered.'

'Why, it sounds defeatist to me.'

'I have to, because otherwise, apparently, I will go mad. Or as we say in the trade, my anxieties will deepen.'

'Fair enough,' Olivia said, turning on to the motorway.

As I counted the lakes, three already in the first few miles of our journey, I thought that Olivia seldom argued, she just accepted that you had a right to your opinion. Audrey never kept up an argument for long, choosing instead to ignore your opinion until it went away. Neither of them had had a nervous breakdown. Perhaps there was a lesson in mental hygiene somewhere there.

'They are giving her pain relief?' I asked as we passed lake number four, just at the outskirts of town.

'Of course they are. Now don't fret so. Anyone would think you were fond of your mother. Now let me tell you who's staying at the moment. There's Linus and little Ivar. Bertil's Uncle Gerald and Gerald's daughter Kerstin, and Aunt Ulla, of course. Ulla is Astrid's, that's Bertil's first wife's, cousin. None of us quite knows how, but she sort of slipped into our summer holidays and now no one can shift her. Actually, someone should warn Ivar; you see, I have this theory that Ulla will outlive us all and end up being handed down through the generations like some cursed parrot. Anyway, they all speak excellent English, even Ivar. Bertil and I speak English between ourselves and we've spoken it to Ivar since he was born.'

'And you're sure that Linus is OK about my being here?'

'Oh, he's fine. He was dreadfully disappointed at first, still is, I suppose, about the cancellation of the project, but he's a very fair-minded man. He knows you were only doing what you thought right. And he knows how fond I am of your mother.'

'I'll keep out of his way,' I said. In the distance an old fort rose up on a hillock, guarding the entrance to the small town of Kungälv halfway up the wide, lazy river. We turned left off the motorway, following the signs to the hospital.

I hadn't realised that it was possible for a fat person to look as small as Audrey did, lying there in her hospital bed. It was odd, because the bed was narrow compared with her own at home; you would have thought she'd overflow like a cuckoo in the nest. Her head was bandaged and her right hip and thigh were set in plaster. At least she wasn't wearing one of those humiliating hospital gowns, but a striped yellow-and-white cotton night-dress, shaped like a long T-shirt. Still, it was nothing like her beloved négligés. Olivia said she had lent the night-dress to her: 'More suitable for a public ward, I thought.'

My mother raised a chubby hand and smiled weakly. 'Hello, Esther darling. You came.'

I bent down and kissed her dry cheek. Where was she, I thought, as I looked into her tired eyes. Where was the old bat from hell, my dear enemy? Gone. Replaced by this frail old lady. I blinked, worried that she'd notice the tears in my eyes.

'Don't look so worried, Esther,' my mother said. 'I'll be fine. Especially now you're here.' She patted the side of her bed for me to sit down. 'You take the chair, Olivia,' she added in passing. 'They made a huge fuss when they heard I hadn't been up, to speak of, for over two years. Apparently, you break easier.'

The pain-killers made her drowsy so we didn't stay long. I left, promising to take the bus in to see her the next day. We got back in the car and drove on out towards the island. Both windows were down, but it was still hot with the sun shining straight into the passenger side. I forced myself to stay awake, to take in the passing landscape. Now we had passed the town of Kungälv, the industrial estates that had lined the road gave way to fields and meadows, and isolated wooden houses painted mostly in a deep coppery red, and sometimes in the softest pastels, lemon-soufflé-yellows, heavenly-blue, baby-pink. We turned a sharp bend and Olivia's gold bangles clanged together as she changed gear. In my first memories of her a single bangle twinkled round her left wrist, but as the years went by they multiplied until they reached half-way to her elbow. I had always admired them, imagining a collection of my own, but strangely I had never bought even one. It was the same with kitchen gadgets. I had noticed how much easier life seemed for people who owned Magi-mixes and blenders, but somehow it never occurred to me to buy them for myself. Certain things, it seemed, one just didn't get oneself: gold bangles, Magimixes, true love.

'Not far now,' Olivia said. 'As we round the next bend, prepare yourself for a great sight.'

I did as I was told. I opened my eyes so wide that they were stung by the sun. And there before me lay the west-coast archipelago, a landscape that seemed to have been formed from an explosion scattering fragments of land across the thunder-blue sea. And taking centre stage was the island of Kilholmen.

Villa Rosengård: summer home of the Stendal family since the turn of the century; constructed from clapper-board like almost every building on the island, painted blue as a summer sky, sprawling at odd angles and with a turret rising from its eastern side. 'Here we are.' Olivia flung the gate open just as a hedgehog crossed our path. 'Only emergency vehicles and delivery vans drive on the island,' she said. 'So we're unusually blessed with hedgehogs.'

I stepped inside the gate, on to the immaculate gravel path, my shoulder aching from carrying the largest of my two cases up from the quay to the house.

'Bertil wanted to meet us at the ferry,' Olivia said, seeing the discomfort on my face, 'but I told him to go off to his golf.'

Golf? Where on this small and hilly granite island did Bertil play golf? Olivia read my thoughts. 'There's a golf course half an hour away, on the mainland.'

The gravel path leading up to the house was flanked on either side by raspberry-red roses. Creamy-white ones, even larger and more lustrous, grew in beds against the blue walls of the house. 'Roses don't seem to thrive anywhere else on the island. Hence the name of the house: Villa Rosengård. Not very original, but then the Stendal family has not been known for its flights of fancy, not until Linus that is. That man has enough flights of fancy to take him to the moon. Now, I've put you in the cottage. You'll have to share the bathroom with Ulla, I'm afraid.'

The cottage, sky-blue with white eaves, like the main house, lay half hidden behind a tall lilac hedge and the door stood open. As our footsteps crunched their way along the gravel path a small elderly woman with a grey pudding-basin haircut materialised like a sullen genie to stand before us, frowning, in the doorway.

'I thought I'd better be here when you arrived, so that I could tell you how we do things,' she called out in heavily accented English. 'The bathroom, for example.' The little woman disappeared inside again, but her voice was carried faintly towards me on the sea breeze.

'That was Ulla,' Olivia said, leading the way inside. 'You'd better join her. Get it over with.'

Ulla was waiting for me. 'I keep my things on the two top shelves and on the right-hand side of the bath taps. Anything blue will be mine: flannel, sponge, soap dish, tooth mug . . .'

'Toothbrush case,' I suggested helpfully.

'I never need one of those. My toothbrush is kept in the specially provided glass, and there it stays, waiting for my next visit, until I decide to remove it.'

'We haven't really met,' I mumbled as I followed Ulla out of the bathroom. 'I'm Esther Fisher. But then you probably knew that.'

Ulla gave me an impatient look over her shoulder. 'Of course you're Esther Fisher,' she snapped. 'Why else would I be showing you around my bathroom? You'll sleep in there,' Ulla continued, as she pointed towards the door across the small hallway.'

Olivia was already in the room. It was large, rectangular, with a window on the far wall. There were two beds, one on either side, both with brass headboards and white crocheted bedspreads. It was a room with an old-fashioned feel to it, dressed in faded rose-patterned paper, its window veiled in white lace. The white-painted floor-boards creaked as I walked up to the bed where Olivia had placed the case she had been carrying for me. 'I hope you'll be comfortable here?' she said.

'Oh, and there are two cans of air freshener in the bathroom,' Ulla announced as she disappeared out of the bedroom. 'Meadow Fresh and Woodland Breeze. I can only tolerate Woodland Breeze.'

'So that's everyone,' Bertil Stendal said, 'apart from Linus. But of course you've met already. Not the most auspicious circumstances, I think one could say, but you both did what you thought was right. Anyway, Linus is in town. Some urgent business he needed to attend to.' As he spoke, the expression on Bertil's handsome face changed from frosty polite, to frosty smiling.

He looked as if he was about to speak again when the child, Ivar, a flaxen-haired little boy with round blue eyes, said instead, 'Linus is my daddy,' before continuing to chat in his own peculiar mix of Swedish and English.

We were sitting in the glass-fronted veranda of the main house: Olivia, Bertil, Gerald, Kerstin, Ulla and Ivar. They were all very friendly, other than Ulla, of course, who behaved like a bear who'd just been told to be nice to Goldilocks. Still, I know what they must all have been thinking.

'I'm really sorry for having mucked up Linus's commission,' I blurted out.

'So why did you do it?' Ulla asked.

That wasn't the reply I was looking for. I turned to her and tried to explain. 'Firstly I was doing my job as a journalist. But also, I really do believe it would be wrong for two old people to lose the only home they've known because bigger interests are at stake. I felt, and still feel, that there's an important principle here. You can build an opera house somewhere else, but you can't shift your principles around. If you do, you render them worthless.'

'So why say you're sorry?' Ulla turned her pale-brown eyes on me.

'It's not that simple to move the site for the building,' Bertil said with a dry smile.

'Daddy met a lady,' Ivar squeaked. 'She's called Pernilla and she's got long yellow hair like a princess. We met her on the quayside and Daddy told me to run along home.' Ivar turned to me and explained, 'He meant Villa Rosengård home, not my home with Mummy, or my home with Daddy in Gothenburg. And then Pernilla . . .'

A glare from Ulla silenced him. 'You talk too much for a child,' she snapped.

Bertil said something in Swedish to her and Gerald added, 'Quite. You're a nasty old woman Ulla Andersson.'

Kerstin, Bertil's cousin, smiled at Ivar. She was a woman of about my age, of medium height and build, but somehow contriving to look like a child. Maybe it was her artless hair; mousey-blonde and cut in a severe bob, and with the fringe held back with a clip, a Minnie Mouse clip I noticed. Or her clothes: a pair of wide sky-blue shorts topped by a sweat-shirt decorated with pigs on skateboards. 'Ivar helped me carry the shopping earlier, all the way up the hill. You're a good boy, aren't you, Ivar?'

'I am a good boy,' Ivar confirmed in his fluting English. 'And when I'm grown-up I'll be a good girl.'

No one seemed willing to put him right on this. I was about to, myself, when I thought better of it. Putting people right can have devastating consequences. Just for example, this friend of Audrey's, Connie Jenkins, had believed that her husband worshipped the ground she walked on, until her sister put her right. The sister told Connie that her husband also worshipped prostitutes carrying truncheons. Poor Connie had killed herself. No, you should always think twice before putting people right.

'I remember Pernilla from Linus's schooldays,' Bertil said. 'Pretty girl, always laughing, forever up to some mischief.'

I had known girls like that at school. I generally wanted to hit them. In fact, I did once hit just such a pretty, laughing, full-of-mischief girl. This one was called Melissa and she had painted 'sunny' faces all over the pages of my new exercise book. I loved my exercise books, especially new ones. Opening the first page was like starting a day full of possibilities. Now Melissa had gone and ruined it. Worst of all, our teacher, Miss Sims, had laughed and said that Esther could sure do with some 'sunny' faces. Later, in the playground I walked up to Melissa and punched her on the nose. When it swelled up and turned red, I laughed and said Melissa could do with a swollen face. I was suspended for two weeks. I had thought it very unfair at the time; my new exercise book, the one I'd have to keep for weeks and weeks before it was filled and I could get another one, was ruined, but Melissa's swollen nose had gone back to normal in a couple of days.

Around me the conversation had tailed off. Ivar was busy plaiting the tassels on the woven rug that covered most of the wooden floor. A fly buzzed round the sun-drenched ceiling, before making for the open glass doors, and from his rocking chair Gerald, who had been dozing most of the time, farted a small smattering fanfare. Kerstin broke into a hearty rendering of some Swedish hymn and Ivar, glancing up from his plaiting, joined in with his squeaky soprano.

We ate our dinner in the garden. In Sweden people eat early, around six for everyday, but we stayed outside, talking and drinking coffee until past nine o'clock. The sun was still high in the sky, but the breeze from the sea was chilly, sending us inside, one by one, for sweaters and shawls. Ivar had gone to bed, cross and disappointed because his father had called to say he was held up with work and wasn't coming home until way after Ivar's bedtime. 'Stupid silly old houses.' He pouted, bashing at the low branch of the apple tree overhead with a small clenched fist.

'Let's have a game of croquet,' Gerald said, leaping up from his chair with surprising agility. There was a moment of breathless silence while we all waited for the fanfare of farts. It didn't come and the conversation resumed. Within minutes he was back, carrying a set of croquet mallets and balls. The hoops were already in place around the side where the old kitchen garden had once been. They seemed to play the game differently in Sweden, and both Gerald and Ulla cheated, edging their balls closer to a hoop or a competitor with the toes of their shoes when they thought no one was looking. Personally I didn't see the point of playing if you were going to cheat, but no one else seemed to mind.

'Villa Rosengård rules, OK.' Olivia smiled at me. By ten thirty we gave up trying to distinguish red from green in the fading light and packed up. Before going off to my own room I phoned the hospital. My mother was comfortable and fast asleep, they assured me.

I was about to go to bed when there was a knock on the door and it was flung open. It was Ulla, garbed in a long white night-dress and with her pudding-basin hair clipped back from her face with Kirby grips. 'I always hang the lavatory paper loose end out,' she said and was gone.

I opened the window and rolled down the blind. I felt lonely. The dark of the night seemed to have driven all the lightness from my mind and turned me morbid and homesick, filled with vague unease. So what? I thought. The lightness had been false anyway, it was borrowed, belonging to people like Posy and, by the sound of things, to the ever-laughing Pernilla. I was better off keeping it at arm's length, treating it with the utmost suspicion, in case I should get used to it and mourn its inevitable passing. To make myself feel better I mumbled all Ulla's rules: 'loo paper loose end out, Woodland Breeze, not Meadow Fresh. Blue for Ulla. Right-hand side of tap . . .' I drifted off to sleep.

I woke the next morning to the sound of gulls screeching and with the sun shining through the white blind. I rolled over and reached for my watch that lay on the bedside table. It was half past five. With a groan I turned on to my stomach and tried to go back to sleep, but the sun and the soft breeze reaching me through the open window beckoned me outside. I slipped into the bathroom and washed in the basin, turning the taps on to just a dribble so as not to wake Ulla. I dressed in a long flowery cotton dress, a Posy dress. She had nagged me to buy it just before I left and it was surprisingly comfortable. I slipped a brown cotton cardigan on top against the wind and against the prettiness of the frock.

As I wandered down the street towards the harbour a hedgehog rattled past, busy, purposeful, blissfully unaware that such bold behaviour would lead to instant squelching anywhere else than on this small island. I reached the harbour as the ferry was about to depart with a handful of commuters. At least I assumed they were commuters, with their formal attire and pale faces. Everyone else on the island was tanned and dressed in those same colourful cotton clothes the Swedes in summer seemed so fond of. I looked at my watch, six o'clock. I turned right, continuing my walk along the harbour towards the eastern point of the island. The sea was calm, and the sun, high in the sky, had turned it into a sheet of glittering foil. It was quite warm and quieter than anywhere I had been for a long time. Pastel-coloured wooden houses lined the quayside, the small gardens sporting nothing much more than a lawn and some shrubs. But almost every house had a glass-enclosed veranda, its windows pointing towards the sea like a large Cyclops eye. A young couple came towards me, hand in hand: lovers, they looked to me as if they had spent the night on the rocks. I smiled in a passing greeting, but they had obviously spotted me as the Antichrist of romance that I was and turned away. Either that or my smile wasn't as pleasant as I thought it was.

I rounded the corner by the old fort which, according to Olivia, guarded the harbour inlet from marauding Norwegians. 'Still?' I had asked.

Olivia had looked gravely at me. 'You never know with Norwegians,' she said. I assumed she was joking.

Here the harbour ended and the granite cliffs took over. I felt as if I was alone at the edge of the world as I faced the open sea and watched the waves crash and break against the rocks. But I was not alone. In the distance I spotted the figure of a man walking down towards the sea from the path ahead, pulling off his shirt as he went. As he reached the cliff's edge he stripped completely until he stood naked in the morning sun. I thought of turning the other way, but he looked so good where he stood, back arched, arms raised high above his head, that I stopped and stared instead. He kicked up his heels and dived, hitting the water almost soundlessly, slicing through the sea leaving only a scattering of droplets to rise in the air.

# Chapter Seventeen

The hospital informed me, over the phone, that my mother had passed a comfortable night. That's how the ward sister put it in her careful English. 'She's passed a comfortable night.'

I had this image of Audrey in the lavatory, passing a night, like a long black fluttering wimple. But I said, 'Could you tell her I'll be in to see her this afternoon.'

I went to sit under the apple tree, a cup of coffee at my side and my laptop on my knee, and tried to write a story for *New Romance*.

A while later, half an hour maybe, I heard my name called and looked up to find Linus coming towards me across the tall grass of the rough-cut lawn. 'I'm sorry about your mother,' he said, sitting down on the grass next to my deck-chair. 'But she's going to be all right, I think.'

'You can't be very happy having me here after what happened with the opera house.'

Linus jabbed his right index finger into a bald spot on the lawn. 'It's fine,' he said, looking down at his soiled finger. 'You did your job.' He looked up at me, squinting against the sun. 'And maybe you have a point. Maybe it was morally wrong. I've railed against that kind of thing myself in the past. The rights of the little man, all that.' He didn't sound as if he was really connected with his own words, I thought. More as if he had picked them up where someone else had left them, thinking they would do as well as any.

'Thank you,' I said. He got up from the ground and brushed down the seat of his trousers, his hand following the curve of his buttocks.

'Were you out on the rocks earlier, swimming?' I asked.

'Yeah, I was.'

'I saw you there. Well, actually, I wasn't sure it was you then.'

Linus looked at me and laughed, that high-pitched giggle of a laugh that bubbled from his firm lips like a tasteless joke.

'I met Ivar,' I said.

Mercifully, he stopped laughing and smiled instead. 'Ah yes, Ivar.'

'He seems a great little kid.'

'The best,' Linus said simply. 'Work?' He nodded at the laptop. Without waiting for a reply he went on, 'I'll leave you to it.' I watched him walk off towards the house. He walked well, with long strides and his legs close together. He didn't amble or waddle, but raised himself slightly on the balls of the feet with each step. For once, I thought, I had no quarrel with God. It had been a kind thing to give such a beautiful man such an utterly ridiculous laugh, thus rendering him safe. I shot a grateful glance up at the heavens before getting back, once more, to work.

I had all but finished the first rough draft of my story, an everyday tale of a thoroughly nice woman being utterly betrayed by a spineless, opportunistic git who wasn't called Angus, when Olivia called me from the terrace.

'It's going to be fine all day,' she said as I approached. 'I've just heard the forecast. It's the perfect day for an excursion.'

An excursion, I soon found out, meant leaving the island, by boat, for an even smaller island, more of a rock, in fact. You brought a picnic (Linus was sent to buy fresh bread and cinnamon buns from the bakery by the harbour) and your bathing costume and a book, and then . . . then, you sat there.

We had arrived, all of us, and successfully disembarked from the little boat. The others were all bustling around, unpacking bathing costumes, searching for suntan lotions, for the most sheltered spot away from the cool breeze.

'It's a bit hard,' I said, looking around for some soft sand, a little piece of grass, a rubber mattress, anything to protect my behind from the hard, ridged granite.

'Of course it's hard,' Olivia agreed. 'What do you expect a rock to be?'

Bertil was in the water, swimming round the white hull of their old fisherman's boat, with a large mop to wash off the smudgy tide-mark. Linus had wandered off crabbing with Ivar. Ulla had picked what seemed to be the only smooth flat part of the whole little island and was busy spreading out her green-and-brown striped beach towel. Next to the towel she placed a voluminous canvas bag out of which she hauled a novel by Selma Lagerlöf. Kerstin, perching on a ledge above, was already reading, something on jogging, I guessed from the title of the yellow-and-blue paperback on her knee.

'Have a swim,' Olivia said as she herself stretched out on the rock right below me. 'The water looks lovely.'

I know it *looked* lovely. It's what it *felt* like that worried me; this, after all, was the North Sea. A North Sea dressed up in the bright blue and turquoise of some Mediterranean temptress, maybe, but I wasn't fooled. 'It's cold.'

'What do you expect?' Olivia said once more. 'It's the sea.'

'I can't help feeling that my body is the temperature it is – about thirty-seven centigrade – for a reason. Chilling it down drastically can't be very healthy.'

'It's very healthy,' Kerstin called from her outpost. 'It's clinically proven that immersing your body in cold water once a day promotes health and long life.'

Clinically proven by whom? I wanted to ask. And where? A clinic for the insane? A clinic for the long-term masochistic? 'Just for today I think I'll pass,' I said. 'Even if it does mean drastically reducing my lifespan.' The bumble-bee drone of a small engine made me turn back towards the sea. A small outboard was speeding towards us, a blonde woman at the helm.

'Over here, Pernilla.' Linus appeared around the western side of the little island, Ivar in tow. 'Tie up alongside us.' The woman waved back with her free hand as she steered confidently towards the Stendals' boat. She manoeuvred alongside, throwing a rope to Linus who had put down the bucket with crabs and scrambled down the rock to help her. She was light on her feet, this Pernilla, I thought. It was obvious from the way she leapt ashore, steadying herself only slightly against the hand proffered by Linus as her feet in their white canvas shoes touched down square on the rock. Like a game-show contestant she looked up and grinned at us all, giving a small triumphant wave as she tossed her fair hair.

'This is Pernilla,' Linus announced.

'We gathered,' Ulla muttered. She wasn't all bad, Ulla. Introductions were made and the picnic was unpacked. Apart from the sandwiches – I had already gathered that they were big on sandwiches in Sweden – and the cinnamon buns, there were thermos flasks of coffee, but no milk or sugar. 'No one in our family takes milk or sugar,' Ulla commented when I asked for some. She pronounced '*our* family' looking as if she were tasting chocolate ice-cream.

Pernilla flung herself down on the hard rock, she didn't even wince, and grabbed the sandwich that Linus handed her. 'So.' She turned to me. 'This is your first visit to Sweden?'

I had been waiting for that question. 'No,' I said.

I felt everyone's eyes on me, surprised. 'You've been here before?' Olivia exclaimed. 'And you never told us.'

Bertil had emerged from the water and now he was rubbing himself down with a much too small blue towel. 'You should have let us know you were coming. We're all very fond of your mother, you know.'

'Obviously these things don't matter to Esther in the same way as they do to us,' Ulla said.

Linus had been busy drying off Ivar who had fallen into the water. 'Esther did let us know she was coming.'

'No, no,' Kerstin contradicted. 'She didn't let us know she was coming *last* time.'

'What last time?'

This was getting out of hand. 'I haven't been to Sweden before,' I said rather quietly.

'But you just said you had.' Pernilla rolled her eyes at Linus. 'I said, "This is your first visit to Sweden?" and you said, "No."'

I squinted up at the sky. A gull circled overhead, its eyes on the crabs in the yellow bucket, no doubt. 'It was a joke,' I said even more quietly, as the gull suddenly swooped, settling a foot or so from the bucket and edging towards it with an awkward gait. Its round black eyes were fixed on the bucket and Ivar's big round blue ones were fixed on the gull. I lit a cigarette and passed the packet to Linus.

'Not a very funny joke, if I may say so.' Ulla poured herself another cup of coffee. 'English humour,' she added. The gull flapped its wings and Ivar let out a piercing scream. 'It bit me! It bit my toe, look!' The gull took flight as Linus rushed forward, but he was soon back again, flapping around close to the bucket. Ivar held up his foot and a few drops of blood fell to the ground, flecking the granite rust-red. Linus gave him a quick hug before turning to the gull and waving his long arms. 'Get away with you! Shove off. Off I said.' The gull hopped back a couple of steps before resuming his bucket vigil. 'Off.' Linus kicked out at the bird who, finally and with a contemptuous look over his right wing, took lazy flight. 'I'm only leaving because I want to,' it seemed to say. 'Not because *you* told me to.'

Ivar was sobbing and rubbing at his toe. 'Dip it in the water,' Olivia said. She got up and took Ivar's hand, leading him down to the water's edge.

'What a drama.' Pernilla gave a lazy little laugh. She turned to me. 'Anyway, you're here and it's a lovely, perfect day, and that's all that matters.' She lay down on the bare rock and the sun turned the tiny hairs on her tanned arms gold. Linus sat down next to her, gazing admiringly at her, and even Ivar seemed to have forgotten his injury and was charmed.

'Do you want to look at my crabs?' He stood by her side holding the yellow bucket out for her inspection. Pernilla opened her eyes and sat up, resting on her elbows. 'Lovely,' she said. 'Really good crabs.'

For a while all was peace. Bertil, Olivia, Ulla and Kerstin read their books. Ivar watched over his crabs, Linus watched over the sleeping Pernilla. I sat wishing she would snore.

'You have a very nasty jealous streak in you,' my father had told me once after I had trimmed his little god-daughter's eyelashes.

'I thought they were too heavy,' I had protested. 'I thought that's why she keeps falling asleep all the time.' The explanation had not convinced anyone.

The breeze from the water grew stronger and I reached for my cotton sweater, draping it across my shoulders. I looked around at them all, so contented. Ivar had pottered down to the edge of the water and was busy chucking stones at a jellyfish. Someone was snoring, but it was Kerstin, not Pernilla. There had to be a trick to this island-sitting, but for now it eluded me. I tried to lie down, a sharp piece of rock cut into my back. I turned on my side, supporting myself on my elbow. That was no better. I sat back up again and picked out a notebook. Maybe I should begin a diary. I should have started one at the time of my breakdown, charting my road to recovery.

Bertil put down his book. 'Linus,' he said. 'Olivia and I have been talking about selling up, buying something in France. What do you think? It's always been a bit of a dream of ours.' He turned to Olivia and smiled. There was an audible intake of breath from Ulla. She too had put down her book. 'We'd keep a *pied-à-terre* in town, but that would be all we'd need.'

Linus was quiet for a moment, then he said, 'If that's what you both want, of course you must do it. I'd buy Villa Rosengård from you, but it's too big for just me and Ivar, and I'd never get the time to spend out here to make it worthwhile. You'll find a buyer easily enough, though. No, go for it. Ivar and I'd miss the old place, but we'll live.'

A small choking sound made me turn round. Ulla was sitting bolt upright, staring at Bertil. She looked like someone who had just been served their pet dog for lunch. 'You're not serious,' she said finally. 'You can't sell Rosengård. It's been in the family for generations. Astrid loved this place. It's hers. You can't sell.'

'I know how you must feel,' Olivia said. What was meant to follow that particular phrase but never did, was *But actually I don't really care.* Instead, Olivia looked concerned. 'It's not an easy step to take, but you only have one life. And as we said, this is something Bertil and I have wanted to do for a very long time. We've got friends over there. We love the food and the people, and the climate will do Bertil's arthritis the world of good.'

'I didn't know you had arthritis,' Kerstin said.

Pernilla had woken up. 'My father had arthritis and I tell you, moving to Spain, getting away from the cold, was the best thing he ever did.' The conversation turned into a medical one and then, when Ivar fell into the water for a second time, it was decided that we should pack up and go back home. Ulla seemed her usual self as we bounced through the choppy sea, but as she lifted her binoculars to study a sea-bird on a buoy I noticed that her hands were shaking.

## Chapter Eighteen

It had rained all day and it was raining still when I left for the hospital. My mother was mending, but it was a slow process. The lack of any exercise (and as I told her, lying on her back and lifting one leg very slowly, then rolling her ankles a few times before repeating the procedure with the other leg, did not count) had made the healing process more complicated, just as it had weakened her bones.

'I'm an old woman,' Audrey stated, 'and old women have weak bones.'

'Old women who sit around in bed all day have especially weak ones,' I chided. 'So don't make excuses.' Sometimes I found the cruel-to-be-kind bit the ward sister had told me about a little too easy. But the hospital still believed that she would be fit enough to be discharged by the weekend.

'I'd better think about getting back to London,' I said. But Audrey begged me to stay on a while longer and I promised to think about it. 'It depends what Olivia feels,' I added. But it was true that I had nothing much to get back to London for. Work didn't start until late August and Posy was looking after the house.

'I know Olivia wants you to stay,' Audrey said. She was sitting up, although her thigh was still in plaster right up to the hip. 'I can't expect her to nurse me. But you are my daughter, after all.'

'Now you admit to it. But I will stay, as long as that's what Olivia wants.'

Back at Villa Rosengård I found Olivia in the kitchen, perched on top of step-ladder, a paintbrush in her hand, squinting at a kitchen cupboard. She turned and smiled at me. 'Audrey all right? I must visit tomorrow.'

'They're thinking of discharging her at the weekend. The problem is, she's not fit to travel back to England yet. Are you sure it's all right for her to stay with you?'

'Of course it's all right. Your mother is my oldest and dearest friend.'

'Would you like me to stay on and help look after her, or is that more trouble than it's worth?'

'We're counting on it. I know I said Audrey is my dearest friend, but that doesn't mean I want to spend my holiday nursing her. I bet she's a shocking patient.'

'Shocking,' I agreed.

Olivia turned her attention back to the cupboard door. 'It needs something.'

I gazed at the white surface. 'Roses.'

'Roses?'

'You should paint a yellow rosebush all across it.' I paused, my head a little to one side, thinking. 'And while you're at it, I'd paint them on the walls of the veranda too.'

Olivia turned and looked sharply at me. 'What makes you say that?'

'Innate bad taste, I expect,' I said airily. Then I saw that she was serious. I shrugged. 'I don't really know. The name of the house, I suppose. Villa Rosengård. Or just a feeling.' I shrugged again.

'When Astrid, Linus's mother, lived here, she papered the veranda with pictures of roses she had cut out from books and catalogues, every inch of wall, apparently. Bertil removed it all after she . . . after she died.'

'What did she look like, Astrid?' I asked. 'Is there a photo somewhere?'

'Linus has a couple. He was only tiny when she died, poor little mite.'

'So what happened? What did she die from?'

Olivia climbed down from the step-ladder and went across to the sink to pour herself a glass of water. With her back turned to me she said, 'I'm not quite sure. Some accident. It's all a very long time ago.'

'Ulla says she adored this place.'

'I expect she did.' Olivia made it clear that she wasn't going to pursue the subject. I walked out on to the veranda and stood there for a moment, trying to imagine it in Astrid's day, when the walls were covered with paper roses.

At lunch, in the kitchen the following day, I sat next to Linus. 'Why is the Lloyd commission so important to you?' I asked him. 'From what I hear you're very successful. You've won prizes, for heaven's sake. You're earning lots of money. I'm the one with the problem. I've just got my old job back, minus some pay and status and freedom. I've never been married and I have no children. I'm the one who should be desperate. I'm thirty-four years old and sometimes I feel as if I've spent my life reading the instructions upside down.' I regretted saying it all as soon as I had spoken because, put like that, it really depressed me. And Linus didn't seem to disagree with anything I'd said, which depressed me even more. What's the point of being self-deprecating if no one disagrees with you?

Then he smiled. 'Can't I be desperate too?' He fixed his dark-grey eyes on me. 'You know, I've yet to see a building I've designed that I'm proud of. I spend my life creating what I know is second-best in order to get the work you're speaking of. Have you any idea, any idea at all what it feels like being forced, over and over again, to create second-rate work when you know you can do first-rate? I tell you.' He hadn't raised his voice but he spoke each word with such emphasis that he might as well have been shouting. 'Sometimes I think it will kill me.'

Then he smiled again, straight at me, eyeball to eyeball, and I found myself smiling back idiotically.

'Pernilla gets very impatient with me,' he went on. 'She never whinges. She says that only privileged people have time to worry about things like that. Try being a single mother on inadequate state support, or terminally ill. She says I'd soon stop worrying about whether or not a building was good, bad or great. She's right, of course. You know, I think that's what I admire most about her. Her life hasn't been easy, but she never wastes time complaining. Instead, she's got this amazing ability to make the most of everything, of living entirely in the present. She never spends a moment on regrets.'

My smile stiffened, then cracked. 'How lovely,' I said. 'But I don't actually agree with her. If you were a single mother architect living on the breadline, you might have other and pressing needs, but I still think you'd worry about some of the same things that bother you now. It's not just a luxury, reserved for the privileged few, it's universally human, in my view. In fact, it's what makes us human. I've interviewed people who've been through the most horrendous experiences and all the while they'd still care about a line of a drawing or a word in a poem, or the state of their hair for that matter. It seems to have been what kept them sane, alive even. Other animals content themselves with survival. A lion who's eaten well and who has shelter from the hot sun lies down to sleep. He doesn't dash about with renewed vigour thinking up how to improve on raw impala or, for that matter, how to build himself a really aesthetically pleasing den. Human beings never rest at the level of survival, or even comfort. We strive on. That's what makes us human.'

Ulla was addressing me in her precise and accented English: 'I'm telling Olivia that she'll miss this place more than she imagines.' She wagged her finger in Linus's direction. 'This place is in your blood, Linus. This was your poor mother's home. You must see that it's a bad decision, selling. Astrid loved this place. How can you even think of letting strangers take over?' She went on about dirty French beaches, syringes in the sand, condoms floating on the waves. 'And what about Ivar?' But Linus wasn't listening any more. He was staring straight in front of him, past Ulla's right shoulder and out at the garden. His cheeks had turned bright pink.

'I know what a condom is,' Ivar said. Today he was wearing pale-blue shorts, a blue-and-green striped T-shirt and a straw hat decorated with daisies and forget-me-nots. 'But I'm afraid I can't tell anyone, because it's rude.'

At the sound of his son's voice Linus had turned round. 'It's not rude, little man. It's very useful sometimes.'

'But Mummy says . . .' Ivar looked confused.

Linus sighed. 'Well if Mummy says . . .'

'Don't be so weak, Linus.' Ulla glared at him.

'Well, we'll just have to visit Ivar, if Ivar can't visit us,' Olivia said. 'Bertil and I are looking forward to the change, especially the weather, condoms or no condoms. Anyway, we only want a very small place. Of course you're all welcome to come, but we want something that suits *us*. Something we can just up and leave if we want to travel. Something that doesn't require much upkeep. We're not young and this place is becoming a burden, not least financially.'

'It makes sense to me.' Linus smiled at her, then he turned back to me. 'I have to admire Pernilla,' he went on, obviously not realising when he'd lost the sympathy of his audience. 'She's not had an easy life.' That perked me up a bit. 'Her first husband was a notorious philanderer. Everyone knew of his affairs, but she stuck by him. The second one – her divorce has just come through – was abusive, not physically, but mentally. He too had affairs. As if that's not enough, she lost her job and her boy-friend, who was also her boss, both at once. Still she manages to be positive and full of enthusiasm. She's a real inspiration, an example to us all.'

I nodded. I suppose she was. But of what, exactly? Courage? Attitude? An inability to learn from past mistakes? But I said nothing. Audrey had always told me that men found envy and spite very unattractive in a woman. Until now I hadn't cared and I always felt that envy and spite were things I did rather well. But now it was different. I wanted to please and the feeling confused me.

'Anyway,' Olivia was saying, 'we might not go that far south. Normandy is lovely.'

Next to me, Linus was still prattling on about Pernilla. 'I feel, well pale, compared with her,' he said.

I looked at him and heard myself simper, 'But you're not pale. You've got a lovely tan.' A look of impatience crossed his face and I could have bitten my tongue off. 'Of course I know that's not what you meant,' I added hastily. Inside I was one big complaint. *I* wanted to be an inspiration. *I* wanted yellow hair to toss and a brave, sunny attitude. Why couldn't I be light-hearted, damn it? Instead I sat there, dark of hair and dark of mind, inside my own little cloud of envy where no amount of Swedish summer sun could reach, longing . . . for what? His approval?

'You've got a very peculiar expression on your face again, Esther,' Olivia said. 'What on earth were you thinking of?'

'Love.' It was out before I could stop myself.

'Oh dear,' Olivia said. 'Oh dear, oh dear.'

'I did tell you that my side was to the right of the bath taps, didn't I?' Ulla asked in a voice with a silky top note but with a sharp undertone, like cheap scent. I looked questioningly at her. 'I thought I saw your flannel on my side,' Ulla explained. She sounded as if she was determined to be patient whatever the provocation.

Fuck your side, I wanted to say. But I had manners. Suddenly I realised that I really cared what these people thought of me, even Ulla. I actually wanted them to like me and to like having me there. 'I'll remove it,' I said, getting up from the table, bringing my empty plate across to the sink.

'Don't be so petty, Ulla,' Olivia scolded.

'You haven't had your coffee.' Linus put his hand out towards me. I looked at it, an artist's hand, long-fingered and strong. 'It's all right,' I said. 'I have to do some reading, anyway.'

'Work?'

I shook my head. 'Just reading.'

'But you have to do it?'

I nodded. 'That's right.'

'Why?' He didn't sound argumentative, just as if he really wanted to know.

'Because I have to. We have one miserable life . . .'

'There I don't agree with you,' Gerald put in. 'I've made a lifelong study of the theories of an afterlife, including reincarnation, and for every year that goes by I get more certain that there is one, an afterlife, that is.'

'For every year that brings you nearer to death you believe in an afterlife, you mean,' Ulla said. 'Anyway, people always assume they'll come back as something worthwhile. But why should they? You might turn out to be a dung-beetle or a fly. Personally, I'd rather stay in my grave than risk returning as something ghastly.'

'You don't have to worry on that score,' Gerald said. 'You never come back as the same thing twice.'

'Has anyone ever told you that you're a deeply unpleasant old man?' Ulla glared at him. The two of them continued their argument in Swedish.

'When I first came here,' Olivia said, 'I used to think how funny it was that everything spoken in Swedish sounded like an argument. Then I realised that in this family it was.'

'That's a little unfair, don't you think?' Bertil protested.

Ivar informed us that it had stopped raining and was now a Perfect Day. 'You should never waste a Perfect Day,' he told no one in particular. No one in particular ignored him.

'I just feel that whatever happens, my chances of returning as something even remotely literate are extremely small,' I ventured. 'I just can't bear to think of the tons of books I will never have read, the places I won't know about, the music I haven't heard, the knowledge that will have passed me by. I don't know why we are here. Who does? But I do know that while I am, I might as well learn as much I can. How else can one even begin to hope to make sense of anything? Once I've saved up some money I'll start to travel. In the meantime, reading and looking at pictures and snooping around other people's minds will have to do.'

'I just want to build good buildings,' Linus said. 'Actually, I want to build great ones.'

'And I stopped you?'

Linus looked up at me with a small smile. 'I didn't say that.'

I exited through the back door to the sound of coffee cups clinking and Ivar chatting on about it being a Perfect Day.

I was sitting by the open window in my room, reading a book on European history, when there was a knock on the door. It was Linus. I put it down, hoping he hadn't come to talk about the fair, the moon-spun Pernilla because, quite frankly, the mere mention of her name made this tight little ball form in my chest. For a moment I wondered if that tight little ball could be my missing heart, but I quickly dismissed the idea. It was jealousy, more like. My stomach simply couldn't digest it. Heartburn, that was it.

Linus had been on his way to sit down in the small white-painted chair by the dressing-table, but instead he straightened up again and turned back towards the door. 'I'm disturbing you, I'm sorry.'

'No, not at all. Sit down, please.' He did as I had asked, legs crossed, leaning back, relaxed. 'I'm just in a bit of a mood,' I explained. 'I often am.'

Linus smiled politely. 'Really, I never would have guessed.'

For a moment, there, I felt pleased. Maybe the step was shorter than I thought to me being described as an inspiration. Then Linus laughed. That figured. He had been joking. And as usual, the sound of his laughter brought everyone, including Linus himself, to stunned silence.

'Olivia asked me to give you a lift to town tomorrow to pick Audrey up,' he said eventually. 'I have to go in to Gothenburg in the morning, I'm meeting a prospective client from Japan and I want to get a little something for Pernilla's birthday. Foreigners don't quite understand the Swedish habit of emptying every office and factory for five weeks of the summer. Anyway, if you'd like to take the opportunity to look around town, we can go and pick up Audrey on our way back. Four o'clock they said, is that right?'

I nodded. 'Thanks, I'd love to have a look around. Gothenburg, city of canals and shipyards, of ancient families cursed with syphilis, of sky-blue trams and of the heavy beating of metal from the shipyards.'

Linus looked at me, eyebrows raised. 'Where did that come from?'

I smiled. 'I used to listen in to Olivia and Audrey chatting. I would curl up in this old chair and nine times out of ten they'd forget I was there.' He still had that question mark in his eyes so I added, 'I might have imagined some of it. You know how it is when you're a child?'

I watched him leave my room and it seemed my good humour went with him, padding along at his heels. At the door, it turned and grinned: Sucker!

# Chapter Nineteen

It had rained again during the night, but by the time I got up it had stopped and the sun was breaking through the clouds, mixing gold with the thunder-grey of the sky. I walked straight out on to the lawn in just my night-dress, my pale-blue-and-white embroidered night-dress. It was a very pretty and expensive night-dress. I might be turned out, during the day, like the prince of darkness's younger sister, but at night I chose to look like the daughter my mother had always wanted. Goodness knows why . . .

The grass was dew-soaked, wet beneath my feet. There was the lightest of breezes from the sea, gently stirring the yellow-and-blue wimple hoisted on the tall flag-pole, and overhead a gull circled, opening its greedy beak to squawk, telling me it was there and watching. (The other day I had made the mistake of peeling the prawns for supper outside in the garden and the gulls had not forgotten.) Otherwise all was still; it was only seven o'clock. I was about to go back to my room to shower and dress when my eye was caught by the sight of a bony behind in cornflower-blue cotton jersey, bent over the bed of moon-white roses: Ulla. I wandered up to her and said good-morning. She raised herself slowly and, wiping her stubby grey fringe from her eyes, she smiled at me. Smiled!

'Astrid planted these,' she said, and her voice held a softness that I had not heard before, caressing the edges of the name. 'She had them brought over from Germany. She spent two years searching for the perfect white rose. Astrid was a true artist. Olivia tries, but Astrid was an aesthete to the very marrow of her being. Linus has something of that.'

'How did she die? Was it a car crash?'

'Why should it have been? She killed herself. Didn't you know?'

'Jesus! Why?'

'I don't know that that's any of your business,' Ulla said, crouching down over the rose bed once more.

Olivia was in the kitchen making lemonade. Her thick dark hair had worked loose from the knot at the back and fell heavy across her face as she forced a lemon half down the white plastic ridges of the juicer. By her side, on the white worktop, lay a weeping pile of squeezed-out lemon halves. I gathered them up and chucked them in the bin. She turned and smiled at me. 'You don't mind helping yourself to breakfast? You know where everything is.'

I brought out the pale syrupy bread from the wooden bread bin and cut myself two thick slices. I spread them with margarine and cut some cheese for one of the slices and some smoked sausage for the other. I ate them at the kitchen table while I leafed through the local paper, trying to decipher the headlines. But I kept thinking about what Ulla had told me. In the end I just had to ask. 'Did Linus's mother really kill herself?'

'Who told you? Not Linus? He never talks about it.'

'Ulla.'

'Ulla? I'm surprised. The whole family treats what happened as a shameful secret. I had been married for a year before I found out, and I mean found out. None of them actually told me. At the time it happened, of course, the whole of Gothenburg was talking about it, but I was living in Stockholm then.'

'So what did happen?'

'Look, Esther. I really don't think it's for me to tell you. If Linus or Bertil chooses to speak of it, that's another matter. Even Ulla, although she's the cagiest one of all normally. Now.' She smiled a brisk, 'all's well with the world if you just don't look too hard' smile. 'You have a nice day in town. I suggest you go to the art museum; there're some lovely things there. And do look at the still life by Erik Johnsson in room fourteen. It used to belong to the Stendals, then Bertil's father sold it to pay for him and Bertil's mother to go for a week to Paris. It's worth an absolute fortune nowadays. Oh, and tell Audrey that we're all set to receive her.'

In the car on the way to town I kept glancing at Linus, trying to summon up the courage to ask him straight out about his mother. *Although a very good student, Esther displays a morbid fascination with*

221

*death and disease that is rather worrying in one so young,* one of my first school reports had read. Well, I wasn't so young any more but otherwise I hadn't changed.

'Do you look like your mother?' I tried feebly. 'I only ask because you don't really look much like your father, not facially at any rate.'

'I'm supposed to look like her.' A lorry rumbled down the opposite carriageway of the narrow coastal road. As it roared towards us, looking as if it were going to run straight into us, I ducked. I always did that. 'Reflex,' I muttered, feeling silly.

'What is?'

'Ducking inside a car when something whizzes towards you, like a bird, or a stone, or another car.'

'Aha.'

'Are you like your mother in temperament?'

'I don't really know. I don't remember her much.' Linus's voice was polite, but the politeness was stretched thinly across something hard and determined, a resistance to speak. Alas, I knew it well, that kind of resistance. In my job you learn to recognise it and to leave well alone; for the moment. We drove on in silence. After a while Linus said, 'You must go to the art museum.'

'Olivia said.'

'I'll drop you there if you like, then I'll pick you up on my way from the office and we can have some lunch.'

'You know, it's very kind of you, putting up with me after everything that's happened,' I said. 'I'm surprised you don't hate me.'

'Well, I don't.' The answer came a little too quickly, as if he had thought about it a lot.

Later, as we drove into town, he told me his mother had been an opera singer. 'She wasn't brilliant or anything.' He gave a little smile. 'Her voice wasn't strong enough for the big stuff, so I've been told, but it was exceptionally sweet and she cared about her music. Passionately. That's one of the reasons I wanted to build the opera house. In my mind, it was my tribute to her.'

'Make me feel really good, why don't you?'

'Don't be silly. As I said, you did what you had to do. It's no point fretting about it. Either you believe that the right of those two old people to remain in their home is paramount, or you don't. I assume you do, or you wouldn't have done what you did. So, nothing I've just said should change that.'

I looked at his profile, long eyelashes, straight nose; not too big, not too small, firm chin, but a surprising softness about the lips. The tip of my index finger wanted to stroke his cheek and the corner of his mouth, but I told it not to be so silly. Instead I thought how right he was, about being certain and not being swayed by others. It was just that kind of certainty I so desperately needed in my life. I decided that this was not the time to confide to him that I was yet to find it and that I had been instrumental in wrecking the most important commission of his career because I *thought* I might be right. There were times when you just had to keep your doubts to yourself.

I looked out of the window, humming a little ditty to myself. When I first arrived, Olivia had bypassed the town centre, driving straight out on to the motorway. This was my first view of the city centre.

'It's kind of ugly.' We crossed a wide, tree-lined avenue and turned left up a hill. 'That's better.' I pointed up at a row of turn-of-the-century apartment buildings. 'You know it worries me that I always like everything old when it comes to buildings. It shouldn't be like that. Architecture, like all creative disciplines, needs to move forward and not just imitate what's gone before. We all know that and yet we all, and by all I mean non-architects, admire the old and wrinkle our noses at most of the new. Something is going wrong there.'

Linus parked the car in a throw-away fashion as if he didn't care if he ever saw it again. 'There's no mystery about it. You just haven't seen enough good modern architecture, that's all. Sometimes, too, you have to go inside a building to appreciate what it's about. It's like it's been designed inside out, if that makes sense to you. It's the proportions of the rooms, the play of the light, those things that make it work.' He pointed towards the top floor of the large Victorian apartment block. 'That's my flat, up there.'

'You've got a turret.'

'Only a little one.' Glancing at his watch he added, 'I'm meeting this guy in twenty minutes, so I'll just have time to walk you to the art museum. Then I'll pick you up at, say, half past twelve and we can have some lunch before we get your mother.'

We walked back down on to the wide avenue and Linus told me how, when his parents were young, the wide street had been lined, not with yellow brick thirties apartment boxes, but Palladian villas in white stucco 'Think about it, the guys who built these are long dead, but the ugliness of their designs lives on to blight the everyday lives of generations to come.' He was walking again, speeding up. 'How can you expect people to think good thoughts and do great things when they're brought up surrounded by soulless crap like this?'

'People create all kinds of beautiful things out of ugliness,' I said.

'Of course they do, and thank God that they do, but somewhere, some time, they will have seen real beauty. But the problem right now is money. Money, as in refusing to spend, and lack of vision. Some of the earlier modernist designs were very much part of a vision, just not one that most of us share today.'

'But you're a modernist.'

Linus smiled down at me. 'Modernist, functionalist, classicist: all these *ists*. For me it's about designing something that perfectly fulfils its purpose, whether that purpose is that of a hospital, a library, a school, private house or indeed an opera house. Beauty is integral to that function and light is what unites it. I don't try to design something new just for the hell of it. I believe in learning from the work of the past, but again, that knowledge has, to my mind, to be used to bring architecture forward. The proportion of a Gustavian room is second to none. You'd be a fool if you didn't study the buildings of that age. The Baroque builder would design, not just doors, but the perfect entrances. You learn and absorb all that knowledge, all those ideas, but if, in the end, all you do is copy you stagnate and we end up living in a world of pale imitations. Anyway, here we are.' He pointed up at the vast pillared museum entrance. 'Have fun. I'll meet you at the bottom of the steps at half past twelve.'

'Don't forget Pernilla's present,' I called after him.

'I won't.' He raised his hand in a salute as he went.

I walked through the vast heavy doors of the museum and up the wide marble staircase towards the rooms, eighteen to twenty-one, that Olivia had recommended me to see. I wondered what Linus would buy Pernilla. What did one buy a moon-spun blonde who lived her life as if it were a permanent audition for the filmatisation of a Scott Fitzgerald novel? Nothing, if you ask me, but of course no one was, so I went on my dark-haired black-thoughted way, up the wide stairs and into room number eighteen. I looked at the pictures: bright blue rooms bathed in sunlight, long-ago celebrations around a table in a garden of tall fresh green trees, beaches and rocks like the ones around the island, and for a while I shed my burden of guilt, my resentments and my petty jealousies, one by one as if they were parts of some tatty and unbecoming costume. For now, life seemed to need no other explanations than what I saw before me. That was art, of course, when it did its stuff. Then my thoughts travelled, uninvited, to Linus's opera house, and I grew muddled and unsure once more. That state of grace, the kind induced by beauty (or a health scare) never lasted very long.

I just had time to look into room fourteen where the picture hung which had once belonged to Bertil's parents. As I looked at the still life of goggle-eyed fish, their rubbery lips puckered as if ready to kiss, their moist scales so real-looking I could smell them, I felt Bertil's parents should not be blamed for preferring a week in Paris to a lifetime of gazing on dead fish.

It was time to go. I looked at my watch, twenty-five minutes past twelve, and began walking towards the exit. Was my hair all right? Lipstick fresh and not all crumbly and dry-looking? I blew into my cupped hand, sniffing the air; breath OK? Yup. Everything was fine as I hurried off to meet my lover.

It was a fantasy, of course, the bit about meeting my lover. Pathetic, really, I thought, so I straightened my shoulders and raised my chin, sprayed myself with romance repellent and hoped for the best as I walked out of the museum. This is Linus you're meeting, I reminded myself. Linus, the environmental vandal. Co-evictor of old dears, giggler of high-pitched giggles . . . admirer of Pernilla the moon goddess.

'Hi Linus,' I said as he came walking towards me up the front steps to the museum entrance.

'Outside all right for lunch?' he asked, waving his arms in the direction of the terrace restaurant next door. I nodded, although I was cold. The sun was still shining, but a strong wind was blowing from the sea. Yet, all around me, people were walking about looking for all the world as if they lived in a warm country, in their bright-coloured shorts and bare tanned arms. They played summer by the rules in this place. On the first of June they donned light, preferably pastel-coloured, clothing, lit barbecues and spent every available moment outside, exclaiming joyously if it happened to be warm and sunny, and exclaiming joyously when it wasn't. This continued until the middle of August when the schools went back for the autumn term and summer was declared officially over. Right now we were lucky to get a table outside, it was so crowded. Most of the others were already well into their meals at the rectangular tables beneath the row of bright-blue-and-yellow flags.

'Did you find something for Pernilla?' I asked as we sat down at a table for two in the furthest corner.

Linus told me he did. 'I especially asked them not to wrap it so that I could show you.' He hauled a box out of his canvas bag full of papers and opened it. Inside was a small glass sculpture in black and gold and midnight-blue, of a head with horns, or was it ears? 'Do you like it?'

I looked some more. 'Can I pick it up?'

Linus nodded. 'Sure.'

I held the head in my hand, turning it this way catching the reflection of the sun. I really didn't like it. I was about to say something honest but tactful, but as I looked into Linus's dark-grey eyes those words came out sounding like this: 'It's lovely, really beautiful. I just love it!' Mercifully Linus didn't pursue the matter, but asked me instead if I had enjoyed the museum.

I showed him the tiny book about one of the artists, Ivar Arosenius, whose work I had particularly liked. 'He died young of course,' I said. 'It's such a smart move, if you take a long-term, posterity kind of view of life.'

'Only if you've achieved your ambition. Nothing is a worse insult than dying before that.'

'Did you call your Ivar after him?'

'No,' Linus said. He scanned the menu before putting it back down on the table and signing to a waiter to take our order. 'But like you, I adore his work.'

I thought how seldom men used words like adore and divine. Linus did, all the time, just as he put his hand up to his cheek in an unconsciously feminine gesture when he was perplexed or deep in thought.

'I used to love painting when I was a child,' I told him. 'I was quite good in a plodding, unimaginative kind of way. It used to drive my mother to despair. "Why is your sun always yellow and your sky always blue or grey and your grass green and your people clean and smiling?" she used to ask. "Where is your imagination?" I told her that was it. That was my imaginary world. A place where the sky was always blue and the sun was shining, and where the people were happy and smiling (I wasn't that bothered about the grass, but green seemed the obvious choice). I knew perfectly well that in reality the sky was black and the sun was an angry orange, and people walked with their heads down so you didn't see if they were smiling or crying.'

'Cheery little soul you were. But I know what you mean. I drew endless cartoons. Ridiculous illustrated stories that I collected in these elaborate notebooks under the heading,' Linus shook his head and smiled, '*My Life as It Ought to Be: A Young Boy's Wonderful Adventures.* I found the lot in a box in my parents' attic the other day. Cringe-making. The drawings weren't bad, but the stories accompanying them, I tell you.' He shook his head again. 'The dreams and aspirations of a podgy, clumsy, rather lonely little boy, so at odds with reality.'

As he spoke, a worry line had appeared between his eyes and suddenly I wanted to reach out and smooth the line away with the tip of my finger. It was a baby-talk feeling, a desire to soothe and to comfort. It was a feeling of . . . of yes . . . of tenderness. My hand lifted from the table and reached across towards him.

Linus had been looking at the menu and now he snapped it shut and said, 'I think I'll have the mushroom risotto.'

My hand dropped back down and I glanced at the list of dishes before me. 'I'll have the fried plaice,' I said, making a quick decision out of pure confusion. But I was soon back into my bad old ways. 'Then again, the risotto sounds delicious. Maybe I should have the risotto. Then I can have red wine, which I prefer.'

'You do find it very difficult to make a decision, don't you?' Linus said.

I looked, shifty-eyed, around the restaurant, then at my right foot that stuck out under the table. I looked up at the sky and a passing seagull. 'Yes,' I said at last, still not looking at Linus. It occurred to me that I hadn't been able to meet anyone's eyes straight on for a long time. I had noticed in my career that neurotics never looked you straight in the eye. Seriously disturbed people had a funny walk too; head down, feet quite wide apart, as if they were checking the ground between them. But, pray God, I wasn't a neurotic, just someone who had had a slight misunderstanding with the world.

I forced myself to meet Linus's gaze and to hold it until I had counted to ten. 'I used to be very decisive,' I said. 'Bossy even. I lived my life according to the rules, albeit my rules. But I had decided early on that you could rely only on yourself. I was very reliable, most of the time. Then stuff happened. I made some seriously flawed decisions. I realised that there were no rules, or if there were, I was damned if I could see them. There are no rules and there are no certainties, we live in the kingdom of randomness and I just can't seem to deal with it very well. It's like I've only just learnt what everyone else seems to have known and accepted all along. So why am *I* so slow-witted? And why can't I deal with the situation now I know it?'

'You are dealing with it,' Linus said. 'You're trying to work out a way of living your life receptive to the changes and the uncertainties, willing to adapt and learn. That's all you can do.'

'Is that all?' I smiled at him.

He nodded gravely. 'That's all.'

'And you have done all of that?'

He shrugged. 'No, of course not. But you're wrong to think everyone else has the answers; they don't. I think it's wrong, too, to say that there are no certainties. There might not be any external ones, but you can have your own. I know I love my son. I know his welfare is paramount. I know I care deeply, passionately, about my work. I don't know *why* I do and sometimes I despair because it seems so futile and so pointless. But most of the time I care. That's one and a bit certainty in my life and that's just about enough to get on with, I think.'

'You're talking about an inner core, aren't you?' I asked suspiciously. 'I don't have one any more. It's crumbled under the weight of my mortal coils. As you've seen, half the time I can't even make a simple decision. It's as if I've got one of these opinion pollsters living inside me. Someone who has to ask a thousand people what they think before knowing what opinion to give. It was quite a gradual thing at first, little things like refusing to be the official executioner at the Tower of London . . .' Linus looked momentarily confused. 'Only joking,' I said hastily. 'Don't worry. My jokes are never very funny.' I paused again as it occurred to me that in that sense we were perfectly matched: I made jokes that weren't funny and Linus was a man who should never be heard laughing.

Our food arrived. As we ate, the sun got hotter. A sky-blue tram rattled past sounding its bell to warn a cyclist who looked as if he was about to hurl himself out on the track.

'You don't become a journalist to win popularity votes,' I said, once we were back in the car.

'I'm sure you don't.'

'One has to stand up for what one believes in.'

'Of course you do.'

'There's no room for compromise.'

'Apparently not.'

'If you don't speak up when you know you should, where will it all end?'

'Where indeed.'

'People need to be kept informed about these petty injustices perpetrated on voiceless people like the Wilsons.'

'Absolutely.'

'You don't agree with me.'

'I've agreed with everything you've said.'

'Not really, you haven't. For heaven's sake, Linus, what do you think, really think?'

'I think that I want to build my opera house.'

'Is that all?'

'Yes.'

'Well, you're a blinkered idiot.'


Audrey was in pain. Her concussion had healed and the bandages had been taken off her head some days earlier, but her broken thigh still hurt. She had dressed in a pink velour gown, the nearest thing to her beloved dressing-gowns she could get without being arrested, I thought, and her faded hair was tied up in a wide white towelling bandanna. 'They've told me to keep moving,' she said disgustedly. 'Exercise, they say. They've even got a physiotherapist coming over twice a week.'

'Welfare Sweden,' I said. 'Most impressive.' But Audrey was not impressed. She sat there, like a bad-tempered powder-puff, in the back of the car, mumbling complaints.

The flag was hoisted at Villa Rosengård in a welcome-back greeting for Audrey, but the household was in turmoil. Bertil had been taken suddenly and violently ill with stomach cramps. The doctor had been called out and had just gone, leaving Bertil resting in bed. 'I don't understand it,' Kerstin said, as Olivia fussed around my mother, a tense-looking Olivia with an overlay of grey across her freckled tanned face. 'Bertil is so fit. Regular exercise, a healthy diet. He doesn't smoke, drinks only in moderation.'

'Maybe it was attempted suicide,' Audrey commented from across the hall. She was still in her fold-up hospital wheelchair – lightweight, chrome, with padded arm-rests. I shot her a hush-up glance.

'What did Dr Blomkvist say it was?' Linus asked Olivia. That little worried line between his eyebrows, not quite central but closer to his left side, had appeared again. He grabbed hold of Audrey's left arm as I took the right. Olivia pulled the wheelchair out of the way and handed Audrey the crutches.

'He doesn't know. He thinks it was just a bad bout of colic, but we're to call him immediately if it happens again. Your father's had his appendix out, otherwise he would have said that was what the problem was.'

I helped a grumbling Audrey into the small bedroom at the back of the kitchen, the maid's room as it was once. 'I'm sorry it's so poky but we were told no stairs,' Olivia, following behind, said. 'The loo and shower are just the other side of the passage, as you know, and you're close enough to the kitchen for you to be able to make yourself a cup of coffee when you feel like it.'

As she neared her bed, Audrey grew happier, like a horse scenting its stable after a long hike. 'You go and see to Bertil,' I said to Olivia. 'I'll look after Audrey. That's why I'm here after all,' I added, glaring at my mother. I still wasn't sure that her fall hadn't been a ploy that got out of hand, to get me across. Audrey read my thoughts. 'Surely you don't think I'd fall and nearly kill myself just to get you to go on holiday with me?'

'Of course not,' I lied. 'Then again, there was the time when you made Madox call and say you thought you had a brain tumour, just to stop me going on that trip.'

'I was worried about you, Esther. You know I never liked that girl, what was her name? Jemima.'

'Katherine.'

'And India . . . Anyway, that was completely different.' My mother settled back in the narrow bed with the crisp white cotton sheets. 'Would you be a dear and see if you can rustle me up some more pillows. Oh, and maybe a little plate of sandwiches, you know the kind I like, and one of those delicious pistachio and jam buns.' She leant back against the bed-rest with a contented little sigh; a horse back in its box with heating, hay and a bucket of oats. 'I am glad you're here, Esther,' she said. 'It's a big comfort.' She wasn't quite looking at me, though. Expressing fine sentiments made us feel awkward, in that we were alike.

'You lose so many people when you get to my age. The links that anchor you to your past snap one by one. That's another reason why Olivia is so important to me. I never had any sisters or brothers and so many childhood friends are gone, and my parents, of course. When there's no one left who remembers you as you were, each time someone from your past dies, the part of you which they remembered, the person you were to them, is buried with them and lost. In the end, you are left with the people who only knew you as this wrinkled old lady. With Olivia I'm still this other person too, the girl I once was lives with her. Does that make sense?'

I stared at her. Of course it did. I just wasn't used to her making much sense at all.

'So you see,' my mother continued, 'she loves Linus and I love you. It is important to us both that there should be no bad blood.'

'You don't have to worry about that any more. Linus understands that I did what I had to do. We get on perfectly well.'

'He's a very good-looking man, don't you agree?'

I felt my face softening and tried to stop it, but it was like trying to prevent a block of butter melting in the sunshine. 'He is when he isn't laughing,' I said and I left the room in rather a hurry.

Audrey refused to get out of bed for dinner. No amount of threats or attempts at persuasion could change her mind. Bertil, too, stayed in his room. The rest of us had supper in the kitchen. Olivia wanted to be within earshot of her 'two invalids', as she put it. Gerald told three sexist, fatist, smoker-friendly jokes, all of which offended his daughter. He told them in Swedish, but Kerstin's reaction needed no translation. She went for a walk, a lonely walk of martyrdom for all women. Linus went off to fetch Ivar who had been staying with a friend, and Ulla, Gerald, Olivia and I played whist. Ulla and Gerald lost four times in a row before Ulla departed, wrapped in ill temper as if it were a shawl. The others followed soon after and I was left feeling much like the last of the ten little Indians, alone.

On my way to my room I paused a while in the garden, taking deep breaths of the cool, fresh night air. I looked up at the star-strewn sky. It looked higher somehow, here on the island, further away. Maybe that was why the Swedes were prone to melancholy, *vemod*, they called it; they knew better than anyone how far away heaven was.

## Chapter Twenty

I had spent the morning reading in the garden and listening to the bees humming in the forsythia shrubs. Bees, busy bees, when they minded their own business and left you alone, were restful little creatures to have around. I yawned and stretched, and got up from my chair, placing my book on the seat. (I was reading Socrates because lately I had decided that without a sound grasp of philosophy I'd never even begin to get the hang of life.) On my way to the house I paused by Astrid's roses, the roses of Astrid, Linus's mother, and bent down to inhale their scent.

'Funny to think of these roses, bought for a few kronor years ago and not much regarded by anyone these days, being alive still and she dead.' Ulla had come up behind me, her feet soundless on the soft grass. 'Yet whose life would you have rated as more important? No, she's been dead for all those years, dead and buried with worms crawling through the space where her lovely eyes once shone.'

I straightened up. 'No one will talk about her.'

'At the time it was a huge scandal. The Stendals are a very old Gothenburg family.' She paused, looking at me with those pale-brown eyes. 'You know, I practically brought Astrid up, me and my parents. The poor girl wanted nothing more than a home and a family of her own. That's why I thought she'd be happy with Bertil.' Her voice hardened and went snappy. 'But it was not to be.' She turned on her heels and was gone in her usual puff of black smoke.

I was in the kitchen of what was now the Invalid House, with the hushed atmosphere and sweet stale air of a place where people walked softly and kept the windows shut. I was making Audrey and me some coffee, having removed an apple core and two banana peels from the tray next to her bed, when Olivia came downstairs. She gave me a quick kiss on the cheek, but she wasn't concentrating and the kiss ended up at the side of my nose. 'Did Audrey have a comfortable night?'

I shook my head. 'Not terribly. And Bertil, how's he?'

'Much better. We're convinced it was a one-off.' She wiped a strand of hair from her eyes. 'I tell you though, Esther, I never want to see anyone in that kind of pain ever again.'

Ulla slid past, something clutched to her bosom; a baby demon possibly, when Olivia stopped her. 'You're not trying to smuggle Bertil food again, are you?'

There was a small pause. *'Lite mjölk bara* (Just a little milk).' Then she added, 'Dear.' I hated it when Ulla used endearments; it made me feel as if the world really was upside down. Olivia rolled her eyes to heaven and made a grab for the milk carton.

'No milk. Dr Blomkvist said no dairy produce whatsoever. Water, weak black tea or Coke, *no* milk.'

'Milk lines the stomach,' Ulla protested as Olivia returned the carton to the fridge.'

'Milk feeds the harmful bacteria. Forgive me if I take the doctor's word over yours.'

'Bacteria,' Ulla muttered as she stomped off. 'Who said anything about bacteria?'

Linus had been upstairs reading the papers to his father but come noon I heard Gerald call him down. I was on my way into Audrey's room with an old transistor radio I'd found in the cottage.

'Linus,' Gerald called. *'Pernilla är här.'*

And Pernilla was indeed there, fair hair dancing round her shoulders as she turned this way and that, greeting us as if she were a princess on a visit to a slightly backward country. 'I heard that Bertil was sick,' she said to the watching masses: Gerald, Kerstin, me, and Olivia who had just appeared from the kitchen. 'I was in the stores getting the groceries and they said that you'd had to have Dr Blomkvist out.'

The Prince of the Slightly Backward Country descended the stairs and the visiting princess turned animated and spoke to him in Swedish. She frowned a pretty frown. She put a comforting hand on his arm. She smiled a rapid smile that cleared the pretty frown. *I* was a bitch. I looked at them, then I looked at Olivia's drawn face, and at Kerstin's, scrubbed and permanently pressed into an expression of hope, and at Gerald's sallow cheeks, and I thought I belonged with them, however much I wanted to be like the moonlit ones.

'Excuse me,' I muttered as I squeezed past with the old transistor in my hand.

'I wish my Swedish were better,' I complained to Audrey as I plugged the radio into a socket by the bed. 'I understand a fair bit, but not enough. I hate not knowing what's going on.'

'You always did,' Audrey said. 'But what's the point, learning more Swedish, I mean. I thought you weren't staying a minute longer than you had to.' She was in a bad mood because there was no aerial for a television in her room. 'They've got the dish so I could get all my programmes,' she complained. 'But not in here.'

'You could get up.'

Audrey gave me an outraged look, as if I had suggested she walked through the house with her nightie pulled up over her head.

'Read,' I suggested.

'I've read everything.'

'Everything? There's a very nice little library on the island and it's even got an English-speaking section.'

'Whatever,' Audrey said, sulking like a child.

'Maybe they've got a Linguaphone course,' I said.

The librarian said they could order one in for me and that I could keep it for three weeks. 'I'll return it before then,' I assured them.

'And is your mother recovering well?' the librarian asked me in careful English. The islanders knew everything.

'Quite well,' I said. 'I hope she'll be fit to travel in the next fortnight or so.'

By the time the cassettes arrived, two days later, Bertil was up and about, and as restless as ever. He spent the morning sanding down the red-and-white painted garden shed and later he announced that he was doing a barbecue that evening. Olivia was playing cards with my mother and Linus was off helping his father paint, so Ivar and I spent the afternoon digging for human remains in the sandy soil of the little playground on the east side of the island. We had just been told by a friend of Olivia's that the plot of land, caught between the small wood and the walls of the old fort, had been used as a burial ground for the prisoners. There had been generations of those and most had died within its walls. The priest and parishioners of Kilholmen had decided, in their compassion, that they didn't want their own tree-lined and tranquil churchyard cluttered up with the likes of the prisoners and their families. Those unfortunate souls, together with the poorest of the soldiers and officers of the fort, had been dumped on a piece of wasteland at the foot of the northernmost wall of their prison. Now it was a playground, but Ivar, who was bored with the swings and the seesaw, wanted to bring his red plastic bucket and spade to see if he could find some bits of the earlier users of the area. I watched him dig, his solid little shape squatting on the ground, as he worked, humming little tuneless tunes, absorbed and completely happy. Once he looked up at me and gave me one of his father's heart-stopping smiles and for the first time in my life I wondered if being childless was such a great idea.

After a while we stopped and had our picnic lunch: a roll with soft blue cheese each, followed by a cinnamon bun. We stretched out on the tall spiky grass and sipped our cartons of pear juice through a straw. Ivar had told me that pear juice went especially well with soft blue cheese and he was right.

'To think there are lots of dead people under us,' Ivar said. The idea seemed to please him and I thought how nice it would have been if I'd had a playmate like Ivar when I was young.

'Look, there's Pappa and Pernilla.' Ivar stood up and waved at the two figures approaching from the harbour.

'I wondered where you two had got to,' Linus said, bending down and kissing the top of his son's fair head.

'We're off for a walk round the island,' Pernilla said. I could see from the way she kept gazing over her shoulder and shifting from foot to foot that she couldn't wait to get away.

'Stay and help us dig,' Ivar said. 'It's really exciting.' He turned to me. 'It's really exciting this digging, isn't it?'

I nodded. 'It certainly is, Ivar.' And in a way it was. To watch a child absorbed in play was a lot more interesting than I would ever have imagined.

Linus looked as if he was about to say yes, when Pernilla tugged at his arm. 'We'd better get on. The forecast said rain in the afternoon.'

Linus looked at Ivar, then at Pernilla. 'You show me what you've found when we get home,' he said to his son. They were off again, up past the playground towards the fort and the cliffs beyond. I watched them go and as they reached the top of the hill, Linus turned, as if he knew I was watching, and for a moment he stopped and smiled, then with a little wave he was gone.

Ivar returned to his digging and I lay back and stared up at the blue cloud-strewn sky. Then he found a bone. Ivar swore it was a man's collar-bone, but I thought it looked more like the kind of bone a large gull would leave behind as his earthly remains.

'It's human,' Ivar said with due solemnity.

'You don't think it looks more like gull?' I asked.

Ivar shook his head. 'No,' he said. And that was that. We returned to Villa Rosengård with the bone rattling gently inside the red plastic bucket.

Bertil was already on the deck, cleaning the barbecue. Ivar rushed over to show him the bone and I wandered back to the cottage to wash and change.

My stomach felt fat and bloated, too much herring the night before, I thought, so I put on a navy-blue dress, long-sleeved and loose-waisted. It was comforting to know that were I to fart, it would almost certainly be blamed on Gerald. My stomach rumbling, I worked out which song to sing, just in case: 'Applejack' by Dolly Parton.

Pernilla had gone back to her place after her walk, but she returned in time for dinner. We were already seated on the deck when she blew in, all dressed in white, lovely and fragile-looking like Blanche Dubois in just the right light. I remembered someone telling me that Marilyn Monroe in the flesh had exuded such radiance that it was as if someone had shoved a light bulb up her bottom. As Pernilla threw herself down in the chair next to Kerstin (opposite Linus), I half expected to hear the sound of crushing glass.

The mackerel was delicious and we lingered as the sun began its slow drop into the sea. It got chilly, and cardigans and pullovers were donned in reverse striptease against the backdrop of the fort and the darkening summer sky. I took a deep breath, filling my lungs with the clear cool air.

'That's good,' Kerstin said, nodding so vigorously that I thought she was going to send her teddy-bear ear-rings flying right into her cup.

'Deep breathing is near the top of my list of tips for staying alive and well.'

'And number one?' I asked. 'Is that the one about not falling under a bus?' It was a churlish remark, but I had just spotted Pernilla leaning her head against Linus's shoulder. I don't know why that should have upset me, but somehow it did.

'Or not have a dime coin fall on your head from the top of the Empire State Building,' Ivar chimed. 'Because that will certainly kill you.' As we all looked at him he added, 'The Empire State Building is in New York.' Misunderstanding the question on our faces.

'You know such a lot for someone so young,' I said to him.

'I'm very advanced for my age,' he managed through a mouthful of ice-cream. 'One of my teachers said.'

'Not to your face.' Ulla looked shocked.

'To another teacher,' Ivar explained. 'Miss Bjork said to Miss Nilsson that I was nosy so Miss Bjork said that I was very advanced for my age.' At the tick-tack sound of a hedgehog rustling through the tall grass he put down his spoon and slid from his chair in pursuit, crawling under the table between our legs and out the other side.

'Children are so natural,' Pernilla said, stretching in her chair. She alone had not wrapped up. I wouldn't have either if I had been dressed in a tiny white shift dress that left acres of tanned and shapely limbs exposed to the soft evening light.

Ivar was put to bed, carried, half asleep already, in his father's arms up to his blue-and-white room. We finished our coffee. Kerstin leant back in her chair and gesticulated up at the star-strewn night sky and at the white roses shining like mini moons. 'Do you really think anything could be better than this? I mean, are you serious about selling up?'

'I'm afraid so,' Bertil said. 'Each place has its time and now it's time for Olivia and me to move on.'

'I know what you mean,' Gerald agreed. 'When Kerstin here was a little girl her mother refused to live anywhere other than the country. But once we had a teenager on our hands and my dear Marie knew that time was running out for her, she couldn't wait to move back into town, the more central the better. With Marie it was as if she had this sudden need to see everything and do everything. Time spent getting to and from a place was time wasted.'

'That is a completely different situation,' Ulla snapped. 'The point is, when you get older and your health isn't what it used to be, you should be near civilisation, among your own kind. Just look at how quickly we got Bertil to the hospital, and dear Dr Blomkvist being on hand at all times.'

'One tummy upset does not an invalid make,' Bertil said. 'And anyway, who said we'd be isolated? They do have doctors in France, you know.'

'It's not the same, being ill abroad.'

'I do wish you'd stop going on about being ill.' Bertil frowned. 'All I've had is a bout of stomach trouble and you seem to be willing it to be something worse.'

'That's a bit unfair, darling.' Olivia smiled at him. 'She's concerned for you, that's all. It might just have been a bout of tummy trouble but it gave us quite a fright, all the same.'

'What about a night swim?' Pernilla turned to Linus who had returned from putting Ivar to bed. I had taken off my grey cardigan and now I pushed up my sleeves, all in the deluded hope that moonlight became me. Pernilla shot me a glance over her shoulder. 'Don't,' she said with a melodious little laugh. 'It makes me shiver just looking at you, all those goose-pimples.'

'Goose-pimples? I'm not cold.' I too laughed, but maybe not quite so melodiously.

'You want a swim, you shall have a swim,' Linus said to Pernilla. 'It's such a lovely night, we should take the boat.'

'I'll join you.' Kerstin got up, taking her cup and saucer with her. 'I need to give my body a little wake-up call.'

'Why?' Olivia asked. 'Where is it going?'

Kerstin ignored her. 'Are you coming, Esther?'

I hesitated. Linus and Pernilla probably wanted to be on their own. I was about to say no, when Pernilla turned to me with a little smile. 'You're not very decisive, are you, Esther?'

'I'd love to come,' I said.

If Pernilla was disappointed she didn't show it, she just put her slender hand on Linus's arm and smiled. 'I always make my mind up just . . .' she snapped her fingers '. . . like that. I simply trust my instincts.'

'I used to be very decisive,' I said, trying to snap my fingers but managing only a sweaty little thud. Pernilla looked as if she was waiting for me to elaborate so I added, 'But circumstances led me to view every decision as a stack of dynamite waiting to be lit.'

'So boom!' Pernilla said, clapping her slender hands together, just as Kerstin appeared with a stack of towels.

'I did,' I said. 'And believe me, the reality of booming is a lot less fun than the idea. I mean if you've ever had your neighbour's arm practically draped across your shoulders . . .'

Linus held the gate open for us and I followed Kerstin and Pernilla out on to the street. 'What's wrong with having your neighbour's arm draped round you? You mustn't be so, so . . .' She searched for the English expression. 'So tight-assed.' She took Linus's hand and pulled his arm up round her shoulders where it stayed. I stared at it, and at the strong hand with its long fingers, transfixed.

'Nothing, really,' I said. 'It's just that in this instance the arm wasn't attached to the neighbour.'

'Oh, my God.' Pernilla put a hand up to her throat.

Squeeze, I thought. Why don't you squeeze? I was never a good-natured drunk and I had had at least five glasses of wine.

Pernilla seemed to feel the need to change the subject. 'Kerstin, what were those rules for a long life you talked about earlier?' she asked.

'An intake of at least five portions of fruit and vegetables a day. Regular exercise and *not* smoking.'

I fished out a cigarette from my navy-blue canvas shoulder-bag and lit it.

'Very funny, I'm sure.' Kerstin shook her head at me. 'But you won't think it so amusing when you lie in a hospital ward breathing through a tube in your throat.'

'Are you listening, Esther and Linus?' Pernilla wagged her finger playfully. 'Not that you smoke that much, Esther.' She sounded almost regretful.

I didn't answer. I was thinking that I liked the sound of our names being linked, even if it was only as smokers: Esther and Linus. Linus and Esther.

'I agree with you about the exercise,' Linus said. 'I mean when did you last see a corpse in the gym?'

Kerstin said something sniffy in Swedish. I recognised the word

240

idiot. It was the same word in Swedish but they emphasised the last syllable, idi*oot*. It sounded sorrowful somehow, as if they regretted the fact as well as deploring it.

Down by the harbour Linus leapt on board the boat, his feet landing on the deck with a barely audible thud. Pernilla jumped after him, landing gracefully, one leg raised slightly behind her as she steadied herself against Linus's outstretched arm. I peered at the gap between the quayside and the boat. With a small sigh I sat down and slid on my bottom until Linus reached my arm and dragged me on board. Kerstin made it by herself, but even her staunchest admirer would not have called her graceful. We travelled along on the still sea, watching the island lights disappear behind us. The world was silent apart from the chug-chugging of the engine. Linus stood at the stern, the tiller in his hand. Kerstin was sitting right up at the front holding a lantern. The light around us was blue, that was the colour of the Swedish summer nights: dark-blue. The sea was calm. I had noticed that often, even after a choppy day, it stilled at night as if it needed a rest from all that pounding of rocks and of boats. It was a sleepy sea we travelled across.

Pernilla lifted her face to the star-strewn sky. I wished I had brought my cardigan. Kerstin turned and smiled at me. 'You're not very athletic.'

There wasn't a lot I could say to that. I could try an 'Oh yes I am', but that would be an obvious lie. I said nothing and forced myself to smile back at her.

'You should go to a gym or something.'

'I do. Well, I did.'

'Really?'

'There are no boats there, though. Not in my gym.'

Linus steered us towards a small rocky island called The Crows. He manoeuvred alongside the rock and Kerstin, taking the rope attached to the front of the boat, leapt ashore. Pernilla was searching for the rubber hammer, and the metal pins that would be knocked into a crevice before Kerstin could tie up.

'Here,' Pernilla handed the hammer and pins to me. 'Take those ashore, will you? I'll do the anchor.'

I clambered up on to the bow of the boat and stood up.

'Coming, Esther?' Kerstin called.

I turned with a quick glance at Pernilla and then, with the hammer and pegs in my left hand, I leapt. I felt the freedom of flying through the air and the hard rock side scraping my legs as I fell into the water.

I surfaced to hear anxious voices calling my name. Hands were stretched out towards me and within seconds I was hauled back on to the boat. Pernilla draped a towel round my shoulders and Linus asked if I was all right. I nodded, shivering in the night air. I attempted a laugh but to my horror it turned into a sob.

'We should take Esther back home,' Linus said.

'No, no, I'm fine. We came to swim after all.' I had managed to steady my voice.

'No.' Pernilla put her hand on Linus's arm. 'You're right. We should go back. We can swim another evening.'

'Make up your minds,' Kerstin called from the shore.

We went back. I sat hunched on the polished wooden seat feeling like the child who's been sick and ruined the party for everyone. They were all very nice about it, of course. 'It can happen to anyone,' Pernilla said.

'Has it happened to you?' I asked hopefully.

She told me that no, it hadn't, actually.

Linus and Pernilla walked me to the cottage door. As I closed it behind me I heard Pernilla say, 'Let's go and swim off the steps. It's such a beautiful evening it would be a shame to spoil it completely.' Looking out of my bedroom window I could see them wander off towards the gate, arm in arm. I stayed staring out into the night long after Linus's back had disappeared from view.

## Chapter Twenty-one

'How long are you planning to stay?' Ulla asked as we bumped into each other outside the bathroom. I was on my way in and so was she, coming up behind me like a revved-up old Austin with her huge sponge-bag before her like a bumper.

'The doctors think that Audrey will be fit to travel in a couple of weeks or so,' I said, backing out of her way. She overtook me in the doorway and turned, triumphant.

'Oh, Ulla.'

'Yes?'

'How old was Linus when his mother died?'

She didn't look surprised at the question. 'Seven,' she said.

'Seven? I always thought he was much younger.'

'Well, he wasn't. He was seven.' She closed the door in my face and seconds later the shower was turned on.

I sat with Olivia and Ulla on the deck, finishing my breakfast. I had left Audrey listening to the radio, a look of suffering on her face and a breakfast tray on her knee. Just as I was about to ask Olivia about Astrid's death, Linus came out on to the deck with Ivar in tow.

'Have you seen your father this morning?' Olivia asked him.

Linus shook his head. 'He wasn't there when I woke up so I assumed he'd gone for one of his walks.'

Olivia poured Ivar out a bowl of sour milk and Rice Krispies, and patted the empty chair next to her. 'You come and sit here with me, darling.' Ivar, dressed in khaki-coloured shorts and a matching T-shirt and with one of Kerstin's 'piggy' hair slides holding back his blond fringe, walked round the table, running his hands along the table top on his way, and slipped on to the chair.

'If I were Bertil', Ulla said, 'I'd take every opportunity there was to

243

walk around this heavenly place.' She gesticulated towards the gate and the road to the harbour beyond. Then Gerald appeared around the corner, hurrying towards us with his stiff-legged old-man's gait. He looked flustered and spoke to Linus in Swedish. Linus got up from the chair and followed Gerald back down the garden towards the shed.

'What was that all about?' Olivia shook her head.

Ivar said in a loud voice but no one seemed to hear – that was often the way with children; the louder they spoke the less one seemed to hear them – 'I need some paper to draw a house.' He used English as Swedish hadn't worked.

'In a minute, darling,' Olivia said.

'But I need it now.'

'If you ask me . . .' Ulla began and was instantly interrupted by Ivar.

'Have *you* got some paper I can have?' he demanded, but was silenced by a glare from Ulla. He sighed theatrically, shrugging his skinny shoulders. 'You said to ask you . . .' he complained.

Ulla carried on as if Ivar had never spoken, '. . . I would tell you that Bertil will end up bitterly regretting selling this place. You both will, I'm telling you this.'

Kerstin turned to her and said something cross in Swedish. I realised I hadn't even noticed her arriving at the table.

'English please,' Olivia said. 'We have to think of our guest.' I didn't contradict her; I hated being left out of things.

'I just can't see', Kerstin went on obediently, 'how you can think that Olivia and Bertil should keep this place simply because we all like to spend our summer holidays here. It's their life.'

The colour rose in Ulla's thin cheeks. Her hand shook as she placed the mug back on the table. 'What do you know?' She spat the words out, making us all turn to look at her. 'What do any of you know with your full lives and your families and friends?' She stopped herself, putting a bony hand to her throat. Then she got up and hurried from the room.

Ivar wanted to know if she'd gone to fetch some paper. I told him that I thought it unlikely.

Moments later, Linus appeared in the doorway. 'It's Father.' He looked straight at Olivia. 'You'd better come. Gerald is calling Dr Blomkvist.'

Bertil was asleep upstairs with Olivia watching over him, seated in a hard chair at his side. He was going to be fine, Dr Blomkvist had said, but he was sending some samples to the laboratory nevertheless and he was consulting a specialist. Ulla had taken to her room and had not been seen for several hours, although Kerstin had left a tray with sandwiches and a flask of coffee outside the room after Ulla refused to come out. 'I want to be alone,' she had snapped, like some Greta Garbo gone wrong. Olivia appeared downstairs just once that afternoon, but when she heard about Ulla, she and Gerald both went across to the cottage to see how she was doing. So that was what families were all about, I thought as I wandered alone between the rose borders, looking out for one another in critical times, even when you couldn't stand the sight of each other. No wonder Ulla was so desperate to belong. I felt an outsider more than ever. Not only was I The Woman Who Had Spiked Linus's Project, but my role in the unfolding drama over Bertil's health was no more than that of a concerned passer-by.

'I feel quite forgotten,' Audrey complained.

I told her that she was. 'But I'm here,' I added, trying to soften the blow.

Audrey continued to look disgruntled. 'When did that Doctor What's-his-name say I could get up and about?'

'You never get up and about.' I was surprised at her question.

'Bed is no place for a sick person,' Audrey said. I didn't feel up to arguing.

The rain had held off for a while but as I passed the apple tree the sleeve of my sweater brushed against the low branches, sending a shower of droplets down the back of my neck and under my collar. I was trying to think of a story for *New Romance* magazine. I had received a letter from Mary, the editor, in reply to mine, saying that they would be happy to look at anything I'd like to send them. *With a bit of heart at their centre, your stories could be excellent,* she had written. *So I hope you've found one.* That last remark had stung me. Of course I had a heart, I'd had one all along. We just hadn't had that much to do with each other until recently.

The weather, after the rains, had turned cooler and the garden had a clean, tousled look, with the tall grass flattened and the leaves heavy with water. I wondered when Linus would be back. He had gone shopping with a list of foodstuffs ordered for Bertil by Dr Blomkvist; clean, dairy-free food that would not feed whatever unfriendly bacteria had taken hold within his inflamed gut.

I was on my way back to the house when he appeared. I watched him push the gate open with his foot, his hands busy with the shopping. I saw him make his way along the narrow gravel path, his cheeks pink and his fair hair curling from the damp. I felt myself grinning and I raised my hand in a wave. Then I spotted Pernilla coming up behind him. She called his name, catching up with him by the sundial and he stopped and turned towards her. I ceased grinning and lowered my hand. He hadn't even seen me and I felt as if someone had switched off the light, just around me. Pernilla and Linus remained in their circle of light. I stood alone in the depths of my black-bottomed mere. I brought it with me as I went, that dark pool.

I stared at him, caressing his features with my gaze, allowing it to wander down the side of his face, along his left arm, down his hip, following the line of the long leg to the ground. I tasted his name, tracing each letter with my tongue. My heart was pounding. I wanted to die. I wanted to live for ever. I wanted to cry. Light flooded my pool of darkness. My God! I was in love.

My first impulse was to call for help: Posy, Chloe, Arabella, Audrey even. Ask them how to stop it. Enquire how to remove these alien sentiments. 'A damp cloth and just the tiniest amount of Woolite,' Audrey would say. Posy, the old romantic, might suggest arsenic. Arabella would probably post me her vibrator. Chloe would laugh. I sank to the ground, careless of the wet grass. I had wondered for so long about what it must be like, being in love, and now it had happened I hated it. I was nothing to him in the shadow of Pernilla's radiance. She gleamed. Her teeth glinted white, her hair shone gold, her skin glowed. I was pretty, I knew that, but even my best friend would not accuse me of radiance. Pernilla joined a gathering as if she knew that everyone had been waiting just for her to get there. I arrived looking as if I wondered where the hell I was and why? As if that wasn't enough, I was everyone's enemy: the journalist! Audrey would have told me that a woman was supposed to help her mate's dream come true, not slash the fabric it was woven from. All in all, my prospects did not look good.

I sat on my bed in the cottage, staring out of the window. 'What is love?' I had scurried around asking, a morning long ago, just days before the wedding that never happened. Now I could answer the question myself. Olivia's vigil by her husband's bedside was love. Ulla's poison-pale face at the thought of no longer belonging was love of sorts. Feeling as if Linus had his finger on the light switch of the world, that too had to be love. I didn't like it. Love was turning me into someone I didn't know. In fact, it was turning me into someone I didn't wish to know. And it hurt.

# Chapter Twenty-two

It had rained for three days now and the wind was up from the sea. In a way I was pleased; this chilly grey state of affairs had just the kind of Ingmar Bergman gloom about it that I had expected from Sweden. But the islanders were still defying type by making the best of things, shouting jolly greetings to each other through the wind and rain and saying, in a very British way, that things could be a lot worse. I searched in vain for my soul mate, that fictional Swede, quiet and dark of mind.

I had managed to finish the story for *Modern Romance* and I had just been to the post office and faxed it to Mary Swanson. Back at the house, I shook the water off Kerstin's oilskin anorak and hung it up on its peg by the back door. I looked in on Audrey. She was asleep and even in sleep her face looked disgruntled. The doctor had said that it was only a matter of days now until she would be fit enough to travel back and I knew she couldn't wait to get home. And me? I had toyed with the idea of breaking a leg or toe myself as a means of being able to remain close to Linus, but a small something inside me, sanity maybe, stopped me. I closed the door to Audrey's room softly behind me and when I heard Linus's voice from the veranda I went out there, grabbing a book from the hall table on my way out. Gerald was there too. I sat down on the small wicker sofa and opened the book.

'. . . and you go on, pushing down, one after the other and nothing comes out, nothing happens and then suddenly . . .' Gerald paused momentarily as I entered before continuing, '. . . out it flies, a big dollop of rotting food. It could be meat or, like this morning, spinach and that Italian cheese, you know the one I mean, Ricco . . . Ricotta, that's the one.'

'Gerald is telling me about the joys of flossing.' Linus rolled his eyes at me, then he laughed – that laugh. It reached me and it sounded good to me. I stared at him and waited for the sound to infuriate me. It didn't. Instead, the sound of Linus's high-pitched giggle of a laugh filled me with happiness and I found myself joining in, hesitantly at first, then hilariously. Gerald looked at us and shook his head, so abruptly we both fell silent. But I couldn't take my eyes off Linus.

'Esther?' Linus said.

'Yes?'

'Why are you reading a book on herring fishing in Swedish?'

'I'm not,' I said. Then I looked down at the book. Maybe I was. 'Whoops,' I said, closing it. 'Wrong one.' I sidled out of the door and once I was back in the hall I slammed the book down on the table under the mirror, hard, to punish it for making me look silly. Then I hurried back to the cottage and my room, and lay down on the bed. I started to cry and once I had started it seemed I just couldn't stop. So that's how I spent the rest of that afternoon, lying on my bed, crying.

When it was time for dinner I took one look at my swollen face in the mirror before rushing outside, down the hill, along the harbour, round to the fort, on to the cliffs. It had stopped raining, but the sky and sea were a dull grey and the wind came from the north. I was alone by the bathing steps. With a quick look round to make sure there was no one approaching I tore off my clothes and shoved them into a crevice. I hurried down the steps and into the sea, gasping as the cold water hit my midriff. Taking a deep breath I dived under the water and swam a couple of lengths. Then I swam back to the steps and clambered back up on the rocks. Damn! No towel.

It's no fun dressing when you're sopping wet. I ran all the way back to the house, my clothes clinging to my body, water dripping from my hair on to my face.

I dashed straight into the kitchen, where they were all about to sit down, and said, 'Sorry I'm late but I just had to go for a swim. I'll get some dry things on. Won't be a tick.' Seven pairs of eyes looked up at me, seven mouths gaped in silence. I dashed off again and as I left the house I heard Ulla's voice, loud, querulous, saying something in Swedish, something unpleasant I shouldn't wonder. Still, I didn't mind. I had achieved what I set out to do; now my red eyes would be down to a swim in the cold, salty sea and not an afternoon of crying.

*

I perched at the foot of Audrey's bed, a mug of coffee in my hand. 'I think that was going too far,' she said. Olivia had already told her about my evening swim and now she had wormed the reason from me. In fact, I had been grateful to have someone to confide in – that is, until I remembered who it was.

'I suppose you wish you had listened to your mother now,' Audrey said. 'I told you nothing good would come of you pursuing that campaign of yours.'

'You mean because it made an adversary of Linus?'

Audrey looked at me with infinite patience. 'Yes, darling.'

'But you can't live your life like that. Either something is right or it isn't. My feelings for Linus should have nothing to do with it.'

'I thought that therapist, what's his name . . .?'

'Peel.'

'That's the one, I thought he was meant to have cured you of all of that.'

I knew it was a mistake to try to talk to my mother. Her mind was a pink cave, which the light of reason never reached.

That night I couldn't sleep for love. My skin was itching, feeling as if it were crawling with insects, ladybirds most probably, cute red ladybirds that itched like fleas from hell. I tossed and turned. I conjured up images to torture myself further, images of Linus with Pernilla, of him smiling down at her, taking her in his arms, pressing her down on to his bed, caressing her . . . 'No!' I cried. 'Enough!' I rolled on to my stomach and buried my face in the pillow. It smelt of shampoo, my cheap and cheerful unscented pharmacy-brand shampoo. I tried to drive away the images of Linus and Pernilla, concentrating instead on the interesting fact that you could always smell unscented shampoo. It didn't work. In my mind Pernilla tossed her head from side to side, her hair fanning across Linus's pillow. I started to sob. I don't know how long I lay there with my face pressed against my own sensibly scented pillowcase, but when eventually I got out of bed to fetch a drink of water the sun, which never rested for long during the short Swedish summer, was already spreading a soft pink light across the horizon.

I went outside and stood for a while on the front step of the cottage, drawing in the morning air. I felt the dew-drenched grass beneath my bare feet as I wandered across the lawn towards the house. The back door was never locked and I pushed it open and continued inside. My heart was pounding as I walked up the stairs, steadying myself with one hand against the wooden banister. The early morning light reaching through the uncurtained windows lit my way. Linus's room was the third on the left. I made my way towards it. The room next to Linus's was Ivar's. His door was ajar, as was his father's, and the faint light from their windows seeped out and met half-way on the landing.

Love, I thought as I stood, my hand on the door handle, was a more desperate emotion than I had ever guessed. I pushed open the door and slipped inside. I had never been into Linus's room, but I knew that it had been his mother's many years ago. Here, as in the rest of the house, the curtains were left open, the light from outside once again showing me the way. Linus slept in a wide, white-painted wooden bed. He had thrown off the duvet and was lying naked on his stomach. I followed the outline of his back and shoulders, the triangle down to his waist and buttocks. I gazed at his long legs, his left one drawn up at an angle, the other straight. I had to touch him. I could die tomorrow without ever having known the touch of his skin on mine. I wanted my lips to touch his. I wanted to kiss the crease where his neck joined with his shoulder and run my finger down the outline of his spine. I wanted him to turn over so that I could bury my face in his stomach. I stepped forward and put out my hand, leaning down over his sleeping profile, catching his warm breath with my own.

Linus startled and turned, shooting out of bed. 'What's happened? What's the matter?' His eyes were barely open and he seemed not to have recognised me at first. As he focused, he grabbed the duvet with one hand and wrapped it round his waist. 'Esther? What on earth is it? Is it Bertil?'

'No.' I took a step backwards. 'No, everything is fine. I just thought I'd . . . I'd . . . I wondered if you had a stamp.'

## Chapter Twenty-three

I woke exhausted, my back and shoulders aching and my mouth dry. It was raining once again. I sat up and as my head moved my brain hit against the hard rock of my forehead. My memory, until now a grey mass, splintered into a thousand shards, each one piercing my consciousness more painfully than the next, as I remembered. I had risen from my bed in the early hours of that morning and wandered across the garden to the house in my oversized T-shirt and nothing else. I had walked upstairs to the room where Linus lay sleeping. I had gone up to the bed where he lay, naked, and he had woken and found me there. I had asked him for a stamp. 'Oh God,' I groaned and buried my head in the pillow, pulling it up around my ears. 'Oh God,' I groaned again.

Linus had been very kind. He had put his arm round my shoulders and given me a little hug. He had told me not to worry. That it had been a traumatic few days for all of us. He had grabbed a bathrobe from a hook on the door and pulled it on, letting the duvet drop as the robe fell down around his feet. He had insisted on walking me back to the cottage. I had allowed myself to be led into my room and up to the bed where he had left me, sitting on the edge, my feet dangling just above the floor. Five minutes later he had returned, carrying a large steaming mug. 'Warm milk, dark rum and sugar,' he had explained with a little smile. 'It'll help you sleep.'

He had been right. I had slept. I hadn't slept so late since I arrived on the island. Already it was ten o'clock.

I had just finished dressing when there was a knock on my door. It was Linus. He was smiling. I looked at him and realised that it was possible to love someone and want to hit them hard in the mouth with a vase of roses, both at the same time.

'I came to see how you were?'

'I'm fine.' I forced myself to smile back. I wished, fleetingly, that I had blackened my teeth as I used to when I was a child. It was a sure-fire way of putting people off what they were thinking. As it was, Linus just looked at me, still smiling, and shook his head.

'Why are you being so kind to me? After what I did.' The words tumbled out of my mouth before I had a chance to stop them. I didn't dare to hold his gaze for fear of my naked love showing, so I studied a fly crawling up the wall just above his left shoulder.

'Why on earth shouldn't I be? You were sleep-walking. It can happen to anyone.'

That wasn't what I was thinking of, but I grasped the excuse gratefully. 'Sleep-walking.' I nodded. '*Of course*. I mean, I *do*. I'm known for it. "That Esther sure is one hell of a sleep-walker," the folks at home say.' I paused. 'But that's not actually what I meant. I was thinking of the opera house.'

Linus sighed. 'I told you before; it was business. I did mine. You did yours. You don't buckle, you remain constant: that's important.' He nodded towards the white-painted chair by the dressing-table. 'May I sit down?'

I nodded back, attempting a relaxed little smile, but inside I was begging him to tell me that it wasn't true, that there was no way he could hate me. *I love you Linus. Love you love you love you. Don't hate me back because I've never loved before and the pain might kill me.* I shrugged my shoulders. 'Oh well.' What a bright, relaxed little thing I was.

'You're sure you're all right?' he said. 'This sleep-walking. You see I know you had that, that . . .'

'Nervous breakdown,' I filled in. It was essential for lovers to be honest with one another and right now I was pretending that was what we were: lovers. Then again, one mustn't forget that even among lovers there was a place for deception. So I sighed and rolled my eyes. 'It's an awful nuisance, though, this sleep-walking. I'm really sorry to have given you such a fright.'

'Don't mention it,' Linus said, giving me another warm smile before getting up. 'I just wanted to make sure you were OK.' As I watched him walk towards the door I wondered if some kind of fit might stop him from leaving. Nothing too dramatic, just some twitching, a quick collapse on to the floor, no the bed, and some gentle foaming at the mouth. Before I had time to reflect further he was gone.

So that was the power of love, I thought, as I listened to his footsteps disappear down the gravel path: to turn you into the kind of person you'd cross the street to avoid.

Bertil was up and about again, and he and Olivia were already busy organising the evening's event. As I walked in through the back door she bustled past me with a vase of rain-drenched roses, Astrid's roses. The scent trailed behind her like a memory. 'We'll just have to be inside.' She peered out of the kitchen window at the sky. There was no sign of any brightening among the solid grey. Olivia had explained to me a couple of days before, when she first suggested the party, that on the island it was considered bad form to issue invitations far in advance. 'People come here to relax. They don't want to be tied down to schedules and checking their diaries every other minute. We all get enough of that in town. No, here spontaneity is the name of the game.'

I felt a tickle of unease. 'I hate not knowing ahead.'

'Why?' Olivia asked me on her way out of the room.

I shrugged. 'I just do. Anyway, I thought Swedes lived organised, planned lives.'

'Not in July,' Olivia said from the doorway.

I followed her out on to the veranda. Gerald was asleep in the rocking chair, and he stirred and mumbled, his mouth making little chewing movements, as Olivia passed, placing the vase of roses on the coffee table in front of him. Next she bustled off again, calling for Linus. He appeared from upstairs, carrying a half-finished Lego model of a racing car.

'Is Pernilla able to come?' Olivia wanted to know. I crossed my fingers behind my back and shut my eyes.

'Of course. She wouldn't miss it for the world,' I heard Linus answer. I should have known better than to trust to superstition rather than good old hands-on measures like locking her in her bedroom or taking her eyes out with hot pokers.

'What are you thinking about?' Olivia asked me.

I started guiltily. 'Anyway,' she went on, not waiting for an answer, 'it looks as if there'll be about thirty of us tonight.' At this, there was a roll of thunder, waking Gerald, and the rain started to fall once more from a blackening sky. How much better it would have sounded, I thought, against the mentioning of Pernilla's name.

'Look.' Ivar came rushing in from upstairs, pointing out of the window at a sudden burst of fork lightning.

'Your Aunt Ulla's being recharged,' Gerald said.

'Is she like Frankenstein's monster?' Ivar asked, turning to look, round-eyed, at Gerald.

'Not as pretty,' Gerald answered. Olivia looked as if she was about to tick him off when Kerstin appeared with a tray with coffee and buns, and those little squares of sugar-sprinkled chocolate biscuits that I had grown particularly fond of. They did a lot of eating at Villa Rosengård: cake and buns and biscuits and little toasted sandwiches with buttered chanterelles and rye cracker bread with strong cheese. In the evening, after supper there were bowlfuls of sweets and plates of green, seedless grapes. At least Audrey couldn't complain about the food. I myself was growing quite plump with it all, my stomach straining against my jeans button.

There was another crash of lightning and Ivar squealed excitedly, running from one of the large windows to the other. Puddles were forming on the gravel path and in the biggest, sparrows were having a bath. By the time Bertil and, moments later, Ulla had joined us, the entire path was flooded.

'You should cancel,' Ulla said.

'Certainly not, I'm British.' Olivia winked at me.

'When it suits you,' Ulla muttered. 'I suppose that next you'll both be wearing berets and serving garlic with everything. As it happens, the educated French abhor garlic in all its forms.'

Bertil, grey-faced under his tan and slightly stooping, as if he was expecting something to collapse on his head at any second, smiled at her and shook his head. 'Whatever are you talking about?'

They said he had made a full recovery, but looking at him, I wondered. Ulla, though, looked perkier than I had seen her for a long time as she bustled across to her favourite chair by the tiled stove with her sewing basket. 'I thought I'd start on the vent pull.' She nodded towards the brass handle up high on the side of the stove. 'I've found a lovely little pattern, forget-me-nots.'

Bertil and Olivia exchanged glances. 'What's the point, you

demented woman,' Gerald scoffed. 'Unless you're planning it as a gift for the new owners.'

'We might decide to stay, after all,' Olivia began. 'These last couple of weeks have shown me the importance of having family and friends close as one gets older.'

Ulla looked up with a little smile, a smug and, for her, curiously gentle smile. 'It's as I've always said, there's nothing more important than family. You know my view on this move. I think it's madness even to contemplate it. You'd regret it, mark my words.'

'Nonsense,' Bertil interrupted. 'And it's not like you to fuss so, Olivia. A bit of tummy trouble, that's all. You heard what the doc said; I simply ate something that didn't agree with me.'

'You ate a bit of Aunt Ulla.' Ivar giggled. 'She doesn't agree with you.' At this he threw himself back on the rug and laughed uproariously.

Ulla glared, but Bertil ignored him. He lowered himself down into the wicker armchair by the window and said, 'If you really want to know, I'm more determined than ever to make the move. While there's still time.' He picked out his pipe from his pocket and lit it, seemingly oblivious of Olivia's worried frown.

Ulla looked at them both. Then, all of a sudden she leapt to her feet like some malevolent jack-in-the-box. 'Is that it? Is no one going to discipline that boy? Is that how he's going to be encouraged to behave?' And she stormed from the room.

'Biscuit anyone?' Olivia passed the plate round.

I looked at my watch; it was gone eleven already. 'What would you like me to do?' I asked Olivia. 'About the party, I mean?' I took the plate and helping myself to a chocolate square, held it out for Ivar who was sitting cross-legged on the floor next to my chair.

Olivia said that everything was under control. 'Fru Sparre will be here in a minute.' She said that in the kind of trusting but awestruck way that is normally reserved for announcements of the coming of the Messiah. I soon saw why. Gertrude Sparre sailed into Villa Rosengård just as the physiotherapist was leaving after a session with Audrey. The two women, who obviously knew each other, stopped and spoke in Swedish, nodding now and then towards my mother's room. After that it took Fru Sparre only moments to assume command of all she surveyed. Audrey, who was about to defy the physiotherapist's instructions and sneak back to bed, was made to hobble out on to the veranda and a hard chair by the window. Gerald was sent off with the newspapers and Kerstin was put to work making meatballs. Bertil was told he looked as if he could do with a rest.

'But I've just had one,' he protested, sounding like Ivar. He was told to have another one and meekly followed Gerald upstairs. 'You,' she said in English, turning to me. 'You shall take the child outside to play so that he does not run between our feet all day.'

'But it's raining,' I protested, sounding as pathetic as Bertil.

Fru Sparre had learnt the first lesson in world domination well: reduce your subjects to the status of children. 'There are rain clothes,' she said and disappeared into the kitchen.

I looked mournfully after her. 'Come on then, Ivar, we'd better go.'

I had just donned a long blue oilskin coat and a bright-yellow sou'wester when there was a knock on the door and Pernilla stepped in, pulling back the hood of her red raincoat. 'I've come to help,' she announced, bending forward and shaking out her hair. I looked around for Fru Sparre; she'd soon sort her out. And there she was, coming out of the kitchen herding Kerstin and Olivia off towards the dining-room ahead of her. She stopped as she spotted Pernilla and her face softened.

'Hello *Sparrhök*.' Pernilla grinned, tossing her head and flipping her hair back over her shoulders.

I looked at her admiringly. She dared to call the Higher Being by a nickname even if it was a butch one like Sparrow Hawk. To my amazement, Fru Sparre smiled. 'How are your parents, my dear? Professor Lindholm's back still playing up?'

I shook my head sadly. How could I hope to compete with a woman who made even Fru Sparre smile. I grabbed Ivar's hand and walked out into the rain.

Wiping the water from my eyes and removing my mascara at the same time, I looked at Ivar. 'So what do we do now?'

'Canals,' Ivar said. Dressed from head to foot in tartan oilskins he was already on his way to the shed. He emerged from there carrying two small buckets and two plastic spades, one blue and one red.

'Canals?' I repeated.

'You dig them and make all the water run down them and then you make dams and all sorts of things. It's really good fun.' He tramped off towards the gate.

'Can't we stay in the garden?' I asked him.

'You like staying in the garden, don't you? You don't like going out much?' Nothing escaped that child, I thought. 'Ulla said you were an agorogo ... agorof ... someone who doesn't like to go out.'

'Agoraphobic,' I interjected. 'And I'm not. Let's go.'

'You see, if I dig canals in the garden I could get into trouble. I might be sent to bed before *The Flintstones*.' He opened the gate. 'Or I might not get my Saturday sweets ...' He shrugged his little shoulders, the palms of his hands raised to the sky. 'Anything could happen.' He gave me one of the buckets and the blue spade. 'So you don't have this *phobia* thing?'

'A *phobia* is being scared of something there's no need to be scared of. It's called an irrational fear.' Ivar looked at me blankly so I tried it again in Swedish. This seemed to confuse him further, so I just told him, 'I'm not scared of going outside, I simply prefer not to sometimes.'

'That's good,' Ivar said. 'My mummy says scared women are a bad example. That's why I have to be extra brave,' he added with his own logic.

'What about scared men?'

Ivar stopped and thought for a moment. 'Oh,' he said. 'I expect they're allowed.' The rain flooded the brim of my sou'wester, dripping down the back of my neck and down my face over the tip of my nose. The street and the harbour below were deserted other than for a solitary Snipa boat, its captain invisible beneath the bright blue awning. A little ghost vessel out to fish. I followed behind Ivar, past the small yellow-painted school and the long, low, red vicarage, down Church Street and up Smugglers' Alley, past the old burial ground and up to the small road that ran along the cliff edge at the eastern side of the island. 'Are you allowed to go this far?' I asked, him.

'If I'm with you, I am,' he said, slipping his small rain-washed hand into mine. The simple gesture of trust in me, of confidence in my superior status as an adult, made me walk taller in spite of the pouring rain. A few yards further along the road Ivar freed his hand and stopped, looking around him before squatting down in the middle of the road. 'Here's a good place to start,' he said, jabbing at the wet dirt with his little plastic spade. I watched him as he dug and scraped, huffing and puffing with the effort.

'But Ivar, if you dig these trenches in the road someone could come along and trip up and hurt themselves.'

Ivar squatted back on his heels and looked up at me through the rain. 'They won't if they look where they're going.'

'But sometimes people don't. What then?'

'Then they'll have to be brave and pick themselves up again. Anyway, Mummy says you should always look where you're going.'

I crouched down next to him. 'And what about your father, what does he say?'

'He says things like "Where people live affects them more than anything and yet no one is prepared to spend any money",' Ivar parroted, word perfect and without looking up from his work. I scraped at the sandy road surface with my blue spade. Ivar worked his way down the hill. After a while he looked up. 'You're not digging very hard.'

I looked at the five feet or so of water-filled trenches running down the street. 'No,' I agreed. 'Maybe I'm not suited to this kind of work?'

'Daddy also says that all work is hard and boring at times, but that if you want to get to the good bits you have to do the bad bits first.'

'So what're going to be the good bits?' I asked, looking up at the dark-grey sky.

Ivar put out his little hands, palms raised. 'Opening the dams, silly.'

My hair was plastered across my cheeks and I could have sworn my gumboots were leaking. Knees creaking, I got to my feet. 'I don't care what Fru Sparre says, I'm going home. Are you coming?'

'We haven't finished yet. You should always finish what you've started.'

I sighed and joined him. 'Where do you want it, this dam?'

'There,' Ivar stabbed at a pot already filling with water. 'I'm going to make it' – he paused and looked at me with eyes just like his father's – 'huge!'

We dug in silence for what seemed like a very long time. 'We've only done it for ten minutes,' Ivar said soothingly when he found me looking at my watch yet again. 'And anyway, Fru Sparre wouldn't like it if you brought me back already.'

'I thought this place was so safe children were allowed out on their own.'

Ivar straightened his back and looked at me primly. 'You mustn't forget that I'm not even seven,' he said. 'I might fall into the sea.'

'Why should you fall into the sea? People don't just walk along and fall into the sea.'

'They do. They do here,' Ivar said.

There was nothing for it but to carry on digging. Soon there was a sizeable puddle before us; Ivar's dam. And at last he seemed satisfied. 'All done?' I got to my feet, my knees creaking.

'We haven't done the canal *from* the dam, silly.' Ivar laughed heartily at my folly. 'That's the most important thing.' As I knelt down once more, spade in hand, I decided I must be very fond indeed of that little boy. I'd like to see anyone else trying to make me spend my day crouching in mud, with rain cascading down my face and neck, and a small plastic spade in my hand.

'Ready!' Ivar shouted triumphantly a few feet down from the dam. 'Open the slush gate.' I removed the stone and mud from the side of the puddle. The water gushed out and down the dug trench as Ivar jumped up and down, clapping his hands in excitement.

We were almost home when we caught up with Pernilla and Linus. 'Whatever have you been doing, Esther?' She stood before me, immaculate even in the pouring rain, her white Capri pants still miraculously white, her face unsmudged and tanned under the baseball cap pulled down across her forehead. Linus had picked up Ivar, who was busy explaining the wonders of his canals, and was carrying him the last bit up the hill to the house. 'I tell you.' Pernilla lowered her voice conspiratorially. 'Chanel's waterproof mascara is incredible. I don't know how I'd get through the summer without it.'

I said I could see it would be a tough call, but inwardly I felt small. A messy appearance hid a messy mind and I couldn't abide mess.

'I'm glad to see you out of the house and garden,' Pernilla continued as we walked back together. 'I was beginning to think you were at risk of becoming agoraphobic.' She was speaking in her careful Swedish-American English. 'That's when you fear open spaces,' she explained helpfully.

'Agoraphobic schmobic.' I sniffed. 'Of course I'm not. In fact, I don't know what you're all talking about. I've already explained to Ivar. It's nothing strange, I'm just a stay-at-home kind of girl at heart, that's all.'

'I think you're having a problem facing up to this one,' Pernilla singsonged. 'Ulla told me your mother has spent the last couple of years in bed although she's physically perfectly healthy, or at least, she was until her fall. Do you think her behaviour has something to do with all of this? I mean, behavioural patterns can be repeated down the generations.' Pernilla was looking earnestly at me as if behind the carefree glamorous exterior there was a psychotherapist waiting to get out, which, come to think of it, there was. She had told me only the other day that she was planning to do a course in Jungian therapy.

I tried my best not to get irritated. 'You don't say?' We had reached the back door and we slopped inside, dripping water on the pale-blue linoleum. 'Anyway, my mother has never been saner,' I said firmly as I divested myself of my oilskins. It didn't mean much, of course, but there was no need for Pernilla to know that.

Linus burst through the door with a laughing, shrieking Ivar in his arms. He pretended to put Ivar down head first before turning him back the right way up and placing him gently on the floor. I decided that if he said 'What are you two girls gossiping about?' I would forget any tender disconcerting feelings I had developed for him and that love would evaporate into the thin air of illusion. It was a test, that was what it was.

'So.' He stopped in front of me, his grey eyes bright and his hair dark from the rain and curling wildly round his head. 'What are you two girls gossiping about?'

My mouth, which was preparing to stay clamped shut and frosty, began to quiver and slowly and against my will, I'm absolutely sure it was against my will, it spread into a wide smile. 'Oh, nothing,' I simpered.

I was horrified. Was this love? After all this time wondering and searching, was this it? Was love acting against your nature and your better judgement? Was it closing your ears to the voice of reason? Was love something that turned you into the kind of woman you would throw a bucket of cold water over had she been someone else?

Fru Sparre appeared and with a withering glance in my direction (had she heard or did she just despise me anyway?) she gathered up our wet clothes in her arms. 'So you're back already,' she said to me. 'With Ivar.' She turned to Linus. 'You've got the wine?'

'I'm collecting it at four.'

'Miss Fisher, you might like to dust the books in the dining-room. They're very nasty.'

'Nasty?'

'Dirt, dust.'

'Oh, right. I'll see to it.' I slunk off to find a duster.

These were holiday bookcases. The books on the shelves were that kind of mix: rows of old detective stories by Agatha Christie and Dorothy Sayers, Ngaio Marsh and Carter Dickson, much read, tattered and smelling softly of mould and dust, the pages stained with dark-yellow spots. There were bound copies of Swedish classics. 'August Strindberg, Selma Lagerlöf, Vilhelm Moberg, Harry Martinson,' I read the names of the authors out loud as I turned the books in my hand, dusting them with the brown feather duster that I had found in the scullery cupboard. There was a whole row of P. G. Wodehouse, all in English, and suddenly, tall and snooty in its pale-blue-and-gold binding, a volume of *Crime and Punishment* in Swedish. I found some children's books, mostly *Just William* stories and an ancient copy of *The House at Pooh Corner*.

Time passed because I was slow about my work, reading a page here and a page there, at random, even wrapping my tongue round the unfamiliar syllables of the Swedish books. I think I understood that in *Hemsöborna* by August Strindberg a man arrived like a whirlwind, and that in a novel by Selma Lagerlöf a boy called Nils rode on the back of a goose. Then I heard Fru Sparre's commanding voice come closer and I speeded up my dusting.

I had to go twice to the window to shake the duster, and the damp air made the dust fall heavy to the ground instead of rising on the air in a powder-puff explosion.

I continued my work. I had started on a row of old volumes of *Reader's Digest* when I found a little parcel tucked in behind, right at the back of the shelf. Inside the layers of paper was a small book bound in red leather, its spine and cover bare of any inscription. I swept the feathers of my duster over its front and back, then opened it to blow across the top of its pages. They were handwritten and I opened the book fully. It was a diary of some sort, had to be, with the dates filled in at the top of each new page. The writing was large and round, and the ink was always blue. The first entry was from the thirtieth of May nineteen sixty-five. Bertil was mentioned and as I flicked through the pages I saw Linus's name too, and Ulla and Gerald, even Fru Sparre. I made a mental note to look more closely at the diary later, before wrapping it up again and putting it back where I'd found it. Last I dusted the photographs – there were four of them, in carved wooden frames. A couple of them were of people I had never seen, but there was one of Olivia, a younger, lighter Olivia, her arm tucked under Bertil's, her face turned upwards towards his. They were smiling. Another showed Ivar as a plump baby held in his father's arms and with a blonde young woman, wholesome-looking, pretty in a pointy-featured kind of way, standing next to them. Lotten, I assumed. Linus preferred blondes. You would have thought he'd have learnt his lesson first time around and that now he'd be happy to settle for a nice dark-haired witch, but oh no, he had to go running after Pernilla.

It was raining still. Linus must have gone out again because I bumped into him in the hallway and he was soaking once more, water dripping from the sleeves of his grey-green fisherman's jersey. I was about to say you're wet, when I decided not to. He probably knew already. It made me think just how much time we spend stating the obvious to each other: 'You must be tired,' we say to the friend who's just flown in from Australia. 'Did that hurt?' we ask solicitously of someone who's just walked into a low beam. Or 'That looks heavy' to the man who, legs buckling, is passing with a load of packing cases in his arms.

'I'm a bit wet.' Linus smiled apologetically.

Then again, stating the obvious was a pretty good way of opening a conversation, I decided quickly. I smiled back at him. 'You are, aren't you, poor thing.' My voice sounded like someone else's, someone fluffy and cute and dimpled. Who was this woman? Love was a disease and as it progressed it changed me, distorted me. Soon I would wake up and be a different person entirely. It was the speed with which love struck that surprised me, the invasiveness of it. There I'd been, much the same as always, and there I was now, covered in attraction, ridden with the aches and pains of love. How had it happened? Why? And at my age.

'I'd better get out of these wet clothes,' Linus said. 'Before Fru Sparre gets me.' He squelched off.

On my way from seeing Audrey, a smaller, fainter Audrey whose voice had been reduced to a soft whine and whose plump prune cheeks sagged, I stumbled over Ivar. He was lying flat on his stomach on the floor outside the kitchen, scribbling in a notebook. 'I'm going to be a journalist when I grow up. Just like Lois Lane.'

'I'm a journalist,' I said. 'But not quite like Lois Lane, not lately, anyway. More like . . .' I thought for a moment '. . . Enid Blyton.'

'I didn't know Enid Blyton was a journalist.' Olivia stood in the kitchen doorway, wiping her large hands on her red apron.

'Who was a journalist?' Ulla had had a nap and now she joined us ready for battle.

'Enid Blyton,' Olivia said.

'Enid Blyton was an author of children's books.' Ulla sniffed. 'Surely you know that.'

'I didn't mean that Enid Blyton was . . .'

'I cannot understand how anyone can have failed to have heard of Enid Blyton's children's novels,' Ulla nagged. '*Famous Five, Secret Seven* . . .'

I escaped back to the cottage. It was time to get ready for the party anyway. Going through my drawers and the white-painted wardrobe I wished, maybe for the first time in my life, that I were more like my mother. Audrey was a woman who thought travelling light was an equation by Einstein. She would have brought just the right outfit for an evening like tonight, an evening spent in a wooden house on an island in the company of the man you loved and the woman he loved. As it was, I had a pair of black cotton trousers and one grey and one black cardigan. I also had my Posy-type dress, and of course some jeans and shorts. I rooted round the shelves and drawers. Surely I had packed something else. Oh yes, a tweed jacket? Why? I chucked it to one side. Then I picked it up and hung it back in the wardrobe. I was fond of that jacket. And it had been very expensive when I bought it five years ago. I looked at my watch. It was almost six. The shops were open until at least seven. The party started at six thirty so if I hurried, I could make it. I rushed out into the rain, down the hill and on to the promenade. There were several shops selling clothes along the harbour front and, blinded by the rain, I dived inside the first.

Summer clothes, sorbet clothes, I touched the sleeve of a tomato-red man's sports jacket. The minutes ticked by as I moved around the shop. There was nothing here for me. The next place was no better, full of hearty shorts and those brightly patterned polo shirts the Swedes seemed so fond of. At last, in the third shop I found the dress I wanted. Actually it was a frock: white with large cornflower-blue flowers strewn across it, tight-bodiced and wide-skirted. I found the right size and held the dress up in front of me in the mirror, there was no time for trying anything on. It looked as if it would fit and the colours suited me. I paid and hurried from the shop, the bag in my hand. I was pleased with myself. I had bought a frock and in no time at all. I had, in fact, been decisive. I clutched the carrier to my chest. Linus had never seen me in a *pretty* dress.

# Chapter Twenty-four

The guests arrived two by two, up the hill and through the gate as rain kept coming from the sky. 'It's like the great flood,' Ulla, who was standing at the window, said. She sounded pleased. 'I expect Olivia intended tonight as a little goodbye party.'

Not many minutes later the rain turned into a light drizzle, then stopped altogether. Ulla turned away from the window with a face like someone who's turned up to see a nice execution only to find there had been a general amnesty.

I went across to the cottage to get a cardigan and on my way back I paused for a moment and looked towards the house. The garden had that new look about it, the leaves of the plants washed clean of dust and grime, the petals of the flowers unfurling. A sparrow appeared cautiously from under a lilac bush and looked around him, before hopping on towards the bird-bath, his head turning rapidly from side to side. From outside, Villa Rosengård looked as if it were ready to split at the joins, there were so many people inside. A back was pressed against the hall window, two or three more against those of the veranda. Then the French doors opened and Olivia led the way out on to the deck, followed by a stream of guests. Blonde, brown-legged women in bright sleeveless dresses bent down and sniffed the water-logged roses. Bertil and Linus walked around their guests refilling glasses. 'What a wonderful night it has turned out to be,' someone exclaimed and out of the corner of my eye I noticed Ulla, standing a little apart, glaring up at the sky as if she could not forgive it for brightening up.

Linus was talking to a middle-aged man to whom I had been introduced, but whose name I couldn't for the life of me remember. Probably something to do with Blom, or Lund, or Berg. Swedes were seen as dour and stolid, but how could they be when they named themselves Björn Blomkvist – Bear Flowerbranch – or Ulf Bergström – Wolf Mountainstream? You could stand in a gathering like this and chuck a brick and be sure it would hit someone with an impossibly poetic name: Smash! straight into Mrs Meadowcops. Bash! a direct hit on old Mr Lindentree. Linus was holding a bottle of wine, gesticulating with his free hand as he leant against the wooden banister of the terrace.

'It was the most amazing sight,' I heard him say as I moved closer. 'This one moment when the setting sun turned the cliff face gold and for a few seconds, no more, the sea was striped in wide bands of yellow and turquoise. It was over in seconds but while it lasted it was heavenly.' '*Himmelskt*,' he said. I drew closer, attracted to the warmth and enthusiasm in his voice and the soft, almost feminine choice of words. I had just finished reading a play by a Swedish eighteenth-century writer about a being, neither male nor female, but whatever you wanted him/her to be. A sprite, a spirit, it captivated anyone who dared come close. It just goes to show how far gone – lovegone, lovelorn – I was that I saw Linus as that being. But the arrival of another creature, all pale hair and golden limbs, wrapped in silver and white, interrupted my thoughts. This one was wearing a frock not unlike mine, but on her it looked as if it had been created straight on to her slim body.

'Linus, I've been looking for you.' Pernilla's voice was thick and a little slurred. Audrey used to sound like that about three hours into a party. I didn't stop to see the delight in Linus's eyes as he looked at her, but turned on my heel and walked straight into an apparition of a different kind. This one was large and elderly, and shrouded in green chiffon, with a huge floppy-brimmed hat in peacock-blue placed low over her forehead, almost obscuring her face. The woman peered at me in the terrace light. She took a step back, still looking, then grabbed me by the elbow and said something in Swedish about a good face. She quickly changed to English. 'You're Esther Fisher,' she announced as if she was glad to be able to tell me. 'I said you've got a good face. I might decide to paint you.' She paused and stared some more. 'Are you bored by this party?'

'Bored? No, no, not at all.'

The woman looked a little surprised but said nothing for a while. Then she pointed towards Linus. 'That one's very pretty,' she said.

'You mean Pernilla?'

'Who? No, no. I'm talking about the young Stendal, Linus.'

'You haven't got a glass, Esther.' Bertil had joined us, a bottle in each hand. He handed them to me and disappeared, returning with a clean glass, swapping it for the bottles. 'Red or white?' he said to me. 'You'll have red, Asta, I know.' I said 'white', before changing my mind and saying, 'No, red actually. But only if you have enough. I would be just as happy with white.' The evening was warm and the air was humid, pregnant with rain. A white-wine evening. 'Actually,' I said as Bertil was about to tip the bottle, 'I'd prefer white.' Bertil gave me a look and poured me some.

'You should learn to be more decisive,' Asta said.

'Oh, I am a very decisive person, really,' I assured her. 'I'm just taking a year out, a kind of gap year where I'm rather indecisive. The year is almost up, though.' Out of the corner of my eye I was watching Linus and Pernilla. Did that girl have *no one* else to talk to? As if in answer to my question, Pernilla laughed and shrugged her bare brown shoulders. I was so busy watching that unintentionally I raised my own in a little shrug and threw my head back in a pretence laugh. Then I noticed Asta's sharp eyes on me and I grinned idiotically.

'He hasn't suggested it, but who knows, I might throw a few things in my rucksack and go,' I heard Pernilla say. In answer to what? I wanted to know.

'Just do it,' Asta said. 'Snap.' For a second I thought she was referring to Pernilla. But love had enhanced my sight and my hearing beyond normal realms. I could see for miles, it seemed, if it were Linus's face in the distance and there were no words too soft or too quiet for me to pick up if they concerned him. Love had made my skin so sensitive that a touch left an imprint that could last for ever. No, Asta had heard nothing of the conversation going on behind her.

'You should always make up your mind like this.' She raised her free hand and snapped her fingers.

'I'm working on it,' I said.

Kerstin appeared beside us. For the evening she was wearing a short flower-sprigged skirt and a sweat-shirt with a pattern of tortoises playing netball. 'What are you working on?' she asked.

I assured her it was nothing and left her with Asta. I liked Asta, but she saw too much.

Linus had his arm round Pernilla's shoulder. 'That's what I adore about this woman; she's so easygoing, no fuss, nothing's a problem.'

'What about me?' I wanted to yell. 'Look at me, I'm easygoing . . .' That's where the thought stopped. Dour? Yes. Sullen? Maybe. Exact and ponderous? Possibly. But easygoing? Not in a million years. With one last look at the tall, fair couple so unlike me, I turned and wandered off into the house.

'There you are.' Fru Sparre handed me a jug of iced water. 'You can pass this round.' She didn't waste time on unnecessary pleasantries, that was for sure. Come to think of it, she didn't seem to waste time on necessary ones either, but like everyone else, I was putty in the woman's hand and I turned and walked meekly back outside with the jug.

Linus was telling some story. All I could hear as I passed through the throng was talk of plastic mouldings, then he laughed, that laugh. It sounded good to me. I asked him if he wanted some water.

He smiled at me, a mocking little smile, fuzzy with alcohol. 'Water,' he said with pretend indignation. 'That's what fish pee in.' He began to recite some Swedish limerick concerning two brothers called Montgomery who drank nothing but Pommery. That's where he lost me. I stood there, wanting to say something sparkling, witty . . . something, anything, but all I could think of was that he'd have a headache the next morning. Pernilla who had disappeared, mercifully but all too briefly, returned and I melted away with my jug of water. I bet she was saying something sparkling, even as I left.

## Chapter Twenty-five

But were was Ivar? It was almost ten o'clock and most of the guests had left when Linus came rushing out of the house asking, 'Has anyone seen Ivar? He's not in his room or anywhere in the house.'

We all searched the garden. We looked in the shed and in the cellar under the house, but there was no sign of him. Linus, Bertil and the remaining guests, men and women alike, disappeared out into the still light night, searching.

Gerald came crawling out from under the deck. 'He and I sometimes look for hedgehogs,' he explained, getting to his feet and brushing down his pale-blue suit.

'He'll probably come bumbling in any minute,' Olivia said, but her face was strained with the effort of staying calm. 'I think I'd better wait here for him.'

I had intended to go along with the search, but now I wondered if I'd be more use staying with Olivia. I was about to offer when Pernilla came up to her, putting her arm round her with easy affection. 'Let me make you a cup of tea, Olivia. You and I'll wait here. There's absolutely no point everyone rushing out.'

I had a sudden vision of our network of canals. 'I think I know where he might have gone,' I said. 'If you see Linus, tell him to go to the little side-street above the old burial ground.'

I ran out of the garden and down the hill, past the school, turning left by the vicarage and down Church Street. The streets were well lit but I still took a wrong turn. At last, sweaty and out of breath, I reached the road where Ivar and I had dug his canals, but there was no sign of him. I had been so sure that that was where he had gone, to check on his work, but the road was deserted. I crouched down by the dam and heard sobbing.

I scrambled to my feet shouting Ivar's name and to my relief he replied, 'Esther. Esther, I'm stuck.' His voice was weak, but I was sure it was coming from the cliffs. I rushed across the road and peered down towards the sea. Then I saw him, a dark shape on a small ledge. 'Ivar, is that you? Are you hurt?'

'I fell and I'm really scared I'll fall more.' Then he said something in Swedish about his leg and the sobbing got worse.

'It's all right, Ivar,' I called down to him. 'I'm here now.' But what to do for the best? Should I try to reach him? But the cliff was steep and smooth, and the chances were I'd fall too and then what use would I be? A rope? I looked around. No rope. Go for help? That was it. But whatever I did, I had to make sure that Ivar remained calm. If he panicked he might fall further and this time he might not survive. I was familiar enough by now with the waters around the island to know that under the surface jagged rocks rose like gravestones, unseen from above. Boats went aground and divers died on those rocks.

'Please, Esther, can you come and get me?'

'Hang in there, Ivar. I just want to think how best to get you up from there.' What to do? What to do? I didn't dare leave him while I ran for help. 'Just hang in there,' I said again. 'I'll get you out of this.' Ivar was crying again. How could I get down to him? And once there, how could I get us both to safety? I needed my thoughts to be orderly, lined up straight, logical and clear. But instead they rushed round my skull, bumping into each other and screaming contradictory instructions like a cinema audience who'd just heard the attendants yell '*Fire!*'

I pressed my hands against the sides of my head. *Easy does it*, I told myself. *Think cool and calm*. I obviously wasn't hearing properly because I was still panicking.

Decision, indecision, bad decision, where were the rules now? Ivar sobbed. I sat down on the cliff's edge and lowered my legs down towards the ledge. 'It's all right, I'm coming down. I'll have you safe in no time.' Scrabbling with my heels I tried in vain to find a foothold, but there was nothing. If I jumped I would land right on top of Ivar. I looked down at the sea. What if I dived in and climbed up? But the cliff was smooth for the last few feet running down to the water and I would have no more chance of scaling it than I would a bare wall.

'Esther, I feel sick.'

I felt sick too. 'I should go for help.'

'Don't go,' Ivar screamed. 'Don't go, Esther.'

'What shall I do?' I screamed back. 'I can't get to you.'

*Please God, tell me what to do.*

A gull circled overhead like a vulture, squawking. Ivar wept. I took a deep breath and then I clambered over the edge of the cliff and down towards him. 'I'm coming,' I said, forcing out the words. 'I'm on my way.' It was getting dark fast now and I peered down to see where to place my sandal-clad foot. Next thing I knew I was sliding down the cliff, the thorns of a wild rose tearing at my hands and wrists. I scrabbled wildly for something to hang on to, to stop the slide, and got hold of the thin branch of a tiny tree. I dislodged a piece of rock with my foot and moments later there was a piercing scream from Ivar.

'What happened?'

'It hurts.' Ivar's voice reached me from below. 'My head hurts.'

I stayed where I was, unable to proceed downwards. Another false step and next time I might kill him. What to do, oh what to do?

'I'm feeling dizzy.'

'It's going to be all right, Ivar. Just stay as you are, absolutely still. No wriggling. If you stay still nothing bad can happen. I'm not leaving you on your own and you are not going to fall. I'll get down to you somehow.'

'Ivar, Ivar are you all right?' It was Linus and his voice was coming from the path above.

'Daddy, Daddy I'm here!' Linus had already run back down the path towards the bathing area, then he jumped. He fell down before me like a giant icicle in his shirt and trousers, and hit the water with a splash. 'Jump, Ivar,' he called as he surfaced. 'Jump into the water and I'll catch you.'

'I'm scared.'

'Don't be. Jump and I'll catch you.'

'I've hurt my leg and my head hurts too.'

'Just let yourself drop into the water. Daddy is here.' There was a silence, then a splash as Ivar rolled like a large caterpillar into the sea. From my vantage point, clinging on to the tiny tree, my feet steadied against a narrow ledge, I watched as Linus swam over to the steps, holding Ivar in a lifeguard's grip. He climbed the steps, Ivar safe in his arms, and at last I dared open my mouth to call for help. But nothing happened. I tried again and all that came out was a small croak as I watched them disappear into the distance. By the time I managed a good loud 'Help!' they were gone. I stayed where I was, clinging on. I didn't have a lot of choice.

'Ivar! Yohoo, Ivar!' It was Ulla's voice reaching out to me in the darkness.

'I'm over here,' I called.

'Who's that?' It was Gerald.

'It's me, Esther. Ivar's all right. He's with Linus.'

'So what are you still doing out here?' Ulla wanted to know.

'I'm stuck.'

'Where?'

'Cliff.'

Two faces, lined and pale in the sparse moonlight, peered over the cliff's edge some feet away. 'Over here,' I called again. The two heads disappeared and reappeared, huffing and puffing, muttering to one another in Swedish.

'Esther, what are you doing down there?' Ulla asked again.

Before I had the chance to answer something witty, like *Just hanging around*, Gerald had said, 'Don't ask such damn stupid questions, woman.' He pronounced it 'voman', Swedish style. 'I shall get a rope.'

'And what will you do with the rope?' Ulla asked. 'You haven't got the strength.'

'Then I shall get help.'

'I think Ivar will have told Linus that I'm here by now,' I said. 'Ivar fell, you see, and I found him, literally clinging on to the rocks and . . .' I paused. I could feel their anticipation in the air. What did the clever girl do?

'And I, I . . . Linus dived into the sea and swam round to just below where Ivar was, then he got Ivar to jump in too. He caught him and swam round to the steps and that was it. They should be home by now.'

'And Ivar is all right?' Ulla asked.

'I think he hurt his leg in the fall and a small rock fell on his head, that was my fault, I'm afraid, and of course he's had a shock, but I think he's fine otherwise.'

'So you jump too,' Ulla said. 'And then you swim round to the steps.'

273

Now why hadn't I thought of that? I was simply no good in a crisis, that's why. 'OK,' I said, getting ready to slip into the water. From where I was, it looked awfully far down. Then Gerald shouted at me to stop.

'Don't! It's shallow where you are. You'll kill yourself. No, you stay there and I'll get help.'

I clung on to where I was, getting used to the thought that I had been but Gerald's breath away from death. 'Linus should be on his way,' I said eventually. 'Ivar will have told him I'm here by now.' I paused. 'Then again, Ivar might have forgotten to mention it. He's probably in shock, poor little mite.'

'I'm off,' Gerald said. I heard him stomp away and I was left with Ulla, the summer sprite of ill will.

For a while we said nothing. I was feeling cold and my arms were aching.

Then Ulla's face appeared over the edge of the cliff. 'You weren't much use then, were you?' For once she didn't sound disapproving, but more like she was making chit-chat to pass the time.

'No,' I said. There was another pause.

'Still, I suppose you did your best.'

'I tried to. I'd like to think that me being here prevented him from panicking and falling further. And I did tell Olivia where to look for Ivar.'

'Astrid wasn't very practical, either,' Ulla went on. 'But you wouldn't expect her to be. *She* was an artist.'

It was obvious that I had no such excuse, but I tried. 'I write short stories, occasionally. And some people would call journalism an art form.'

'Really?'

I twisted a little to one side, making myself more comfortable. 'Why *did* she kill herself?'

There was a pause, which Ulla filled with sighs, before saying, 'I don't think now is the time to talk about it; you're hanging from a cliff.'

'I'm not really hanging, more perching. It would take my mind off it.'

There was another pause, then Ulla asked, perfectly politely for her, 'Are you mad?'

I told her that I wasn't. Not really. Disturbed, maybe, I mean who wasn't these days? But mad, no, I didn't think so. 'I'm just really curious. I want to know. I hate not knowing. It's by way of being a compulsion. But I'm being rude. I should respect your wish not to talk about it.' I looked up. The clouds had cleared and there were stars everywhere, little holes of light as if a thousand moths had eaten away at the fabric of the sky. I could smell the sea. No wonder Astrid had loved this island and her home on it. What had made her leave it all behind? And what about her child? How could she have done it, abandoned him so completely?

Ulla's head appeared again, gargoyle-like in the moonlight. 'We all failed her. None of us understood.'

In the silence that followed I tried to imagine her, Astrid of the full-blown, heavy-scented roses, Bertil's young bride, Linus's mother.

'She was a singer, you know that. They say her voice wasn't strong enough ever for her to have made the big league, but what do they know? It takes time for a voice to mature and she had so little time.' Ulla's voice had been brittle, coated in ancient resentments, but now it softened and became dreamy. 'Her parents died in an aeroplane crash when she was just a baby. The poor little thing grew up being passed from relative to relative like an unwanted parcel. Then my parents took her in and gave her a home. My father and her mother were brother and sister. Of course I was almost grown up by that time. She was happy with us, but her early childhood had left its scars. A feeling of being in the way, of being unwanted. She felt her parents' death as an abandonment. Logic had nothing to do with it. "Why wasn't I with them?" I remember her saying. "Why did they go off without me?" When it came to love she was like a leaking vessel; she could never have enough. I think she thought that having a home and a family of her own would be the solution to everything. Bertil offered her all the things she needed so badly. He was older, steady and successful. He was ready to have children and had the money to look after a family. And at first everything was good. Then she met *him*.'

'Who's him?'

'We're here.' I heard Bertil's voice. 'We'll have you up from there in no time.'

'So then what happened?' I asked Ulla as we trailed behind Bertil and Gerald on the road home.

'I'm tired,' Ulla snapped. The spell had been broken and she had turned back into a toad. 'Is it not an English expression *Curiosity killed the cat?*' she said.

'It was a car,' I said. 'I have it on good authority that it was a car. Anyway, you've told me so much, you can't just leave it like that, all up in the air.'

'Oh can't I.' Ulla muttered into the night.

I was in bed, still cold under the thin duvet, when there was a knock on my door. 'It's me, Linus. Can I come in?'

I sat up in the bed. 'Yeah, sure.'

There he was. I would like to say that he was framed in the doorway, but he was too big, it was more as if he were prising it apart to get in. 'You're in bed, I'm sorry.'

I could have pointed out that it was to be expected that I was in bed at one o'clock in the morning, especially after the night I'd had, but I didn't. Instead I sat up straight and pulled the duvet up under my chin. 'Did Ivar get to sleep all right?'

'Like a lamb.'

'I'm afraid I was pretty useless.'

'You weren't useless at all,' Linus protested. It was the kind of polite throw-away line one reaches for to avoid embarrassment (unless one's Ulla, of course) but coming as it did from Linus, I plucked it out and held it close, smiling with unexpected happiness. 'You really mean that? You don't think I was useless?'

'By what Ivar tells me we've got you to thank that nothing worse happened. I'm the one who's sorry, leaving you quite literally hanging. Ivar was in such a state he didn't think to tell me until he was safely tucked up in bed. I can't believe I didn't hear you calling.'

I shrugged, still smiling idiotically as if the air between us was made up of illegal substances. 'I was in a bit of a state myself. At first I didn't want to deflect you from getting to Ivar and then, well I kind of lost my voice, temporarily. You know I'm no good in a crisis any more. It's like any action has to be put before a judge and jury residing permanently inside my head, examined and argued over until no reasonable doubt remains.'

'Can't you just accept that life is a bit of a muddle?'

'No.' I banged my fist down on the bed, forgetting for a moment that I was in love with him.

Linus, leaning against the doorpost, gazed down on me like some benevolent deity, or so it seemed to me because I had remembered again. 'Try looking at it this way . . .'

'What way?' I interrupted in my eagerness to follow his every word.

'Think of it like this vast mural covered in so many layers of grime that you can't actually see the picture underneath. But you know it's there, all of it, that's the important thing and that all you can do is to get on and rub away at your own little corner, cleaning it up, making it clear. The thing is, you know the picture is worthwhile, just from the glimpses you get as you work away. The chance of you ever getting to see the whole is infinitesimal, but you know you have to keep going even unto your last gasp of breath.'

I had been busy visualising that darkened mural – I'd always enjoyed listening to stories – but now I had to ask why. 'Why should you keep trying when you know you'll never get there?'

'I told you, because otherwise all there is is darkness.'

'That's a cop-out ending,' I complained. 'It's like saying, "and the hero and heroine lived happily ever after . . . unless, of course, you know differently, in which case we'd like to hear from you on e dot lin dot inc dot."'

'What do you want me to do? Lie?'

I sat there looking at him and thought I could always say yes, then ask him really quickly if he loved me.

But before I got a chance he said, 'But all that matters right now is that you're both all right.' All at once there was such unexpected tenderness in his eyes that I had to look away. It was either that or throwing off my duvet and rushing into his arms. That would have been a high-risk strategy at the best of times, but tonight especially, because Kerstin had lent me her warmest pyjamas and they were baby-blue and had the legend *Cute and Pretty* embossed on the chest. Personally I think a black-and-white striped number with Alcatraz printed on it would have been more alluring.

'But you're tired. I must leave you to get some sleep.'

'No! I mean, I don't think I could sleep. I'd like the company.'

Linus smiled at me, then perched on the empty bed opposite. He looked funny, sitting there among all that lace. 'What are you grinning about?' he asked.

'You look funny, and . . . I'm just happy,' I said.

'Why?'

'I'm glad Ivar is all right. I'm glad you think I was of help after all and . . .' I shrugged.

'And?'

'Being with you right now makes me happy, all right?'

'Very all right.'

In the silence that followed I thought the beating of my heart could be heard right across the room to where Linus was sitting. He stood up. 'I suppose I should be off back to my own bed.' But he lingered for a moment and looked down at me, and now the tenderness was mixed with something else, was it amusement? What was so funny? I smiled back at him and put out my hand. He stepped forward and took it, turning it over in his larger ones. Then he bent down and kissed it lightly. 'Good-night.'

He was gone so quickly, but I stayed sitting up in bed, resting my hand, the right one, the hand that he had kissed, reverently in my left one. If I closed my eyes I could still feel the warmth of his lips against my skin.

## Chapter Twenty-six

'Aren't they beautiful?' I pointed at Astrid's roses. Audrey, squinting against the morning sun, bent down awkwardly over her crutches, muttered agreement, but there was no doubt she would have preferred to have seen them on telly or read about them in some beautifully illustrated book.

'You must be up and about at least for some part of the day,' I said, touching her elbow to make her move on. 'You know what the doctors said. Stay in bed and you'll most probably develop a blood clot.'

I walked a reluctant, hobbling Audrey along the gravel path and on to the lawn, an older, thinner Audrey in spite of all the Swedish syrup bread and custard buns and platefuls of fish and smoked sausage. I helped her to sit down on the small wooden bench beneath the apple tree, which was covered now with tiny leaf-green fruit, little sour promises of things to come. I sat myself down next to her on the grass, leaning my back against the seat. Soon Audrey was asleep, the trouble-free sleep of the just, or in the case of Audrey, the just-not-troubled-by-much-thought. I listened to her soft snoring and leant back on my elbows, my face lifted to the sun.

I must have gone over the events of the night before so many times I had worn a groove in the memory: the look of tenderness in his eyes, his lips pressed against my hand. He had gone into town this morning, Olivia had told me over breakfast. I was quite content not to see him because daylight might have changed the look in his eyes and for now I was happy with my dreams. Closing my eyes, I lifted my hand to my lips in a tender second-hand kiss.

I must have dozed off like Audrey, because I looked up with a start as Ulla, black in thought and tooth (yes really, she had slipped in the shower that morning and blackened her front tooth) stood over me. 'How are you today?' she asked.

'Fine,' I said. I noticed a small book in her hand and it reminded me of the diary I'd found the day before on the sitting-room shelves. 'Do you keep a diary?' I asked her.

'Yes, yes I do.' She didn't actually say what has it got to do with you, but I could see that was what she was thinking.

'I think it might have been an old one of yours that I found when I dusted the bookcase.'

'I shouldn't think so. I keep only my current one with me, the others are in my little flat in Gothenburg.' She stomped off towards the cottage.

A few minutes later I got to my feet; Audrey was still snoring softly in her chair. I wiped off a silvery thread of saliva from the corner of her mouth – I knew she liked to look good at all times – and went over to the house, I could hear Gerald's voice from the veranda, but no one else was about as I wandered into the sitting-room, scrabbling around behind the *Reader's Digests* until I found the diary.

Later that morning, once I'd settled Audrey back in her bed, I went into my room and had a good look at it. Once I saw the name Jonas coupled with Bertil and Linus, I was convinced it was Astrid's diary. Snooping in other people's diaries was not nice, but I understood very little. I could either put the little book back where I'd found it or I could show it to one of the family: to Linus or Olivia? It worried me that its existence might in fact be unknown to them as neither of them seemed very clear about what drove Astrid to take her own life. Checking the dates of the last entry I saw that it was made the year Linus would have been seven, so just before she died. But even as I went in search of Olivia, I changed my mind. I had no idea what was hidden among those pages, but it was bound to concern Bertil. The picture painted of a man by his first wife might well be one best not shown to his second, especially given what happened. So should I hand the diary to Linus, Astrid's son? But what reasons might she give for abandoning her son and were they reasons he could live with? He would know the truth and so would Olivia, but truth left corpses in its wake and I was frightened of what might be set in motion. And what about Astrid? Would she have wanted her son, let alone her husband's new wife, to read her heart and soul? What to do? Oh, what to do for the best?

I should give the diary to Bertil. He probably knew of its existence anyway. But if he didn't? Bertil had not been well. Reading his dead wife's thoughts on him and their life together, and of the man she left him for, could hardly be conducive to peace of mind.

There was a tentative little knock on my door and Ivar appeared with a message that my mother wanted me. I got up, complimenting him on his pale-green-and-turquoise chiffon scarf, and put the diary away at the bottom of my underwear drawer.

'Why did you hide that book?' Ivar wanted to know.

'What book?'

'The book you hided.'

'Hid,' I corrected to gain time as we wandered across the grass.

'Hid,' Ivar repeated, and then his attention was caught by Linus and Pernilla struggling through the gate with a cartload of bags and boxes. I stared at them too and the little bubble of delight in which I had resided since Linus left my room the night before burst and I was left shrouded in a sticky film of disappointment. How good they looked together, how at ease with one another. To anyone but me they would be 'that lovely couple'. And the lovely couple waved at me, each with their free hand, and Ivar rushed off to greet them. I went on my dark and jealous way, wanting badly, in the midst of all that bruising of the heart, to know what was in that diary.

The next two hours were taken up with trying to coax Audrey into doing her exercises. 'Why?' asked my mother.

'Because if you don't move you'll die,' I said.

'It was because I moved that I almost did die. None of this would have happened if I had stayed at home in my own bed.'

'But you didn't and . . .'

'. . . and whose fault is that?'

'Don't blame me. Roll the ankle, roll it. Just *roll* it for heaven's sake.'

I needed to take a long walk after that. The sun was out, turning the sea into that bright blue temptress once more. 'Come into my arms,' she called to me as I walked alongside her, turning the western corner of the island and continuing towards the woods. But I knew better than to trust that sincere blue, that free-of-jellyfish, clear and sparkling sea. 'I know you,' I muttered. 'You're cold.'

The boat bringing passengers from Gothenburg out on to the islands of the archipelago turned the southern point and steamed towards the harbour. The deck was crowded with holiday-makers and the vast sky-blue-and-yellow flag at the bow of the boat moved in the soft breeze. It was a day for optimists, so what was I doing out? I made my way back towards Villa Rosengård, the harbour way this time, weaving between the trippers and the helmeted children on bicycles and the shoppers with their baskets. The shoppers on this island were not like ordinary ones, I had noticed. These were *Brigadoon* shoppers, smiling, chatting, unhurried and unfrazzled, but set to disappear, to sink without trace once the month of July came to an end.

At the newsagent I stopped and bought the American edition of *Vogue* for Audrey. As I stepped outside, I bumped into Linus. He was alone, Pernilla-less, but, I thought bitterly, he probably carried her in his heart, like a little picture . . . or a malign growth . . .

'Hi there, Esther.'

'Hi there, Linus.' We started walking back together. I asked him what was in all those boxes he and Pernilla had carted up to the house.

'My office,' he said. 'I don't know how you'll take this, but I've just had a fax from Stuart Lloyd. He wants to resurrect the plans for the People's Glyndebourne. I should really have stayed in town, but I don't want to leave Ivar. He's due to go back to his mother next week anyway. So the work had to come to me.'

I said nothing so he asked me again if I minded. I thought about it and the more I thought the more confused I got; this was often the way. But I did know that I loved Linus and I also knew that two old people should not be evicted from the only home they'd known because they were in someone's way. So I answered truthfully, 'I'm not sure.'

'People fighting causes are the most dangerous ones,' Audrey had said to me the other day. She had looked stern. 'They feel they answer to a higher authority than the rest of us. You caused havoc with your articles about Linus's building, havoc, that's what you caused.' She had sighed and leant back against her pillows, closing her eyes. Opening them again she looked at me and said, 'Then you always did.' Out of the mouths of babes and demented old bats, I had thought at the time, but then I had been stung.

Linus stopped walking. 'You're not *sure*! You say that now?' His smile had vanished and his cheeks were slowly turning pink. '*I'm not sure*, you say. After everything you did. I believed you were passionate about what you were doing. I mean, I could understand someone acting out of passion, but to all but destroy someone's dream on an "I'm not sure"?'

Did the sun disappear behind a cloud? Like hell it did. Did the waves cease their beating of the rocks? They most certainly didn't. But I felt an icy hand grip my heart and squeeze and as it squeezed the tears rose in my eyes. They felt as if they were blood.

Doesn't that just show how fanciful love had made me?

I trundled on a couple of steps behind him, like a child in the wake of an angry adult. I loved him, but not even the most determinedly pastel-clad Swedish optimist could have found anything promising in Linus's and my relationship: my relationship with the man I loved. 'Oh Pastel-clad Swedish Optimist,' I'd query. 'Pray tell me what my chances are to live happily ever after with the man of my dreams?'

'None whatsoever, oh Dark-haired, Dark-minded Stranger,' the reply would come.

I sighed. Linus, deep in dark thoughts of his own, did not seem to notice. I sighed again, louder now. I wanted so badly to reach to him, to communicate with him, if only by me sighing and him asking what the hell was the matter? Or, miraculously, to ask me tenderly if all was well? But Linus said nothing and we reached the house in silence. He opened the gate and stood back to let me pass, then he followed. I had to explain. Before the anger took root in him I had to tell him that it wasn't how he thought it was; not that crass, not that simple, but where to begin? There were so many thoughts behind the actions that trying to pull them out was like sticking your hand inside a bag of maggots and choosing the plumpest.

I opened my mouth to speak. But it was too late. Gerald must have been looking out for us because he was already hurrying towards us on his stiff, thin legs, calling out to Linus.

'Go and see your parents,' he shouted and his old face was sagging more than ever, as if all the cares of the household had assembled like dust in the bags under his eyes and the pouches of his cheeks. 'Hurry, hurry.'

The colour drained from Linus's cheeks. He dropped the basket of shopping and hurried towards the house.

Gerald told me that Bertil had been taken ill again and that this time the attack had been worse, far worse, than the last. They were waiting for the ambulance and Dr Blomkvist was on his way.

A cheery hello made us turn, two actors in a drama facing a stray extra from the comedy show on the next-door set.

'Oh hello, Pernilla,' Gerald said, his voice distracted.

*Stay away you scarlet-princess-type person*, I wanted to cry. *This is family business.* But if it was, what business was it of mine? It was odd, but it was now more than ever, when things seemed to be going continuously wrong, that I wanted to belong with them all, be one of the family, not this English trouble-maker, this outsider.

Gerald was filling Pernilla in on the latest news. 'I'd better go and see what I can do,' she said, marching off as if to war. I wished she were marching off to war, that is. A really bloody one, just for a day or so, to give me a chance. Then I thought of Bertil and I felt ashamed.

'Don't.' Gerald's voice, surprisingly firm, called Pernilla to a halt. 'There's enough people fussing about in there. But if you want to help you might like to go and find Ivar. He was looking for hedgehogs, but I haven't seen him for a while.'

I went with her. We found him on his hands and knees among the lilac bushes. 'I saw one, a baby one, a tiny tiny one.'

I tickled the grubby soles of his little feet and he squirmed and giggled. It struck me how comforting the sight and sound of a child were in times of crisis.

'You really don't think there's anything I can do?' Pernilla asked me. 'It's just that I've got a tennis court booked.'

I forced myself to consider the question. Could she be of any help? Gerald had said not. Maybe she could be of comfort to Linus? 'You go off to your tennis.'

'But you'll let me know if there's anything I can do,' Pernilla said as she strode off down the gravel path. As she rounded the corner she turned and called, 'And tell Linus I was here, will you?'

I raised my hand in a reassuring little wave before turning to Ivar, who had scrambled to his feet. 'What say I shout you an ice-cream?' I asked. Ivar wanted to know how one shouted an ice-cream and I was just about to explain when the ambulance screeched up the hill, coming to a halt outside the gate. It wasn't using its siren, there was no need on the island. The sound of the engine and the tyres on the small street were enough to get people out of their houses and front gardens, and to send old Mrs Palme next door scurrying to her open window, her head full of pink curlers. I held Ivar's hand as they brought the stretcher from the back of the ambulance.

Linus emerged from the house, his mouth set in a grim line. 'You wait here with me, darling,' I told Ivar as he made to run towards his father. 'That will be the best help, right now.'

I sat on my bed in the cottage, fingering Astrid's diary. There was no news, as yet, of Bertil. Audrey was happily ensconced in bed with a pile of English magazines I had ordered and which had finally arrived. Olivia and Linus were at the hospital with Bertil. Kerstin had taken a grey-faced and trembling Gerald to visit friends on a nearby island. Ivar was staying the night with the family in the yellow house two doors down the hill. It was nine o'clock and the blue of the sky was beginning to darken as the sun set behind the western point of the fort. A couple of hours earlier I'd called the hospital, but as I wasn't family they would not tell me anything. What about Ulla? Where did she fit in? In fact, where was she? And then, like a genie whose lamp had been rubbed the wrong way, she stood in my doorway, her small triangular face set in an angry frown.

'What are you reading?'

'Oh nothing,' I answered, truthfully as it happens. Ulla marched forward and before I knew it she had snatched the diary from my hand.

'Have you heard any news of Bertil?' I asked her, hoping to divert her attention while I decided what to do next.

She shook her head. 'Nothing. No one has seen fit to let me know what's going on. Not that that should surprise me.'

Before I had a chance to snatch it back she had opened the small book. She scanned the first page and looked at me. It was hard to read her expression: surprise, anger, sadness? 'Where did you get this?'

'I told you the other day, remember. It was in the bookcase. I found it behind some of the other books when I was dusting. It's Astrid's, isn't it?'

Ulla nodded, silent. She looked around for somewhere to sit and sank down in the wicker chair by the window. 'You haven't read it?' She shook her head. 'No, of course you haven't. You can't. For someone who says they've had lessons your Swedish is appalling.'

'Thank you,' I said. 'But I wouldn't have read it all even if I could, of course I wouldn't. I had a fair idea that no one else had seen it. My first thought was to give it to Linus, but I got worried. I mean, should a son read his mother's diary, especially a mother who'd killed herself? And Bertil and Olivia? Would Astrid have wanted them to see it? The same thing went for you. And yet, for all of you, Astrid's death is unfinished business; you said she left no note, no letters and, until now, no diary. It's hard not to know. Anyway, I'm sorry to have kept it to myself but I was in a quandary.'

'I understand that.'

'You do?'

'I just told you I did, didn't I? I've noticed that you care about this family. I'm glad of that.'

To my horror I started to cry, in front of Ulla of all people. Thank God she made no attempt at comforting me. Instead she said, 'Are you in love with Linus?'

I stopped crying and stared at her. Ulla nodded, a self-satisfied little smile on her thin lips. 'I thought as much. I can't say I'm surprised; he's Astrid's son, after all. But he wouldn't go for you. Not just because of all that trouble over the opera house. I'm not saying you're not pretty, but you're too intense. Too serious. Always frowning and brooding. Men don't like that kind of thing. Men like women who are easy, uncomplicated, cheerful. Then they can save their real energies for the important things in life.' Her smile widened. 'All those things mattered to me once, you know.'

My feelings were all over the place; surprise at this sudden show of humanity, like seeing a glimpse of lace below a guardsman's tunic. Surprise, too, that she had guessed. And horror when I realised she saw something of herself in me. Was that it? For weeks I had struggled to emulate Pernilla with the result that I had picked up bits of Ulla. Ulla!

She patted the diary. 'I'll take this into my room.'

'Are you sure that's the right thing to do? I mean, she might not have wanted anyone to read it. It was hidden, after all.'

'Not that well hidden by the look of things. I'm her closest surviving relative, apart from Linus of course and, as you said with some wisdom, it's probably not appropriate for a son to read his mother's diary.'

She was right, rightish, at least, and that, I was beginning to see, was about the best you could hope for in life.

After she had gone, I stayed on my bed, eyes closed. She would be in her own room now, crouched over poor Astrid's diary. But at least she had loved her. I had noticed the way her pale-brown eyes softened at the mention of Astrid's name the way they never softened, not even when looking at Ivar dressed in one of his most mixed-up outfits, or a baby hedgehog tick-tacking across the gravel path.

I would like to have said that I was woken that night by my door quietly opening and soft footsteps on the floor-boards. (At least then I wouldn't be sitting as I was now, bolt upright in bed, my eyes wide and my heart thumping.) But Ulla came bursting through my door, an avenging gnome, shouting, 'You want to know about Astrid? Well I'll tell you. In fact, I'll tell everyone.'

I switched on the light. 'Ulla. Are you all right?'

'Of course I'm not all right.' And to my horror she began to cry, her skinny shoulders heaving with unlovely sobs. I got out of bed and walked up to her, put my arm round her and she shrugged it off, of course. Instead she fished a large white handkerchief from the inside of her sleeve and trumpeted into it, before plonking herself down into the chair by the window. I perched on the bed, looking at her where she sat, just outside the circle of light.

'We drove her to it,' she said, her voice hoarse. 'Bertil and Gerald and I. And that man, of course.' She looked up at me. '*He* became a grand old man of music. *He* might still be alive for all I know. Whereas she, my little Astrid, lies in her grave nothing more than a bundle of bones.' Again she clenched her fists. 'If I had known . . . Bertil too. He showed no mercy. He felt no compassion. That man deserves everything that's happened to him. And worse.'

'You don't really mean that?' I said stupidly.

Ulla returned to her old self for long enough to snap, 'Then why would I say it?' But then she added, so quietly that I had to strain to hear, 'But I am to blame too. I just never realised how much.' When she looked up again her face was contorted with pain. 'I loved her and when she needed me I let her down. She died thinking I didn't care. Me, Bertil, that man, all of us.'

I put out my hand to take hers, but she pretended not to see. 'What does it say, that diary? What is it that's upset you so?'

'What's upset me? I'll tell you what's upset me. I'll read it to you.' And she did.

# Chapter Twenty-seven

## ASTRID'S STORY

I wonder what is wrong with me. Maybe if I write things down, I'll see it more clearly. Maybe I love people too much, so that I end up driving them away. I used to wonder if my parents really were dead, or if they had just grown tired of their small daughter and her entwining arms. I used to picture them sneaking off across the border to another country, on exaggerated tiptoes like pantomime burglars, suitcases in hand. I used to imagine them on some sunny tropical shore, under the palm trees, laughing, drinking wonderful things from coconut shells, swimming in the clear, warm sea; without me. I still do, sometimes.

Bertil might as well be in another country for all the attention he pays me, although I can't see him doing much laughing or drinking from coconut shells. I'm not alone among the women I know to complain that my husband doesn't notice me. Of course he does, sometimes. Usually it's with a frown, because I'm late, or early, or chatty, or silent, or disorganised, or fussing. But it's at night I mind the most. Gunilla, plain, homely Gunilla, told me today over lunch how her husband would sometimes gaze upon her with a look of almost awe. She giggled when she told me that. She was embarrassed but delighted too, I could see from the flush on her cheeks and the way her eyes grew bright at the memory.

'You're so beautiful,' he would say. 'With your wide womanly hips and your soft breasts.' Gunilla had giggled even more, but I believed her, I had seen her husband look at her and that was when she was dressed and out in public.

I'm pleased for Gunilla, but sad for me. What's wrong with me? I'm young. I'm beautiful, so everyone tells me, everyone but my husband.

'You look very well tonight,' he says sometimes as we go out. He doesn't look at me when I undress. He doesn't look away either. Soon I'll be old and not worth looking at at all.

My birthday. Bertil came home early from the office and Fru Sparre had been at it all day, organising a family dinner. Ulla came, of course, dear, funny Ulla, with her pepper-and-salt hair freshly permed on account of Pastor Bergström. I think Ulla harbours dreams of marriage to the pastor. Gerda returned from a field trip to South America just in time for the party, and Gerald and Marie came with little Kerstin to keep Linus company. I never thought it was possible to care so much for another human being as I care for that little boy. And he depends on me utterly and loves me. No one has ever depended on me before.

Bertil was sweet. He had bought me a woven platinum bracelet. Linus gave me an ashtray, blue-and-green-coloured Kosta glass. Bertil swears he chose it all by himself. He's only five, but he's got an eye for beautiful things already. Later in bed, Bertil made love to me, but I couldn't help feeling he saw me as a house with the entrance in an impractical place.

Tonight I did a recital at Stenhammar Salon. I was one of four performers; a tenor, a baritone, a mezzo and me. The recital went well. When I had finished my last piece, Jonas Aminoff, the conductor, and the orchestra applauded me. They don't always do that. Bertil told me he thought I had done well.

'I want you to be proud of me,' I said, putting my arms around his neck.

'I am proud of you,' he said, giving me a little push away. 'Very proud, my dear.'

Tomorrow we move out to the island for the summer months. At least, Linus and I do. Bertil and the others will come on Midsummer Eve as usual. I picked up Linus from kindergarten and we went to Paleys for hot chocolate and buns. He looked so serious where he sat, on his chair opposite me, so careful not to spill his drink or put crumbs on the floor. 'Let's have a conversation,' he said.

'What do you want to have a conversation about?' I asked him.

He thought for a moment. 'Fire engines,' he said. 'Let's have a conversation about fire engines.'

Linus was beside himself with excitement at his pappa joining us at Villa Rosengård at last and he insisted on wearing his patent leather shoes with silver buckles. They all arrived together: Bertil, Gerald, Marie and little Kerstin. I wish Bertil would pay more attention to Linus. He barely spoke to the poor little boy and when he did it was only to tell him off for being over-excited. He never even noticed the new shoes.

It rained most of the afternoon, thank goodness, so there was no inspection of the garden. I don't know what he'll make of my rose beds.

Ulla arrived today, thin as a crow, her hair a dry frizz, as she scattered criticisms like shards of glass: Linus's laugh was too loud. Why was Kerstin's nose always running? Had Bertil not noticed the paint flaking on the west gable?

Pastor Bergström has gone to be a missionary in Madagascar and her heart is broken. My poor cousin, so full of love no one seems to need. Compared with her I'm lucky, I've got Linus, after all, and Bertil. Sometimes he looks at me as if he really does care.

Gerald went fishing and brought home five mackerel for supper. Bertil grilled them outdoors. They were delicious.

I can't believe that summer is over already. Linus has grown a full centimetre. He is as brown as a nut and full of energy. Bertil left for town last week. He seemed relieved to get back to work and what he would term 'sensible people'. I know when we married some of my friends said I was wise marrying a man who was ten years older. 'He'll carry you through life on his hands,' they said. 'And what's more, he won't find it easy to run off with someone younger.'

I don't think Bertil is interested in other women, but then he isn't terribly interested in me either. Linus and I seem mostly to irritate him. 'You're all emotion,' he said to me the night before he left for town. I asked him what else there was. I hated the look he gave me as he answered in that cool, low voice he seems to reserve just for Linus and me, 'Try common sense, a sense of proportion, intellect.'

But he is not unkind, Bertil. When he saw the expression on my face he came over to me and put his hands on my shoulders. 'I love you very much.' He gave my bottom a little pat. 'Now off you go and get ready for bed.'

We made love. I kept my night-dress on, as usual. I always wait for him to undress me, but he never does.

Tonight was the first of the Strauss evenings. The audience loved it and afterwards Jonas Aminoff came round to our dressing-room to congratulate us.

I saw Jonas at the party for the cast and orchestra. We were both hot, so we wandered out on to one of the balconies and talked for ages. He really listens when I speak, as if he truly wants to hear what I have to say, not because he's decided to indulge me.

Bertil's birthday. Where have the weeks gone? Gerda gave a dinner in his honour at the university. The family was there, of course. And the people from the office. Linus was allowed to come too. We had gone shopping together and he fell in love with a pair of bright-red corduroy trousers. He got himself ready for the party hours early and then, when we were ready to go, it all got too much for him and he was sick all over his new trousers. He was in such a state that we had to put him to bed. Linda next door came over to baby-sit. Later she told me that as soon as we'd left he had got out of bed and dashed into the hall. He had stayed there, pressed against the door, sobbing, and for most of the evening she couldn't persuade him to move, until finally he'd gone to sleep in a little heap on the floor. I can't get his little stricken face as we left without him out of my mind. I sometimes understand Bertil's aloofness. It must be so comfortable loving someone just a little, but never so much that it hurts.

Bertil and I went to the Mayor's party. Jonas was there. I was wearing my black lace dress and wished I hadn't as the rooms of the palace were far from warm. Bertil told me I should learn to be practical in my dress. Jonas went and asked our hostess for a shawl. It was such a kind thing to do. 'But you're freezing,' he said, looking at me with such concern. I don't know why, but it made me want to cry.

Last time we rehearsed with the full orchestra Jonas had talked to me about my future as a singer. He told me he'd love to talk some more if I thought it would be useful and I said that of course it would. Very helpful indeed. So last week he called and we decided to meet for lunch at Park Hotel. I can't remember a happier afternoon. It was like stepping out from a black-and-white film right into the middle of a Technicolor one. As I looked around me at the other guests I found myself pitying them, just for not being me. He is a widower. I never knew that. He talked about his wife and of how he missed her, and I told him about Linus. Jonas said he sounded lovely and that he'd love to meet him some day.

The third of December and the festival of St Lucia. Linus and I brought Bertil coffee and Lucia buns in bed. I was Lucia of course, with my crown of electric lights in my hair and my white gown, and Linus was the sweetest little Star boy you ever saw. Bertil was thrilled and said he was a very lucky man.

There's a Sibelius concert tonight. I've got tickets, but Bertil says he has to work late.

Jonas came out to look for me in the intermission. He told me he was doing *Finlandia* just for me.

Christmas was lovely. Then again, right now everything is lovely. Linus still believes that it really is Father Christmas coming with the sack of presents, not Ulla in a red-and-grey suit and a big grey beard. 'The child is a moron,' Bertil said, but he was smiling.

Every year I'm taken by surprise at how naked the flat looks once the decorations are down, like a face after a party, all make-up removed and the hair scraped back. This year, though, the sight doesn't depress me. Nothing does. I'm floating.

Lately I've taken to worrying that I might die without ever having known what loving Jonas would be like.

'With my body I Thee worship.' It's ironic that it's only now that I know fully what that means. Ironic, sinful, because I know from being with a man who is *not* my husband.

I had told Bertil that I was staying the night with Ulla who wasn't well. Linus didn't like me leaving, but I promised him I'd be back before he woke in the morning and that I would take him to Paleys for hot chocolate.

He gave me the strangest look when I returned. A look that did not belong to a six-year-old. He was up already and I said I was sorry I was late. He just fixed those great big grey eyes on me and then, suddenly, he smiled. 'You look very pretty today,' he said. Later, we walked back from Paleys and it began to snow. Linus ran up and down the pavement trying to catch the snowflakes falling in the light of the street lamp, and when he got tired he came back to me and buried his face in the sleeve of my fur coat. How I longed for him and Jonas to meet. I know they'd adore each other, I just know it.

I've lived just for today to come. Jonas returned from the tour late last night and early this morning we met at Delsjön. The lake is completely frozen over so we could walk right across it. I love this winter landscape. The ice, blue almost, as you get further out, and the branches of the pine trees frosted with snow. The stillness. It was as if we were alone at the end of the world. We held hands and barely spoke. It seemed sacrilege to break that other-wordly silence. I felt so happy it scared me. Some people wear their happiness lightly, almost nonchalantly. I have noticed Jonas does. Others, like me, carry it gingerly, fearfully, as if it were a shell filled with precious liquid.

I had brought a flask of coffee and some sandwiches, and we ate them in his car. It was the first time in days that I had been able to eat and not feel as if I were swallowing sandpaper. When I drove off, leaving him standing in the snow, I felt I was tied to him by my very guts, and as I went further and further away my entrails unfurled and stretched until the pain became unbearable. When I got home I had to rush straight to the bathroom and rub concealer on my lips; they were so swollen and blotchy from kissing.

I can't go on any longer. I will have to tell Bertil.

Today I had to return Linus to his father. Bertil has gone to court to claim that our son is in moral danger living with his mother and her lover. In the meantime, while they decide, these strangers, the fate of all of us, they have awarded Bertil temporary custody. I try not to think about what that might mean. I rang the bell of the place that was my home not long ago. When Bertil opened the door, Linus buried his face in my coat and clung on to my waist. Then, as if he understood that he had no choice, he just put his little hand into his father's and went inside. I met Bertil's eyes, they were cold and polite, and I implored him with mine to show some pity. The door closed and for a moment I stood there, this scream inside me that never reached the air. I wanted to bang on the door and beg Bertil's forgiveness, implore him to take me back so that I could have my child. I closed my eyes, my fist raised, and I couldn't do it. I couldn't return to my dark prison, knowing that I would never again see the sunlight.

Jonas is wonderful. He understands how much I miss Linus and he's never other than gentle and loving with me. 'Astrid, my love, my life,' he whispers to me as we make love. 'Astrid, my love, my life.' He says I'm everything he's ever wanted and that now he needs nothing else.

My solicitor rang to tell me the judge has awarded Bertil sole custody of our child. I plummeted like a fallen angel to earth, and down some more to hell.

Jonas is changing towards me. I don't know if I've done something wrong, but nothing is the same. He used to hurry home after a performance, just wanting to be with me, and now he often doesn't come back until the early hours of the morning. When I ask him to be home with me he gets angry and shouts that he's been neglecting his orchestra for too long. 'Get your own life,' he yelled last night. I thought I had, going with him. I wanted to ask him why he was being so unfair. It wasn't long ago, after all, that he had told me how he wanted me all to himself and that he needed nothing else. But he had left already, slamming the door behind him. I think he's feeling guilty and that is what makes him especially cruel.

So I sit alone in this small flat that reeks of other people's cooking. My friends won't have anything to do with me. Even Ulla won't speak to me. Two days ago I went to Metz for afternoon tea and Fru Granberg, the manageress, looked at me as if she had never seen me before and said there were no tables available although I could clearly see three. Worst of all, this morning that ghastly weekly printed a story: *Singer Wife of Star Architect Bertil Stendal elopes with orchestra conductor*. I was due to take Linus out for the day, but now, because of the article, Bertil has forbidden it. I pleaded with him, but he said he wasn't having his son gaped at by the gossip-mongers of Gothenburg. I lost my control then. 'You're a monster,' I screamed down the phone. 'I'm his mother and he needs me.'

Bertil's voice came back to me, quiet and dry. 'Well, you should have thought about that earlier,' he said.

'I should have, I know, but I didn't, I didn't.' I was sobbing and then I heard the click as the phone went dead.

My roses will be in their second flowering now. I close my eyes and remember their scent and the feel of the fresh sea breeze on my face. We're in Spain now. We've travelled Europe for three months. I don't seem to have had the energy to write my diary until now.

The first five weeks of our trip were part of the orchestra tour, the rest has been part of Jonas's dream of seeing the world. I haven't been doing any singing. Jonas says it wouldn't look good if we performed together as people might accuse him of favouritism. I tried to say that I had been getting work long before I knew him, but he hasn't got the patience to listen. To begin with, as we travelled, he was loving and considerate, almost like the old Jonas, but as the days and the tour progressed he grew more and more irritable and impatient with me. I tried to be cheerful and not let him see how desperately I miss my son, but nothing I do nowadays seems to please him. I think up things to tell him about my day that might amuse him, but everything comes out wrong and we usually end up having a row. How different it all seemed a year ago!

We returned home last night. I telephoned Bertil to ask when I could see Linus. He said he would think about it and ring me back. He told me that Linus seemed more settled and that he had stopped calling out for me in his sleep. I started screaming down the phone that he had never told me that my son had called for me in the night. Bertil asked, in the same cool quiet voice, if telling me would have made me give up Jonas and return home? I asked him if I could have Linus back if I gave Jonas up. Bertil told me that if I ever tried to take Linus back he would destroy me. 'You have no fixed job, no money and you are morally bankrupt. Do you think any court would hand over a child to you?'

I put the phone down and I didn't seem to be able to stop crying.

Maybe Jonas is right to be bored with me. I must try harder. I went and had my hair cut short, like Audrey Hepburn in *Roman Holiday*. I've put flowers on the table and tidied up, and done all the laundry and the ironing, so that when he comes home from rehearsals there will be nothing for him to get annoyed about. I'll make a paella for dinner, just the way they did it in that little restaurant in Toledo that he liked so much. If I just try harder he'll love me again. He has to love me. After all, I have nothing else.

Jonas came home too late to have supper. He had been drinking. He went to sleep on the sofa in the drawing-room and I threw the paella in the bin. I didn't even bother to take it out of the dish. I found myself listening out for Bertil admonishing me for being such a wastrel and just then, I missed him. Most of all, of course, I long for my son. There has to be a way for us to be together!

I called Gerald and begged him to plead my case to Bertil so that I could see my son. Gerald was polite but cold. He told me he'd see what he could do. Then I took the tram across to Örgryte to Ulla's. I hadn't been to her flat in almost a year and it felt strange stepping into the entrance hall and walking up those wooden stairs to the first floor. I knew she would be in, Ulla was always in around six. She opened the door nearly the moment I rang the bell. Almost as if she had been waiting for me all this time, I thought, and I gave her a big smile.

She didn't smile back. 'It's you,' she said.

I asked if I could come in and she stood back, but so grudgingly that I had to squeeze past her to get through the door. She never asked me to sit down. I stood in her parlour and remembered how I had been the most welcome visitor in the world in that sparse little room.

'So what do you want?' she asked me, unsmiling and unyielding.

It seemed to me then that there were faces like hers everywhere, looking back at me with cold eyes, disapproving eyes, eyes without love. I took a step towards her and she took a step back. 'It's Linus,' I said. 'It's breaking my heart not seeing him. I thought maybe you could talk to Bertil.'

'You broke all our hearts when you ran off with that man. And now you want me to help you.' She shook her head. 'I will never understand you. Bertil is a good man. He loved you and he would have looked after you for the rest of your life.' She looked at me and for a moment her eyes softened, or maybe I just imagined that they did because she went on to say, 'When I introduced you to him and he took such an interest I knew you'd be all right. I did that for you and then you go and throw it all away, and for what? Eh?'

'Love,' I whispered.

'Phaa! And what about your child?'

'I know,' I screamed. 'That's what I came to you for. I can't stand it any more. Don't you understand, *it was never meant to happen like this*!'

Ulla looked at me and said, 'You must have things to do.'

Bertil rang the next evening. 'There's no point you getting the family to speak for you. I'm not trying to be difficult, but I have to think what is best for Linus. He seems to have settled down at last,' he said.

'You mean he's forgotten me?'

There was a pause, then he said, 'If you like.'

Being a sinner, I had no rights.

Last night Jonas took me out to dinner. To begin with it was wonderful, just like the old days and his smiles and tender looks, the hand he put over mine across the table, all acted like a balm to soothe the pain in my heart. He asked me what I was doing about Linus. I told him how desperate I was to have my child back and he seemed to understand at last. 'Perhaps you should try a different solicitor,' he said. Maybe everything will be all right, after all. If Jonas still loved me, maybe he'd marry me when my divorce came through. And if I were married to Jonas, possibly I could convince a judge that I was not an unfit mother. Slowly that dead place at the centre of my being began to stir and come alive again. I smiled and reached out for his hand, which had left mine some time ago. Then, idiot that I am, I spilled my glass of wine right across the table and over his new suit.

He disappeared to the men's room before I had a chance to say sorry and when he returned his jaw was set tight with disapproval. After that everything I said and did was wrong. Why did I smile at the waiters in that nervous way? Why did I eat so slowly? Why did I gulp down my wine with no thought of its taste and quality? By the time we left I was in tears, which made him even more cross. I lay awake that night, staring at his beautiful profile lit by the faint glow from the street light outside the window. I wondered how I could still love him, but I do.

Bertil called to tell me that I could take Linus out for the afternoon. Six months! That's how long it's been. I didn't sleep at all last night I was so terrified that he'd find some reason to call off the visit.

All morning I paced the flat, dreading the phone ringing and Bertil telling me I couldn't see my son. All the way on the tram my heart was pounding and the ride seemed to last an eternity. At last I was there. Back outside my old home. I didn't bother to wait for the lift, but ran up all five flights of stairs so that when I rang the doorbell . . . (how odd that still felt, ringing the bell to what had once been my home, standing there waiting to be let in).

At first I thought Linus didn't recognise me, he just stood there, his face immobile. Then he sobbed, a hoarse, choked-back sob, and ran into my arms and burrowed his face into my coat and wouldn't let me go. Finally, gently, I prised his strong little hands from around my waist. 'Let's go to Paleys for hot chocolate,' I said. Once there, seated at our table by the window, looking out across the Avenue, I gave him his Christmas gift: a pair of skating boots, black like the big boys wear. He wanted me to take him to the skating pond and I said that I would, soon. He's grown some more, he's quite tall now for his age and Bertil had cut his hair very short, but it didn't take long before it felt as if we've never been apart. We stayed as long as I dared. When, finally, I said it was time to go, he got up, as good as gold and pushed his chair in neatly. Once out on the street he put his hand in mine and said, 'Are we going home now?'

'Oh, my darling,' I said, kneeling in front of him, doing up his little camel-hair coat. 'Mummy can't live with you at the moment, but soon we'll be back together again, properly, and then I'll never ever leave you again. I promise.'

He was so quiet on our walk back. As we stood by the front door he started to cry, clinging to me and refusing to let go. Bertil came out and pulled him away. I screamed at him to let me in, but he closed the door in my face. I could hear Linus crying for me. It went on for ever. I couldn't bring myself to leave, so I stayed, pressed against the door, listening to him cry and crying with him, soundlessly, until my face ached. Eventually Linus stopped crying. It was late when I finally got to my feet and walked home. Jonas had left a note on the table saying that as I hadn't been there when he got back he'd gone out for the evening with some friends. 'Don't wait up,' the note said.

Ulla closed the diary. 'That was the last entry,' she said.

I lay in my bed, eyes closed, awake. Newspaper headlines floated past my eyes like so many sheep being counted on the way to sleep. *The Decline of Morality! Back to Basics! A Return to Old-fashioned Values! Is there no Shame Any More?* Black on white, the messages that spelt our desire for order and security and rules. And then there was Astrid's story.

## Chapter Twenty-eight

'Imagine the sea under ice.' Ulla pointed across the water. We were standing together on the island's highest point.

'The whole world seems frozen, the sea, the branches of the trees, the grass. Astrid came out here alone on Christmas Eve that year. They found her body under the ice two weeks later.'

She turned round, her mouth twisted in pain. 'The moment she left me on her last visit I wanted to run after her and tell her I would do everything I could to help. I phoned Bertil and begged him to let her see more of the boy.' Her voice sank to a whisper. 'She never realised.'

'But why did it take you so long? You loved her. Surely if you love someone you'll forgive them anything.' And I thought of Linus. Was there anything he could do that I wouldn't be able to forgive if he asked me to?

'You don't understand,' Ulla said. She wasn't looking at me any more, but staring out across the sea again. 'It was because I loved her that it took me so long to forgive her. And then there was Bertil. He had been *my* friend long before he knew Astrid. I introduced them. You could say I gave him to her. She took him and then, when she got bored, she threw him away. At least . . .' she turned that pained face towards me again '. . . that's how it seemed to me then, all those years ago. I didn't understand what her marriage was like. Maybe I hadn't wanted to understand. I had been so proud of my gift to her of a husband, a wealthy, steady, suitable husband who I thought would give her everything she'd ever need. I just didn't want to know that he couldn't give her the one thing she needed most.'

I stared at her. Ulla and Bertil. Had Ulla loved him? Then again, why should that seem so impossible? They were the same age. Judging by a couple of blurred family snapshots she had been quite attractive in a perky Scandinavian-troll kind of way. I wondered if Olivia knew? Then again, why should she? It was all a very long time ago.

'Did you ever resent Olivia? Did you mind her stepping into Astrid's shoes, coming here?'

Ulla shook her head. 'I did at first, but she loved Bertil and Linus. I didn't know then that he had made Astrid so unhappy. Of course, at the time I thought Olivia rather a poor substitute, so large, coarse even, compared with my Astrid. But she was always careful not to tread on Astrid's memory. She didn't demand for things to change. Bertil offered to sell up, both the flat and Villa Rosengård, but Olivia said no, why should he? He and Linus loved this place and the flat was perfect for their needs and in the nicest part of town. So I told myself that she could have been a lot worse.'

'I'm glad you told me everything. I mean, not just because I'm a nosy old thing but because, well you know because of how I feel about Linus.' I gave her a sideways look. 'I didn't think you even particularly liked me.'

Ulla gave me a small smile. 'I don't *not* particularly like you. And you asked me about her. You were interested. I believe you felt her presence in this place, the way I always have. I've seen you look at her roses. And you're a journalist. It's your job to spread news. I want people to know how that man, Jonas Aminoff, killed Astrid. All those people at the time, her so-called friends, who acted as judge and jury. She got all the blame, then. She was the hussy, the flighty one, the scarlet woman. The men got away scot-free. Maybe that's the way of the world, but why should we put up with it? No, I want you to put the record straight.'

'But Ulla, a journalist deals with news. This happened a long time ago and most of the people who cared then wouldn't care now, if they're even alive.'

Ulla stamped her foot like a child. 'Why should he get away with it? And her, Astrid, what about her reputation? All those evil things they wrote about her.'

'Bertil is a sick old man. Jonas Aminoff does seem to have been a grade A bastard, but we only have Astrid's side of the story. Maybe it wasn't quite as black and white as she makes out?'

'I didn't think you were much for moderation.'

'I'm getting to be. I've learnt the hard way about the beiges and greys that make up our world. It's easier to live your life in black and white, but it's not truth. I'm finding it increasingly hard to judge.'

'I don't,' Ulla said.

'Thank God I didn't give the diary to Linus. He probably should see it some day, but not without some kind of careful preparation. I dread to think what it might do to his relationship with his father . . . Actually, how much does Linus know?'

'Some. He seemed early on to have given up asking the questions that might provide a painful answer. I think he's frightened of what he might find out. So he asks instead about what she was like when she was a child or as a young girl. Or what she used to like to cook. If she had some pet names for him that he hadn't remembered. No, as I said, I think he's frightened to ask too much.'

I found myself staring at Ulla. Where had she hidden all this understanding and sympathy? Under her helmet of hair?

'And now Bertil is abandoning Villa Rosengård, *her* home,' she said. 'As if he hasn't done enough.' Her voice was quiet, her words carried out over the water by the wind. 'She loved that place. He's prepared to hand it over to strangers. It's *her* house and we, all there together, her family, are all that's left of her. He and Olivia were prepared to break that up, scatter what was left of Astrid as if it were her ashes all over again. I've watched over that family, over that house, for all these years and now he's throwing it away. That seems to be what people do; they throw away your life's gifts as if they were nothing much more than an empty cigarette packet.' She looked straight ahead as she walked. 'Well, I've had enough. And you, you do what you will with what I've told you.'

What could I do – other than love Linus all the more?

He was there when we returned from our walk. Sitting at the kitchen table drinking coffee.

'Linus, you're back,' I said unnecessarily. And I thought it was unfair to blame the dumbing down of the population on television when romantic love was so obviously the greater culprit. He looked up at me and smiled, a small, tired smile. He hadn't shaved.

All at once I felt worried. 'Bertil is all right, isn't he?'

'He'll be OK.'

'That's what the hospital told Ulla. But you got me worried, sitting there looking so glum.' I took a step towards him and put my hand, just lightly, on his shoulder.

'What's wrong? Is there something else?'

Linus stared down into his mug of coffee. 'My father has been poisoned. They analysed some samples and they've concluded that he's been poisoned, some stuff you find in mushrooms. Every time, it's been the same. The thing is, Bertil never eats mushrooms. He says they give him wind.' Linus smiled, a joyless smile.

I sat down next to him. 'So what are you saying?'

'Not me, the police. They say someone has deliberately poisoned my father and that the someone is likely to be a member of his own household. They also told me that this person, whoever he or she is, is apparently either inept or not serious about killing him. I suppose that's meant to be comforting. I'm afraid I don't find it makes things that much easier.' His voice broke and he flopped down across the table, resting his head in the crook of his arm. I realised that he was crying and, before I could stop myself, I was sobbing too. A man weeping was always a pitiful sight, but when you loved the man it was almost unbearable.

'Linus, darling Linus,' I mumbled. I slipped down on to my knees in front of him, turning him gently towards me. I put my arms round his waist and leant my face against his knees. 'It'll be all right,' I mumbled. But how could it be?

'Esther!' Audrey called from her bedroom. I pretended not to hear. 'Esther!' she called again. Audrey might have had the body of a weak and feeble old woman, but her voice had all the carrying power of a middle-class matron at bay.

Linus straightened up. 'Your mother is calling.'

I got up. 'So she is.'


Audrey was sitting up in her narrow bed, a baby-blue shawl draped round her shoulders. She was looking displeased. 'What's going on, Esther? Something is going on.'

I sighed. *Of course it is*, I thought. *You're wrecking my life*. I didn't say that, though. And anyway, it was unfair. 'Of course something is going on,' I said instead. 'Bertil is in hospital, you know that.'

'Something else. There's something else.'

So I told her. As I spoke, I looked at her cheeks: they were growing pink; and at her eyes: they sparkled. There was nothing as certain to perk up an invalid as other people's trouble, I thought.

'So who is it? Who's done it?' Audrey asked, practically levitating from the bed with excitement.

'I thought Olivia was your best friend in the world,' I replied. 'Shouldn't you at least pretend to be worried?'

'Of course I'm worried. But you say that Bertil will be fine and it obviously isn't Olivia, so . . .'

'Can I rely on you not to blab?' I asked her.

Audrey looked indignant. 'Do you need to ask?'

'Yes,' I said.

'Well you can rely on me entirely.' I decided to trust her; after all, she was my mother and I needed to talk to someone. 'Well, the thing is, had it happened only once and had that once been today, I would have said it was Ulla.'

'Ulla?'

I told Audrey all about the diary. She looked genuinely shocked. 'That poor woman. And little Linus.' Sometimes my mother surprised me by showing normal human emotions. I liked it every time.

'But you see,' I continued, 'Ulla only read the diary last night and by then Bertil was already in hospital. Anyway, they think that he was poisoned the same way on the other occasions too.'

'So who?'

I shrugged. 'I keep thinking it's some awful mistake. That Bertil has been secretly feasting on dodgy mushrooms, not knowing they were dodgy of course, and hang the consequences; he could always pass his wind on to Gerald, so to speak.' I looked hopefully at Audrey.

She shook her head. 'I don't think so, darling.'

I sighed. 'Neither do I.'

Then the police arrived. Two of them, a man and a woman. They asked to look around the house. Who was going to refuse them? They went into every room, turning out the kitchen cupboards and bathroom cabinets. They searched through the rubbish, both from the kitchen bin and the dustbin outside. They asked to see the cottage. I told them I would alert Ulla so as not to give her a fright, the police turning up on her threshold like that. But Ulla was on her way over already; I met her half-way. We left the police to their search, but it wasn't long before they were back in the house. They asked when

Olivia was due back, and Gerald and Kerstin. Linus told them Kerstin and Gerald were expected later that day, but that Olivia was staying another night at the hospital. They left, saying they would return the next day to speak to everyone. They had been polite enough right through, but I had noticed that smiling at them was a waste of time, they never smiled back.

'What did they ask you?' Kerstin, looking old in her little-girl's clothes, grabbed my arm as I returned to the sitting-room after my interview.

'Nothing much,' I said. I was tired. I hadn't slept much that night, then again, I don't suppose any of us had. 'They wanted to know which meals I had prepared and who with. How long I had been staying here. Whether I knew of any family quarrels or tensions, that kind of thing.'

'Ah.' Kerstin nodded and went to join the police officers in the dining-room.

'This is a nightmare,' Olivia whispered. She seemed to have shrunk in the last few hours, withered and wilted, and the sparkle had left her brown eyes. 'It's been bad enough Bertil being taken ill, but this, that it's some kind of deliberate attack and by one of us. Ulla is right, it's like some stupid detective story. But it isn't a story, it's us and it's real.' She buried her head in her hands and wept. I went up to her, patting her awkwardly on the shoulder while all kinds of inane words of comfort auditioned in my head. *The police might have got it wrong. The hospital might have got it wrong. Maybe there was a mix-up of samples.* None of them passed muster, so I stood there wordless, patting away at her shoulder.

I was alone in the garden. The late sun bathed it in golden light. The wind had stilled. Across the street they were having a party. In normal circumstances, non-poisoning circumstances, I would have said it was a lovely evening.

'What's going on?' Pernilla came striding towards me, fair hair dancing. She seemed to have got even more tanned in the last day, her bare arms and her legs under the white shorts the colour of the ginger biscuits Ivar liked for his elevenses. 'How is Bertil?'

I filled her in on what had happened about Bertil's progress, but I didn't say anything about the police's suspicions. I didn't think that having a poisoner in the family was something the Stendals would want known at this stage. Pernilla tut-tutted, then she asked where Linus was. I told her he was inside. I added that I thought he was just about to go off to the hospital. Actually, I wanted to run inside and put a screen around him so that she wouldn't find him.

'Pernilla! Oh Pernilla, it's all so dreadful.' Kerstin came running towards us, tottering slightly as her bare feet hit the gravel. She said something to Pernilla in Swedish, but I recognised the word police.

Pernilla turned to me, her eyes wide and hostile. 'Why didn't you tell me? This is unbelievable, awful.' She pronounced the *aw* in awful in a mournful elongated way, as she looked accusingly at me. Kerstin, too, turned to me, eyebrows raised.

I hung my head. 'I wasn't sure how much I was supposed to tell anyone.'

Kerstin gave a little laugh. 'Pernilla isn't anyone, Esther.'

I agreed there. Pernilla certainly wasn't anyone, she was a ginger-biscuit princess with fair hair, green eyes and right now I wanted to push her down on to the ground and sit on her head.

Kerstin was speaking to Pernilla in Swedish again as they walked towards the house. I went back to the cottage.

I sat on my bed thinking over and over about the ease with which the dream had turned into a nightmare and how seamlessly it had happened. What a surprise it all was. You could be the most inveterate pessimist and yet, when it happened, when that giant boot in the sky descended on your head, you were left disbelieving. Crushed too, obviously, but disbelieving to the last.

Bertil remained in hospital. His heart was not as strong as it could be and it had been weakened further by the latest ordeal.

'I'm glad, really,' Olivia told me. 'At least there he's safe.'

'As soon as the police say we can, Audrey and I will be leaving,' I told her. 'I spoke to Dr Blomkvist and he said she'll be OK to travel. At least then you won't have us to worry about.'

'Oh Esther, you know how we've enjoyed having you here. But I admit that once this is over all I'll want to do is go away somewhere with Bertil, just the two of us.' She sank down on to the chair next to me at the kitchen table. 'The worst is not knowing who did this dreadful thing. It doesn't matter how many times the police tell me it had to be someone here, I still can't believe it. I mean Gerald, or Kerstin? Linus, Ulla? You, or your mother? Me? It's all crazy.'

'What's crazy?' Pernilla stood in the doorway. I hadn't heard her come in. 'I let myself in,' she said. 'The door was open.'

Olivia made a half-hearted attempt to get up, but she didn't make it to her feet. She collapsed back into the chair and burst out crying. After all the weeping there had been at Villa Rosengård lately you would have thought I'd got used to dealing with it, but I hadn't. As usual, I just stood there feeling hopeless and like someone getting a glimpse through a door that should be shut.

By the time I had thought to ask if she wanted a cup of tea, Pernilla was at her side. 'You're still in shock,' she said. 'Let me take you to your room. *Du borde vila.*' She switched to speaking Swedish as they disappeared upstairs, Olivia allowing herself to be led by Pernilla, the daughter-in-law in waiting.

I was appalled at myself. How low could I get? To think like that at a time like this. It was the problem with love, another problem, it had no respect for the accepted rules of behaviour. Love had no decorum, it just barged in where you least wanted it, however unsuitable the occasion, bringing with it, as likely as not, its unattractive offspring, jealousy and selfishness. And I'm ashamed to say that in my mind they were both blondes.

I went in to see how Audrey was. 'How's Bertil taking the news?' she asked as soon as I got through the door. I noticed that she was looking perkier than she had for a long time. Disaster obviously became her.

'What news in particular?'

'About the police believing he's been deliberately poisoned.'

I shrugged. 'I don't know.'

'What do you mean, you don't know?'

'I *don't* know.' As I spoke, I wondered how many mothers and daughters across the world were at that moment exchanging just those words.

'How can you *not* know?'

I felt that the conversation wasn't getting anywhere, so I asked her instead if I could get her some books from the library. She said, sulkily, as she always did, that she had read them all. I looked at my watch. 'The physio will be here in a minute.'

Audrey leant back against her pillows. 'I'm feeling quite weak,' she said. I had noticed lately that she affected some undetermined middle-European accent when she wanted sympathy. 'Be a darlink and get me some of those heavenly white roses from the garden. I need something beautiful to look at.'

'You've got me,' I said and I was not entirely joking. I mean, what hope had I to turn Linus's eye from Pernilla if my mother didn't think I was pretty?

Audrey sat back up and peered at me through those great big baby-blue eyes. Then she sighed and fell back once more against the pillows. I got up from the bed. 'I'll get you some roses.'

'Esther.' Audrey called me back. 'If you would only stop scowling you could be quite lovely.' My heart did a little leap in my chest. 'But then, what do I know? I'm your mother.' My heart moved back to its normal place, skulking in the depth of my chest cavity.

I thought the kitchen was empty until I spotted Linus in the corner by the scullery door where the light never quite reached. He was standing completely still, leaning against the cupboard. I didn't know if he'd noticed me coming in.

'How's Audrey?' His voice came from the shadows.

I turned and walked up to him, smiling, because however awful things were, his mere presence made me smile. I couldn't see his eyes, but as I came closer I could feel his pain; it hung in the air around him like an A note at the end of a song.

'Audrey's fine,' I told him. 'In fact, you should be getting rid of us as soon as the police confirm it's OK for us to leave. Dr Blomkvist says she's well enough to travel whenever we're ready.'

'I can't believe this is happening,' he said. 'Isn't that what everyone says?' He looked up at me suddenly and the hurt in his eyes made me want to rush up to him and take him in my arms. 'You step from the light into darkness.' He clicked his fingers. 'Like that. In a second everything has changed. Someone in this house has poisoned my father. How are we supposed to live with that?'

'I didn't do it,' I said quickly.

He gave me a small smile. 'Of course you didn't. You English don't know a poisoned mushroom from a good one.' He raised his hand and it hovered between us, then his fingers touched down lightly on my cheek. I closed my eyes for a second and his touch was like a branding iron. As I walked out into the garden, I was sure the mark, his mark, was there for everyone to see.

I fetched a pair of secateurs from the small red-painted shed and went to cut some roses, Astrid's roses. I never did find out if Bertil had approved of her planting them, that summer all those years ago.

## Chapter Twenty-nine

Ulla had spent the day in her room refusing to come out. Earlier, I had left a plate of sandwiches and a mug of coffee outside the door, and when I returned an hour later the plate and mug were gone. Linus and Olivia were over at the hospital, and Gerald and Kerstin and I ate our supper on our own in the kitchen. Audrey, as usual, had refused to get out of bed. I looked around the table at the empty chairs. The ghosts of happy families looked back at me.

On my way to my room I knocked on Ulla's door. 'Are you all right? Would you like me to bring you something more to eat?'

There was no answer and I knocked again, then, suddenly worried, I opened the door and stepped inside. Ulla was fast asleep in her armchair. I stopped and stared at her. Ulla the helmet-haired harridan was draped in a rose-pink silk dressing-gown and her feet were shod in white down slippers. The grey helmet of hair was a helmet no more, but a fluffy bird's nest of wiry curls. Astrid's diary lay on the small desk by the window and next to it was a black-and-white photograph. I bent down and looked at a female version of Linus: same fair hair and large dark eyes – I expect hers were grey as well – same curved top lip, same expression of slight surprise in those eyes as they looked out at the world. So that was Astrid, Astrid who had died under the icy sea around the island all for the lack of love.

In her sleep Ulla stirred and muttered, and I tiptoed from the room, closing the door softly behind me.

That night I slept, exhausted. I woke to the sound of doors slamming and a cat shrieking as if it had been kicked. Next I heard Ulla's voice so it probably had been. She was speaking in Swedish and an unfamiliar voice, a man's, answered her. I got out of bed and on my way to the shower I bumped into Ulla and a police officer. She didn't seem to notice me. The policeman nodded briefly in my direction before disappearing into Ulla's room.

What was going on?

I had resisted listening at the door. Or rather, I'd realised that it would not do me much good as the conversation inside was both low and in Swedish. The sun was shining from a clear blue sky and it was warm to the point of mugginess. I sat on the terrace having my breakfast. Kerstin joined me with a cup of coffee and the papers. Neither of us felt like speaking.

Olivia came out through the French windows, her face grey in the sharp light, blinking at the sun as if she was surprised that it was still there. She sat down beside me and after a while she said, 'Ulla is a bit of an expert on mushrooms. She took us mushroom picking once and she knew exactly which were edible and which were not. I told the police.'

As if on cue, Ulla came out of the cottage followed closely by the police officer. They didn't approach us where we sat, staring, on the terrace. We kept staring as they disappeared out of the gate. Then, suddenly, Olivia leapt from the chair and hurried after them. After a moment's hesitation I followed, then Kerstin. We must have looked pretty silly as we ran down the path. Half-way down the hill we caught up with them. Ulla stopped and turned to look at us. Her pale-brown eyes were blank, as if all the seeing had been turned inwards. A sparrow hopped round her feet and down in the harbour the ferry bell rang to announce its departure. The church clock rang out the half-hour, half past eleven.

Olivia said something in Swedish; I think she asked where they were going. She was panting, out of breath already from running. I sometimes forgot that she was not a young woman.

I heard the words Miss Andersson, that was Ulla, and police station. Ulla still said nothing. Kerstin suddenly reached out to touch her shoulder, but Ulla shrugged her off. We stood there watching them walk away. Ulla looked like a steel-helmeted child as she kept pace with the tall policeman.

Ulla! Who could believe it? Well, everyone actually. She had been formally charged with the attempted murder of Bertil Stendal, but the next day we were told that the charges had been reduced to grievous bodily harm. Everyone liked that a lot better, not only Ulla. Having an attempted murderess in the family left a much darker stain than a batty old aunt (not quite aunt) who indulged in a bit of recreational poisoning, because that was all it had been, the family decided. Bertil was back home and fit enough, give or take a weakened heart and liver. Olivia visited Ulla in her holding cell in Ytterby on the mainland. She returned to tell us that Ulla had never meant to kill Bertil or anything close, she had only wanted to scare him into believing he wasn't strong enough to make the move to another country. We all believed this to be true. I was silently grateful that Bertil had been harmed enough to be out of Ulla's way now she had read the diary, or she might have mixed an extra toadstool with his morning porridge.

I was walking round the island for the last time. When I reached the point where I had seen Linus, that first morning, dive naked into the sea I sat down and wept, my head in my hands. Now I knew only too well what love was and I wished I didn't. It was like giving a blind person sight for just long enough to take in the wonders of the world only to take it away again, plunging him back into darkness. But now it would be a different, crueller darkness, the darkness of absence: of light, of colour, of sunsets and sea, of trees and mountains, of paintings and the infinite variety of human faces. That's how my life would feel without Linus.

I reached in my bag for a tissue and then, instead of blowing my nose, I took out my pen and wrote his name on the pale-pink paper. *Linus. Linus I Love You*, and the ink bled into the tissue, blurring the lines of the words. But at last they were out, those words that had lain like a weight at the base of my heart, making it heavy.

What a fool love had made of me, because when I stumbled over an empty bottle of pear juice, discarded at the edge of the path, I picked it up. I unscrewed the top and then, having rolled the tissue into a cigar shape, I pushed it down the neck of the bottle and replaced the top. I turned to the sea and as I raised my arm I called out his name to the wind and the gulls, and hurled my message into the water.

'Goodbye Gerald and Kerstin, goodbye Bertil.' I stood with Olivia on the departing ferry, Audrey was seated in a collapsible wheelchair lent to us by the hospital. Once we reached the airport she would be transferred into one belonging to the airline and Olivia would return this one to the hospital. I tried to concentrate on practical things, like wheelchairs, to take my mind off the pain of leaving. The last passengers walked aboard and the barriers went down. The bell rang and we were off. The sun glittered on the soft waves, a seagull circled squawking overhead. Up ahead I glimpsed the blue gable of Villa Rosengård. I lifted my face to the sun.

'Be careful,' Olivia said. 'Looking straight into the sun like that. You'll blind yourself. See, your eyes are watering already.'

On the quayside Bertil, Gerald and Kerstin gave one last wave before turning round and walking back up the hill.

I lifted my face to the sun once more; it was too good an excuse for my tears to pass up.


Ivar was splashing around in the small rock pool by the bathing steps. 'Look Pappa! Look at me, I'm swimming underwater.'

Linus looked as the head and the feet of Ivar disappeared below the surface, leaving his bottom in its blue bathing trunks sticking up in the air like the tail of a duck. 'Very good, Ivar,' he called back.

Ivar surfaced and announced that he was diving for treasures. Some minutes later he scrambled up from the pool, a bottle in his hand. 'Look at this. It's a message. A message in a bottle.' He climbed up the rocks until he stood in front of Linus, water dripping from his slicked-back hair. 'Here. Do you think it's a treasure map? I bet it's a treasure map.' He handed the bottle to Linus who took it, turning it round in his hand.

'It looks more like an old tissue to me. Go and chuck it in the bin will you, there's a good boy.' He lay back on the warm rock and closed his eyes against the glare of the sun.

But Ivar was curious. It might look like a boring old pink tissue, but maybe that's just what the pirates wanted you to think. Out of sight of his father he unscrewed the top and fished out the tissue.

# PART FOUR

# Chapter Thirty

Lives are shattered, your heart breaks and yet you can wake up in your own bed as if nothing at all had changed. 'Tap tap tap.' Posy knocked on my bedroom door. 'I've made you some breakfast.'

'Did you miss me while I was away?' I asked her as we faced each other across the kitchen table.

Posy thought about it. 'Sort of,' she said finally.

'But you're glad to have me back?' I seemed to have this need to be loved nowadays, to belong somewhere.

Posy was studying me, her pretty head a little to one side. 'Mm.'

I must have looked downcast because she tried to explain. 'Of course I'm really glad you're back. Of course I've missed you. It's been restful, that's all.' This might have been a fair reply, but not the one I had hoped for. She told me her brother had asked after me. 'Have you missed Angus very much?'

I told her as tactfully as I could that no, I had not.

'He still cares about you a great deal.'

'Look,' I said. 'He's a nice man. But I have this thing against deserters.'

Posy looked shocked. 'That's a bit harsh, don't you think?'

I sighed and looked down at my hands. Then I looked up again, not straight at Posy, but just to the side of her. 'I'm in love with someone else. I mean really in love. Gut-wrenchingly, knee-weakeningly, stargazingly, moon-madly in love.' Now I looked at her.

She was about to laugh. But something in my expression must have stopped her. 'You mean it, don't you,' she said. 'You're serious? Who is it?'

'Linus.'

'The architect. Crikey! And what about him? Is he in love with you?'

It took me some time to force the word from my lips, this bad, wrong word. 'No.'

'Ah!' Posy said. 'Now that would explain why you didn't miss Angus.'

After breakfast I went to see Audrey. There were still a couple of weeks to go before I started work. It was just as well; for the moment my mother needed a lot of organising. Still, as she herself had said with characteristic disregard for normal human decency, 'Such a stroke of luck that Janet's mother died while we were away, because now Janet can live in.'

'You know,' she said now, as I sat down on the chair by her bed. 'You're far too worried about what people might think. I told Janet that we would have been in a right pickle had her mother not died this summer and she saw my point completely.'

'She knows you,' I said. 'That's why she wasn't surprised.'

My mother looked pleased, as if she was glad I agreed with her for once. 'Now,' she said. 'Before you start lecturing me, I know I have to do my exercises.'

'You're staying in bed? I mean, you haven't decided to rejoin life after everything that's happened?'

Audrey looked at me, her baby-blue eyes opened wide in surprise. 'Whyever should I want to, especially after everything that's happened?' I had to admit that she had a point.

'Come and sit here, Esther.' Audrey patted the side of the bed. I moved over from the chair. 'Don't look so suspicious.' My mother gave a little laugh. I laughed back, every bit as insincerely, as she took my hand in hers. I looked embarrassed. Audrey and I had managed thirty-four years with just a bare minimum of physical contact between us. Why should we change now?

'When I was a little girl,' Audrey began, 'I used to love to visit my Aunt Leouora. I never saw her in any pose other than reclining on the *chaise longue* in her sitting-room. She had a dear little house in Bloomsbury. I went back there some years ago, but it had been turned into some sort of take-away place. They had something large and brown and unspeakable turning round and round on a spit, and the smell was dreadful. Someone told me it was a donor kebab. Awful name, makes me think of kidneys, as in donor organs. Anyway, I digress.

'I can remember to this day seeing her there so peaceful, a tray with coffee and a box of chocolates on the small table by her side, a novel in her hand. And don't think that Leouora was a dull woman, or that her life lacked excitement. This was no escape. She loved life. She was better read than any man or woman I have met since. She spoke four languages fluently and read Latin as well as any priest. She embroidered. She listened to all the new plays on the wireless. The only thing she missed was her music. Her teacher said she would never succeed while she insisted on singing in a reclining position. Otherwise, her life was fuller than most. She wasted no time dawdling about, or sitting in traffic jams, not that there were many in those days, but you know what I mean. So, while other girls my age talked of marrying dashing men, soldiers maybe, who would whisk them away to exotic places, or having masses of babies (Gillian Barton wanted her own hunter and Shirley James, bless her, dreamt of becoming a missionary) I told them I wanted to lie on a *chaise longue* and read. I don't think they ever took me seriously.' Audrey fell silent.

'You're saying that you have, at last, fulfilled a lifetime's ambition?'

'I suppose I am,' Audrey said, removing her hand from mine and reaching out, instead, for a doughnut. I left her sitting there, contented.

*Good to have you back.*

Now Chloe didn't really say that. It was me imagining, as I faced her in her office two weeks later. What she actually said was, 'So?' Then she looked hard at me, studying me for signs of madness I expect. She should meet Ulla, I thought. But I wasn't thinking this unkindly. I missed them all, even her. Linus I missed with never-diminishing intensity. No, that wasn't true. Sometimes I dreamt of him and then I didn't miss him because we were together. But it was a short respite because waking up was parting from him all over again.

I realised that Chloe was speaking to me and as I looked at her I noticed that her skin had a new tautness; pig-pink it stretched across her cheek-bones with no visible lines or wrinkles. 'You're saying you really are back to your old self?'

I nodded. I didn't tell her that I had also moved *forward* to a *new* self. I didn't want to confuse her just as we were about to sign my new contract of employment.

'As you know, you can't step into your old job, Charlie's there now.'

'Charlie from Sport?'

Chloe nodded. The sun broke through a cloud and shone straight in through the fifth-floor window, hitting her profile. She rose from her chair and went across, shielding her face as she drew the blind. 'But we still want you to work on some specific features the way you have been doing as a free-lance, as well as taking over from Alison on "*Chronicle* Woman".' She sat down again.

'I thought I was going back to features full time.'

'Sorry.' Chloe shrugged. 'I wouldn't complain if I were you. "Woman" is being expanded to three pages and we're aiming to make it far more hard-hitting. Out with the "Ten Ways to Catch a Man for Christmas" and in with "Ten Ways to Beat the Ageing Process the Natural Way". Investigative stuff. "Where to go for HRT". "The Truth about Long-Lasting Lipstick". That kind of thing. Look upon it as a challenge.'

'And you think I'm the right person for the job?'

'You'd better be. And there's that People's Glyndebourne thing. It looks like it's on the cards again – Terra Nova have launched their chain of travel agents very successfully, so I suppose they feel they can take a bit of adverse publicity for now. Charlie agrees with me that as you started the reporting you might as well wrap it up.'

'They're going ahead, are they? Wow. I'll have to think about that one.'

'What's there to think about?'

I looked at her. If I told her love, she'd collapse with laughter. 'It's laser,' I said instead. 'That's what you've had done, you've laser-treated your face. That's why your skin's so smooth and pink, and why you can't face the sun.'

'You noticed.' Chloe looked pleased. 'I did it as part of our series on cosmetic surgery, but I'm thrilled with the result. I'm recommending it to everyone.' She got up too. 'I'll walk out with you, I'm off to the City for our "Why Smart Women Are City Women" series.'

As we stepped out into the sunshine, the New Vampire at my side pulled her straw hat down lower and pushed her silk scarf closer round her neck. We walked off in opposite directions.

I sat on the tiny lawn at the back of the house pulling the petals off a daisy: integrity, no integrity, integrity, no integrity, integrity, no integrity, integrity . . . Bugger!

When Chloe told me that Stuart Lloyd had announced his intention to restart the opera house project I had thought about one thing, and one alone: *Linus! Linus will be coming over, a lot.*

After lunch I had gone back to see Charlie, the Charlie who had taken over my old job on features.

'So,' Charlie had said. 'It looks like we'll be doing a follow-up on the Wilsons.'

'Ah.'

'"Just as the clouds lifted above their heads the Sword of Damocles descends once more on brave George and Dora Wilson". You know the kind of thing.'

'You mean we should try to stop the building of the opera house again?'

Charlie took on a look of Patience Barely Endured. 'We are continuing our campaign of justice for the Wilsons, yes. Oh, and did you know?' He had called me back from the doorway. 'Barry Jones, you know the guy; used to be someone in television . . .' I winced at the 'used to be' bit. 'Apparently he lives near the Wilsons and he called up to say he'd like to back our campaign in any way we'd want. He's attempting a come-back and I think it might well happen for him. He's been to a sex addiction clinic (that's for learning not to need sex, not how to do it).' I thanked Charlie for that explanation. 'And', Charlie had continued, 'he's on the wagon. His family is right behind him, and he and his wife are renewing their marriage vows in a moving ceremony near their country cottage, so I think all the pieces are in place for him. See if you can get him "Having tea with his good neighbours Dora and George in their farmhouse kitchen"-type thing. Get on it right away.'

I pulled up another daisy from the uncut lawn. 'Integrity, no integrity, integrity . . .'

Back inside I read John Donne: *No man is an island, entire of itself; every man is a piece of the continent, a part of the main. If a clod be washed away by the sea, Europe is the less, as well as if a promontory were, as well as if a manor of thy friend's or of thine own were. Any man's death diminishes me, because I am involved in mankind. And therefore never send to know for whom the bell tolls: it tolls for thee.*

I read it again, out loud, to Posy. I thought that no more beautiful words had been written or worthy sentiments expressed. 'What is one woman's unrequited love for a man compared with that?' I asked her. 'And the clod, or clods in question right now are the poor Wilsons. Could I just stand idly by and watch them being washed away on a tide of progress?' Before she had a chance to reply I answered myself. 'Yes, yes I could, but I won't. Maybe there have to be victims for progress to be made, but if I know nothing else I do know that I don't want to be part of a society where the victims have no voice. I'm the attorney for the defence.' I looked at up at her. 'That's an important job, isn't it?'

Posy nodded. 'Yes it is, but what about Linus?'

I slept badly that night. My mind was just one big, aching mess. I missed him. I missed the sight of him and the smell of him (salt air and a faint trace of the vanilla-scented soap that Ivar had given him as a present). I even missed his laugh. When I faced myself in the mirror in the morning I half expected my cheek still to burn from that one touch, and my hand to wear the imprint of his lips. It didn't. I knew about lust, but love . . . that all that aching of the heart and longing of the soul could actually hurt? I even missed the island. And as I walked through the London streets, adjusting my pace according to that of the pedestrian traffic jam ahead, trying not to inhale the air, which was still and so heavy with fumes it felt as if at any moment it might drop like a metal sheet on to the ground, I closed my eyes and imagined a cool breeze from the sea and the crying of the gulls. At night I went to bed again, wondering in whose arms Linus rested right now, as I lay alone.

Silly question; Pernilla's, of course.

*And therefore never send to know for whom the bell tolls: it tolls for thee.* I rose, bleary-eyed and heavy-brained, and with that line ringing in my ears. I showered and had some coffee and two cigarettes, then I picked up my bag and went down to Rookery Cottage.

It had taken Ivar two days to admit to having disobeyed his father, fishing out the tissue from that bottle of pear juice instead of chucking it away as he had been told to.

He had sidled into Linus's room on the morning of their departure from the island and held out his hand with the tissue crumpled in it. 'I think it's for you. It says your name.'

Linus was packing, but he had reached out for the paper, smoothing it out and reading the message.

'It just fell out of the bottle.' Ivar shrugged. 'Just like that, plop.'

His father wasn't listening, but kept on staring at the paper and Ivar made his escape.

Later Linus asked Pernilla if she had written the message in the bottle. Pernilla laughed until he thought she was going to choke. Then she coughed and through the coughing she said she thought it was probably Esther.

'Esther?'

'Of course Esther. Don't tell me you never noticed that she'd fallen for you in a big way. God, men are so blind.'

'It was probably some joke of hers,' he had said quickly, hiding his embarrassment.

Now Linus had returned to work and Ivar was back with his mother. The Swedish summer was all but over and autumn was in the air.

Linus sat at his table, drawing. He was doing it the old-fashioned way, with a pencil on paper – the computer would come later – and with each stroke of his pen he demolished the picture in his mind of his mother's anguish, erecting in its place a monument to his love for her.

The week of reading Astrid's diary he had been carried forward on a tide of anger; anger at Esther, a comparative stranger, knowing so much before he did and at Ulla, paradoxically, for sending him the letter telling him where to find the book. Most of all he felt fury towards the two men, Bertil and Jonas, who had driven his mother to take her life. He had felt her agony seeping from the pages and he had wanted to murder the bastards, both of them, his father and Jonas Aminoff. But slowly the rage had subsided.

It was Esther he had forgiven first. In spite of everything that had been going on between them, he liked her. He liked her a lot and as soon as she had left the island he had missed her. Was it she who wrote that note? Was she really in love with him? He kept thinking about her and bit by bit, things came back to him, things that had not meant anything much at the time: that night, for example, when he found her in his bedroom. The way she had looked at him the next morning in hers. How he'd look up sometimes and find those big, serious eyes fixed on him. Of course he had seen longing, but he'd never thought it was longing for him. If Pernilla was right he had been blind indeed. So in the midst of all the confusion and pain over Ulla and Bertil and Astrid, and the betrayal of all of them, thoughts of Esther wouldn't leave him alone, like a sweet but annoying tune you just couldn't get out of your head.

Once, when he was at his angriest with her, with Bertil, Ulla, his mother, the lot of them, when he felt that all he could rely on was the stones he fashioned into buildings, her small face had appeared before him. Suddenly he wasn't angry any more, instead he wanted to touch her pale cheek and kiss her grumpy mouth. He liked the way she looked; the fragile-looking body that hid the stubborn mind. She was really very pretty, in spite of the crabbiness that seemed to hover, almost permanently, just at the back of the blue eyes. He liked her sense of humour and the way she moved, neat and awkward both at once. She was kind, too; he had seen her with Ivar. And she was bright and she thought about things.

God! he hoped she wasn't going to start that campaign of hers again. Old dears or no old dears, newspapers or no newspapers, this time the building was going up.

*Architecture in general is frozen music.* And another picture appeared in his mind, that of his mother walking across the ice until it gave way under her feet and she fell into the freezing water. Had she been frightened or had she given in to death with relief? And where had he been, her son who loved her so much? Too small, too helpless and pathetic. Well, no more. He, Linus, was what she had left behind and he was going to make her proud.

It had taken longer to get through his anger towards Bertil. For one, he had realised that the anger was not new, but that it had been there for as long as he could remember, lurking in the shadows of his heart and never allowed to come out in the open; not until now, that was. How could he forgive him? The cruelty to Astrid, the way he had refused to tell his son the truth about her death. All the little half-truths, all that rewriting of history. It had been years before he knew that Astrid had killed herself. At first it had been: 'Your mother had an accident. She had been ill for a long time.'

'But Bosse says my mother didn't love us any more so she ran away,' Linus had cried one day after school.

Bertil had told him never to listen to gossip. 'Your mother met with an accident, she died. There really is no more to say.' But there had been, lots more, and Linus had always known it and that knowledge, unadmitted, had worn a hollow at his very centre where love and security should have been.

Had Bertil really acted out of concern for Linus when he took custody of him, or had he been motivated by pique and a need for revenge? Bertil himself seemed unsure of the answer and the truth no doubt lay somewhere in between. When confronted, Bertil had shied away as if he'd been struck. 'It's such a long time ago. Attitudes are different now.' His old-man's voice had been pleading and his old-man's eyes had turned moist. 'As far as I'm concerned she was ill. There was no need for her to run off with that man. And as for taking her own life . . . It was all madness.'

Madness seemed to run in his mother's family. Look at Ulla. And what about him, Linus? He had certainly worked like a madman these last few days; seeing the engineer and the surveyor, the lighting and acoustics experts, and drawing, sometimes all night so that he was still in the office, bleary-eyed and stubbled, when the others arrived for the next day's work.

It hadn't taken him long to feel grateful to Ulla for helping him to find the truth. In her letter she had told him everything that was known about how his mother died and she had filled in as many gaps as she could about the time leading up her suicide. Bertil had dropped all charges against Ulla. That way, the family could re-form, closing up like a jellyfish that had lost a small and unimportant part of its body. Soon everything would be much the same as it always had been. Only a little less. The condition of Ulla's release from custody had been her voluntary confinement to a mental hospital. That was where Linus had visited her the other day.

'Did you mean to kill Bertil?' he had asked her because he thought he should. In a funny way, though, he didn't really care, it was as if all of that episode was buried far down in the past, overtaken by the strange immediacy of his mother's death.

Ulla had raised tired eyes to his face. 'No, of course I didn't. I wanted to give him a fright, that's all. Make him stop and think, and see what a stupid idea it was for him and Olivia to sell up and move away.'

She had paused and when she began to speak again her voice was quiet, her tone even. 'None of you has any idea what it's like not to belong with anyone, not really. To be essential to no one. To be tolerated rather than loved. To come first with no one. Why should you know?' She gave a small smile. 'Whatever happened to you, you were your mother's best love and your father's. Your wife's, too, before it all went wrong. You've had all that and you'll have it again. In the meantime you've got your son. To him, you and his mother are the universe. Bertil and Olivia are sufficient to themselves. Even Kerstin has that old fool Gerald who cares for her. But I, I knew I was only ever around on sufferance. And the worst of it is that in the end you make do with that, with being tolerated rather than loved. You cling to the only thing you've got. What I had were those few weeks every summer at Villa Rosengård. For that brief period I could pretend that I was part of a family. Your father was going to take that away from me.' She had leant closer to him, fixing his gaze with hers. 'Do you have any idea what it's like to know that there is no one, no one at all, who cares that much whether you live or die? Well, I do, only too well.' As he stood up to leave she had added suddenly, 'If I had seen the diary in time it might all have been different.'

He had turned round and looked at her. 'Oh?'

'Then I might well have killed him.' She had smiled that joyless smile at him. 'Only joking, of course.'

Pernilla had gone back to Stockholm and her job in the PR agency and he was glad to see her go. It had been fun, the time they spent together. In bed it had been sex more than love-making, but that was OK. If she had looked for more commitment from him she hadn't said so. But in the last couple of weeks of the holidays she had begun to irritate him. It was little things at first, like her constant cheerfulness. No one had a right to be so damned cheerful all the time, it wasn't natural. And he had thought of Esther and smiled. One could never accuse that woman of being overly cheerful.

And Pernilla always wanted to *do* things. She was never content just to *be*, to look and listen and just be. Esther had that capacity for stillness and for silence. She understood that for the activity to matter there had to be lulls. She was the kind of woman with whom you could just lie back in the grass and watch the clouds on their endless travels across the sky. Pernilla would want to play tennis. And he remembered how, disconcertingly, he had thought of Esther the last time he had been in bed with Pernilla. There she'd been, small, neat and scowling, popping up before his mind's eye when that mind should rightfully have been busy with Pernilla who at that very moment was lying in his arms, her large, even teeth nibbling his left earlobe, her legs encircling his hips. And all that time she, Esther, had been in love with him, if Pernilla was to be believed. The thought made him curiously happy.

He worked on, perfecting the details of the design, translating them on to the computer and now, finally, preparing to hand them over to the model makers. And he thought of the old brother and sister, the Wilsons. Every step he took towards the fulfilment of his dream was a step nearer to the destruction of theirs. But this was no time for doubts, so he swiped them away with an impatient gesture of his hand across his forehead and carried on with his drawing.

The next day, half-way through the morning, he telephoned Esther in London. He asked her straight out if she had written the message in the bottle.

There had been a long pause. Then: 'Oh my God!'

'So you did.' Linus felt himself smile.

'I feel like a complete idiot.' She sounded cross. 'I mean never in a million years did I imagine it'd actually get to you.'

'Well it did. Ivar found it.'

'Ivar did?' There was another pause. 'Oh, well.'

'Maybe we should talk about this,' Linus said. 'I mean, this is the kind of thing one needs to talk about.'

'It's bloody embarrassing.' Esther sounded as if she were close to tears.

'Well if you'd rather not . . . so how's everything else? You heard the news about the opera house?'

'Yes, yes I did.' She paused and swallowed before saying, 'I'm working on a piece about it now.'

'You're doing what? I don't believe this. You say you love me and then you set about destroying my life.'

'I'm not trying to destroy your life. I'm trying to behave in a way that makes me able to live with myself.'

'God, do you remind me of someone. You write about love with one hand while the other is busy unstitching the very fabric of my existence.' He slammed down the phone. Bloody women! You couldn't trust them, not any of them. It was a good half-hour before he had calmed down enough to get back to work.

At ten o'clock he finally left the office. Buildings, he thought, as he switched off the light behind him, buildings, solid, lasting, they were what mattered.

# Chapter Thirty-one

I would never have thought of myself as a likely suicide candidate. Yet, after that phone conversation with Linus, the one when I added hatred to the list of reasons he could give for never loving me back, there were moments when death seemed an option. *It's better to have loved and lost than never to have loved at all*, I kept telling myself. The trouble was that for most of the time it sounded like a load of bull.

So I worked. I did my pieces for '*Chronicle* Woman'. I did a charming and sympathetic feature on Barry Jones and his new-found passion for charity work. I kept in touch with the developments in the Wilson saga, feeling sick at heart all the while. 'Linus, my love, this will hurt me more than you,' I muttered as I prepared to leave for Kent. As if that were going to help either of us.

The Wilsons' dog was dead. 'How did it happen?'

'It were in the way,' George said.

'In the way of what?' I wondered.

'Machinery,' George replied.

'Oh. Oh dear, how dreadful. You must miss him.'

'He were an old dog, but I miss him.'

Maybe it was the newly planted roses blooming against the cottage wall, or the warm sunshine of an Indian summer, but Rookery Cottage looked an altogether different place from the one I had visited two months earlier. The hens were still picking their way up and down the mud-track drive, but their harassed pecking had given way to a leisurely strut and there seemed to be a new shine to their feathers. Even the evidence of George's scrap business had been tidied away beneath a newly renovated open shed.

George had been out at the front when I arrived and in the space it took for us to reach the front door a white Ford Fiesta drove up and a middle-aged woman, her ample form clad in a dark-blue track suit, got out and hailed him. Having caught up with us she introduced herself to me, breathlessly, as Penny Perkins, Chair of the Save George and Dora's Home campaign. I looked at George.

'It's the locals,' he muttered. 'They've sort of taken up our cause, if you like.'

Penny Perkins's face relaxed into a pleased smile. 'We had the local TV news down the other day. They were doing a follow-up.' She pronounced the last words carefully, as if she had just learnt them. 'It was marvellous, actually. We all gathered round in George and Dora's kitchen and had a little singsong. Someone said it must have been like that during the war, that community spirit, everyone looking out for everyone else and keeping each other cheerful.'

She paused and Dora, who had appeared in the doorway, took the opportunity to point at me and say, 'That there's Miss Fisher. She's the one from the paper.'

'Oh, right. Well, we have a lot to thank you for, then,' Penny Perkins said. 'Without you Dora and George might have lost their home already.' A frown creased her brow and she sighed. 'But I'm almost forgetting. I came to tell you that they're saying now the building's going ahead for certain. You wouldn't believe it, would you, after everything. But Ted was down at the council offices and he heard Mary Trilby tell Joan and that's how Ted knew.'

I nodded. 'I'm afraid it's true. As you know, your side lost the appeal against the compulsory purchase order and Terra Nova has decided to go ahead with the opera house project, so unless public opinion causes the council to relent I'm afraid the eviction will be enforced in the next few weeks.'

The gummy grin on Dora's face shrank to a frightened O. 'What are you going to do?' The three of them turned and looked at me.

It was all very well to be considered a source of power, but this was ridiculous: I was a journalist, not God. Then again, maybe the differences had been somewhat blurred over the last couple of years. I suggested we went inside. 'I must tell you that I think the chances of the compulsory purchase *not* going ahead are slim.' I sat down at the kitchen table, taking the mug of tea handed to me by Dora.

'But what about the media?' Penny Perkins spoke the word with the reverence normally reserved for the Almighty and she clearly expected a miracle.

I had to tell them: 'There are limits to what we can achieve.' Penny seemed amazed, looking at me like a pilgrim who'd just seen her wine turned into water. 'It doesn't mean we won't keep trying.' I attempted to soften the blow. 'That's why I'm here now. We know we've got huge public support for George and Dora.' I nodded at them across the table. 'But as I said, there are limits to what we can do. I'm sorry,' I added. Then I thought of Linus and I'm ashamed to say I wasn't so sure.

We drank our tea in gloomy silence interrupted only by the slurping as George sucked the liquid from his dunking biscuit. 'I'm here to do a follow-up piece,' I said eventually. 'Who knows what might come of a renewed campaign?'

'You can show me with my jams,' Dora said.

'Your jams?'

'I've done them all summer. There's been a real run on them these last few weeks.' By way of explanation she waddled up to the larder, bringing out three different jams in their jars.

'Dora's Real Country Apricot' I read on one. 'Dora's Real Country Strawberry' and 'Dora's Real Country Kiwi'. 'Kiwi? You surely can't grow kiwi fruit around here? Come to think of it, what about the apricot? Do you buy the fruit?'

Dora winked at Penny. ''Course not. Whoever could afford that? No, I just buy the jam off the shelf. Then I put it in my own jars with my own label and no one knows the difference.'

'It's not very honest.'

Dora looked at me reproachfully. 'What harm is it doing? People like bringing back little souvenirs. We're quite the celebrities nowadays.' The thought seemed to cheer her up. 'Shop jam's much nicer anyway, sweeter,' she added.

Penny Perkins nodded. 'They are, you know. We get people coming from all over asking for George and Dora.'

'It's good jam, that,' George muttered. 'Nothing wrong with it at all.'

'But surely making your own from local fruit would work out cheaper and so give you a higher profit?'

'I can't be doing with all of that.' Dora shrugged. 'That's what you've got your shops for. Now where do you want us for your picture?'

I sat in front of the computer, but instead of the blank screen I saw the new opera house rise in splendour above the lake, there to offer solace to generations, to educate and inspire. And there was Linus, its creator. His image was so real that I found myself whispering to him, little words of endearment that could only be thought up by a brain shrouded in mist, love-mist.

His image faded and in its place came a tumble-down cottage with roses round the door and rusty machine parts in an open shed at the front, and a surprisingly fertile vegetable plot at the back, Rookery Cottage. Now I saw George's sharp features and Dora's unlovely virtually toothless grin. But I was the attorney for the defence and my clients did not have to be lovable or even especially good to deserve my services. I struck the letters on the keyboard with the force of my heavy heart.

When he was a young boy Linus had often dreamt that he was big and powerful, and that he rescued his mother. He had never known just what it was he should have rescued her from, so in his dreams it varied. Sometimes it was from a giant with eyes the size of wagon wheels and teeth like slabs of granite (that had been when he was very young). Sometimes it was from Red Indians and once it had been a wolf. He saved her from robbers and kidnappers, and as he got older he found ways of curing what had made her sick. But always the dreams would end the same. His mother would open her eyes, and smile at him and say, 'Thank you, Linus. Whatever would I have done without you.' For that brief moment he was a king, filled with pride and happiness; complete. Then, as the dream subsided into reality he'd cry, drained, empty of hope, and each time the tears were more bitter than the last because the truth was that he would never save his mother. She was gone; for ever beyond his reach and, dream as he might, there was nothing, nothing at all he could do to change that. When it had mattered, when his mother had needed him, when he could have made a difference, he had been too young, too stupid, too small and puny and powerless. He grew up. He grew strong, but the sense of powerlessness remained.

But now, as he stood before the completed model of his opera house, he felt the same elation as when he had dreamt and found his mother's eyes smiling up at him, thanking him, her rescuer.

He had learnt from so many previous occasions that no drawings, no computer images could ever quite prepare you for the sight of the finished model. Sometimes it fell short of your expectations, at others it lived up to them, but rarely did it exceed them. This was one of those rare moments. His creation rose before him, perfect and true to life in every detail but size, and it was a beauty. He moved around the model table. Not only was the opera house gorgeous, but the days and nights spent working had made sure that it was perfect, too, for its purpose and for its setting by the lake. He bent down and peered into the main auditorium, the cocoon. Every acoustic panel was in place, every seat – stalls, dress circle and balconies. Even the lights were in place, perfect scale models of the chandeliers, which he had commissioned from Olle Holm, the glass sculptor. He straightened up and stood back, getting a whole view of the model. Then, before him, like an overlay on a computer image, came the vision of two old people who had lost their home. 'An Englishman's home is his castle,' he mumbled. But not any more, it wasn't, and he, Linus, was party to the deconstruction of their lives. 'Oh Esther,' he groaned. 'What the hell am I doing?' And he felt like crying the way he had when he was a child who had just seen his dream slip away.

# Chapter Thirty-two

The compulsory purchase order against Rookery Cottage had gone through and the eviction notice was about to be served. I didn't know they served eviction notices at the weekends. Penny Perkins and her fellow campaigners were waiting for the council officer as he arrived, driving up to the gate in his red Vauxhall, and so were I and a photographer, Paul, from the paper. I had been talking to some of the protesters. 'You must care deeply about George and Dora to do this?' I asked one.

The woman, in her twenties with lank mid-blonde hair, looked blankly at me. Then her brow cleared. 'Yeah, them. 'Course I do. I've seen them on telly. It's diabolical.'

'I don't actually know the Wilsons,' a middle-aged woman in baggy jeans and a multicoloured knitted jersey confessed. 'Not many of us around here do, but I simply couldn't sit idly by and let this kind of thing happen.'

A man, fiftyish and wearing a bright-blue V-neck sweater with a small eagle motif, told me he was the local publican. 'We don't often see them down at the pub and when we do they keep themselves much to themselves, but you have to do your bit for the community, know what I mean.'

A man stepped out from behind the crowd and into the line of Paul's lens, pointing at the red Vauxhall. It was Barry Jones. A thinner Barry Jones with a less extravagantly bouffant hair-style, but Barry Jones nevertheless. 'This is it, girls and boys, so let's show 'em what we British are made of.' His voice soared above the din of a passing harvester as the campaigners formed a ring round the cottage. Fists were raised in victory salutes. The council officer stepped out from his car and, with barely a glance in our direction, walked up to the gate and nailed the eviction notice to the post. Then he turned on his heels and walked back.

The campaigners, led by Penny and Barry Jones, were too busy shouting their slogan – 'What do we want? Justice for George and Dora. When do we want it? Now!' – to notice that he had gone, his business done. When they did realise there was a moment's silence before one of the campaigners, a burly man in his sixties, balding and red-faced, took up the chant: 'We shall not we shall not give in, we shall not we shall not give in.' That seemed to perk them up as they linked hands once more for the camera. Suddenly a huge cheer went up. I turned round to see if the notice had been torn down, but it was still there, neatly pinned to the gatepost. The cause of the good cheer was the arrival of the crew from a local TV station. Penny raised her fist. 'What do we want? Justice for George and Dora. When do we want it? We want it now!' Lights, Camera, Go! Barry Jones linked arms with the nearest protester, a woman with long grey hair cascading down her back. 'This is a human rights issue,' he pronounced and when he realised that the crew had missed it the first time, he said it again, twice, adding, 'I care not a jot for my own safety,' as if he were expecting an armoured car full of secret police to storm through the gate at any time. The crew moved closer. 'As I said, this is a human rights issue . . .' The protesters surged forward drowning out his words with their chanting.

'Is this how Frankenstein would have felt, do you think?' I asked Paul, as I watched my unlovely creation form and swell before us.

'Monsters don't have feelings,' he replied. 'That's the point of them.'

'But Frankenstein wasn't the monster. Frankenstein created the monster,' I explained. 'Surely you knew that?'

'Whatever.' Paul shrugged.

I hadn't reread my last article when it appeared the previous week, but I knew it by heart, line by manipulative line. And the line had been swallowed, gratefully, by our readers and the letters of support were arriving by the sackful. But it looked as if this time nothing I could do would stop the eviction of the Wilsons from their home. For their sakes, if nothing else, maybe it was time to face up to the inevitable and stop campaigning. But would Charlie agree?

I had written to Linus, trying to explain my actions. I had avoided phoning because I knew that once I heard his voice I would melt: first it would be my heart, then my brain and finally the telephone receiver itself, until there was no logic, no determination, no creditable defence, but just a soggy mess of blood and guts and plastic. So I had written this letter instead.

Dear Linus,

I know you're very angry with me. I know you feel betrayed. I also know all too well what this project means to you and on one level I hate what I'm doing. And it's not as if the project is without its merits.

But are you sure that Stuart Lloyd's insistence on it being built on the land adjoining his estate is not more to do with personal ambitions than thoughts of the importance of bringing culture to the masses?

Dora and George Wilson are not the world's most attractive people. They don't contribute anything very special to the sum total of human greatness or happiness. They're not terribly bright, nor are they especially good. But Rookery Cottage is their home, the only one they've known. It's pretty well the only worthwhile thing they've ever had; as I said, God not having been overly generous with his gifts to them. There they are in all their frailty and they are powerless. I don't think there's anything worse than to be powerless.

Individuals have always been sacrificed for causes. Maybe that's how it has to be? But the day it happens silently, without debate, without the victim being heard, that's the day a new order dawns, one of which I don't ever want to be a part. I have to do what I think is right and believe me, Linus, it's harder than you'll ever know for me to go against you like this.

Please try and understand why I'm doing what I am doing and that it's not a betrayal of my feelings for you. But what kind of lover would I be for you if I betrayed everything I believed in to try to make you love me?

I was still hoping for a reply.

\*

The TV crew had left Rookery Cottage and so had the campaigners. Even Barry Jones had gone. He had vanished with the TV crew. All that remained was the eviction notice on the gatepost and the scent of self-righteousness in the air.

'Bric-à-brac business's doing well,' George said on our way back up the drive. 'Them squirrels in particular. People like to say they bought from us.' He bent down and picked up a mess of crushed egg and chicken foetus underfoot, chucking it on the compost heap as we passed on the way to the door.

'So that young man who carves them must be earning some real money,' I said, as we sat down in the kitchen. Dora was already by the stove, making the tea. She and her brother exchanged looks.

'He's not all that young either. Just seems that way. But he does all right for someone who's not right in the head,' George said. 'We see to that.'

'What's his name?'

'Frank. Frank Wilson, same as his grandfather although Father would turn in his grave knowing his daughter's bastard were named after him.'

'He's your nephew?'

'He is that,' George said. Dora looked troubled.

'So the lady who was here the other day, showing you some antiques, is your sister?'

Dora and George nodded grudgingly. Dora sat down heavily on the chair opposite mine. 'It was a bad business back then and our father was a hard man. But they're all right now,' George said.

'She had to go once we learnt the babby was on the way,' Dora said, her head lowered. Then she looked up at me. 'I was sorry about that. I like little babbies.'

'Your sister wasn't married to Frank's father?'

Dora sniffed. 'She wasn't married to anyone, that was the trouble. Wouldn't even say who the father was although we had our suspicions, didn't we, George?' George nodded. 'Then when Jack Grant let her have that Railway Cottage rent free and gave her a load of things to furnish, well then we knew. Anyway, Aggie came back to the village and the boy with her.'

'Some folk thought Frank should be put away on account of him not being right in the head,' George said. 'And Aggie was fretting what would happen to him when she goes, she's older than us both, see, because the cottage is for her, not for Frank. But we told Aggie there was no need for that. Father is long since gone and we own this place. "No, Aggie," I said. "There's no need for anyone to be put away, thank you very much."'

'And there's no harm in Frank,' Dora said. 'And he's ever so good at his carving. It's on account of Aggie going through the change when he came along, him being funny like. Well, that's what doctor said.'

'You do understand that if the worst comes to the worst and you have to leave Rookery Cottage the council will have to pay the true market value of the house? You would get somewhere else to live. Somewhere where Frank could go too.'

'They say that,' George almost shouted. 'But this is our home. People around here understand our ways. Frank's too. Being a Wilson in these parts means something. There are no houses in the village for sale and if they were the money we'd get for this place wouldn't buy any, not the way they've all been tarted up. This is our home. We bought it. We struggled half our lives to be able to. What was the point if they can just come along and take it away?' George was red in the face and his eyes were watering as he banged his fist on the table. 'What is the point?' And then he leant his head on his arms and wept.

My reporting of the eviction notice being served on George and Dora Wilson got a huge response. I had to stop reading the letters of support because it threatened my resolve. Too many of my correspondents were agreeing for all the wrong reasons, venting feelings of spite and envy, backing up their arguments with emotive and badly argued points. There was, clinging to some of the letters, the scent of the lynch mob. They bore the signature of the Seriously Ill-informed Readers or SIRs as they were known. But, I kept reminding myself, it was no good blaming Dora and George for the failings of some of their supporters.

'So?' Charlie perched on my desk. 'How are we doing with dear old George and Dora? I reckon we've got another week's worth.'

'I don't know, Charlie. Maybe we should quit.'

'What do you mean, quit? The readers have been with us this far. They'll want to be in on the final act. "Axe descends on brave George and Dora Wilson." That kind of thing.'

I looked up at his eager face and the small bright eyes darting from side to side as we spoke, as if he was anxious to make sure he wasn't missing something more interesting going on in another corner of the room. I told him I had spoken to Simon Fuller at Terra Nova Enterprises. 'He's the new right-hand man, it seems. Work on the access road, that's the bit which is going through the Wilsons' front room, is scheduled to begin the first Monday of next month. That's just about three weeks from today.' I shook my head. 'I don't know, Charlie. All we would be doing now is to give George and Dora hope when there is none. Nothing short of a miracle can save Rookery Cottage.'

'What say we create a miracle?' Charlie looked upwards into the distance, the way he did when he had just spotted a headline, and made a sweeping gesture with his arm as if to clear the way for his vision. "Victory for the People's Paper, as *Chronicle* readers save brave George and Dora".' Then he too shook his head. 'No, I can't see that happen, you're right. But I want to run the finale nevertheless. Our readers expect it.'

I shook my head, about to protest when he went on, 'Oh, and I've had Barry Jones on the phone, offering his help again. Apparently he's got a new TV show coming: *The Smallest Room in the House*.'

'I don't think that's the miracle we need.' I was struck by a new thought, a little hopeful thought. 'Oh, Charlie, that thing, you know the Barry Jones scandal, it might even have been a blessing in disguise, do you think? Strengthened his marriage, given his career a new impetus?' I made my voice light and unconcerned, but I knew my eyes were fixed on him, hopeful.

'Nah.' Charlie got up from the desk and brushed down his trousers although they looked perfectly fluff-free to me. 'No, he's still miles away from where he was before all of that stuff. I doubt if he'll ever get back to the top. Anyway, the Wilson thing is your call, just make it good. I want a great exit from this one.'

'It's bloody typical,' I complained to Posy that evening, over supper. It was her turn to cook and she had made couscous with spring onions and sundried tomatoes. 'I spend my life searching for absolutes, pining for certainties. I strive to prove to myself that something in this life is steadfast and sure – even if it's only me. And then . . . when I do, that very proof is what wrecks things for me.'

I stabbed the couscous with my fork. 'Not that Linus was about to leap into my arms anyway. And now bloody Charlie wants me to be some kind of peeping Tom at the Wilsons' wake for the benefit of our concerned readership. I tell you, those two old things have come to rely on the publicity. They like being in the limelight. But once they're out, they'll lose that too. I tell you . . .'

Posy helped herself to some more couscous. 'I thought you had realised at last that you'd have to relax your principles a little. You are a journalist, after all.' She looked pleased with herself when she said that. People always did look pleased with themselves when they had a go at journalists. They, together with psychiatrists and lawyers, formed the unholy trinity of our society and I had considered becoming all three.

'But seriously,' Posy said. 'Relax a little or you'll go mad – again.'

I sighed. 'I know, I know, principles, like spots and braces on your teeth are adolescent afflictions; you're meant to grow out of them. But surely there's got to be a limit to how much we're prepared to buckle and bend to squeeze ourselves into the life we think we want.' A tear escaped from my eyes, landing on a sundried tomato on my plate. 'Or maybe not. Linus feels I've betrayed him. He thinks I'm like his mother. And George and Dora will feel betrayed too, whatever I do.' I wiped my eyes with the back of my hand. 'So I can look back with satisfaction at yet another successful period in my life.'

'I thought he adored his mother,' Posy said. 'I thought this opera house was partly about her. His Taj Mahal, you said once.'

'He does love her, but he hates her too. You can do that with mothers.' I tried to eat my food, but it seemed to grow in my mouth until I was unable to swallow and I pushed the plate away. Then I was struck by a frightening thought. 'Do you think God is a four-year-old? Could that be the answer to all these imponderables of existence?'

'Isn't it enough that He's a He?'

I nodded. She had a point there.

I was getting ready for bed when the phone rang. It was Linus. My heart thumped against my rib-cage as I took the receiver from Posy. 'Yes.' My voice came out a squeak. 'Yes,' I tried again, an octave deeper.

'It's me, Linus. I'm coming over next week to meet with Stuart Lloyd. I thought we might have dinner one night.'

'You got my letter?' My voice sounded small, as if it didn't want to be found.

'Yes, I did. I'm sorry not to have written back, but I've been snowed under with the project and anyway, I'm a lousy correspondent.'

'You must be thrilled it's definitely going ahead?'

'I can't tell you how much.' He paused. 'I'm sorry. I shouldn't have said what I did the other day. You don't owe me anything. I'd like us to be friends. Especially now I've got what I want.' There was another pause. 'That was a joke, kind of.'

We decided on dinner Monday evening, then he hung up before I'd even had a chance to ask how everybody was.

'I can't tell you how much this thing means to me.' Linus stood with Stuart Lloyd before a computer image of the People's Glyndebourne.

Stuart Lloyd nodded. 'You and me both.' He turned to Linus, a huge grin on his face. 'It's going to be fantastic. I knew you were the man for the job the moment I saw those preliminary designs. The person to turn my dream into reality.' He looked sideways at Linus, an embarrassed little smile on his face. 'But enough of this sentimentality. Still, I tell you there was a time when I thought we'd lost. With the launch of the travel agents being imminent I simply couldn't afford all that negative publicity, but people have moved on. These days people's outrage lasts about as long as their breakfast cereal. In a couple of weeks it will all be forgotten. There's always a new story, a new outrage. Right now this thing about the woman who had her baby's sex changed at a private clinic in Switzerland seems to take up a lot of space.' As Linus looked blank, he explained: 'Her husband had four sons already from a previous marriage so when she gave birth to yet another boy she had him operated on. There's been quite a fuss about it, as you can imagine.'

'Still, it's a pity we couldn't have done it without robbing the Wilsons of their home,' Linus said. 'This project is everything I've dreamt of. The "Now I Can Die Happy" thing of my life. But it turns out to be built, literally, on someone else's misery.'

'You know that journalist, don't you?'

'Yeah.'

Stuart Lloyd shook his head. 'Look here, Linus. Do you want to see your opera house built?'

Linus sighed. 'Yes, more than anything.'

'Well, there you are. I mean, look, we'd all like to get our own way *and* be smelling of roses while we go about it. But life isn't like that. Most actions are compromised, whether by self-interest or by it buggering up someone somewhere along the line. Nothing comes clean, everything is tainted. That's just life, take it or leave it.'

Linus thought of Astrid. 'I'll take it,' he said. 'All of it.'

'Good. And by the way, with or without you, I'd still build. The difference is that your design is a great one and the others weren't, which is worth thinking about; long after we're all gone and our petty squabbles are over that building will contribute to the cultural well-being of the nation. So, Linus, there's no place here for faint hearts.'

'Quite,' Linus said, feeling curiously light, as if he hadn't got a heart in the first place. It felt good. Peaceful. 'Where do you want me to sign?'

Stuart Lloyd looked puzzled. 'Sign?'

'Soul, devil . . .'

'Ah. I see what you mean. A fax will do. We've even got faxes in hell these days.'

# Chapter Thirty-three

'So here we are,' I said stupidly, as the waiter at Lincoln's seated us at a table for two right by a trolley laden with shellfish, some dead; the lobsters, some alive; the oysters, but whatever their status they were lying in state on the same bed of ice. Lincoln's was famous for its seafood. Linus and I had arrived at the door of the restaurant at the same time, punctuality being one thing we had in common. I tried to think of something else, but my mind was as still as my heart was furious. I looked across the table at Linus, my eyes drinking from his, my lips trying to catch his breath as he leant across to light my cigarette. When I could bear it no more I looked around me instead.

Linus appeared to have a fondness, shared by many of his countrymen, for what they thought of as English Style. Lincoln's was a restaurant so ancient in tradition you half expected to pay the bill in shillings and pounds.

'Bertil told me about this place,' Linus said. 'He used to eat at Lincoln's whenever he was in London. The first time was in nineteen forty-nine, would you believe it?'

I looked around at the other diners, men mostly, plump and florid; a gathering of elderly Billy Bunters. I nodded towards one of them, sitting on his own at a tiny table in a corner below a still-life painting of dead game, silently tucking into a large plate of oysters, his napkin pulled up under his chin. 'Do you think he stayed on, since forty-nine, I mean?'

We ordered: crab salad for both of us to start with, then grilled Dover sole for Linus and scallops for me. Linus relayed his conversation with Stuart Lloyd. 'I felt a little like Faust must have done when he signed away his soul.' He gave me a wry little smile across the restaurant table.

343

I put my hand on his, just for a second. 'I'm glad for you, I really am. And I am your . . . friend, but no one needs friends with feet of clay. You're the architect, you know better than anyone what happens to constructions built on clay.' As I spoke I hoped I was right in thinking that sooner or later they cracked.

'Actually,' Linus said, 'they sometimes last for a surprisingly long time.'

Did he have to make things even more awkward? 'Well, as I said, you're the architect.' Then our first course arrived.

'How's your mother?' Linus asked.

'Audrey?'

'That's the one.'

'Fine.'

'So how is everyone your end? I spoke to Olivia last week and she sounded OK, not great, but OK.'

'That's just it, they're both OK, but only just. I'm afraid I gave Bertil a very hard time after I'd read the diary. And I did resent half the world knowing its contents before I did.' I blushed and looked away. 'Don't worry,' he said quickly. 'I know you were in a difficult position. Anyway, Bertil is fine now, physically, but emotionally?' He shook his head. 'I don't know. We all went out to the island last weekend, Olivia and Bertil, Kerstin and Gerald and me and Ivar. It was as if nothing had happened, that's how it seemed to begin with, anyway. We just closed over the wound and went on as before, but of course things have changed irrevocably. For Bertil and Olivia; all those years of thinking we were all one big happy family while all the time we were actually nurturing this particular serpent at its very bosom.'

I found it hard to picture Ulla nursing at anyone's bosom, but I let that pass. 'I still find the whole thing a bit unreal,' I said instead. 'It's modern manners to view the dark in life, not as a tragic but integral part of living, but more like a breach of contract, of our rights. I can see the scenes at the pearly gates, all those people lining up for compensation.'

Linus smiled at me and put his hand over mine. I had left it there, lying nonchalantly on the white table-cloth, waiting for just such a gesture from him, and as I felt the warmth of his skin against mine little starbursts of excitement shot through my stomach and up to my chest. We sat like that, facing each other over the restaurant table, the one candle and the four glasses, the plates and the crumbs and the large red wine stain next to my glass. The moment seemed an eternity, but it was still too short. Then he retrieved his hand, leaving mine in mourning. 'I really wish I could make you understand.'

I gazed into his eyes. 'Mmm,' I said. He looked nonplussed. What had he said? Was my response adequate? I checked my face mentally; had it forgotten to put its knickers on? Was it baring all?

Linus looked sad as he lifted his glass to his lips. I too felt sad. It seemed that doom and gloom was what we did best. But what the hell? Anything that we had in common was fine with me.

'How's Pernilla?' I had to enquire rather in the way you'd feel the need to ask the doctor if it was six days or six months he'd said you had left to live.

'She's fine.' What was that in his voice? A distinct lack of interest, that's what it was if I was not mistaken. Dear God, don't let me be mistaken. 'I haven't really seen her since the summer. You know how it is. We're both busy. She's in Stockholm. I'm, well, I'm all over the place.' He shrugged.

Had I mentioned doom and gloom? Absolutely not. I was the girl with a song in her heart and fireworks going off in the pit of her stomach. 'Oh, I'm sorry,' Esther Insincerity Fisher replied.

'It's nothing to be sorry about.'

I glittered. I twinkled. Just let them ask me to be the Good Tooth Fairy now.

The waiter appeared soundlessly and poured us some more wine. When he left us Linus spoke, and all of a sudden his voice was intense and his jaw was set tight as if he had a problem keeping it under control. 'Have you any idea what it feels like, knowing that your own mother ended her life in such misery, such absolute despair and loneliness, and that you were too young, too dumb to do a thing to help her?'

I sobered up, like a fairy who's had all her sparkly bits washed off. 'Please, Linus, don't do this to yourself. You can't think like that. No six-year-old would have the kind of wisdom and maturity to help in such circumstances, you know that. Just think of Ivar. Bright as he is, what could he do in a similar situation?'

He relaxed a little. 'I know. It's a totally illogical feeling, but I feel it nevertheless. That and this . . . this anger. With her, too.' He looked at me with unhappy eyes. His mother's eyes? They certainly weren't a bit like Bertil's cool pale-blue ones.

'How could she choose to die, to leave me like that, for ever, with no road back? Why couldn't I make her stay? I was her son. Wasn't I enough? Did I mean so little? What's *wrong* with me, Esther, that I'm never enough?'

'That's not how it is. That's not how it is at all.' I looked into his eyes, willing him to see all the love in mine. But I couldn't give him a satisfactory answer. All the tender feelings in the world were jostling for space in my mind. I ached with love and pity for him, but I sat there silent. Like a dog that had been sent off to its basket one too many times, my emotions refused to come out to play. All I could do was be practical while my heart wept all the tears my eyes couldn't manage. 'But you read the diary,' I said at last. 'It was because she loved you so much that she couldn't bear to live without you.'

Linus shook his head. 'She didn't have the courage for battle. She kept writing, over and over, how much she loved me, but when it came down to it the love wasn't enough to make her fight on. But she must have known that things would change once I got older. No, the truth I have to face is that I wasn't enough. And why should I have been?'

'I think you've got that wrong,' I said. I put my hand out towards him and he laughed. The silly, high-pitched laugh made the other diners turn round in their seats to see where the offending sound came from. Normally, while dying quietly of embarrassment, I would have made sure that everyone knew that the noise did not come from me. But not now, not with him. Instead, I just sat there, looking at him as pleased as a mother whose first-born had just burped. God, how I must I love that man!

'So how is Ulla?' I asked when it was quiet again.

'Oh she's fine, busy knitting strait-jackets, getting treatment. There's no question of her going to prison. I've been to see her in hospital. She is a bit mad, there's no doubt about it. At the same time I can understand where she's coming from. She's had so little in her life. No lover, or husband, or children. She cared genuinely for my mother, but she lost her. I hadn't realised, I hadn't bothered to realise how hard things were for her. She was always just there, my silly old not-quite-aunt Ulla. Every family has one. And they have their uses.

They unite the rest of the relatives by their sheer awfulness. They make us feel blessed in comparison, superior. And we feel good about "having her". But those short weeks every summer were her life and now even those were going to be taken away from her. She felt absolutely powerless.'

'Like the Wilsons. Now do you see what I've been on about?' I didn't mean to say it and as soon as the words escaped my mouth I wanted to shove them back in like spat-out crumbs. But it was too late, they were there, in the air between us, doing their damnedest.

Linus sat back in his chair. When he looked at me it was with a stranger's eyes, all warmth and intimacy gone. 'You don't give up, do you?' He signalled the waiter for the bill. Then he turned back to me. 'I really don't need this. Not now and not from you.' He signed the credit-card slip, drained his glass and stood up. 'Shall we go?'

My mind said yes and gave the order to my legs. They refused. *Come on, guys*, my mind pleaded. *We're talking dignity here*. My legs replied, *Fuck dignity* and remained under the table. Linus looked at me, eyebrows raised.

'I don't want to go,' I said rather quietly.

'What?'

'I don't want to go,' I said, a little bit louder now.

'What do you mean, you don't want to go?' All around us the other diners abandoned their own conversations for the promise of a public spectacle.

'What do you think I mean?' I whispered.

'Will you speak up, I can't hear a word.'

'*What the hell do you think I mean?*' I yelled.

'Will you stop screaming,' Linus snapped. 'I'll be waiting outside.'

'Don't bother,' I called after him. Then I turned round and glared at as many people as I could. It was embarrassing to sit there, but it was better than running after him. Who did he think he was? Men! Bastards! I should have known! They're all the same: vain, touchy, controlling, unable to take criticism. Bastards!

After five minutes or so Linus strode back into the restaurant. 'Are you coming or not? I've got an early appointment tomorrow morning so I'm not going to hang around waiting for you all night.'

'I'm very happy here, thank you. You go off and get your beauty sleep. It must be hard work wrecking people's lives.'

Now I probably shouldn't have said that. Linus just stood there looking at me and suddenly my anger disappeared and I felt scared. I had gone too far. I could see it in his eyes. But I didn't have a chance to say sorry. He turned on his heel and was off. I sat there, forcing myself to finish my pudding, as if I wanted to be on my own. I sipped my wine. I sipped my water. I ate some more *crème brûlée*, making myself feel quite sick. Finally I stood up and walked out of the restaurant, forcing myself not to hurry.

'Enjoyed your meal, madam?' the waiter asked as I passed.

'Immeasurably,' I said.


The scale model of the opera house had arrived in a sea container that morning. Stuart Lloyd had just said, 'Wow!' Now he said it again: 'Wow!'

'So you like it,' Linus asked unnecessarily. His cheeks still turned pink when he was pleased or excited, damn it.

Stuart Lloyd took a step towards him and shook his hand. He said, 'And no more worries now about this business with the Wilsons?'

Linus pulled a face and shrugged. 'I can't say it doesn't still concern me. In fact, what should have been a really good evening last night, with Esther Fisher, turned into an embarrassing nightmare.'

'Oh yes, your little friend in the enemy camp? I must say I've had a gutful of her and all her ilk.'

To his surprise, Linus found himself defending her. 'It's not as simple as that,' he said. 'She really believes that what is happening to the Wilsons is wrong and that matters more to her than her relationship with me. I have to respect her for that.'

Stuart Lloyd looked at him, eyebrows raised. 'Do you? Anyway, she doesn't sound a very comfortable person to be with.'

Linus smiled. 'Oh, she can be, surprisingly so. And I don't think this is easy for her. She had some sort of breakdown earlier in the year. All to do with the consequences of doing her job, trusting her instincts and getting it wrong, that kind of thing. In the end she wasn't sure of anything. She didn't dare to make any kind of statement. She even lost her job at one point.'

'How lucky that she recovered just in time to bugger us up. Anyway, we've won. The People's Glyndebourne is happening and that's what matters.' He nodded towards the model. 'That's going to win awards.'

Linus grinned at him. 'Might do. And you have no problems with anything so far? You don't think it's too costly, or that this or that material is wrong, or that you would after all prefer something with a few Palladian columns or a gargoyle or two?'

'A gargoyle is always nice, but no.' Stuart Lloyd shook his head. 'No. I told you before, I aim to give you a free hand. By the way, you're happy with Pelling & Son?'

'The builders. Yup. They seem extremely on the ball.'

'You've got a site meeting when?'

'Friday. Oh, and I've found a marvellous guy to do the glass engraving on the north window.' They submerged themselves in the details of the work ahead and Linus felt the kind of excitement he knew other people had to go to drugs or sex to find. This was what being alive was all about. It was what he had been put on this earth to do, to build.

# Chapter Thirty-four

So, I had finally proved to myself beyond a doubt that I was to romantic love what Attila the Hun was to world peace.

I was visiting Audrey and trying hard to pretend that I was on top of the world. She certainly was. Her thigh was out of plaster and she had put on some weight. To look at her, so comfortable against the mountain of pillows in her large bed, it was hard to believe that she had ever left to go on that ill-fated trip.

My lips brushed her cheek and as I straightened up she said, 'You look awful.' I thanked her. She peered at me. 'What's wrong?'

'Nothing is wrong,' I snapped and then, as I sat down in the chair by her bed, I began to cry. I don't know who was most horrified, Audrey or I.

After a while, I felt a hand on my shoulder; pat, pat. 'There, there.' The hand was withdrawn. 'Is it your . . . you know, that time of the month?' My mother had never felt at ease around bodily fluids.

'You mean my period? No, it isn't. And even if it were, do you really think I would be sitting here snivelling about it?'

'It's just that I don't think I've seen you cry since you lost that pig of yours. Oh, and that time in Sweden.'

'Pigotty.' I sniffed, wiping my nose with the back of my hand. 'His name was Pigotty.'

'Whatever.' There was a silence broken only by the rhythmic sound of Audrey's hand dipping in and out of a bag of liquorice allsorts. Finally she said, 'I spoke to Olivia today. They still can't make up their minds whether or not to sell. Ulla has started crocheting. She's working on some kind of patchwork blanket, apparently. Olivia says that the hospital has the most wonderful craft workshop. She's thinking of displaying some of what's made there at the gallery. And they're delighted about the go-ahead for the opera house, of course, and so am I. Dear Linus.'

I glared at her. 'Oh treachery, thy name is Audrey.'

Audrey ignored me. That was why she looked so well, in spite of her accident, in spite of her age; she just ignored anything that might possibly cause her stress, pretended it wasn't there, denied its existence. 'I'm very fond of Linus,' she said.

'You barely know him. I hate it when you do that, when you "really like" people in that indiscriminate fashion.'

'I don't think I'm very fond of you when you're in this mood. If you ask me, it's that . . . you know, your . . . whether you know it or not.'

'Stress might just wash off you,' I said. 'But on me it droppeth like the gentle rain, turning me into a homicidal maniac!' I realised that I had shouted the last bit of that sentence.

'And I suppose it's too early for . . . you know . . . your . . . the change,' Audrey mused. I gripped the doughnut on the plate on my lap, squeezing every last drop of jam from its plump body. Then I stood up. 'I think I'd better go.' I grabbed a paper napkin on my way.

'If you must,' Audrey said. 'Bye-bye, darling.'


I had barely got my feet under my desk when my phone rang. It was Dora Wilson. She got straight to the point. 'I'm worried about George. Really worried.'

'OK, Dora, what's up?'

'He's been watching that show again, you know that American one, *My True Life Drama*?'

'I think I know the one.'

'Well, this time it was about folks just like George and me, only they were American. They were about to lose their house and the husband, they were married like, so in that sense they weren't like me and George . . .'

Out of the corner of my eye I saw Chloe enter the room – she was trying to get my attention. 'Yes?' I said into the mouthpiece.

'And so he tricked the man, this one was a lawyer, into their cottage, only they called it a cabin, and put a shotgun to his head and I said to George, that's how they do it over there, all those Westerns and guns and what-nots, and he said, what's good for the goose is good for the gander . . .'

'Hey, Dora, what are you saying?' I waved to Chloe with my free hand, mouthing to her to wait.

Dora sounded impatient. 'I told you, George saw that show . . .'

'Yes, I heard all that. But what are you saying about guns and geese and ganders?'

'George said that what's good for the goose is good for the gander.' She was speaking slowly now, as if to an idiot, so she wasn't far off the mark. 'And that he has his shotgun and he knows how to use it, which is true because he used to win prizes for his clay pigeon shooting in the old days when they still had a . . .'

'Wait wait wait, are you saying that George is threatening to shoot someone?'

'I don't know,' Dora said. 'But he's been ever so agitated, what with them coming for us Monday and you saying there's nothing more you can do . . .'

'I'm afraid that's true. We've done everything we can and we've come to the end of the line. But there's a tremendous lot of goodwill out there for the two of you . . .'

'So George keeps muttering to himself, and not half an hour ago, he brought the shotgun out from the cupboard and he had a really peculiar look on his face.'

'What would you like me to do?'

'Mabbe if you came down. Talked to him. Mabbe if you took some more pictures, made him feel he still mattered like, that people were still reading about him. He'd think there was still some hope.' That was the other problem. We picked up people, lifted them up and put them down in a circle of light and attention, and then, when we had had enough of that particular spectacle we turned our backs, switched off the light and walked away to the next attraction. 'It would be lying,' I said.

Dora sighed. It was a wonder of modern communications, I thought, that such a heavy sigh could travel through the wires all the way from Kent. 'It might calm him down.'

'But what happens then? The eviction is being enforced on Monday and that really is it. I'm so sorry, you know I am, but I can't really see that lying will achieve anything.'

Chloe was gesticulating frantically from the doorway. 'Look, Dora, maybe you should call your doctor. It does sound as if George is getting rather agitated. The doctor could give him something to calm him down. And talking to someone he knows and trusts . . .'

'He don't trust no whipper-snapper wet-behind-the-ears lady doctor. It was different when it was Dr Crabshaw, now he was what you'd call a real doctor . . .'

'Look, Dora, I have to go. Call the doctor anyway and lock away the shotgun just in case. I'll call you in a while to check that everything's all right.' I put down the phone.

'Yes?' I said to Chloe.

'About bloody time. We have a complete crisis on "Woman" and you'd better sort it out.'

'What?'

'You said last week that Cameron Diaz uses Rosewood lipgloss by Pascal to get that famous pout. You just forgot to mention that you can only get that particular shade in the States. I've had the PR from Pascal calling to complain that their counters are being overrun with customers all wanting Rosewood, which they haven't got, and poor Roz is getting about ten calls a minute, some of them abusive.'

'What do you want me to do about it?'

'I don't know. Just do something.'

I tried, but if asked I'd have to say that my mind wasn't one hundred per cent on the job. I kept thinking about my conversation with Dora. George had had hare-brained ideas before, most of them inspired by what he'd seen on TV, but it had all just been bluster. But back then he'd had hope, I thought, as I dialled the number of the spokeswoman for Sugar Candy, the new all-girls group. (I wanted to ask her if Candy Floss, the lead singer, would care to share the secret of her much-talked-of new cleavage, thinking that would take our readers' minds off Cameron's pout.) It was then I had my premonition. All right, so maybe it was just a bad feeling, but it *was* bad and it involved the Wilsons. I dialled the number of Dora's mobile. There was no answer, so I tried George's. Still no answer. I grew increasingly uneasy.

Five minutes later my phone rang. It was Simon Fuller from Terra Nova Enterprises. 'We've just had a rather disturbing message from your friends the Wilsons. I didn't quite get it all, but the old boy kept shouting about geese. He said he had a gun and wouldn't worry about using it if he didn't get his way.' Simon Fuller's voice was smooth and matter-of-fact, and it didn't alter as he went on, 'And I have to say that we hold you and your cronies at the *Chronicle* entirely responsible for any trouble the Wilsons might cause.'

'Hang on a minute. That's ridiculous.'

'Think what you like. Oh, and there's a site meeting this afternoon. The architect, the council and the builders. I really hope you haven't stirred up more trouble than you can handle.'

So did I, oh my God, so did I. I dialled the Wilsons again, both numbers. Still no reply from Dora's. George's phone was switched off. I looked at my watch; twelve o'clock noon. 'Hey, Roz,' I called across to my colleague on 'Woman'. 'I'm going down to Kent. Oh, and when Chloe gets back, could you tell her I've got Candy Floss's cleavage for Saturday.'

The site meeting had finished and the others had left. Linus remained, transfixed by the image of his building as he gazed at the plot of land adjoining the manor. At this hour – he glanced down at his watch, it was just after one o'clock – and at this time of year, early autumn, the sun would stream in through the glass crescent, welcoming you inside, filling the foyer with light. It would merge with that from several skylights to form an ever-shifting pattern on the white-and-black polished floors. At night the sunlight would give way to artificial light, ascending, descending, flowing in from the sides. And beyond, the cocoon of the auditorium.

He was so deep in reverie that at first he didn't hear the man addressing him.

'Afternoon,' the voice said again.

Linus looked up and saw a small man in his seventies approach, a flat tweed cap on his head and a shotgun cocked over his arm. 'Afternoon.' Linus smiled at him.

'So you're here to see about that there People's Glyndebourne?'

Linus nodded. 'Absolutely. I'm the architect. Are you local?' The man nodded, his small eyes fixed intently on Linus's face. 'So what do you think about what we're doing?'

'Everyone's got their opinion around here,' the man said. 'But if you're the architect I reckon you'd be interested to see this cottage that's in the way.'

Linus looked more closely at the man. 'You wouldn't be George Wilson, would you?'

'That I am.'

Linus felt himself turn pink as he rolled up the drawings and placed them back in the cardboard container. What the hell was he supposed to say now? He bent down and closed his document case, which sat on the ground by his feet. Straightening up, he looked at George and said, 'I know how very difficult this has all been for you and your sister.'

'If you come with me I'll show you the cottage. Dora will give us some tea. I'm sure you'd like a cup of tea.'

'That's very kind of you.' Linus tried not to look at the shotgun as he spoke. 'But I'm afraid I've got to get back to London. Another meeting.'

'I reckon that meeting can wait,' George said.

'I'm afraid it ca . . .' Linus paused as he found himself looking down the end of a shotgun barrel. 'Then again, if you say so.' He started walking towards the ramshackle building in the distance, which he knew from his map to be Rookery Cottage. 'Actually,' he said without turning round, you don't have to point that thing at me. I'm quite happy to go back with you and see your . . . the house. Anyway, what would you do if someone saw us? We must look a bit odd.'

'There's no one that will come here this time of day,' George said firmly.

As they approached the front door an elderly woman, larger than George but with the same small sharp eyes, appeared.

'I brought the architect with me. Thought we could have a cup of tea and a chat,' George called out to her.

Linus said, 'Hello, you must be Miss Wilson?' trying to behave as if he often came to tea with a shotgun at his back. They all turned at the sound of tyres skidding on mud. The car, which was small and black, screeched to a halt and its only passenger stepped out. It was Esther Fisher.

'Esther Fisher! What's she doing here?' Linus wanted to know.

'I called her,' George said. 'We need publicity.'

'That's what his film said,' Dora agreed. '"Without publicity you are lost in the shadows of life."' Her voice had taken on a High Priestess quality as she quoted the programme's American voice-over.

'That's right.' George fixed his eyes on Linus.

'Esther!' Linus called to her. 'Get back in the car . . .' He got no further as George, with surprising speed, shoved him in through the cottage door, slamming it shut.

## Chapter Thirty-five

Linus was inside the cottage with a shotgun held to his head, or it might be his chest or his stomach. I was alone outside.

A minute or so before, Dora had stuck her head out of the first-floor window, and called out, 'I'm ever so sorry, Esther, but George says to tell you that if council don't stop that eviction he's going to shoot the architect.'

I stared up at her face, which looked pretty much its usual florid self, only a little better, framed as it was by the late-flowering autumn roses growing on the climber.

'Tell me this is all a bad joke,' I pleaded with her.

Dora shook her head, regretfully, it seemed. 'It's that TV show I told you about. George says that if this kind of thing helped in America then it can help us over here. "Don't give up when everything seems lost because that's the time the Good Lord picks up His fists on your behalf. And with His help, and the power of the media, you will win through!" That's what they said on that show and George believes them. So if you'd just call those people at the council and tell them.' Her head disappeared and the window was slammed shut. It was opened again almost immediately. 'Oh, and George says if you call the police he'll shoot for sure.'

My hands trembled as I dialled Directory Enquiries for the number of the local council. I got through to Maureen. She was sorry but she was the only one there apart from Jason Shaw and he was in Refuse and Sanitation anyway. Maureen wondered if she might help.

I asked where everyone else was. Maureen told me that they were out of the office, but could she help?

I explained it was an emergency and that I needed to talk to the chief planning officer and the chair of the council. Maureen explained that the emergency number was only in operation between five p.m. and nine a.m.

I wondered if I could persuade George to shoot Maureen instead. 'Is there any way I can get hold of anyone?' I asked, my voice rising in desperation.

Maureen explained that in her view there was no need to shout. Then she asked me if she could help.

I pushed the off switch and called up at the window for Dora. After a couple of minutes it opened and there she was, popping out like some malignant cuckoo.

'Dora, please tell George that there's *no one* in *any* position of authority at the *council offices*.'

After another brief wait she reappeared. 'George says then you'd better get that Stuart Lloyd. He started it, he can put a stop to't.'

'Is Linus all right?'

Dora's face softened. 'Don't you fret about him, Esther. He's having a cup of tea with George.'

'Is George still pointing that gun at him?'

Dora's head disappeared. Then she was back again. 'Yes. But you're not to fret. Just call that Stuart Lloyd, George says.' She leant out a little further, stretching her heavy neck. 'It'll soon be over, you'll see.' I think she meant to comfort me.

Had I made an appointment? the receptionist at Terra Nova asked. I explained that I simply had to speak to Mr Lloyd. I just wanted a quick word on the phone, but it was extremely urgent.

The receptionist was sorry but without an appointment I couldn't speak to Mr Lloyd.

'Oh, but didn't I say, I've got an appointment,' I said quickly.

The receptionist told me she was sorry but that Mr Lloyd was unavailable right now.

'But you said I couldn't speak to him without an appointment,' I yelled.

The receptionist told me, with infinite patience, that this was indeed so. Without an appointment I could not speak to Stuart Lloyd.

'But I've got an appointment!'

'I'm afraid Mr Lloyd is unavailable right now,' the receptionist said, but would I like to speak to his secretary?

I screamed that I would.

'No,' the new voice on the other end of the line informed me, this wasn't actually Stuart Lloyd's secretary. She was unavailable right now, this was Lindsey, the assistant. I started to cry.

Lindsey asked if she could help.

I stopped crying and asked, very slowly, if she could get me on to Stuart Lloyd as it was a matter of life and death.

There was a pause and my heartbeat quickened. 'No.' Lindsey was ever so sorry but Mr Lloyd was unavailable right now.

'Dora!' I yelled. 'Dora, I can't get hold of Stuart Lloyd either.' Dora looked displeased. 'It's not a trick. You don't understand, it's impossible to get hold of anyone. Please could you just let Linus Stendal go and we can try to sort this out sensibly.'

Dora returned to the window. 'George says that trying to sort things out sensibly got us nowhere, so if it's all the same to you he'll try it this way.'

'It's not all the same to me,' I shouted. 'Please, Dora, don't do this. I'm your friend, for heaven's sake. I got them to stop once, I might be able to do it again. You just have to give me time.'

Dora pondered for a moment. 'I don't suppose there's that much of a hurry.' The window slammed shut.

What now? I searched for a tissue in my fashionable 'go anywhere' J. P. Todd bag, which I had paid over four hundred pounds for in the belief that it would add to my sum of happiness. Well, what good was it to me now (and the tissue turned out to be in my jacket pocket anyway), when the man I loved more than life itself was held hostage by a crazy old man with a shotgun? How had George and Dora changed from being poor put-upon old Dora and George into some kind of geriatric Bonnie and Clyde? It was more shocking by far than Ulla's bit of witchery and that had seemed bad enough at the time. There was a lot of talk about the evil influence of television on the behaviour of children. But what about its effect on pensioners?

I looked up at the perfect blue sky. Maybe it was all bluster; a last-minute gesture that was a little too dramatic for comfort. 'Dora,' I called. 'Dora, can I speak to Linus?'

'He's in the bathroom,' she said. 'Seems he's got trouble with his stomach.'

The second she disappeared from the window I dashed round to the side of the house where I knew the WC was. I ran up to the small window. 'Linus,' I whispered. I could see a shadow moving inside. A pair of hands appeared behind the frosted pane and the window was eased open. I glimpsed Linus's face, pale in the gloom of the tiny room, and I put my hand out towards him. A voice, George's, called out, 'What are you up to in there?' Linus turned round and shouted, 'Just the usual. I'll be out in a minute.'

He turned back to me and pushed the window wide open. I was face to face with him for the first time since it had all begun and just seeing him made the chaos melt away. I found myself grinning idiotically.

'I've got the car keys,' I mouthed as he heaved himself up on the window-sill. He was half-way out of the window when the door burst open, sending the metal eye which had held the hook in place flying across the room. I ducked out of sight. If George realised that I was helping Linus escape I would be even less use than I was now. There was a thud as Linus jumped back down on to the floor.

'Now why would you want to be doing something silly like that?' George scolded. But he sounded disappointed rather than angry.

I sank to the ground and hid my face in my hands. I sat like that for a minute or two, then I walked back to the front of the house and picked up the mobile. I dialled the number of Terra Nova Enterprises again and this time I managed to get through to Simon Fuller. He did sound just a little bit alarmed at what I had to tell him and he promised me he'd get a message to Stuart Lloyd. 'Give me your number and I'll call you the moment I've spoken to Stuart.'

Ten minutes later my phone rang. 'Esther, it's Audrey here.' There was a pause while I gathered up my screams. 'Your mother,' she went on.

'Not now!' I yelled and pushed the off switch so hard I thought that stupid little black button would break right off.

A few seconds later the phone went again. 'It's your mother, Esther. You seem upset.' This time I didn't even bother to yell at her.

While I waited for the right call I kept myself busy thinking of how I would cut the legs off Audrey's bed when I got back to London. The phone rang again. 'It's Simon Fuller here. I got hold of Stuart, but I'm afraid that he feels, as do I, that this is really a matter for the police. It would be most unwise for Terra Nova to get involved.'

'But the guy is threatening to shoot your architect.'

'That's why we believe it to be a matter for the police. Anyway, it's bad policy to give in to hostage-taking. Sets a dangerous precedent.'

'Your architect being threatened with a shotgun is a very dangerous precedent,' I argued. 'Let me talk to Stuart Lloyd, will you?'

'I'm afraid he's unavailable.'

I took a deep breath so as to calm myself. 'But you said that you'd just spoken to him.'

'That was then. Now he's unavailable.'

'So you're washing your hands of this whole thing?'

'Certainly not. We've called the police.'

'You've done what! No, no, don't bother to repeat it, I heard you the first time. And just remember, if things go really wrong it'll be Linus's blood on your hands.' I didn't wait for him to finish telling me not to get hysterical.

'Dora,' I yelled. The first-floor window opened and she appeared. 'I'm sorry, really I am, but those idiots at Terra Nova have called the police. I told them not to, I really did.' Dora didn't answer, her head just vanished.

After a few minutes George took her place. 'I said no police.'

'I know, George. It really isn't my doing. But no one listens.'

'So you know how Dora and me feels then,' George said. 'I told you . . .' He was interrupted by the sound of a gunshot. He yelled, 'What the heck!'

I screamed, 'Oh my God!' I rushed to the door and banged it, screaming for them to let me in.

'Don't fret, Esther.' I heard Dora's voice from above. 'I was making us a cup of tea and the gun went off like, but there's no harm done. Shots went into the pantry door and George can soon fix that.'

'Is Linus all right?'

'Of course he's all right. Why shouldn't he be?'

'Dora, for heaven's sake, you're holding him hostage with a gun to his head.'

Dora's face took on a disgruntled air. 'Well, if you put it like that.' And then we heard the sirens. Two police cars and an ambulance screeched up the muddy track to the gate.

'Tell George not to panic,' I called. 'And, please God, not to shoot. I'm here. I'll negotiate on your behalf, just don't shoot!'

# Chapter Thirty-six

I was alone no more. Rookery Cottage was surrounded by armed police. A female negotiator, looking pretty in a long flowery skirt and soft white blouse – 'It's about looking normal,' she had explained. 'Non-threatening' – stood poised below the closed first-floor window. The ambulance and its crew were ready and waiting by the open gate. Dora had appeared once, to say that George was not best pleased. She had lowered her voice, leaning out further towards us. 'This wasn't how it was in that programme.'

I explained to the negotiator – her name was Wendy – about George and his TV show. I had been allowed to stay on site because of my knowledge of the suspect, as Wendy put it.

'So will you tell the council, then?' Dora asked. 'You'll tell them we're staying on.'

'I'm afraid we can't do that,' Wendy said. 'But if you could persuade your brother to put away the gun we can all sit down and have a sensible chat.'

Dora disappeared. She left the window open and was back within minutes. 'George says he'll shoot if he doesn't see that eviction notice torn up. He says you should all go home and send someone from the council instead.'

Wendy asked to speak to Linus. My heart raced as his face appeared in Dora's place. 'I love you,' I mouthed silently. I don't think he saw.

'Are you all right?' Wendy asked him.

He nodded. 'Just don't give in to him.'

'Linus, for heaven's sake!' I pleaded with him. He ignored me. 'I'm absolutely fine. Now remember, no giving in.' He was gone.

An hour dragged by. 'Now what?' Wendy exclaimed as a white van followed by a dark-blue Jaguar drove up to the gate.

An officer hurried towards us. 'It's the bloody TV people,' he called. 'Local news station. And that guy Barry Jones. Claims he's a friend of the Wilsons.'

'Send him up,' Wendy said. 'Keep the TV crew away, but tell them to stay in their van.' She turned to me. 'You think George would respond in a positive manner to the TV crew?'

I nodded. 'He might well.'

'We'll let Barry Jones, that is *the* Barry Jones by the way?' I nodded again. 'OK, so we'll let him try to talk to George first.' Wendy signalled to one of the officers, a tall dark man in his thirties, his cap pressed down low on his forehead. 'Get Barry Jones up here, will you?'

'George, Dora,' Barry Jones called up at the open window. 'It's Barry Jones here. Hello, friends!'

Dora appeared. 'It's nice to see you again, Mr Jones,' she said. 'George says to tell you he'll shoot if they don't tear up that eviction order.'

'Now now, Dora, tell him not to be hasty. I'm sure we can sort this out without resorting to violence. Violence never solved anything.'

Dora seemed to think about it. 'It did in that film George saw,' she said.

'I've got the boys from the station with me. You remember Tom? He did you last time. Why don't you tell George to come out and speak to Tom? It'll be on the news tonight.' Barry Jones's voice was coaxing, as if he was trying to lure a dog with a stolen slipper from its hiding place under the bed. 'Go on, Dora, you tell him.'

Dora disappeared and came back. 'George says he wants the telly people right up front with you lot. Says you won't try any hanky-panky with them there.'

'Get them over here,' Wendy ordered.

Within seconds of the TV crew being in place, the door of the cottage opened and Linus stepped out followed closely by George. George had the gun pointing at Linus's back.

'Let him go, George,' Wendy coaxed. 'Put the gun down and let's talk.'

'Why should I listen to you? You don't care.' George spat the words out. 'None of you do. Me and Dora are just two old nuisances. We're in the way. I fought in the war, do you know that? And Dora lost her young man on the railway, that's the Burma railway to you. We've

363

worked hard, been a burden to no one, but now we're in the way so that's it. No one cares.'

'People do care,' Wendy tried. 'But sometimes . . .'

But George wasn't listening. 'But you should care.' He looked straight at the camera. 'To you we're just two useless old people, but you look properly, why don't you? We've got eyes, same as you. Hands, not soft lily-white ones like this here architect, but hands all the same that have worked this land for near seventy years. Do you think we can't feel things same as you, because we're old and poorly educated? Well, we had no time for such things, for all that reading and learning. We were too busy working for a living. This is what we've got.' He waved his free arm at the cottage walls. 'This is where we've lived our lives. It's been a good place, cosy enough in winter, cool in the summer. We know about your opera. It's nice music if you've got the time and the money to go and listen to it. Makes you laugh too, the way they carry on.' He paused. 'We don't matter, Dora and me, but we bleed same as you.'

It happened so fast. George swung the shotgun round, pressed it into his mouth and pulled the trigger. The shot rang out. Dora's scream turned mute as blood and brain matter and splinters of bone splattered her face and neck, and the top of her yellow jumper. Linus caught George in his arms as he slumped backwards. The gun fell to the ground. Wendy screamed for the ambulance crew. The front doorstep of Rookery Cottage coloured red.

## Chapter Thirty-seven

The world stopped as the mind and matter of George Wilson flowed out on to the steps of his home.

Then it turned again. Linus was covered with George's blood. I wanted to take him in my arms, but I couldn't. Dora sat on the ground, rocking back and forth, a medic trying to get her to her feet. When finally she stood up she stumbled and fell back against him. He steadied her and helped her with the short walk down the drive to the waiting ambulance. She didn't look back once.

Wendy was discussing what she should maybe have done with two other officers. Barry Jones was sick in a shrub. The television crew had been cleared.

Linus stood a few feet away, looking at me. His eyes were huge and splashes of red stained his white face. Never had I seen a face that colour, plaster-white. I put out my hand towards him. He took it and fell into my arms, sobbing. A doctor, just arrived, offered to help, but I waved him away. I don't know how long we stood there, Linus and I, but my arms were numb by the time we moved, walking slowly back to my car.

Linus spent the night with me. He lay on his front, one arm thrown above his head, one leg curled up, the foot of the other sticking out from under the duvet. He had fallen asleep in my arms and then, when I was sure I wouldn't wake him, I had wriggled free and got out of bed. I stood there watching him, my perfect love, with me at last. And I felt nothing.

I walked out of the room and downstairs to the kitchen where I had left my laptop. Then I wrote my piece. By midnight I had faxed it to the paper; it would be in time for the later editions.

Charlie was on the phone again at seven the following morning. He wanted me to do a feature. 'Recap on the events of the last year. Reintroduce the main players, that kind of thing.'

I told him no.

'What was that you said?'

'I said no, I won't do it. And once the inquest is over I'm going away for a couple of weeks.'

'You can't. We need you here.'

'Yes I can. Ask the union.'

A week later Linus and I were at the airport, waiting for our flight to Gothenburg. I bought the paper from the news-stand. On page four was printed the result of the inquest on George Wilson's death. Suicide while the balance of his mind was disturbed.

Linus didn't make any comment. He had barely spoken since the day George died. Actually, it was OK with me, him being silent. After all, what was there to say? I played out an imaginary conversation in my mind:

LINUS: I drove that man to his death.

ESTHER: Well, don't you worry about that, Linus dear, these things happen. Anyway, who am I to speak? I betrayed them by my incompetence just as I betrayed you with my misguided ideals.

No, better to say nothing.

After that first night he had moved his few things across from the hotel – Posy didn't mind – and had stayed with me. We had slept every night in each other's arms but we hadn't made love. In the morning we had risen, two strangers, to another silent day.

'What's going on with you and this guy?' Posy had asked me one afternoon when we were alone in the kitchen. 'I thought you were meant to be in the throes of this great love.'

'We are,' I had said tiredly.

In Gothenburg Olivia met us at the airport. This time the place was almost empty. The few people waiting were dressed in anoraks and large coats; it was already winter there. Olivia hugged us both. 'My poor children,' she said. 'My poor, poor children.'

She drove us all the way out to the island. She asked after Audrey,

366

and I said that she was well and not unduly put out by what had happened. Olivia, in turn, told us that Ulla was making excellent progress and that she was expected to be discharged any time. 'We've arranged for her to go away to a retreat up north. It's run by a marvellous woman, a nun. We're taking her up there. We felt it would be a good thing. Show her we had put it all behind us. It was a wicked, irresponsible thing she did, but we're convinced she's speaking the truth when she says she never meant any real harm. As long as she takes her medication she should be absolutely fine.'

I was glad to hear it. Or at least I knew that I would have been glad to hear it if only I could feel something, anything.

Olivia crossed over with us; she had decided to stay the night, before returning to town the next morning. It was hard to believe that only two months had passed since I'd left. The quayside was empty but for an old couple, waiting. The sea was slate-grey and calm, and the few boats left in the water rocked gently in the wake of the ferry.

At Villa Rosengård none of the blooms remained on Astrid's roses. 'I thought I'd put you in Ivar's room,' Olivia said as she unlocked the front door. 'You'll be cosier there than on your own in the cottage.'

That night, like every night since George had shot his brains out, Linus joined me in bed. As always, when I felt his warm skin against mine, a flash of excitement shot down my belly. But before anything could happen the feeling died, as it did every night, and we were left with a melancholy tenderness, lying in each other's arms, united by our common terrors. That night he cried. He hadn't cried since it happened. I suppose it was the relief of being home that did it, that released all those tears. I held him close, whispering to him as if he were a child, telling him that he was handsome and brave and clever and kind. I told him I loved him. Eventually he fell asleep, still sobbing.

Most days we rose early, except for the first morning when we slept until gone eleven. Linus did a lot of work in the garden and I took my time shopping, preparing lunch. We ate together. On one day it was so mild we could sit outside on the deck. I noticed that the lawn was turning yellow. In the afternoon we took a walk round the island. Some days we walked from the east side to the west and sometimes from the west side round to the east. Some days we met other walkers, stood aside or passed with a polite nod, on others there was only us.

Linus seemed happier on these walks. He even talked a little. But he never spoke of George and Dora or the opera house. To anyone observing we might have seemed like a prematurely middle-aged couple, happy enough in each other's company, but curiously alone. It happens, I believe, when people have been together a long time and the spark has gone and they've forgotten exactly what it was they had so loved in each other once upon a time. But of course it wasn't like that with us. There were times when the love between us was tangible. You could just put your hand in the air and feel it burn. But we stayed at a distance, kept apart by the contempt we feared we'd see in the other's eyes if we looked closely.

This particular day we were making our way from the west around to the east, and had got about half-way, when he stopped me, putting his hands on my shoulders and turning me round to face him.

'Esther, what's wrong?' Before I had a chance to answer, he continued, 'I don't mean just with you, but with us?'

I looked away out across the slate-grey water, then into his eyes that were the colour of the sea in winter. 'I don't know.' I shook my head. Then I smiled a weary smile. 'It's not exactly how I had pictured it, my first grand love affair.'

He smiled back, his eyes serious as he studied my face. 'No, I don't expect it is.'

'I had sort of imagined that if you loved someone, really loved them the way I love you, then you'd want to be with them. But I don't think we can be together.'

He lifted his hand to my cheek, touching it with the tips of his fingers. 'No, no, I don't think we can.'

I left the island the next morning on the seven o'clock ferry.

# Epilogue

It's two years to the day since I left Linus asleep in the blue house. In those two years I've done a lot of travelling. It took some persuading, and some gentle emotional blackmail, to get the paper to allow me to write the features that I now wished to write. Once the readers began to respond, Chloe of course wanted to know why it had taken me such an age to find my 'niche'. My niche was foreign reporting of the in-depth kind. I was a roving Jonah, trawling the globe for the inhumane, the worst, the most sad. Where I found it the misery was such that I could do no further harm, but, and it was a big but, there was always the possibility that I might do some good. It was what kept me going. And there were times when I felt a small bud of satisfaction form inside me. Times when, because of what I had seen and written about, money was raised that made a difference somewhere where people were suffering. Occasions when pressure was put on politicians and some broken victim of tortured imprisonment was allowed to remain in our country.

I learnt, too, that it wasn't through what was perfect that greatness was shown, but rather that it was the inconstancies, the randomness of life, which most brought our humanity to the fore.

I had just returned to England from Brazil. This time I'd been away almost three months. I was pleased with the work I'd done on the children of the sewers and the priest who tried to save them.

I still wrote, occasionally, for the women's pages; I needed to prove to myself that I wasn't a prig. And anyway, I had never quite lost my belief in the uplifting power of the right lipstick.

Linus was often on my mind; mostly when I woke in the morning, or when I went to bed at night. Sometimes I thought of him when I was saddened by what I saw and then again when I was happy. But as the weeks and months passed by I thought of him less and I had trouble remembering his face, but not his laugh. The startling imperfection that had made the whole so endearing to me echoed around the rooms of my mind when I least expected it.

The last I heard he had taken up again with Pernilla.

I never spoke of him. The final time I did I had said it all. Curiously, maybe, it was in Audrey of all people that I had confided two years before, when I returned home.

'But darling, I don't understand.' Audrey had patted the side of her bed for me to sit down. 'You say you love him and he loves you. So what are you doing back here without him?'

'I suppose that sometimes love isn't enough.'

'You mean you don't love each other enough?'

I had looked at her, shaking my head. 'No. I mean that sometimes loving someone, however much, isn't enough. I never would have thought it. It's almost funny, isn't it,' I added, not feeling in the least like laughing. 'All those years dying to know what love was, what it felt like. It never occurred to me that I might find it only to have to leave it behind.'

'But Esther, why do you have to? I don't understand.'

I had sighed and lain back across the bed, my head resting somewhere along Audrey's legs. 'We're never alone. George walks between us and he tucks himself up next to us in bed at night. I look at Linus and I see George's blood on his face. God only knows what he sees when he looks at me. It's as if while we're together we can never be free of it. We love each other, but we can't find peace in each other's presence. I am the salt in his wounds and he is the salt in mine. You can't live like that.'

'No,' she had said. 'I do see that.' I felt her hand on my forehead. It felt cool. I closed my eyes. 'I'm here, if that's any help. I always am.'

I remember opening my eyes and looking up at her. 'You are, aren't you. I don't think I've appreciated that enough.'

'You do now, that's sufficient. It takes time for children to appreciate their parents.'

I sat up. 'Maybe we could go shopping together sometimes. Or go to see a show, or just out to dinner.'

There was a pause, then Audrey said, 'Now don't let's get carried away. You know I don't go out.'

I looked at her and smiled. 'At last you're being utterly consistent. It's what I always wanted.'

My mother smiled back. 'Good, darling. I'm pleased you're pleased. Now, if you don't mind.' She grabbed the television remote. 'I'm going to watch my programme.'

That had been that, everything the same and yet so utterly different. Does that make sense? I don't know.

But it made sense for him to be back with her, with Pernilla. The reflection he saw in her eyes was easier to live with than the one he'd see in mine.

He had written a couple of times. A few months after we parted it was to tell me of his decision to continue the work on the opera house, now officially named the People's Opera.

*The most persuasive argument for going through with it* [he wrote] *came from Stuart Lloyd. Dora had stated that she never wanted to return to the cottage after what had happened. George had killed himself, the dreadful damage was done. We had wanted to build the opera house because we believed it was a right and good thing to do. Whom would we help but our own consciences if we scrapped the project? What earthly good would it do? Much better, then, to build and to make the building the best and most beautiful in our power. Anything else would be a meaningless gesture.*

*So much for the official argument* [he had gone on to say], *the truth of the mind, not the heart. But really I went ahead with the project because I wanted more than anything to build that house. I went ahead because the Opera would be the fulfilment of all my dreams and would make my life worthwhile. I'm being as honest with you as I can although I know it might drive us even further apart.*

I wrote back saying 'Good Luck!'. But that was a long time ago. And now the building of the opera house was complete. Tonight was the opening, with a performance of *Madam Butterfly* in front of a huge invited audience. As Stuart Lloyd had promised, it really was the people's opera. The usual dignitaries had been invited, of course, but mostly the guests were what politicians loved to call Ordinary People. There were even buses laid on, from all over the country, that's how ordinary those people were.

I had refused to cover the occasion for the paper, but knew I could use my pass to get in. I needed to be there. I wanted to see Linus's building, of course, but more than that it seemed important, too, that we were there, if not together, at least in the same place, that place, at the conclusion.

And I wished him well. But I told myself that the love had melted into an easy stream of affection capable of no great waves. It was a comfort.

I had seen photographs of the opera house as the work progressed. The papers had been full of reports lately, for good and for bad. The good being the mentions of the many awards already given: *For beauty and innovation of design: The People's Opera, Kent.*

*For bringing together design and location in an outstanding manner: The People's Opera, Kent.*

*For acoustics: The People's Opera, Kent.*

Then there was the headline which read, THE OPERA HOUSE WITH BLOOD ON ITS STEPS.

I arrived early and, as it was a fine evening, parked my car at the lower car-park and walked up towards the lake. I was wearing a Pernilla dress: a short pink shift embroidered with tiny silver and pink beads, although when I bought it I hadn't thought of it that way, and I wore a floaty white wrap round my shoulders.

It was only half past six, but the moon and the sun were out together. I walked up the road in my silver sandals, turning now and then as a car with another early guest drove past. Two stopped and offered me a lift. I told them I was happy walking. I rounded the corner where the gate to Rookery Cottage had been and that's when I first saw the opera house. It stood, slightly raised on the hillock above the lake; a square of white stone with the crescent-shaped foyer all in glass reaching into the water, connecting with the old manor house via a series of covered bridges. It was beautiful, of that I was in no doubt.

Linus Stendal stood alone on one of the three small bridges which connected the restaurant on the tiny island in the lake to the main part of his building.

The day before he had stood in that same place, and he had seen his

372

building free, at last, from its cage of scaffolding and netting. And at that moment, for the first time in his life, he felt complete. 'That's it,' he had said out loud. 'I've done it. Now I can rest.' It had been an instant of true happiness. He was a lucky man. Many people went through life without ever having that moment.

And then it was gone. All those doubts and fears, all that guilt which he had repressed for so long, rose, as in revolution and squeezed the happiness from him until he was left standing there, empty before his creation.

He had returned to his car and driven back to London, drowning his thoughts in music, telling himself that he was tired, that was all. Tomorrow everything would seem different.

But it wasn't, much. He gazed at the building before him. It was a triumph. He knew that. But try as he might, he could not recapture that feeling of yesterday, the one he had waited for all his life. He scrabbled around among his memories, brought each of them out and inspected them for shards of happiness: the day he was told he'd got the commission, when he first saw the model of the design, the praise when it was shown, the awards. But although he felt a great sense of relief at the project having been completed, and a real sense of achievement, the joy eluded him. Then again, why was he complaining? No one ever said you were put on this earth to be happy.

He looked at his watch. It was ten to seven, time to go inside. And the date, well it was the same as that day, two years ago, when Esther had left him asleep in his room at Villa Rosengård. He had woken up to find her gone and had wanted to die. But he wasn't like his mother. He would never do to Ivar, or the others, what she had done. Instead, he had picked up the fragments of his existence and tried as best he could to unite them into something resembling a life.

And one day he had awoken and realised that for a while now he hadn't had to work so hard at it. He found himself laughing, not because he knew it was a laughing moment but because he genuinely felt like it. And his work with the opera house was not only absorbing and fulfilling in itself, it also led to other work, commissions interesting and challenging. Not quite like this one, but that was all right too, he wasn't expecting that, not yet.

Pernilla had moved back to Gothenburg and they had started seeing each other again. At first it had been good. 'A healing experience,' as she put it. But he couldn't make it last. He just couldn't love her. Not the way he could have loved Esther. He'd rather have nothing than some pale imitation. So, lovewise, that's exactly what he was left with: nothing. But that too was all right. And he had the other, different kinds of loves. He had his son. Ivar was nine years old now. Tall and thin, not plump the way Linus had been at that age. He had stopped wanting to grow up to be a woman and spent most of his time playing sport: football in the summer, ice hockey in winter. He was pretty good too. So, Linus thought, as he wandered back across the bridge, it was all mostly quite all right.

But as he reached the side entrance to the crescent foyer and faced the first guests, the trays of food and glasses of champagne, as he spotted Stuart Lloyd at the far end, he dived outside again, using one of the small fire exits that brought you straight out. He told himself that all he needed was some air.

Below him to the left, just where the road curved, was the place where Rookery Cottage had once stood. He looked away, he always did, but then he forced himself to look again, centre, right and left; he could not allow himself the luxury of not seeing. He walked on down, smoking a cigarette. The sky was dark now, but the moon and the stars and the headlights of the cars lit up the evening so that he could see where he was going.

In the distance, about half-way up the road, he saw the lone figure of a woman coming towards him. She was quite small and she was wearing a dress that reflected the light. Her hair was dark. He walked a little faster and crossed over to the same side as her. By now he was all but running. Then he stopped and waited.

I wished now that I had brought a coat, or a cardigan at least, because it had grown cold all of a sudden. No matter. It was time to go inside anyway, to join the party. I quickened my steps and then I saw him, this man, crossing the road towards me. A car passed close to him and at the moment his face caught the headlights I recognised him. I stopped walking and raised my arm in a wave.

'Linus,' I called. 'Linus, it's me, Esther.' I started walking again, as fast as I decently could. When we were but a few inches apart we both stopped, abruptly, as if we were covered in thorns and could reach no further.

'Hi,' I said. I never was that good at chit-chat.

'Hi,' he said. He used to be better.

'Nice place you've got here.'

'Oh, it's just a little something I dreamt up. I'm glad you like it.'

Enough, I thought, of taking it lightly. 'I love it, Linus. It's a truly wonderful building and I haven't even been inside to see all that miracle of light you told me about.'

'The inside will knock you out, so to speak.'

'You must be happy with what you've done here. Tell me you are.' I watched his face in the comings and goings of headlights. It was hard to read his expression.

'Of course I'm happy with it. It's good and I know that. It's just . . .' He shrugged. 'Well, you know how it is.'

'You did what you wanted to do,' I said to him. 'You built your opera house and it's beautiful. It's a great thing you've done here. But now you want it all pure and untainted as well. But you can't. Life isn't like that.'

He laughed. Not the high-pitched giggle of a laugh that I remembered, but softly, quite normally, in fact. 'That's pretty well what Stuart Lloyd said to me once.' He remained where he was, about ten inches away, but he reached out and put his hands on my shoulders. I could feel the warmth of his touch through the thin shawl.

'I had my moment last night,' he said. 'I stood there, looking at the building, and I knew that I had created something beautiful. We can do that sometimes, make a whole of far greater value than the sum of our own pitiful parts. I felt I'd done just that.' There was a smile in his voice. 'You see, I'm not afflicted with modesty.'

I smiled back. 'You know, Dora is doing all right,' I said.

'I had heard.'

'I've visited her a few times. It took her a while, obviously, to get used to the new place. But now she quite likes it. Apparently the neighbours treat her like a bit of a star. She likes that too. Of course, she misses her brother horribly, but all in all she could be worse.'

'Dead like George, you mean?' Linus said.

I smiled. 'No, I think it's a little better than that.' Then I lowered my voice because I didn't really want to hear what I was saying myself, 'But in a strange kind of way, although I'm glad she's all right, it almost makes what happened to George worse. Anyway,' I shivered, 'shall we go inside? I'm a little cold.'

Although I didn't know it as I spoke, that was just the best thing I could have said, because all of a sudden, Linus came alive before me. I felt his fingers grip my shoulders as he pulled me towards him, taking me in his arms. I heard him mumble my name, his breath hot against my hair.

I pulled back a little, looking up into his face. It was pale in the moonlight, but now I saw only his beloved eyes, his adored lips; George was gone.

'I love you,' I said. 'It's pretty well the only thing that matters to me. And I want you to trust me, please. You can trust me.'

'Will you stay with me this time?'

I lifted my hand to his face, caressing his cheek with the tips of my fingers, running them down to the corner of his mouth. I smiled at him and felt him smile back. 'I'll never leave you again, I promise.'

I heard him sigh, a contented little sigh. 'I believe you. You're not a quitter.'

We walked together up the road towards the opera house as the floodlights on the lake were switched on. They shone into the glass crescent, blinding us to the people inside, merging them into the light.